VILLA
APHRODITE

OTHER BOOKS BY THOMAS BAIRD

Novels

Poor Millie
The Way to the Old Sailors Home
Losing People
People Who Pull You Down
Finding Out
Nice Try
Sheba's Landing
The Old Masters
Triumphal Entry

Novels for Young Adults

Walk Out a Brother
Finding Fever

VILLA
APHRODITE

THOMAS BAIRD

A
Joan
Kahn
BOOK

St. Martin's Press
New York

Copy Editor: David Wade Smith

Library of Congress Cataloging in Publication Data

Baird, Thomas P., 1923-
  Villa Aphrodite.

  "A Joan Kahn book."
  I. Title.
PS3552.A39V5   1984   813'.54   84-13331
ISBN 0-312-84679-7

First Edition

10 9 8 7 6 5 4 3 2 1

For Ralph Kirkpatrick

PART

one

PART

one

At first, Signora Benassi thought it was the climb—her mother's grave was up at the top of the slope, near the ancient, crumbling, mossy back wall of the Protestant Cemetery. It was also, perhaps, the heat—warm for Rome in May—though the walks were shaded. Whatever the cause, her dizziness would pass in a moment. She placed her feet wide apart and, to distract herself, tried to say aloud the inscription that was carved on the block of Vermont marble that had been brought all this way, at her mother's wish, to mark her resting place. Its lettering, fine as that on a Flavian entablature, swam before Signora Benassi's eyes. Awful!

When the dizziness had persisted beyond all reason, she dropped her bouquet of flowers and leaned against a cypress tree. Leaning not being enough by then, she clung to it with her left arm. In a panic, she looked around. She needed help.

What if she should die?

Not far away was a young man, the only person in sight, except for the custodian who was watering the shrubbery down near the entrance, too far to be of any use. She called to the young man in Italian, and beckoned with her free hand. He came toward her. When she could see him better, though he swam too, she marked his appearance; one had to be careful of strangers these days, even in a cemetery. Wavy brown hair, worn not too long, thank goodness. Strong and fit—he was coming fast. Dressed in a navy-blue polo shirt and khaki trousers, and—now she could see!—he had nice blue eyes and was worried, not bored, by her plight. British? Dutch? German? Most likely American. She tried English.

"I'm . . . dizzy," she breathed. "From the climb." She looked back down the narrow, graveled path. "You take it like a greyhound, but it's steep for someone like—like me. Could you help me a moment?"

"Certainly," he said. "Glad to." She was right. An American. "What can I do?" He considered his options, first with a careful look at her, then with a quick overview of the cemetery, its variously shaped monuments bristling—the crowded dead whom Rome wouldn't let lie anywhere else. He tucked the book he was

3

carrying between his belly and his belt and opened his arms. "Do you want me to—?"

Signora Benassi laughed, and felt better for it. "Carry me? Heavens, no. Just let me hang on to you while we walk through that gate into the other part." She drew a new breath. "Into the park by the pyramid, where there are benches rather than gravestones. I'd prefer not to sit on someone else if I don't have to."

He matched his pace to hers, with the gentleness some strong people use toward the weak, as they stepped slowly and silently forward. Meanwhile, she'd put her right hand through his left arm and could tell from his tautness that he was ready to grab her if she should start to fall. She was grateful for her long gray kid glove, her own forearm and wrist and hand being so wrinkled and spotted, and his smooth and muscular. They came to the gateway, from which one could see the whole parklike extension of the cemetery, walled and fenced and tended: a broad sweep of grass and beyond it, sitting squatly within its moat, the famous Roman funerary monument known as the Pyramid of Cestius; then, to the left, trees and benches, and the oleander coming into bloom, and finally, down in the corner, the humble marker that was the cemetery's pride.

"Have you been to this part yet?" Signora Benassi asked. "It's a surprise, isn't it? Grass is such a rarity in Italy—it's an English idea, really." The young man said no, he hadn't been here yet, he'd just come into the cemetery when she'd called to him. "Well, you surely knew about Keats. Keats is almost the only reason anybody ever visits this place," she said. Then, to keep the young man near her, in case she should need him, the signora had him take her to the corner bench. "I'll sit here while you go look at the grave."

"Will you be all right?"

"We shall see—as we shall see if you have a dry eye afterwards," she said.

And she thought, as she waited, of her own burial place beside her mother, and then thought, *What if I had died just now?*

The young man went first to the plaque in the wall, read it, then turned to the grave itself. "'Here lies one whose name was writ in water,'" he quoted from it, so she could hear.

"I've always thought it self-important of Keats to have asked to have that put on the stone," the signora said. "I mean, he was posturing, don't you think? His letters read so charmingly, yet I'm not sure I'd have altogether liked him at the end. I'm old enough to have seen people die of tuberculosis. Self-pity's not inevitable." She paused. "Any more than it is when we die of whatever we die of now."

The young man looked around. Nobody was anywhere nearby, only an elderly couple nodding side by side on a bench back by the gate. He stooped quickly and picked a leaf from the lush ground cover, which looked like violets but wasn't, planted in front of Keats' stone. "There. That's done." He took the book out of his belt, put the leaf in it, and closed it again.

"It used to be the fashion for sentimental ladies and melancholy gentlemen to pick leaves from the graves of famous people—it made Westminster Abbey rather a disappointment!—but I didn't know anybody still did it." Signora Benassi was surprised that her impression of the young man was so off. "I certainly wouldn't have guessed you were the type."

"I'm not. I did it for someone I used to work for. He had an old guidebook to Rome given to him by his grandmother, maybe, or maybe it was one of his schoolteachers. Anyway, it had a dried leaf from this grave in it, right at the place where the cemetery is described."

"And he lost it? Writ in water indeed!"

The young man smiled. "No. The guidebook was a rarity—I guess they mostly get used up and thrown away—and he sold it to a collector. He's a rare-book dealer. He asked me to bring him a replacement—for the leaf part."

"Do pick me one," Signora Benassi said. The young man did so, and she put it in her handbag, which dangled by its strap from her left elbow. She searched for another subject of conversation. "What's the book you're carrying?" she asked.

The Companion Guide to Rome."

Not unwilling to make some small impression, the signora said, "By Georgina Masson—a friend of mine. She lived for a while near Florence. Had an impossible big dog named Willy, which kept people away—that's how she got her work done. A remarkable woman."

The signora shifted on the bench to test herself. Nothing hap-

5

pened—inside her head. "I'm feeling better now. Let's go back where we came from—if you're through here." The young man helped her to her feet, and she took a step or two. "Yes, I do think I'm going to live," she said.

And thought, If I had died just now, what confusion I'd have left behind!

As they made their slow return, following the wider circle this time, past the oleanders, she established a few useful facts. "You are an American, aren't you?" she asked. He was. "And where do you come from?" He came from California. Once that was settled, she asked him his name.

"Mark Stapleton," he said. "Are you an American?"

"It's complicated, in my case," Signora Benassi replied. "My mother was an American, married to an Italian, but she went home to bear me and get me citizenship, and I've kept it, my American citizenship, as she did hers. I am Madeleine Benassi."

They had reached the gateway. Mark stopped to look back. "So I can describe it to Peter Tremper—he's the book dealer I mentioned. Are you Miss or Mrs. Benassi?"

"I am Signora Benassi," she replied. "And I'm relieved you didn't call me Madeleine, Mr. Stapleton. Americans use first names so quickly nowadays."

"I couldn't possibly call you Madeleine."

"Why not?"

He grinned. "Because of your hat."

Signora Benassi laughed. "It's pure Queen Mother, isn't it— pale mauve-gray flowers and all?" Then she said, "I, too, was married to an Italian. Benassi knew virtually all of Petrarch's *Canzoniere* by heart. He and Georgina Masson would have hit it off tremendously well, but they never met." She looked over the grid of paths, which crisscrossed the cemetery from where they stood to its farthest reaches several hundred yards away. "Would you like me to point out some of the curious tombstones as we walk along?" She chose a route. "Go straight ahead here. So. Now down these three little steps."

They looked at the marker of Jeremiah Sands, born in 1835 in Worcester, Massachusetts, died in Rome in 1911. His inscription read: HIS VIRTUES WERE NUMBERLESS. OF VICES HE HAD NONE.

"There. Isn't that amusing?"

"Do you think it's true?" Mark asked.

Not interested in his point, in part because she'd never known any Sandses from Worcester, the signora said, "It couldn't go on my stone, either part. 'She had a minimum of virtues, and not too many vices'—that would do better for me." A brief return of lightheadedness made Signora Benassi want to stand still a few moments longer. To keep her companion entertained, she said, "What about you, Mr. Stapleton? Tell me what would go on your stone. Come. Be honest."

Mark said, very tentatively. "I'm . . . friendly."

"Don't I know it!"

"And I like to try new things. I guess you could say I'm ready to experiment."

"A tricky list—to experiment and to please so often don't go together. What about vices?"

"That's easy," Mark replied, obviously unrepentant. "I have a problem with follow-through. Live for today, and so on."

"That's neither a virtue nor a vice, of itself," Signora Benassi said. "It's no vice not to follow through on murder."

"What about you?" Mark asked—clearly she was entertaining him, which was, oddly, a relief; dying people don't entertain anybody. "You weren't specific—about your virtues and vices."

"Me? You won't believe it, but my chief virtue is balance." They both laughed at that. "Of mind, I mean. Good sound worldly sense, and balance, the kind Molière approved of. And as for a vice—well, I do like to get my own way. Because it's the way of good sense, of course." Signora Benassi paused. Where was the good sense if a woman almost seventy-five left her affairs as if death had taken her by surprise? "And often I succeed—in getting my way," she said slowly, "though not always."

Her head was stable again. "Now, then—should we look at more tombstones?" She steered Mark here and there, stopping to point out the odd detail, until they'd come back to the cypress they'd started from. "And this is my mother's grave, Mr. Stapleton."

CONTESSA DAISY FOWLES RINUCCINI
New York, April 11, 1870—Florence, May 16, 1951
NAM VENUSTAS QUOQUE
INDICAT GRATIAM DEI

Mark gave Signora Benassi time with her thoughts—the loving remembrance blended with reservations that filled her heart each year when she stood on this day in this place.

"You will note the date of her death."

"May sixteenth," he said. "Same as today. That's why the fresh flowers."

"And the long gray dress, and the gray stockings and gloves and shoes and hat. When I come here, I like to come in old-fashioned mourning. As for the flowers, I dropped them when I got dizzy, but there's a vase—you see it?—and a water tap over there. Could you fill it and put the flowers in it?"

After Mark had done so, he stood once again at the signora's side and read the inscription aloud in a schoolboy's halting Latin. "What does it mean?" he asked.

Signora Benassi translated. "'For beauty, too, is a sign of God's grace.' Not a quotation, as you might think, but composed by my late husband. My mother was, you see, a famous 'beauty' as they then said. Admired by Edward VII. Though pure Yankee, she was very exotic looking. She started a rumor that there's a red Indian somewhere in the family tree—or hiding behind it—back in the seventeenth century. My mother had black eyes, like that."

Young Mark Stapleton, who'd never in his life heard anybody say such things, gazed at the signora as if he were looking at a manifestation.

Warmed by it, she said, "As you see, I got brownish eyes, and a rather foolish little nose, whereas Mama's was imperious, and my hair, before it was white, wasn't any particular color. Hers was black. Black as black. And fine. Another gift from that Iroquois. And Mama was quite tall." Deliberately, Signora Benassi set out to flatter Mark, to pay him in advance for the trouble she would put him to when she asked him to take her out of the cemetery and deliver her to her driver, who was waiting with the car near the entrance. "Mama would have liked your looks," she said, "because they're not obvious. She was very outspoken about things like that, particularly as she grew older. She'd have described you as 'blooded.' Or perhaps 'racé.'"

Mark didn't seem to understand—or didn't want to.

Signora Benassi went on, "Mama's taste didn't run to classical male beauty, like that of—oh, I think of John Barrymore, the typical matinee idol, or—who else?—someone you don't know, the great nephew of a friend of mine. He's got a name as handsome as his face—Tiberio—isn't that splendid? Your chin has force, Mr. Stapleton, and your eyes have candor, I think. Mama'd have liked that." She glanced at him again. "And the friendliness you mentioned—it's all there. Actually, that's the best part."

"Tiberio," Mark repeated. "Classical male beauty," he said, as if testing out the concept and not too much liking it.

Signora Benassi thought of Tiberio's great-uncle; if she had died, she'd not have had a chance to say good-bye to Ricky, and what would have become of him? "As for me, I don't know who I'd put first, you or Tiberio. Tell me where you're staying."

"At a hostel, all male, up on the Aventine, run by monks. It's right by the square of the Knights of Malta."

"I'm at a hotel not far from there. I can take you home. I've got a car outside. I can take you home if you're quite sure you're ready to go."

Mark was quite ready. In the car, which she'd hired for her week in Rome, as they went the short distance from the Protestant Cemetery to his hotel, she asked him how long he'd been in Rome, and if it was his first trip, and if he liked it.

Then, "Will you be coming to Florence?" she asked. "I live in Florence."

"Day after tomorrow."

"That will be Thursday—a few days before me." The driver stopped in front of Mark's door, a mere opening in the otherwise formidable blank wall that the hostel, once a large Franciscan monastery, turned as its face to the world. Signora Benassi drew a calling card from her pocketbook. "Here. Take this. Keep it. Call me." She gave him her telephone number to write on the back of the card. "You will call, won't you? After the weekend?" Mark promised that he would, and got out of the car.

She leaned forward. "I haven't forgotten what you did for me. Thank you," she said simply.

Mark took her small gloved hand through the open door and bowed awkwardly over it.

"Aha!" she cried, amused by his effort. "Not *quite* up to Tiberio; still, he'll have to watch out."

"Brother Ninian," Mark said, "do you think it's possible to have numberless virtues and not a single vice?"

"For God. Not for you."

"It's something I saw just now, down in the Protestant Cemetery, written on the tombstone of Jeremiah Sands. 'His virtues were numberless. Of vices he had none.'"

"*Protestant* cemetery!"

"We have to go somewhere."

"No harm's done by letting you sleep awhile in Rome, but remember, it's not your final destination."

"That's not very ecumenical of you, Brother Ninian. Would it be true, about my final destination, in your opinion, even if I did have numberless virtues and no vices?"

"Hell is a hard fact, Mark."

"Actually, I just confessed my vices. Doesn't that get me some credit, even under your system? I confessed them to this really ancient lady I met, who was there at the cemetery to put flowers on her mother's grave, and almost keeled over from the strain. She confessed her vices to me, too. So you see, we aren't entirely bad. Confession is confession."

"And penance is penance," Brother Ninian said dryly. "Not to mention absolution."

Mark and Brother Ninian, an elderly English Franciscan, were out behind the monastery, where there were almost two acres of open land, right at the most precipitous edge of the Aventine Hill. The higher part of the grounds, near the monastery buildings, was shaded by pines; there were chairs and benches there, and some graveled walks, partly roofed over, that had once served as a cloister, and there was a fine view, up toward the island in the Tiber and Trastevere. The rest of the land was planted as a garden, where the monks raised vegetables for themselves and their boarders. Brother Ninian, who was in charge of the garden, was picking for dinner; as he had arthritis and disliked plants, his life and duties were a burden to him.

Mark, who'd been trying for almost two weeks to bring him

around to a smile, tried yet again. "Do you want me to pick some zucchini for you?"

"Of course not. You'd only get the wrong size and we'd have to throw them out."

"You could tell me the right size and then I'd pick the right size. I'd like to help. A virtue I confessed to—we confessed to our virtues, too—is that I'm *very* friendly, Brother Ninian."

"If that is one of your virtues," Brother Ninian said sarcastically, "I wonder what your vices can be."

"Signora Benassi's vice is that she's bossy."

"Signora Benassi!" the old man said.

"Have you ever heard of her?"

"Of course not."

"Oh. I thought she might be famous. She kind of had that air. Are you going to pick tomatoes? Even I can see the difference between a ripe and a green tomato."

"Then you'll realize, if you'll look, that they're all still green."

Brother Ninian was indeed a hard man to please. Perhaps one could do it by displeasing him.

"Maybe your tomato plants would grow better if there weren't so many weeds around them," Mark said.

"The day has only twenty-four hours, and I have only two hands."

"The weeds seem to make better use of those twenty-four hours than your two hands do, Brother Ninian."

It worked. Brother Ninian smiled, just a little, and, to be sure, grimly. "Perhaps you'd like to pull some of them."

"I'm a paying guest."

The monk nodded. "Idle," he said. "Idle and lazy. Sloth— that's a real sin. A weed of a sin."

Mark laughed. "I feel kind of weedy, as a matter of fact." He stretched his body, rising on the balls of his feet, and raised his hands over his head. Then he trotted the path to the retaining wall, which was about ten feet high. He called back, just too low to carry to Brother Ninian's hearing, "Weedy and raunchy. In need of getting laid." He scrambled to the top of the wall by putting his toes and fingers into gaps left where bricks had fallen out, and looked down the steep part of the Aventine onto the street below, just to show it could be done—and because he knew Brother Ninian would be watching him and would disapprove. "What's more, I'm going to do it tonight," he called, in the same tone of voice. He returned, whistling. Brother Ninian wouldn't like that, either.

"You could have hurt yourself, going up that wall, you know. They'd have said I was responsible, because I saw you do it and didn't try to stop you."

"I could have, but I didn't. Success is a hard fact, too."

"Uccellino, uccellino," Brother Ninian said. "Some people talk the way a little bird twitters. And sometimes I can see why the orders in which they take vows of silence have their appeal. Come. Bring that other basket, if you want something to do, and help me get these things to the kitchen."

Mark whistled more of his song—something about love and midnight that was on Italian radio a lot—as he carried the vegetables inside. To have been asked to do it was, he thought, a sign of favor, the first Brother Ninian had shown him; Mark didn't like to fail when he'd set out to please someone. Also, he'd never been allowed in the monastery kitchen before, and he had the chance to look around and see how they did things. Brother Nepomuk, who cooked, and who seemed to find something likable in everybody who stayed at the monastery, allowed him to take a handful of cherries, too.

Signora Benassi dismissed her car for the evening when she reached her hotel, but told her driver to be on hand at ten in the morning; they'd have many places to go. She then went upstairs to cancel her dinner engagement and to talk to her doctor in Florence.

Her room was large and airy, its furniture old-fashioned—a brass bedstead, wooden desk and chest of drawers and clothes press, and no plastics at all, except in the bathroom. She felt better as soon as she got there. Dr. Greghi listened to her story and her brief list of symptoms when she was able to reach him on the telephone. His only recommendation for the moment was rest, but he said she'd had a warning and must come and see him when she got back home. She made an appointment for the following Monday; she'd already decided that she was going to move her return date up to Friday.

Thereafter she lay on her bed to reflect upon the wider implications of her seizure, and came to two decisions. The first: whatever else that seizure may have meant, it was indeed a reminder that the years were running out; it was, therefore, time she and Ricky got married. The second: she'd have a birthday party. The two things could be done together.

Relieved to have made up her mind, she slept awhile. When she awakened, she ordered her dinner sent up. Light things— boiled chicken and cold green beans, and strawberries, which were just in season, with, to be sure, some cream, for she was partial to the Anglo-Saxon way of eating them. White wine and mineral water, too.

When she'd almost but not quite finished the strawberries, she got paper and made a list of her next day's activities. A dozen people to telephone—engagements for lunch and dinner to be changed or canceled, and appointments to be made. A visit to her notary and to her lawyer, who was at a firm that did business on both sides of the Atlantic. One to her man of business, who also had affiliations in America. Her dressmaker—that was important. She'd better plan to go to Signora Martelli every day until she left town. It was a heavy schedule, maybe too much for her, but Dr. Greghi really hadn't been all that alarming, only grave, and she'd watch herself for signs.

A little after ten o'clock she reached for the telephone, dialed a number in Florence, but changed her mind and hung up before the call went through. The later one called Ricky, the better the mood he was apt to be in; he would agree to almost anything when he was sleepy. She put on her nightgown and robe, then put the bowl with its remaining strawberries and her napkin on her bedside table, along with the rest of her bottle of mineral water and a glass.

She went to the tall double windows to open them for the night; it was too early for mosquitoes, and as for prowlers, well, she was on the top floor and the hotel had quite amazing privacy because, like Mark's monastery, it was situated on the crest of the

Aventine, far out of the way. From her tiny balcony she could look across miles of the city toward the Pincian Hill, and such was the magic of height and distance, and perhaps of her mood, that she could think away the noise and confusion of modern Rome and return to her earliest memories of the city, before all the seepage and leak of progress had silted up with high-rise apartment buildings a Campagna where her mother had once ridden a horse as freely as she might have in the eighteenth century. An absolute loss, for which there was, for someone like Signora Benassi, no compensation.

She gave a little shrug; it wasn't in her to be melancholy for very long over human folly. She turned to her bed, got in, and fed herself a strawberry so good it made her smile. She dialed Florence once again, this time seriously.

Ricky was there.

"It's me. Madeleine. I'm in my bed."

"I wish I were in it with you."

She laughed. Ricky was there—and in a teasing mood.

"And I'm eating strawberries. They're delicious."

"*Ma—che lusso!*" he said, although in general they spoke English together.

"I called to tell you that I've changed my plans. I'm going to come back to Villa Arberoni on Friday, on the midafternoon train. We'll have dinner in, just the two of us. Gina won't be back, but Costanza can take care of us. I'll call her first thing in the morning. Or we can go out. You're free, I hope."

"Entirely."

"Now tell me, is everything working all right?"

"There seem to be lights on. Obviously the telephone is in order."

"Stop it, Ricky. You know what I mean."

"I believe the buses are running—is that it?"

"Ricky—your insides."

"My heart? How nice of you to ask. Yes, it's beating—what a wonder! Am I breathing? I seem to be. My brain? Who can say?"

Signora Benassi had squashed the last strawberry between her tongue and the roof of her mouth. As she was spooning up the rest of the cream, she said, amused, "At your age you needn't deal with my question quite so delicately. You said you were off, just when I left, and I've . . . wondered."

"That's probably why I said it—to keep me in your mind. Though I no longer remember. But in any case—yes, everything seems to be working, Madeleine, thank you."

She used a little joke they always included in their letters to one another. "You haven't done anything foolish?"

"No. And you?"

She could have told him then about her attack, told it very lightly, explained it as a result of overdoing, her own fault for climbing that hill too rapidly in the heat, but she left him ignorant, lest he worry. "No," she said. "But let me tell you what I have done." She then spoke of this and that, ending with her visit to the cemetery; told him about Mark, too, though she concealed how she'd happened to meet him. Then she came to a more important point. "You know how visiting Mama makes me think of things, Ricky. Puts ideas in my head. I've decided to have a birthday party this year. Like the old days. I'll open the *salone*, definitely. I think I'll have music, too—maybe I'll ask Iris Siswick to play for us, though not if all she'll do is Haydn. And then afterwards—because of the heat, I'm going to have it in the evening—afterwards a little orchestra, just three or four musicians. Dancing for those of our friends who still can, and for the young. Tiberio and his generation. Supper, too. Won't that be fun?" She wiggled her feet under the sheet with pleasure, like a little girl. "I've been thinking of a dress."

"Have you! You *are* planning a party. Tell me about it."

"I'm going to see my dressmaker tomorrow. I want her to do something out of silk the color of the palest café au lait, and trim it with a really innocent blue—do you know what I mean? Lots of ruffles and ribbons. Does that remind you of anything? It should. It's very like, really very like the dress Mama's wearing in the big portrait—which is the reason, of course. I'll send Signora Martelli a color slide. She'll have trouble matching the hues exactly, because they've changed dyes since 1910, but she's very resourceful. Do you think it's too daring, Ricky, to dress rather like Mama?"

15

"I think it's a charming idea," Ricky said.

"Well, then—there's the party. I have other things I could say to you, too."

"Ah?" His sudden wariness was clear in his voice.

"But they'll wait. Have you been eating regularly?"

"Mmm. The Davenports asked me out to dinner last night. I ran into James Molyneux today, and we arranged to have a little picnic in his rooms this evening. Bought food at the *tavola calda* up on Via Romana. I just got back."

"Then *he's* eating, too. That's a relief. We'll all have dinner on Saturday, as usual. Meanwhile—nothing foolish."

"I promise, my dear," Ricky said. "There are, after all, few opportunities at my age."

The signora hung up, turned out her light, and was soon asleep, but not before she'd added one small task to her next day's list: a note to Mark Stapleton, which she'd leave for him at his hostel, to tell him she was returning early to Florence, and that he should call her Saturday morning and plan to come to her to dinner that night. And to tell him that if he did, he shouldn't mention her little difficulty, that she'd called her doctor, who'd assured her it was nothing serious, and one didn't want needlessly to alarm one's friends.

After dinner, Mark read awhile; then, when it was late enough for the chance of an adventure, he put a couple of condoms in his pocket and went strolling. He'd liked his stay in Rome, in general, except he hadn't yet met the girl he could travel with, which was something he'd counted on doing—an important ingredient in his itinerary. He'd been told it would be easy, that Europe would be full of single girls, but he was a month too early. The big crowds come in June, he'd come in May. Even so, he'd had bad luck, and he wasn't used to that, with girls or anything else.

He went into the park near Santa Sabina, where packs of well-to-do young Romans about his age gathered at this hour, to play their radios, to flirt, to take drugs, or just to talk.

As he walked under the pines, he observed the dome of St. Peter's on the skyline and also made note of what single girls were around. None that interested him was interested in him. Busy, all of them. He was good looking; his white shirt, open halfway down his chest, and his soft white trousers flattered him, but he was too obviously a foreigner and promised no future. After a while he left the park, descended the hill, and went around Circo Massimo, then over toward the Colosseum and the Arch of Constantine. He wouldn't be back this way again, not at night, so he stopped to admire the ruins. Then he continued along the flank of the Forum and eventually climbed the Capitoline Hill to the Campidoglio.

He stood there a long time, leaning on the balustrade, watching the crowd below on the approaches to Piazza Venezia, and also the sightseers who came up to admire Michelangelo's architecture by night. He was feeling alone. Not lonely, not homesick, just alone. Then five Americans arrived—two middle-aged men and a middle-aged woman, one angular old woman with bright red hair, and—at last!—the perfect girl. Beautiful! Medium height, nice tits and ass, slender but strong looking, cool—not smiling much. You'd have to work a little to please her, but once you had . . . He followed her with his eyes, wondering if there was any way on earth he could insert himself into her group. "Do you know how I get to the Trevi Fountain?" Something like that? He didn't have the nerve—they were too well dressed for that kind of pickup. When they went away, Mark wondered where they'd be staying. Surely at one of the expensive hotels toward the center of town— or maybe at the Hilton, up on the hill beyond the Vatican. No way to trace the girl, even if he hadn't been leaving Rome, he knew that, but the sight of her had left him feeling more alone than before, and with an ache of desire, too.

It was time to go back; tomorrow would be filled with the places and things he hadn't yet seen.

There was only a scattering of people in the Aventine park as he walked by it this time, but he entered it again. Last chance before the certain defeat of the monastery. Not far from the entrance was a single girl, smoking, who returned his smile. She was in blue jeans and a pale yellow shirt and loafers—definitely not a prostitute. He drifted to her side and they walked together toward the great dome, which, softly lighted, now floated above the darkened city. She had long hair, worn in a wild, windswept way, almost a tangle, that suggested she might be imitating a minor movie star. Her name, rather boringly, was Maria, and she didn't speak any English. Mark spoke little Italian, but conversation wasn't the point.

She had a car. After they'd driven only a few blocks, to a deserted street beside the city's rose garden, she parked and let him move his hands over all her body—and smooth her hair—while they kissed. Then she took him to an apartment in the direction of Via Appia. Inside, where the light was better, he realized she was at least thirty—he was only twenty-four. A fairly used thirty, at that, which was why she'd been where she was when she was. It was too bad; nevertheless, he made love to her, not in her bed but on the living room couch. When he tried to go to the bedroom she made him come back, as if the bed were out of bounds. Perhaps it had to do with a man; there was some slight evidence of one in the bathroom—some shaving soap never thrown out, but no brush. A husband, probably—she wore a wedding ring. Had he walked out on her? Maybe. She also wore a little chain around her waist that had a clasp just at her navel with ornate initials on it, tacky but sexy. Mark played with it, got his hands between it and her skin as they made love. At the climax, she said his name over and over, "Marco, Marco, Marco," but then said another name— "Mario."

So she was a loser.

As Mark lay naked beside her afterwards, the plush of the upholstery prickly on his buttocks and legs and shoulders, he knew from the continuing eagerness of her touching that despite that "Mario," what they'd just done had meant more to her than it had to him. He told her he was leaving Rome in the morning, and that she'd given him a real send-off, that she was what he'd most remember about it. *"Maria, e il Parco dell'Aventino,"* he said, putting the phrase together carefully as he smiled across the pillows at her. She was pleased. When he was ready again, he got her to take off the chain. "Wrap it around my cock and balls," he said— he'd taught her some of the English already, and he showed her the meaning of the rest. After they'd made love a second time, she had to look between the cushions of the couch, because the chain had fallen off in the midst of the action. She called a taxi to take Mark home; she didn't want to drive out again that night, for fear she'd lose her parking place.

You weren't supposed to take showers at the monastery after ten o'clock, because the pipes banged and groaned when the hot water went through them and disturbed people who were sleeping, but Mark took one anyway, using only the cold water. He also rinsed Maria out of his briefs and hung them up to dry in his room. He estimated the evening as better than nothing, but it had put him no closer to a solution to his travel problems; he really didn't want to fill his months in Europe with a series of Marias. It was too bad about the American girl he'd seen that night.

The next morning he slept until eight and almost missed breakfast, then spent the day sightseeing. He found Signora Benassi's note when he got back to the monastery, where he stayed all evening, for fear he might run into Maria if he walked around again. It had been his last full day in Rome. His train for Florence left at three o'clock the following afternoon.

As Ricoverino, the Marchese dei Guidoni, was putting in his cufflinks, he noticed that the cuffs of his shirt were giving out and that the collar, where it met the clean-shaven skin beneath his chin, was abraded. The shirt itself had been carefully laundered and admirably pressed by the servants over at Villa Arberoni, but after a few more washings it would be indisputably frayed, no longer to be worn in public except perhaps to the theater, if one had on an overcoat and shied away from the scrutinies of the lobby. However, the worn shirt would do for today, so Ricky slipped into it and buttoned it up and, by way of compensation, put on a necktie that was in virtual mint condition.

He reviewed himself in the mirror above his dressing table, not so much from vanity as from habit. He was thin and erect for an old man, and people remembered him because of his thick white hair; the way it was brushed up into a kind of military ruff made him look like a general of the time of the first Napoleon. Why not? There'd been plenty of Guidoni warriors in past centuries. He arranged a blue-bordered handkerchief in the left breast pocket of his newest suit, and behind it he tucked his ancient spectacles, so the silver mountings would glitter a bit from among the cloth points.

He stopped when he was going through his library, which was as big as the drawing room of his apartment, had nine-foot-high bookshelves on all four walls, and two book ladders. He picked up one volume, lying all alone on a table, which was small enough to go into an inner breast pocket without causing too disfiguring a bulge. Bait for his proposal to James Molyneux, with whom he had an appointment. The hallway, when he'd let himself out of the apartment, smelled of food, because the window that ventilated it, and gave onto the court above the exhaust fans of the commercial kitchen downstairs, didn't properly close. The marchese tested the air, speculating. Cannelloni? Something of the sort. And that typical Florentine specialty, *arista*—a roast of pork with rosemary and garlic. And wasn't a fish being poached— to be served cold, with mayonnaise? Perhaps one should lunch downstairs. Yet perhaps not. The owners were strict with their landlord; they paid their rent on time and extended him no credit. If one had to pay cash, there were more agreeable places to eat—if none quite so nearby.

He slammed his door and tested it to make sure the latch had caught. No. He did it again. Yes. It ought to be repaired, too, but everything cost so much money in these trying times, when even one's locksmith wanted to own a fast car and a shooting dog. He descended to street level.

It was eleven o'clock, a fine late-spring morning. The sunshine that flooded much of the small piazzetta in front of his palace dazzled the marchese's eyes as he pushed ajar the left valve of the front doors, as ponderous as part of a fortification, and stepped out onto the pavement. To his right were the tables of the caffè-trattoria that occupied much of his ground floor, to his left the motorcycle shop and the shop where they repaired television sets, and then the street, Via dei Guidoni, that came from the direction of Santo Spirito and stopped at the palace façade (attributed to Ammanati). Piazzetta Guidoni was virtually a cul-de-sac. People didn't careen through, leaning on their automobile accelerators, in order to get from nowhere to nowhere else, unless they didn't know where they were, or thought you could reach the side entrance of the Boboli Gardens that way; and the only tourists who came were those who were seeing absolutely everything old in Florence—American or German art historians, mostly, every one of them a friend of that ass Davenport.

The Marchese dei Guidoni, standing at the edge of the shadow cast by his own cornice, surveyed his square like the lord he was meant to be, his frown severe, the ruff of his hair intimidating. All was in order. The tubs of bushes that demarked the outside space allotted to the Trattoria da Nardo were correctly placed and had just been watered. The tables were set out, ready for—among other things—his midmorning coffee. The truck belonging to the television repair man was parked somewhere else, as the marchese had requested it be. He glanced at his watch. It was just eleven, but his kind of people were in general at least a little late lest they be a little early. He walked down Via dei Guidoni for a newspaper and a package of cigarettes. That errand accomplished, he returned to the café and took a table. It wasn't in the sun and wouldn't be until late afternoon; nevertheless, when the elderly waiter, who'd been serving the marchese for a decade, came to take his order, he respectfully adjusted its sunshade, as if an unpleasant glare might otherwise reflect from the old stones of the buildings on the north side of the piazzetta.

Soon the marchese was sipping a cappuccino and reading his newspaper, only pausing now and then to listen to the birds whose cages hung back in the arches between the inside and outside dining areas of the trattoria—the sound of them reminded him of his childhood, when his English governess had left a canary in his bedroom to keep him company whenever he was sick. He was, seemingly, so at ease that one would never have guessed he was at all anxious about his appointment. To the contrary, for all one could see, looking in from the borders of his life (James Molyneux did just that as he approached, thought to himself, Ricky has the real aristocrat's talent for indolence) it was but a moment in the day of a gentleman who had many other things to do—or very few, it didn't matter which. The one was quite the same as the other.

. . .

Guidoni looked up. There was James, emaciated and high-strung. All nerves and not enough digestion. The sun caught his face—he was just outside the shade. That nose of his, long and inquisitive, not unlike Lorenzo the Magnificent's. A complexion as dark as any Italian's, and liquid brown eyes—unlike the marchese himself, who had the pale skin and intense blue eyes not uncommon in onetime Ghibelline families. The two shook hands. James sat down and ordered himself a glass of mineral water with lemon in it. Ricoverino put his glasses on the table and beside them laid his newspaper, folded open to the report of yesterday's activity on the Milan stock market, by which he intended to suggest delicately that money might be at least part of the point of this meeting.

"I hope you didn't mind my calling you so late last night to ask you to come today—and after we'd spent the whole evening together, too, James, but sometimes one has thoughts toward midnight that don't come earlier. By the way, Madeleine phoned in the meantime—I mean between the time I left you and the time I called—did I tell you? She's returning day after tomorrow, in the afternoon. We spoke of you—nicely." Ricky smiled. "I didn't mention this appointment, because of course I hadn't yet made it. There'll be dinner as usual on Saturday."

James nodded. "I know, Ricky. She called me herself earlier this morning."

"Ah? And . . . did you mention that we were meeting?"

James shook his head, waiting now. He'd noticed the newspaper and only hoped Ricky wouldn't ask to borrow money.

Ricky turned to listen to the birds. "Good Lord!" he exclaimed. "The nightingale's started up, and it's morning. They get confused in cages." He touched the first button on the cuff of his left suit sleeve. "Loose already, and the suit's almost new. Not yet paid for. I must do that, I suppose, before I go back for a reattachment."

When James looked at the button, he also noticed the cuff on the shirt—something Ricky hadn't intended. And at the same time, he found himself faintly surprised that Ricky, given how old he was and how poor—and how poor was as much of a certainty as how old—was still buying suits.

22

Ricky had cocked his head again. "That's the really good canary. An absolute Farinelli." After a moment he said, "Well, I still have a few things I can sell, if necessary."

So that was it!

James said, "Lucky you!"

"One doesn't *like* to sell, naturally. Because of sentiment—the idea that something one's family has owned for half a millenium should, as a matter of principle, be passed on to Tiberio."

"He'll have to make his own way—as he's trying to do," James said. Tiberio dei Guidoni hoped to recoup his fortunes by making a good wine for export on the remnants of the family estates down between Arezzo and Siena in an area recently given its own legally controlled denomination of origin: Val di Chiara. "I should think he has more to hope for from his grapes than he does from you, Ricky."

"But you know, James, he simply doesn't have enough land to be profitable today. We've sold off so much of it. Not me, in this case, but his grandfather, my older brother, you know. His father, too—my nephew was no more provident than any of the rest of us. Tiberio seems to be provident, but he hasn't anything much to be provident with." Ricky sighed. "Even when he inherits this palace, if I still own it when I die, it's not going to help much. The rents barely pay the interest on the mortgage I took on when I had it modernized."

James clucked sympathetically.

"Tell me, James. You still do . . . do act as a kind of . . . would 'agent' be the right word?"

"Oh, absolutely. I'll always try to find someone who'd like to buy anything old, for someone who's got it to sell. Providing," James added carefully, "it doesn't arouse any scruples."

Both of them looked at the other side of the piazzetta. They'd had conversations like this before, which had ended with James taking some Guidoni possession into his charge, but they'd had none recently, because of Signora Benassi. She thought it very wrong of Ricky to sell his heirlooms, and had warned James not to help him do so.

"I was thinking of books."

"My specialty," James murmured. "You do have a lot that are

old? I've never had a look at your library, you know."

"You must . . . some time," Ricky said vaguely. He disliked having anybody around, because everything in his apartment was so dilapidated, including the two book ladders, which he was quite uneasy about using himself and certainly couldn't let anybody else use. "The library came to me along with the palace when my brother and I divided our father's estate up, after entail was made illegal. There were two cardinals in my family in the sixteenth century, James. The first hat came as a reward for being loyal to the Medici after the expulsion of 1494—we'd turned Guelph long since, and part of the family had already moved up to Florence by then. The Guidoni bishop of that generation stuck by Cardinal Giovanni, and when Giovanni became Leo X, our bishop got his reward. The second was arranged by Cosimo I—it was another Guidoni bishop who saluted him by the title of Duke, from the pulpit of the Duomo here, as a matter of fact, after the assassination of Duke Alessandro. Both of these princes of the Church were rather extravagant bibliophiles. I've got oodles of theology and philosophy and church history. A dozen Bibles—four in manuscript, and the rest printed. Psalters. Lectionaries. The Fathers—particularly Augustine. Commentaries, too. But other things, of wider interest, bought by them and their relatives, my more direct ancestors. There are, I believe, some quite important early editions of Tasso and Ariosto. On and on. It occurred to me that someone in the world might want such things more than I do."

"It seems very likely," James said.

"Oh yes, and there are some early bindings, of course, in quite good condition—the books have never left here." Ricky indicated his palace. "Do people nowadays like bindings?"

"Enormously. Some people," James said in a noncommittal way.

"Would these things interest you, James?"

"Except for one thing: Signora Benassi."

Both were silent a moment, thinking of her.

"Who does like to have her way, Ricky."

"As I well know." The marchese lifted an eyebrow. "But apart from her?"

"Apart from her, yes."

"Just as a for-instance, I slipped this in my pocket." The marchese drew forth the little volume and handed it over.

James wiped his hands on his own clean handkerchief, to be sure they were free of moisture from his glass of iced mineral water, and took the book. His lean fingers manipulated it with respect as he examined the main panels and the back strip and the edges of the paper. He opened the front cover, noted the treatment of the interiors of the binding—it was too early for marbled endpapers—then turned to the title page. He pursed his lips and gave a little whistle. He translated the Italian into English. "'On the Voyage lately undertaken by the Pilot-Major of their most Catholic Majesties . . .' That would be Amerigo Vespucci, would it not?" Ricky nodded. "Written by Fra Antonello da Settignano. So—the author was from around here. And dedicated to Anselmo dei Guidoni."

"He was the first of our cardinals. And of course, Vespucci was a Florentine, too."

"A fact you can hardly miss if you live in this city." James looked a little longer at the book. "The friar was taken along to see to conversions, if they ran into natives. Oh, this one would go very easily, this one would. Anything about the age of discovery and exploration sells." He handed it back. "It can't be a unicum, but it surely can't be common, either. And of course, to be coming from the very library of the prelate to whom it's dedicated— that adds luster."

"That's just what worries me. Couldn't the books be sold someplace where nobody would know me? It's not the government I'm worried about—I mean, those people who try to keep things in Italy. It's Madeleine. And then also Tiberio. I don't want him to know and resent it."

"California?" James said. "Is that far enough away? I know a book dealer in California—just got a letter from him this morning I haven't even had a chance to read. He tells me people collect old books and drawings and such things in Los Angeles now the way they used to collect the autographs of movie stars."

"California would be perfect," said the marchese. "Quite, quite unimaginably distant. So, then, you will take them, James?"

James shook his head. "I can't afford to offend Signora Benassi. I haven't paid her a penny for my room and board in four months."

Ricky's face fell. "Then what will I do?" he said despondently.

"Have you some urgent need for money?"

"Well . . . yes. Something *has* come up."

"I don't have any I can lend you, damn it all. Never been lower. Things have gone from bad to worse for me. If only Hilda were here." Hilda Molyneux, James's cousin, usually lived in the studio at Villa Arberoni, but she was currently in America getting a divorce. "She always has her reserves, but it may be weeks before she returns."

"If you were to take the books, would I get some money fast?" the marchese inquired.

"Not really. I'd want to get you as much as possible—and that goes for my commission, too. Auctions take time, and generate far too much publicity. And if you sell outright, for cash, you'll get gypped. The best thing to do would be to place the books on consignment with a dependable dealer. He'll take a percentage, the way I do, when they're sold, and send you the rest—the way my friend in Munich sold your Sustermans—which means no money until there's been a sale to a collector, although Tremper, out in Los Angeles, is a pretty good friend of mine and might be understanding. Up to a point. I mean, might advance you a bit."

Ricky put a hand on James's arm—a significant gesture from a man who was usually so reserved. "At least think it over, James. I know we could keep it a secret. And it's only books."

"The signora is the signora," James said. "I'm sorry for that obstinate fact—for both of our sakes."

"But if you should take them—" Ricky said, pleadingly. "*If* you should—she's away now, and Antonio's off duty, I believe, until Friday—we could get them to your rooms at Villa Arberoni before either of them is back. Then you could ship them out one by one, and nobody would ever know where they came from—except for the bindings that have my coat of arms on them—nobody in my family ever used a bookplate, thank goodness. Word's not going to get back to her from Los Angeles. Please." Ricky tried a last argument. "We're poor together, James. It's easy enough for her to say don't do it. She's rich."

"I agree it isn't fair to have standards set by people whom they don't in the least try."

Ricky sensed that James might be weakening. "Telephone me," he said quickly. "Don't say no now. Telephone me tonight. And remember, there's not much time if you're to have them safely in your place before Madeleine returns."

"Very well. Why shouldn't I think it over? Perhaps I'll get used to the idea," James said. "But perhaps not."

"One thing," Ricky said. "You and I can surely trust each other."

"That we can," said James. "That we can."

Ricky probably ought to have paid for the mineral water, since he'd invited James to meet him, and the meeting was about his business; nevertheless, James put down some money for it—that particular morning, Ricky seemed to be feeling poorer than James did—then cut through the hedge and strode briskly off toward Piazza Santo Spirito and the river, swinging the cane he always carried, but mostly used only when he was tired. As Ricky dei Guidoni watched him go, he couldn't help but deplore that left leg, several inches shorter than the right one, which gave James Molyneux his bad limp and surely had shaped his misanthropy. Without it, James, who was forceful and clever, cultivated and honorable, might have gone a long way. Might have excelled in some fine career. Or made a great marriage—had his tastes leaned in that direction.

Left by himself, Ricky considered for a bit the occasion of his special and urgent need for money.

If Madeleine was going to have the seventy-fifth birthday party she had described to him, she would no doubt tell people there were to be no presents; nevertheless, they would offer them, small and large, scaled according to their relationships with her. And they would certainly be curious, every old man and old woman would be, some of the youngsters too, to see what he had given her. She had, after all, been his mistress for twenty-five years. She must, simply must, as her gift from him, have something as splendid as the room and the dress and her mother's portrait to show off, or people would talk and laugh. So that was the kind of man he was, they would say. A penniless parasite. Living off La

Benassi, and she didn't even mind, they'd say about Madeleine. She felt no shame over it. And they'd lean their white heads together and whisper, "Of course, when you think of her mother and her history, what used to go on at Villa Aphrodite—you remember, *caro*, that was what we called Villa Arberoni then— well, after all," they'd say, "what can you expect, under the circumstances? Rinuccini out of the picture years before Madeleine was born, and the Belgian prince, for all his dash, was no Louis XIV to push her precedence, certainly. Poor Madeleine, first married off to that intellectual from Bologna, and now she ends up with an aging mackerel of a marchese, who scarcely gives her a birthday card."

No, it couldn't be. Ricky had to get some money. For both his own self-respect and Madeleine's figure in the world, so that people wouldn't sneer at her at her own birthday party, he had to give her something quite special. And that would cost money. James, he suspected, would in the end come around about the books; whether he did or not, however, the gift must be ordered. It couldn't wait.

Ricky finished his newspaper and left his table at the café about noon. He headed, as had James, toward the center of town, toward the best place in all Florence to get old silver and jewelry, a shop where they also made things to order. Not one of the tourist places with their trays of trinkets, such as line the Ponte Vecchio, but a place of an entirely different kind—one had to ring a bell in order to get into the dark little rooms of the Fratelli Sulmona, the Sulmona Brothers, over near Palazzo Strozzi. Giacobbe Sulmona, the elder of the two brothers, a man of about sixty, some eighteen years younger than the marchese, came to the door and admitted him. There was a small gallery in front with showcases in it, but little of importance was ever there, and Giacobbe didn't even bother to light the vitrines, nor did Ricky try to look. He wasn't after anything ready-made, in any case.

"A dear friend of mine is having a birthday on July twenty-second," he said, after he'd been invited to take a seat in the rear room, at a table that was covered with a piece of worn red and gold brocade. "I had thought to have something made. Would there be time?"

"Certainly, Marchese," Giacobbe Sulmona said. He made an elaborate reference to a bequest, now on exhibition at the Bargello, that Ricky's grandfather had left to the city. "Not, to be sure, time for a suit of parade armor such as was worn by your ancestor at the great Tournament of Love held in the courtyard of Palazzo Pitti in 1583."

"That fancy old tin can!" Ricky said, smiling. "Well, it wouldn't be appropriate, as the friend is a lady. Signora Benassi." Sulmona bowed; he knew her, of course—indeed, he owed his life to her, and of course he knew of the Marchese dei Guidoni's connection with her.

"I was thinking of a necklace and earrings. Matching. Designed around the motif of nautilus shells—you know she has that famous one by Cellini. A chain of nautilus, carved from jasper or whatever, but set in silver—the metal of Florence. A touch here and there of gilt where it won't rub, if you like. The shells starting small, here near the shoulder, and getting larger toward the bottom, woven together somehow, as it were, amongst aquatic plants. And then similar shells for the two earrings."

Sulmona reached for a pad of paper and a pen and began to sketch. "Something like this?"

Ricky nodded. "Yes. That was my idea."

"It would be splendid. A touch of Fabergé. And more than a hint of the art nouveau."

"The allusion is deliberate—you may also have seen Signora Benassi's mother's wonderful art nouveau furniture—a royal gift. Could something like that be ready in two months? It absolutely must not, under any circumstances, be late. She must have it by that day."

"Oh, no worry. It will involve some rush, but—I'd have the first shell made by the workers in *pietre dure* and the silversmiths, and if you approved it, we could proceed, making small variations, to be sure, and not just of scale, between the creatures, and improvising with their setting, as seemed beautiful. The stone can be cut and polished fairly quickly, once we get the idea right. And of course the silver is our profession. It will be . . . wonderful, Marchese. I dare to say that Signora Benassi will be ecstatic."

"Yes. I think it will please her." Ricky tapped his fingers on the table, which was foolish; Sulmona noticed the frayed cuff of his shirt and knew at once from that. "There is a problem."

Sulmona shrugged just a little. "For me too, Marchese," he said, looking quite unhappy. "I would, of course, be glad to go ahead with the design. I happen to have jasper in hand that will do. Very fine. But the silver I must buy, and silver is now so expensive. I would need enough at least to cover that expense."

It wasn't true. His shop would have pounds of silver too, but the message was clear. The necklace and earrings were going to be moderately costly, though no precious stones would be used, and he was unwilling to undertake it entirely on credit. They sat a moment. Ricky took out his cigarette case, which was itself of silver, and quite heavy, and had his arms on it. He offered Sulmona a cigarette. It was refused. He lighted one for himself. After a moment he let his fingers approach the case, which he'd left lying on the table as he always did for politeness' sake when he was smoking and another wasn't, so the other person might have the opportunity to change his mind and take a cigarette after all. He gave the case just the slightest push in the direction of the jeweler.

"No. *No!*" Giacobbe Sulmona cried. He had made the case himself, four years before—a commission from Signora Benassi. "She would surely—"

"I'd say I lost it."

Sulmona shook his head. "I couldn't. I'm afraid you'll have to go elsewhere, if you are determined on that."

Ricky sighed and took the case back. "Scruples, scruples. Everyone has scruples today," he murmured. "But I suppose you're right, and you know perfectly well there's no 'elsewhere' to go to. When would be the last moment you could begin?"

"A week or so, perhaps. One will want to be sure such a fine thing is done correctly."

"Naturally." Ricky sat and smoked without saying anything more until he had finished his cigarette. He prepared to leave. "Let me see what I can do. In the meantime, why don't you go ahead with a drawing? And of course, you won't mention any of this. It is to be a surprise."

Sulmona didn't need to reply. He was discreet to a wonder.

Ricky returned to his palace, stopping for a sandwich along the way; it would be nice when Madeleine was back and his meals were more substantial. Before he took his nap, he went to his library and, just in case, chose the books he'd send around to James Molyneux. All from bottom shelves. He'd tackle the ladders only when, as his library was decimated of its lower treasures, he absolutely had to climb for more.

The mails in Italy were deplorably undependable. It was not just that they were slow, they were also so erratic that sometimes letters mailed weeks and leagues apart would arrive at once, all in a bunch. That very day, for instance, James Molyneux's morning post, which he'd found on the table as he left Villa Arberoni, contained a letter from Lugano, mailed four days before, one from Munich mailed a week ago, one from Detroit mailed on the first of the month, and one from Los Angeles, from Peter Tremper, mailed nearly three weeks earlier. And then a postcard from his cousin Hilda, which she hadn't bothered to date.

James had time to read all of them while he waited to cash his monthly check, which had been in the letter from Detroit, sent from the bank where his small fund of money was managed. Unfortunately, his father had invested in real estate in that city. A disaster, like everything else about Detroit. Hilda's money came from real estate in Ann Arbor. Thriving. Things were always thriving for Hilda. She even sold her sculpture fairly regularly.

Along with the check had come a discouraging letter from the trust department of the bank. James could expect his stipend to decrease. A little commercial building had been sold for almost nothing. The capital realized, reinvested, would result in an annual loss of income. And the cost of keeping his senile mother in her nursing home had gone up. Hilda's card, as crammed with information as a letter from most people would have been, mentioned her divorce, which was now finished, her return to Florence, which would be fairly soon, the possibility of a show in New York next year, and the sale of a piece to a collector on Long Island, who'd also commissioned a bronze portrait of his wife, who had a beak like a magpie that was sure to give problems when it came to making the cast.

Well—good for Hilda. Competitive, difficult Cousin Hilda, whom one loved but sometimes didn't like.

The other letters, including the one from Tremper, were about business. James sold books mostly in America, but many of the small things—drawings, a few minor objets d'art—that came into his hands he sold in Switzerland and Germany. Tremper's letter included a check for a hundred and five dollars, which James also cashed. Not large, but unexpected.

But there was more than business in the letter. Tremper was also writing to introduce someone.

> . . . Mark Stapleton. His *first* time in Europe. Making the rounds on a Eurail pass. He'll be coming to Florence sometime after the middle of May. His father is a lawyer in San Diego, and his uncle is *the* librarian at the University of Arizona, where Mark went to college. He's a gymnast, incidentally. Perhaps *the* most beautifully coordinated young fellow you'll *ever* see do cartwheels down Rodeo Drive. Anyway, Mark has been working for me for nearly two years—his uncle got him the job after he graduated. But some aunt died and left him a few thousand dollars, and I advised *him* to see the world—and to let the world see *him!* You'll understand *just* what I mean when you meet him.
>
> I've given him your number and told him to call you. He's *eager* to learn things and not at all stupid, might even make a book dealer someday, though I doubt it. *Very* West Coast—but a short time with you ought to rub a lot of that off. I think it would do him good to have a look at your complicated way of seeing things, and I hope you'll take him in hand while he's in Florence and teach him *what's what.* I don't think you'll find it a burden.

They were a little insinuating, all the italics, but Peter Tremper could never keep them out of his letters. As if one were going to cancel everything in order to show one of his catamites around the Uffizi!

There was a postscript to the letter, written in longhand down below the signature, and on the back of the sheet.

> I've just this second finished a *long* conference here at the shop with Dr. Wesley Knuckles—*unbelievable* name, no?—who's been

out here looking at the Getty and especially the Huntington Library with Emilene Ladore—does her name mean anything to you? *Megabucks!* Tex-ass at its biggest. Her father died last fall, and now she's got to spend *all* his money. Knuckles (and don't ever let him get 'em in your eyes)—former president of at least one college and one university, and of the Sentinel Foundation, on lots of boards, etc. etc.—your real high-academic operator—is angling for the privileges of spending it for her. Or with her. Anyway, he's got her onto the idea of some kind of place for Renaissance studies. They'll have to create an *instant* library, and he wanted to talk to me about books for it. They'll have money for important items, rare stuff, not just modern stuff, and I told him to look you up—they're on *their* way to Italy, too. You would be an ideal person to act as their sleuth and procurer. BE CIVIL TO HIM! If it all goes through, the funds will be bottomless. Maybe the boredom, too, but it could mean a real job for you. Security at last, etc. etc. If they decide to go really big—drawings and paintings and the like—you might be able to get in on that, too. Use *all* your arts. Take Knuckles and Ladore around Florence. Help persuade her of the *sublimities* of the Quattrocento. *Nobody* can do the job better. P.T.

That was more interesting, but James had heard nothing from a Wesley Knuckles. Maybe he'd come and gone, unannounced.

James spent part of the afternoon at the German Art Historical Library on Via Giuseppe Giusti, behind the Annunziata, looking up a little drawing that had just come into his hands. Not worth much. By a minor follower of Vasari—about as minor as anything could get. Eventually he bought some cheese and bread and wine, and took them home, intending to have them for his supper.

As he was crossing Ponte Santa Trínita, he stopped to look up the river. How he loved the city, even this dirty water, and disliked the United States by just as much; but as things were going, he couldn't hold out here. He'd have to go back. Get a job somewhere—clerk in a bookstore, maybe for Tremper. Listen to his italicized banter day in and day out. Scrape along somehow until he got old and died. Be poor, back where to be poor was really ugly, and where all his associations were crushing to the spirit. Was it possible something would come of the man Peter Tremper had mentioned? Rescue in the nick of time? James didn't count on it.

There was certainly some money in the Guidoni books. James suspected the little volume on the voyage of Amerigo Vespucci was an expensive item, worth perhaps as much as five thousand dollars—five hundred for him—perhaps as much as ten. There might be more like it. Everything was high these days, if it was really good. Even ten percent of the sale of some of Ricky's books might amount to enough to keep James in Florence another year or two. He didn't need much. He was a fool not to sell them, just because of Madeleine Benassi's caveat. If he didn't, someone else would—now that Ricky had it in his head.

Ricky was right: they could trust each other. Together they could keep it from her—and from Tiberio. James could help himself by helping Ricky, whom he much liked.

James limped back to Villa Arberoni, where he lived, and when he reached his rooms at about five-thirty, he spoke to Ricky and said the deal was on. And then changed his supper plans.

He telephoned his young friend Bruno, who worked in a shop where they made picture frames and furniture, off to the north of Santa Croce, and asked him if they could have dinner together and spend some time afterwards. Bruno, now twenty-six, had a very fractional part-ownership in the shop, thanks to James, but he'd been only an apprentice helping to put up scaffolding in the cathedral at Prato at the time they were restoring the Filippo Lippi frescoes there when James first noticed him and contrived to meet him.

Bruno, as usual, could manage: he picked James up outside of Porta Romana—James didn't drive himself—then drove to the outskirts of town, where they ate at a bar, and afterwards returned to the empty shop in Borgo Allegri. A couch, covered with a couple of old U.S. Army blankets left from World War II, sat in a little room to the rear. They sat on it and talked, then made love, and afterwards washed up at the basin whose white porcelain was flecked with bits of gold leaf off the hands of the artisans. They talked some more.

Nowadays, Bruno always wanted to talk about the same thing: emigrating to North America with his wife and two small children. His brother Sandro, who'd modeled for Hilda Molyneux, had gone there this past year and was now living in Vancouver.

James, as usual, listened and agreed—but with a certain detachment. He had years ago got over his infatuation, and Bruno bored him now; nevertheless, if he went to America, James would—occasionally—miss him. Perhaps there would be more money presently, James said, to help make the plan come true, but right now there was none.

Before they left the shop, James shared part of his unexpected hundred dollars with Bruno. The grateful Bruno took him all the way to Piazza Santo Spirito, not far from Villa Arberoni, though it was quite the opposite of the direction he had to go to get back to his family.

James slept better when he'd been with Bruno than he often did at other times. He was asleep by midnight, which meant that he was up quite early the following morning and made plans. First he called Bruno at the shop and told him to go to Palazzo Guidoni at ten-thirty. Then he called Ricky to alert him to that arrangement. By eleven, Bruno had delivered the books to James's rooms, two cartons of them. James gave him a glass of wine, and they made love quickly again before Bruno went back to work. James saw him out and shook hands with him at the truck and thanked him, and said to tell the shop owner that he'd pay for the service as soon as he could.

As he watched the delivery van drive off toward the other bank and the other end of town, James became aware that Signora Benassi's porter, Antonio, was standing at the entrance to the villa, watching. He'd come back early from a stay with his brother in the country, no doubt because the signora was returning early, too. Nothing to worry about. If he'd seen the cartons come in, he'd have had no idea they came from Ricky, would have nothing to gossip about with the other servants that might reach the signora's ears. If he knew Bruno had stayed awhile upstairs, he'd think Bruno had been unpacking. There was no harm in people's seeing James and Bruno together, providing Bruno always appeared to be doing some kind of manual work.

PART

two

PART

TWO

This foreign custom of eating breakfast by yourself in your hotel room, though rationalized by Wesley Knuckles (who could probably rationalize killing his own baby), struck Miss Emilene Ladore as just intolerable. She slept alone by night, that was the way it was and always had been and she was used to it, but the diversions of the day, offering company and conversation, were supposed to begin with fruit juice and toast and coffee, etcetera. She and her father, Billy Abilene Ladore, had eaten breakfast together for seventy years; it was something she'd counted on, one meal he always showed up for, even when he was skunk-drunk. It was at the breakfast table that he'd made many of his sharpest comments on life and the times, the state of the nation and the State of Texas, also ranching and the natural-gas business and her own shortcomings—increasingly, toward the end, on what she should do if she kept her senses after he was dead and she had all his money. On *now*.

She'd put up with these solitary breakfasts in Lisbon and Madrid, but she wasn't going to put up with them any longer. Rome was the end of it.

She telephoned Wesley's niece, Laurie Walker, whose bedroom was just down the hall and around a corner, to tell her to come over and eat with her. Not just this morning, but all the other mornings that lay ahead of them, too.

No answer.

Miss Emilene was in a quilted pink bathrobe, zipped up around her big-boned body from corded neck to blue-veined shins. It was perfectly decent for her to go stand in her open windows, though you couldn't be sure who might be able to see in—a priest with a telescope, peeping from one of their innumerable churches, maybe. If she could see Rome from up here on top of the Spanish Steps, Rome could see her. Not that it mattered. A city of strangers—for which, from time to time already during this visit, when something struck her as nasty, like the half-wild cats that lolled and fornicated in the caves of the Forum, she thanked God. For five minutes or more she stood there, not really looking at the view, though it was one of the most celebrated on the planet, but rather remembering her father. Remembering Billy Abilene. Remembering his feet, thrust out from under the breakfast table because of the way he slouched in his chair. Showing his seedy boots—he never bought those expensive ones they went in for in Houston and Dallas, said he worked in his. Asking Billy's advice, in a hopeless way—was this project sound or silly? was she doing the right thing?—because it was really he who'd got her into this, and it hadn't been just orneriness, terminal or otherwise.

She returned to the telephone and tried Laurie again. Pretty, delicate Laurie, so quiet and sweet—but not to be trusted. Wesley's spy.

Still no answer.

That was funny. Where could Laurie have gone this early in the morning? Or—one of those sudden ideas that come into a person's mind came into Miss Ladore's, like a mouse that runs to the center of a room, then scampers back out of sight—had Laurie been out all night?

Maybe not so quiet.

Holding the telephone receiver at some distance from her head, Miss Emilene yelled in her order for her own breakfast. When the waiter came up with it, she had him put it and the table that it went on more or less in the middle of the room. There the light from the two great windows fell on either side but left the chair and the tray in shadow so that, telescope or not, nobody could watch her eat. She tried Laurie yet again, for it wasn't too late to order her tray sent up too. Again, no answer.

When some kind of wasp flew in to get at the strawberry jam in its little silver pot on the tray, the old woman lurched, angular as a scarecrow, into her simply huge bathroom for a hand towel. Deftly, on the first try, she swatted it dead—something familiar, something she knew how to do, kill wasps and bees and spiders and moths and, occasionally, a scorpion—the undesirable small fauna of west-central Texas. She sat down, buttered a piece off one of the rolls, and chewed on it a little. She mucked the spoon around in the jam but didn't really want any; at home she'd have had chokecherry jelly, put up for her on the big ranch each fall. She didn't really like the rolls. Didn't much like the coffee, either. Wished she could have had some Wonder Bread toast, and a patty of homemade sausage, and eggs scrambled up with a few diced onions and maybe bits of chili pepper. Wished she had no responsibilities, had only a tenth of her money, twenty or thirty million instead of three hundred in her own name—plus the trust to worry about. Decided to call Wesley Knuckles. He was no snug harbor, and she knew it, but she wasn't calling him for support. She wanted to complain, and he was ideal for that.

She lifted the receiver. After a worrisome number of rings, there he was.

Wesley, his room on a different floor by his own careful arrangement, was lying flat on his bed, his rolls and butter and preserves already finished, his coffee cup nested on his sternum—the chest above and the belly below rising just enough to hold it steady. His head was tilted so he could read the guidebook he held by resting his elbows on his ribs. He was naked. He'd already shaved but hadn't yet showered. His smooth face was calm and satisfied, his mouth shapely with pure contentment; his silver hair, which was tousled from the night, made him look quite a lot like the busts said to be of the great Pompey.

The ringing of the telephone surprised him into a jiggle that spilled some of the coffee before he could steady the cup and saucer. One little rivulet trickled toward his navel, following the incline of his belly as he half sat, and a little dribbled down onto the bottom sheet—what would the maid think? What did it matter? He reached for the receiver.

"*Pronto,*" he said, though it was unlikely it would be an Italian calling.

"Oh. You're there," said Miss Emilene Ladore.

"And wherever did you think I'd be, Miss Emilene?"

"I was beginning to wonder."

"I can hardly hear you. Can you speak a little louder?" Wesley reached for his napkin and dabbed at the coffee. "Beginning to wonder what?" he asked.

Miss Emilene's volume went up. "I had the mouthpiece too far from my mouth. Daddy said more germs get passed along by telephones than any other single way, except one-dollar bills. I was beginning to wonder if maybe you'd both ditched me, you and Laurie."

"Ditched you?" Wesley hesitated, searching for the ulterior meanings behind this latest notion. "I haven't gone anywhere. Neither has she. She's right there in the room next to yours, don't you worry."

"It isn't next to mine, and no she isn't. I've tried to get her."

"She's probably in the tub."

"No she isn't. I've tried her three times over the last twenty-five minutes. She's gone out of her room, I tell you. I wanted her to come and have breakfast with me. I don't like this European system, Wesley. In Texas you have breakfast with other people, if there're any handy." Miss Emilene played one of her large run of trumps. "It's enough to make me want to pack my bag and go home."

Wesley threw his napkin as violently as he could toward his own tray, but his voice was all bluff heartiness. "Oh, come on. *Come on.* Quit? Over a thing like that? *Quit?* With the job barely begun? Come on, Miss Emilene. What would your father say? I tell you what. I'll try to locate Laurie and send her right in to you."

"Don't fuss at her. There's no use now—it's too late. Leave her alone for today. But after today—I guess my point's been made clear enough." Miss Emilene's attention wavered. "Do you suppose she could be corner-kissing that handsome elevator operator?"

After he got over his shock at the non sequitur, Wesley laughed. "Don't you think the other passengers in the car might notice?" His face, when it settled down, was, however, far from jolly. Miss Emilene, for all her eccentricities, might have an insight. "What elevator operator?" he asked.

"Last night's. When we came in from dinner and walking around the ruins and so on with that couple who tried to get me to take the spaghetti that had rabbit livers on it and wanted some of my money—I don't remember their name."

Wesley laughed again. "You do have a gift for vivid characterizations. Lanahan is the name, and he's the director of the American Academy in Rome—I trust you remember that part.

42

And I don't think he was after your money all that much, though he wouldn't turn a bit of it down. Anyway, I also hope you remember some of the very interesting and very wise things he had to say after dinner about the history of the Capitoline Hill—and before dinner about our project. Go on about the elevator operator."

"The boy couldn't take his eyes off Laurie. If I noticed—and you could hardly miss it—she must have. What did you mean about the other passengers? Oh, I see. I'm not crazy, Wesley. I didn't mean she'd be kissing him if he was still on duty. I didn't really mean any of it anyway. I take it back. It was just a thought that crossed my mind."

"I'm glad to hear that," said Wesley. He asked delicately, "Apart from wanting Laurie to have breakfast with you, was there anything else? Anything you particularly needed her for?" Miss Emilene couldn't tolerate the idea that a stranger might have sat on her toilet seat, hence one of Laurie's duties was to wash it each day with soap and water.

"No, no, no, no. *No!* That's only when we first move in, or after the maids and whatnot have fixed up the room."

"Of course. Quite right, too. I was just checking. Now give me ten minutes to find Laurie for you. And remember, the car will be here at nine-thirty."

Wesley tried his niece's room himself. No reply, so he called the hotel's penthouse, a bar and restaurant by night, where one could, however, take breakfast while looking at the extraordinary view of the city if one wanted to—a fact nobody had told Miss Emilene. The headwaiter who answered the telephone knew at once. Yes, Miss Walker was there. Wesley sent a message to her to wait for him, then showered and dressed quickly. Last of all, after he'd combed his hair into a more artful disorder, he put on an ample bow tie rather than a four-in-hand. Fat blue polka dots on a yellow ground. Jaunty. A touch assertive. Just right for a day when Miss Emilene was feeling rambunctious and Laurie independent. Those polka dots might help a bit to put them in their place.

Laurie was at the very best table, though there were guests who looked far more important: Swiss bankers, French art dealers, oil sheiks, and so on. "Well, well," Wesley said pleasantly, as he trailed quasi-avuncular fingers over her shoulder before he sat down. "I'll just have . . . nothing, I think," he said to the head-waiter—and had to repeat himself, because the man was ogling Laurie and hadn't heard him. "So this is where you are."

If Laurie was glad to see her uncle, she certainly didn't show it with a smile, or tell him so.

"But now you've been found out," he said. The back of the breakfast menu had on it a key to the view, some lines that wavered up and down, with humps for the hills and bumps for the domes, and place names printed nearby. "The Quirinal. The Colosseum. The Esquiline. The summit of the Aventine back there. The dome of the Gesù. The Pantheon. I quite understand your wanting to come up here for breakfast." Wesley continued his identifications. "Sant' Andrea della Valle. Something about that name rings a bell." Laurie still didn't say anything; she was definitely being sullen. "Of course! It's where Tosca goes to meet her lover."

Wesley glanced quickly at Laurie, then away again, reminded of the elevator boy and, by a sideways jump, of her affair with the youth who delivered goat's milk to her father. He looked at her again; she was rather pointedly *not* looking at him. Beautiful girl, no doubt about that. She'd always been his favorite of the Walker children. Wonderful lips, not quite pouting, but brimful of promises. High-arching eyebrows. Her mother's light hair, her father's dark eyes. Wesley felt a little stirring of desire, intensified, if anything, by the incest angle.

"Let's see," he went on, as he was deciding exactly how to rebuke her. "There are the towers of Sant' Agnese, and of course dear old St. Peter's—and I don't in the least blame you for feeling a little rebellious now and then."

Laurie did look at him. Right at him—those pretty eyes could bore in. "I don't think I've been rebellious," she said coldly.

"I said *feel*, not *been*," he replied.

She moistened that upper lip with the the tip of her tongue, and Wesley was stirred again. "Feel?" she said. "How I feel? My feelings are not quite the point of this . . . expedition, are they?"

"No, and I shouldn't want them to become so."

"Uncle Wesley, what are you getting at?"

"I don't know exactly. I mean, it's just a sense I have. A sense of an attitude." He put down his menu and placed both his clumsy hands on the table, then dropped them into his lap. "Miss Emilene has been trying to get your room already this morning. She wanted you to come in and have breakfast with her today. And from now on."

"Christ!"

"When she couldn't get you, she called me about it. She said if she had to continue to have breakfast alone, she might pack up and return to Texas."

Laurie said angrily, "We agreed on separate rooms, Uncle Wesley, and you said that included breakfast alone—over here. It's too much."

"Nothing is too much if it serves our cause. And why make such a big thing of this, considering some of the other duties you must put up with?"

Laurie said, "Call her off."

"And then," Wesley said smoothly, as if he hadn't heard, "there's simple kindness to be remembered. Miss Emilene's a very old woman, old for her age, I mean—which is already considerable. And there's her strange life. Almost a prisoner, it's said, of that alcoholic old pirate. She's sad right now. Lonely, too." He smiled slightly. "You know all the lines, Laurie."

"I'm doing the best I can," Laurie said, "but breakfast?" She herself looked at the Roman skyline. "Damn dear old St. Peter's."

"Hardly possible," Wesley murmured, "considering who lives near there." He spoke more severely, giving orders now. "Miss Emilene is going to have her wish. Henceforth she will have someone to have breakfast with. Since the only choices are you or me, and since I can't go to her bedroom—you know, she's got a rather prurient streak in her—strange old ruin—anyway, I can't, so it will have to be you. I'll spell you now and then, when facilities like this room we're in right now permit it."

"Uncle Wesley," Laurie said surprisingly, "I'm lonely too."

"Lonely? Nonsense. How could you be? You're never alone. You mean . . . lonely for someone your own age?"

"That isn't exactly what I mean, though I don't see why it would be all that unreasonable. I'm lonely for someone I can say things to."

"Try *me*. I have an ear as big as my heart," Wesley said softly, then quickly returned to his severe style. "In any case, you agreed to the terms. I told them to you and made you repeat them aloud. You can't say I didn't."

"That was supposed to be a joke. We were all laughing, you and Mom and I. Even Pop sort of chuckled."

"Into his glass of goat's milk. Well, it was no joke. I warned you of everything, and you agreed." Wesley used the fingers of his hand rhetorically as he itemized. "Agreed, one, to be Miss Emilene's companion day and night—with the exception you've mentioned of having your own bedroom—and to help her in any way you could. Two, agreed to be pleasant to her, no matter how irritating she got to be—don't forget that one. Three, agreed to run interference for her where matters sanitary were concerned. Four, agreed to help me in any way you could to further my plans. In return, you're not only getting well paid, you're also getting about as first-class a trip as anybody your age ever took to Europe." He gestured at the view. "There ain't anything like that in Baltimore, Maryland, Laurie. You've met some interesting people already. More coming up—wait till you see John Battle Davenport. That's the positive part of the trip." The headwaiter was watching Laurie again from the back of the room. Wesley stared till the man noticed and looked away, as he concluded harshly, "But don't forget, the basic premise, if you are to carry out your part of the agreement, is that, like a seeing-eye dog, you can have no life of your own while we're over here. No likes. No dislikes. No boys."

Laurie didn't change expressions. Was she practiced in deceit?

Wesley stubbed his fingers together, then hid them again. "None of which means you can't have a perfectly good time."

He'd made her laugh, though it hadn't been his intention. He relaxed.

"In the end," he said, "good times don't matter, either. Only our project matters."

"Uncle Wesley, I didn't quite realize it when I signed up, and neither did you, I suppose, but I'm not well cast in this role."

"Oh, come, come. You've done very well so far. Miss Ladore actually likes you, I think. Now go to her. Tell her that henceforth you will have breakfast together—in the public place, if there is one. She tells me that in Texas they like to eat breakfast in public. Help her get ready. We have sightseeing to do—and an appointment."

Laurie didn't argue further with him. She was strong-minded, but she was also smart and, though only twenty-three, knew enough not to waste her ammunition. If there was going to be shooting, it would be at least the rebellion her uncle had alluded to, if not a full-scale revolution.

As Laurie was adjusting the red wig prior to their setting forth, Miss Ladore said, "Child, I'm sorry."

"About what?"

"Sorry you don't have more time to yourself. Sorry you aren't having more fun."

"And are *you* having fun?"

"Me? No. But I'm not supposed to, I guess. And I'm sorry you're going to have to eat breakfast with me. But I just can't help it. When you've had someone across the breakfast table from you for as long as you can remember, it's hard to get used to being alone."

"I know that," Laurie said, contrite.

"You may know it, but that doesn't mean you like it."

"Really, I don't mind. I'm sorry about something too, Miss Ladore. I'm sorry you miss your father so."

"Miss him? Well, yes, I do." Miss Ladore gave a little tug of her own at the wig; sometimes it seemed as if she preferred it to be off-center. "Love? I'm not so sure. The morning he died, it was like someone came to me and said, 'Take up your bed and walk.' Only, after seventy years, Laurie, you just can't learn to walk by yourself overnight."

"**G**ood morning, Brother Ninian," Mark said, as he came up behind the old monk. Brother Ninian was kneeling at the near end of one of his rows of tomato plants, the sleeves of his habit turned back to reveal skinny arms and bony elbows, an old white Panama hat on his head to protect it against the sun, though it was early in the morning. His sandaled feet were already dusty. "You're weeding, eh?"

"Of course—after your remark the other afternoon." Brother Ninian turned his head and noted Mark's near nakedness. "Running? Again? Where? How far this time?"

"Mostly along the Tiber embankments, for I think about seven miles."

"Seven miles—and all to no useful end."

"It's given me an appetite for breakfast." Mark pulled up a weed the monk had missed, dangled it a moment between his fingers to show it off, then tossed it to one side. "And it's how I hope to keep ahead of the devil," he said. "I doubt if he's much of a runner."

"He doesn't need to be," Brother Ninian replied, not amused. "People run to him."

"I plan to go by him so fast he won't notice me," Mark said. "Can I help you?"

It was tempting. The time it took Brother Ninian to reply showed it was tempting. But at length he said, "No. I can't say this part of my duties is easy, but I'll continue to do it as long as God gives me the strength."

"It's not the strength, it's the bending," Mark said. "It's my last day here. I suppose you know that."

"Yes, I suppose I do."

Mark, without asking again, began to weed a short distance away from Brother Ninian, who didn't tell him to stop. "I've really liked it at the monastery. It'd be a perfect place if it weren't for the shortage of women."

"We don't think of it that way."

"I've even liked talking to you, Brother Ninian, though you're such a hard man to please."

"You can please me best by keeping quiet as we work—if you insist on working. I can't forget that you're a paying guest."

A few minutes later Mark said, "Ouch! Damn! I scratched my

48

side on one of those trellis things you have the tomatoes trained on." He looked. "No blood."

"You should wear more clothes."

"Adam didn't."

"That was a different kind of garden. And I don't think it can be said that Adam's stay in his was a great success."

They worked on, until Mark began to get bored, but he was determined to finish one row. When he had, he stopped, raked up his weeds, and put them in a barrel nearby. He walked up to the monk.

"I demand my wages," he said.

"What's that? What is it you want?"

"I want your blessing."

There was a long silence; Brother Ninian had stopped working. Slowly he got to his feet. "That is surely one thing I do have to give." He touched Mark's forehead. "God bless you and keep you, Mark," he said.

"Can't you make it more personal than that?"

Brother Ninian thought a moment. "And teach you how to love more than your own reflection in other people's eyes."

"Ouch . . . again."

"But not," Brother Ninian concluded, with a thin smile, "at the cost of the loss of your good heart."

"That's better."

"And now—off with you. Do you go home by way of Rome after your travels are ended? So. Stop by, then. I want you to see that there'll be no weeds in my tomatoes."

After Mark had showered and eaten breakfast, he carried his backpack and oversized shoulder tote down to the little storage room behind the lobby of the hostel, paid his bill, and set forth for his last partial day in Rome. He took the street that led past the park where he'd met Maria, stopped for a last look in Santa Sabina, glanced toward the view of St. Peter's, seen down an avenue of baby carriages at this hour of the day, then descended to the Tiber. He walked along until the river made its left turn, then he cut into the city toward the Corso Vittorio Emanuele, going nowhere in particular. Sometime after ten o'clock he entered Piazza Navona.

There she was. The beautiful American girl from the Campidoglio. She was standing beside the middle fountain, trying to see what went on behind the splashing water. Mark moved closer. She was wearing a sweater, though it really wasn't cool enough for it, a gray flannel skirt, and, to his surprise, stockings.

At first he thought she was alone, but in a moment she turned and rejoined two of the people she'd been with before, the strange old woman with the red hair, and one of the middle-aged men, the one who was a little plump and spoiled-looking, now dressed in a dark suit and a bow tie. They were up at the far fountain, and the man, too, Mark realized, was, like him, looking at the girl. Mark drifted after her. There were always such crowds in Piazza Navona that nobody would notice.

The man read to the girl and the old woman from a book he was carrying—not any guidebook that Mark recognized, yet that was what it appeared to be from the way they'd listen, then look, listen, then look. Mark speculated on their relationship. Grandmother, father, daughter? Possibly, though it didn't seem exactly like that.

After a visit to the inside of Sant' Agnese, where Mark didn't follow them, the trio left Piazza Navona and made their way by side streets to the entrance of San Luigi dei Francesi. A big Mercedes was parked in front of it, and the man in the bow tie leaned in to speak to the driver. Then they went into the church.

This time Mark did follow. He'd stalk the girl until she'd noticed him. There'd be some satisfaction even in that.

"Let's see," Wesley said. "We go down the nave." He led the way. "And turn left." He wheeled his two companions as if they were on the drill field. "Our objective should be just short of the chancel." He waved toward it and, as he did so, looked back through the exceptionally wide side aisle. "Quite the junkyard, isn't it? If God were to have a garage sale, it'd look just like this church. Ah yes. There we are. The Contarelli Chapel. Gets stars from everyone, you know. Not just in John Battle Davenport's guide." He waggled his book. "Miss Emilene, does Caravaggio ring a bell?"

"Is it something they eat?" she said.

As Laurie glanced at the old woman to see if she was serious, she noticed a young man about her own age, who was walking behind them—at a distance. When he saw her see him, he smiled at her. As she was to have no life of her own, she didn't smile back.

"Caravaggio was, of course, a painter," Wesley said, "and everyone in the art business agrees we should stop short of him. No longer Renaissance, and so on. They made that point quite strongly when we had our luncheon conference with the directors of the College Art Association."

"I thought the point they made was the same point those people last night made, that I ought to give them some money," Miss Emilene said.

"That was *after* lunch," said Wesley. "Here we are." They stood just outside the small chapel and peered in. "Even darker than the rest of the church." Wesley fed a coin to the meter that turned on the lights. "That's more like it. Now then, let's see what Davenport has to say. Here he goes. 'The Contarelli Chapel contains—'"

Miss Ladore, like Laurie, was tired of Wesley's guidance; unlike Laurie, she felt free to say so. "I don't see why you always have to read about things."

Wesley stopped, offended. "I'm just trying to help. Davenport's very famous. Taught generations of Vassar girls. Handed down from mother to daughter. It's said some never looked at his slides, only at their adorable Battsie, as they called him—meanwhile swooning in the front row. Personally, I find his handbook charming and illuminating, but if you'd rather . . ."

With a little toss of his head, Wesley shut his book, but kept his finger in his place. They pressed in as close as they could, but were held outside the chapel by a low balustrade, whose gate was locked. "There and there and there they are." Wesley pointed to the painting over the altar facing them and to those on each of the lateral walls, so intent on what he was doing that he didn't notice the young man who had now come up quite close behind his little group and was looking at the pictures on their electricity.

Time passed. Everybody was respectfully quiet. When the lights went off again, Wesley pushed past the young man without seeing him—tourists in Rome are like beggars in India—and dropped in another coin.

"Now I'll read," he said, and ignored Miss Emilene's deep sigh. "'The Contarelli Chapel contains three great religious paintings which established Caravaggio's importance for the seventeenth century, and whose example led many a lesser follower into coarse and tedious attempts at imitation. *Matthew and the Angel,* over the altar, is, in the opinion of this admittedly idiosyncratic observer, one of the duller works of an artist whose inventions usually have shock value, poor substitute though it may be for purity of feeling and elevation of style.'" Wesley chuckled. "That's pure Battsie. Couldn't miss it. I like it more than that gushing eulogy we read on the Raphael Stanze. He writes about Raphael as if he were something you ate with a long-handled spoon. Battsie's more readable on the attack."

Mark, pretending that he was following what was being read, moved in so close to Laurie that the back of his bare right forearm touched her; she was on one side of Miss Emilene, Wesley on the other. When she drew away, though not by very much, he ran the fingers of his left hand over the place where he'd felt her skin against his.

"Here's what Battsie says about *The Calling of Matthew,* there on the left wall. 'Our artist has chosen to represent the moment when Christ summons the tax-gatherer Levi, later known as Matthew, to become his apostle. The gesture of Christ is an unusually happy use of quotation, worthy of Giulio Romano, by an artist who, often unwisely, preferred to depend upon the mere facts of nature. Christ's right arm and hand are extended like those of God the Father in the *Creation of Adam* on the Sistine ceiling, the fingers similarly drooping. As in Michelangelo's original, the action here seems to generate spiritual force. It passes above the heads of the two foppishly dressed youths nearest to Christ, over the table and its compromising still-life of money and moneybags, passes, so to speak, across the things and creatures of this world to reach directly into Matthew's soul and to say to him: I want you.' There. You see that, Miss Emilene?"

"Of course I see that, Wesley," said Miss Emilene. She added, looking around—and noticing Mark for the first time—"I don't like this church. Where is it we go next?"

"The Vatican Library," Wesley said. He looked at his watch. "We'd be a little early, though."

Mark eased around behind Laurie and gave a signal. She turned and looked at him with with what was perhaps a little more interest than was permissible in her situation. He mouthed three words. "Me? You? Vatican?" And raised his eyebrows in a question. She gave a little frown and a shake of her head that seemed intended to warn him about something.

Meanwhile, Wesley read on. "'Matthew's response is equally dramatic. His gesture and his face both seem to say, as he sees the figure in the doorway, Truly is it I whom you want, Lord?' That's enough of Battsie for the moment—but there it is, you see?" Wesley waved at the painting. "'I want you,' and 'Is it I you want?' So much for *The Calling of Matthew.* Now let's see what our grand professor has to say about Matthew's martyrdom."

A commotion at the back of the church made him pause. A bit later a group of almost a hundred Japanese tourists, milling toward the chapel, separated the Americans. Wesley was shoved toward the electricity box. Miss Emilene was pushed up against the low railing that separated chapel from aisle. Laurie tried to stay with her but couldn't and was squeezed to the rear. Mark, being stronger than the others, dug in and held his ground. The hurrying newcomers parted and flowed around him to get close to their guide, who jumped up on the balustrade and began to discourse in Japanese. He paused. There were exclamations. More discourse. Then came the inevitable photography—click, click, click. When the photographers pressed forward to get different angles, Miss Emilene, waving her long arms, started to topple. She cried out, whereupon several of the Japanese men politely got hold of her and kept her from falling, and one of the women straightened her wig. The cameras were turned on all that, too.

Wesley cried, "Help is coming!" and pried his way rudely toward her.

Laurie looked around to see what had become of the young man who'd touched her and suggested they meet at the Vatican. There he was. Their eyes met, and this time held. He raised his right arm, the fingers drooping a little, and pointed at her over the heads of all those intervening Japanese. Again he mouthed some words: "I want you."

Laurie broke into a radiant smile, and the young man grinned back.

Wesley had by then reached Miss Emilene. He took her arm and dragged her from the chapel. "Make way there. Make way there," he said gruffly. Miss Emilene, who had turned so she was facing the church, saw Mark's gesture and Laurie's smile, and got the point. As far as she was concerned, it was the most interesting thing that had happened that morning, by quite a lot.

When the three Americans were reunited, and Mark once more at a discreet distance, though still within earshot, Wesley said, "How irritating! I'm so sorry, Miss Emilene—you might have been hurt. We'll forget about *The Martyrdom of Matthew*. Martyrdoms are all the same, anyway, except for details. Come on." He led his group back to the entrance of the church.

Their driver had moved the car to get out of the way of the two tour buses that had brought the Japanese group. While they were waiting for him to pull back up, Laurie asked, in quite a loud tone of voice, "What are we going to do in the Vatican Library, Uncle Wesley?"

So he was her uncle! Mark moved closer to catch the reply to her question.

"See how they've set up their facility. Get their ideas."

"Would it be all right if I went to have another look at the Sistine Chapel while you're talking to them?"

"Another look? Well—I don't know."

"I'd really, really like to see THE SISTINE CHAPEL AND THE RAPHAEL ROOMS AGAIN," Laurie said, loud and clear.

Miss Emilene said, "Why not let her do it? It's not as if we won't all be under the same roof."

Wesley consented, and they drove off without his noticing the young man who was right behind them as they were waiting outside the church. And of course Wesley didn't see him break into a run toward the river and the bridge and the street that led to the

Vatican. Given Roman traffic, it was not unlikely he'd get there almost as fast as the car. He, of course, would be entering the vast complex of museums and library through the lobby everybody unimportant came in by, whereas the car would be going to the entrance nearer the square of St. Peter's, where one went if one had official business. But they'd all be together, as Miss Emilene had pointed out, in the buildings that surround Bramante's Belvedere.

❧❧

"Itiss a great pleasure to receive you, Miss Ladore, yessitiss," said Dr. Voluminis, the bald, pink-cheeked official who had come to meet the three Americans as they were being brought up to the Library by a page, "and to show you how sinkss work here." He led them behind doors that shut out the general public. "La Biblioteca Aposstolica Vaticana," he said, "which iss to say, the Aposstolic Vatsican Library."

As he took Wesley, Laurie, and Miss Emilene through the different rooms, he explained something of the Library's history, how it originated in the practiss of the pops to collect manuscriptss during the medieval agiss, how more systematic collecting began in the Renaissanss, continued greatly augmented in the seventeenth century. One after another, he mentioned the great bequestss: Carafa, the Elector Palatine, Montefeltro, Borghese, Chigi, and so on, not omitting that of Qveen Crisstina. He explained about the archifss and the buildingss and the visiting hourss. He took them to the Sala Sisstina, but there was nothing to see there, because the usual things were put away in anticipation of a great exhibition of material relating to Firgil. After that he took them to his office for conversationss.

At this point they were joined by two monsignors. Monsignor Lalumia, a rotund, gentle man, whose fingers were inkstained, was an expert on Church history at the Gregorian University and an important figure in the cultural activities of the Vatican. Monsignor Dugan was there because he was an American, subspecies sidewalks of New York, with plenty of that accent, plus a tactical brogue he'd learned over the years.

Though Miss Ladore was, of course, the Prime Mover, she was

expected not to speak but to listen, and she and Laurie were given armchairs somewhat separate from the posts taken by the clergy and the learneds.

The discussion was opened by a brief and deliberately vague presentation on the part of Wesley Knuckles. He told the three other men how Miss Ladore was the chief trustee of a foundation set up in her late father's will, and that she wished to establish some kind of an institute with the money.

"Part of it," Miss Ladore called from her place on the fringe. Wesley corrected himself. "With part of the money." She and the other trustees had come to him for suggestions, since he'd had wide experience both in the academic world and with foundations. After giving the matter much thought, and consulting with a number of scholars and administrators, he had suggested a research center. Not just one more miscellaneous think tank like—

"Ssinktank?" Dr. Voluminis asked. "What iss a ssinktank?"

"The Institute for Advanced Studies at Princeton would be an example," Wesley replied. "We want something with more focus."

"Uncle Wesley," Laurie whispered from afar, "what about the Sistine Chapel?"

He ignored her—or perhaps he didn't even hear her. "Are you gentlemen familiar with the Hellenic Center and Dumbarton Oaks in Washington, for instance? Or the center for the study of British art at Yale?" They all knew the former but not the latter. "Well, perhaps something like Dumbarton Oaks, only not limited to so minor an area of studies as Byzantium, and certainly not limited to art."

Monsignor Lalumia coughed gently, and when Wesley turned to him, he asked just what would go on in such a place.

Wesley said, "We don't exactly know. Faculty? Perhaps. Teaching? Possibly. But possibly not. Facilities for study suggest themselves; a library would seem indicated, in that case. It's all still blurred in our minds, gentlemen. As I say, I've gone around in the United States, looking at places and talking to people. Miss Ladore has done some of it with me. The Smithsonian, the National Gallery of Art—it has that big new art-history center, you know. Invented out of nothing—just what we have to do. Oh, I've been to about every place you could imagine, and some"—

Wesley smiled slightly as he recalled his afternoon at the Kinsey Institute—"you couldn't. And now we're in Europe, doing the same thing. We've just been to the Gulbenkian in Lisbon, to start with."

"Is it true, Dr. Knuckles," said Monsignor Dugan, "that you're thinking of concentrating your interests on the Renaissance?"

Wesley pretended surprise. "Where did you hear that?"

Dugan chuckled. "The Vatican is the place where rumors were invented."

"It's also no secret, then, I daresay," said Wesley, "that whatever we do will be done as splendidly as possible."

Monsignor Dugan said, "If a thing is worth doing, 'tis worth doing well."

"My daddy used to say that the only things worth doing well are the things that aren't worth doing at all," said Miss Emilene from beyond the pale.

"Where iss thiss insstitute to be?" asked Dr. Voluminis, frowning at Billy Abilene's crackerbox cynicism.

The temperature in the room rose by several degrees once that question was asked.

Laurie said, "Uncle Wesley—the Sistine Chapel," but nobody paid any attention to her.

Monsignor Lalumia said, "If it will have to do with *Il Rinascimento,* it ought to be in Italy. And in Italy—well, surely the place where there are already the finest minds at work, the place where more people would more like to come, is Rome."

"In which case your activitiss and facilitiss could be coordinated with thoss here at the Vatsican," said Dr. Voluminis. "Were there more fundtss available to uss, we could do far more sinkss like our forthcoming great Firgil exhibition. Such are our richess in incunabula alone, for example, that—"

Monsignor Dugan interrupted. "But it should be pointed out that there is also great interest in the Renaissance in America," he said. His tone of voice grew a touch unctuous. "The authorities of the Church have traditionally supported historical and cultural studies, Dr. Knuckles. They might be able to facilitate your start-up—if that's the way to put it. The Renaissance has so often been treated as a secular event, whereas it was a great age of the

Church. I need mention only Julius II della Rovere, Leo X de'Medici, and Paul IV Farnese. Diocesan land, buildings, and so on might be made available, in one of the older centers, and with it would go our help in every way." He mentioned the city to which he would be sent when his tour of duty at the Vatican was up. "I'm thinking particularly of Chicago."

"There's also Texas," called Miss Ladore.

"*Il Rinascimento nel Texas?*" said Monsignor Lalumia.

There was a knock on the door. A very old priest, stooped and doddering, entered the room and was introduced as Father Wrzesnia.

Dr. Voluminis repeated what Wesley had said, and told the old priest they were now discussing where the Renaissance Institute might be located.

"Rome is the obvious place," said Monsignor Lalumia.

"Not to all of us," said Monsignor Dugan, with a tight little smile.

"Your dilemma is easy to resolve," croaked Father Wrzesnia. "It should be in Poland." He looked sorrowfully at Miss Ladore. "But if it cannot be there because of historical circumstances, then at least the Polish Renaissance should be the heart of the curriculum."

"What curriculum?" said Monsignor Dugan.

"*Il Rinascimento in Polonia?*" said Monsignor Lalumia. "*Volete scherzare!*"

Father Wrzesnia peered at him. "Remember that between 1500 and 1540 more books were printed in Cracow than in the whole of England."

"Oh, *England*," said Monsignor Lalumia.

"An interesting idea, Monsignor Wrzesnia," Wesley said, "but—"

The old priest held up a deprecatory hand. When Wesley didn't understand, Monsignor Dugan corrected him. "*Father* Wrzesnia."

"Sorry. Father Wrzesnia, of course," said Wesley. "But as we'd have to draw the line somewhere, as far as our range of interests is concerned, I rather fancy it might be to the west of Poland."

Said Monsignor Lalumia, "*Il Rinascimento* belongs to the country of Petrarch, of Aeneas Silvius Piccolomini, of—"

"But it has fallen to the New World to study these things from its special perspective, as it was Rome that truly defined and preserved the glories of Greece for posterity," said Monsignor Dugan.

"Poland," wheezed Father Wrzesnia.

"Uncle Wesley, how about the Sistine Chapel?" Laurie said. This time she got to her feet.

Wesley turned again. "Oh. Laurie. I quite forgot. My niece wanted to spend a little time, while we were talking here, with Michelangelo. Would it be too much to ask—?"

"Voluminis," said Monsignor Dugan, "why don't you take her to the Sistine by the secret passageways?"

Voluminis took Laurie away.

"Sigismund I and his queen, Bona Sforza, surrounded themselves with scholars," said Father Wrzesnia. "The Polish Renaissance cannot be overlooked."

"Sure now, and doesn't it seem as if you're the only one who thinks so?" said Monsignor Dugan, with a wink at Wesley.

"Not the only one," said Father Wrzesnia softly.

Monsignor Dugan lowered his eyes. "I forgot myself," he said humbly. He turned to Wesley. "Couldn't you stretch yourselves as far as Poland?" He brightened. "In which case, a site in or near Chicago would seem just right, would it not?"

"Nice going."

"Sorry it took so long."

"Where're you from?"

"Baltimore."

"I'm from California. Born in San Diego. Just recently I've been living in L.A. I don't think I'll go back there, though."

"Where'll you go?"

"Maybe to Baltimore."

"I'm not sure I'll go back there."

"Then I won't go there either. What do you say we get out of here and go to the Raphael rooms. They don't have these crowds."

Mark and Laurie departed the Sistine Chapel.

"What's your name?"

"Laurie Walker."

"I'm Mark Stapleton. How long have you been in Rome?"

"Five days. How about you?"

"Two weeks. I'm going to Florence this afternoon."

"We're going to be in Florence by the middle of next week."

"Where'll you be staying?"

Laurie had to think a moment. "I believe it's called the Granduca."

"Sounds expensive."

"I'm sure it is. What about you?"

"Probably a youth hostel, only I've been staying in a kind of hostel in Rome, and I've had enough of them, I think." Mark added, "I'm traveling alone."

"I'm not."

"I know. Your uncle. And is the old woman a relative?" Laurie shook her head, and let Mark take her left hand as they paused in front of the School of Athens.

She pointed to a figure in the foreground. "According to the guidebook Uncle Wesley has, that person, who's supposed to be Euclid—you know, who wrote about the hypotenuse of a triangle—is actually a portrait of Michelangelo."

"Yeah, only it's Heraclitus, not Euclid," Mark said. "Euclid's over there—with the compass."

"I might have known I'd get it mixed up." Laurie gave a little laugh, Mark a little squeeze. "It's because I don't listen very carefully to Uncle Wesley when he reads."

"Think of all we could have done together if we'd met five days ago."

"We couldn't have, though. I'm under contract. As the old lady's traveling companion."

"So that's why you have to wear stockings. Who is she?"

Laurie hesitated, but she could see no harm in telling him. "It's Emilene Ladore."

"No kidding! Does she have bodyguards and stuff?"

"No. The Italian police told Uncle Wesley it was safer not to. They said bodyguards were asking for trouble, because the only good ones are kidnappers or Mafia to begin with—it's how they learn their job."

"When her father died last year, the papers said he was right up there with Hughes and the Hunt brothers and Getty."

"I believe it. You can't imagine the way people are after her," Laurie said, with sudden sharpness. "People you wouldn't expect it of. It made me sick, last night at dinner. Just now, too. They're like pigs. Oink, oink, oink. Everybody we've met so far—including my uncle, of course. It makes me furious. It really does. She's not dumb, but she's kind of innocent, as if she hadn't ever grown up in some ways. I guess her father was a hard man to live with. She quotes him all the time. Things like, 'My daddy always said that the one thing you should never forget about is the one thing you'll never see—germs.' She's a germ crank, kind of. One of the things I have to do is sterilize the toilet seat for her once a day."

Mark said, "Germs are a thing of the past. If you're going to worry about anything, it should be viruses." He grinned. "I'm a good clean kid, by the way, even though I'm not in a suit and tie. Guaranteed not to have herpes."

"Who cares? Let's go to the next room."

They went into the Stanza of Heliodorus. Two guards who were talking to each other stopped long enough to look at Laurie, then went on with their conversation. Mark and she went to stand in front of *The Mass at Bolsena*.

"Julius II," she said. "Have I got that right?"

Mark nodded. "Yeah. Can't you get away at all? I mean, couldn't you try, if you had a good enough reason?"

"It could cause so much trouble the reason would have to be pretty good."

"Would I be a good enough reason?"

Laurie looked him over. "You might."

"I'll leave you a note at the Granduca, telling you where I'm staying."

"What if Uncle Wesley sees it?"

Mark said, "I'll sign it with a fake name, but you'll know it's me. Mark Stapleton."

They moved toward the fresco of *The Expulsion of Heliodorus*. "I know it's a heavy question, but—you aren't in love or engaged or anything like that to some guy back in Baltimore, are you, Laurie?"

She shook her head. "No ties—except for Uncle Wesley and Miss Ladore."

"Me neither. It could lead to some really good times in Florence."

"I doubt it," Laurie said. Her eyes filled with tears, and Mark squeezed harder. "You really can't imagine how awful it is. My God!" She gasped. "Here comes one of those monsignors. They must have finished their conference. Get away from me, quick."

Monsignor Dugan noticed that the beautiful young niece of Wesley Knuckles was talking to a young American, and that when she saw him approach, she sent the young man away to look at the fresco called *The Repulse of Attila.* But Dugan didn't think much about it, much less mention it to anybody. The young seemed to pick each other up everywhere these days, and drop each other just as casually, even in the Vatican.

James Molyneux had spent the better part of two days working on a brief catalog of the books Ricky had given to him to sell. When it drew close to four-thirty on Friday afternoon, the time for which he'd invited Mark Stapleton, he had only six entries left. He'd finish easily by early in the evening, despite the interruption. The letter he'd then write to Peter Tremper could be not only about the books but also about Mark, could tell Peter his impressions of Mark, and that he'd gone out of his way to be nice to him, had him around the very day he'd called—which just might make Tremper a little more willing to send an advance to Ricky. James had left the largest volumes till last, had them in a pile on his table. Folio volumes, all of them, big and awkward to handle—and by no means necessarily interesting in proportion to their weight; his first quick glance had indicated that they were all about theology.

Would Mark be on time, or should James begin a new entry? He'd like Mark better for being punctual, but given what American youth, as one saw it in Florence these days, seemed mostly to be like—wandering *bouche ouverte*, if not in a daze, through the city where intelligence had been invented—he didn't count on it.

He decided to go ahead with his work, which was, moreover, engrossing.

He lifted the topmost of the folio volumes off the pile, laid it on the working area of his library table, measured its dimensions, and noted them—it was some 18¼ by 13⅛ inches in size—then made a brief description of the binding. After that, he went through the first pages one by one, taking more notes where it was appropriate. Then, when he'd reached the text and quickly riffled through the rest of the book to get an idea of its general condition—was it stained or foxed, were any of its pages torn or crumpled?—he discovered an oddity about it. Two pages, almost at the back, were stuck together, and something flat was imprisoned inside them. He investigated. It was as if the two pages of the book had been turned into a kind of envelope by having their borders glued around some other sheets of paper; the whole thing was too thick to be only one sheet. He squeezed lightly. The inserted sheets, if that was what they were, were slightly smaller than the pages of the book, no doubt about that, and it felt as if they were folded together in such a way that there were ridges at their borders. He did find some places where he could get a finger through holes between the sealed pages, but in doing so he discovered nothing new. The book's secret eluded any casual investigation.

He sat back, puzzled. This would make a strange descriptive note in his list for Tremper. Should he attempt to separate the pages? He knew a restorer who worked with paper, Egidio Ferrante, but he'd charge the earth, and there was no reason to think it would be worth it; moreover, he just might recognize the Guidoni coat of arms on the binding. While not as famous as the Medici arms, they were still to be found here and there in Florence, carved over the doors of Ricky's palace, for instance, and prominent in the Guidoni chapel at Santa Croce. Probably it would be best just to note the peculiarity and send the book along to Tremper as it was, and let him worry about it. No doubt he had people who charged less for routine repairs than did a restorer of fine prints and drawings, like Ferrante. On the other hand, it did make one curious.

The bell rang to inform James that his visitor had arrived. "Damn!" he said, irritated that he had to stop just when there was this new development to fuss over. He closed the book. Further investigations would have to wait. He also quickly turned over any other books that displayed the Guidoni arms—an unnecessary precaution, no doubt, where Mark Stapleton was concerned, but Ricky would certainly be uneasy if he knew that James was letting even the most naïve strange eyes see the one thing that would surely give away their transaction.

He put on his jacket, went downstairs and out of the building, and crossed the courtyard to the high metal door that gave onto Piazza San Doroteo.

"Sorry to keep you waiting out here," he said, as he was shaking hands with Mark, "but the porter who usually lets people in is sort of on vacation. He's around somewhere, I saw him only yesterday, but he isn't technically on duty, and when he's not here or it's after hours, the outside bells ring in our rooms instead of his, and we have to come down. I hope you had no trouble finding our obscure piazza."

He closed the door behind them, then led Mark into the vestibule of Villa Arberoni. There was a stairway to one side, but James used his key to open the door that led to the interior of the building and the elevator.

Mark, very curious about James—more curious than James appeared to be about him; James hadn't looked at him, not really, not even when they were shaking hands—had noticed immediately how James found ways, such as a gesture—the sudden leaning on a doorjamb or reaching to touch the vestibule table— or a quick turn of direction, to hide his limp. Peter Tremper had prepared Mark for that, but he hadn't prepared him for the keen intensity of James's face, its utter lack of complacence. A disturbing face. Then Mark got distracted by the place. There'd been an enticing glimpse of a garden—huge cypresses and a path— through a grille to the left as they crossed the courtyard where lemon trees grew in terra-cotta tubs, placed so they'd get the sun, and now he had a view of a long dim corridor that appeared to stretch the full length of the building, some hundred and seventy feet, for at the far end, glimmering like hope, there was another wide door with a window in it that was bright with daylight. The floor was of hexagonal terra-cotta tiles, the walls freshly white-washed, the air cool and still, not unlike his Roman monastery. Several other, smaller doors gave off the corridor, all of them closed. It was as if the place were used as an institution, a school where the children made no noise; the quiet here, in contrast to the relentless din of commercial Florence, was striking. After they'd got inside the elevator, James Molyneux pushed the top button on the command panel, and with a sigh, like a weary animal prodded to its feet, the elevator shuddered and rose.

James said nothing during their slow ascent, which seemed to Mark to take a long time, and the silence seemed as long as waiting for a gun to go off. He recalled Tremper's remarks about James: that he was likely to be prickly but that one shouldn't be put off by it, that it was because of his limp and his "disappointments"—whatever Tremper meant by that—not because of a bad disposition. "Actually, James can be almost lovable. Almost. And," Tremper had said, "if you're lucky, and he takes a liking to you, he might show you a little of Florence one morning, and there's nobody, absolutely nobody, who makes a better guide. Earned his money at it for a while. Take advantage of him." Tremper had added, with one of those little smiles—he was not particularly guarded around Mark—"If I didn't think he'd find things about you to like, Marco Polo, I wouldn't send you to him. Because his bite, when he doesn't like someone, is no joke."

Hence this morning's early telephone call to James, on Mark's first day in Florence. And what had resulted from it? An invitation to tea. Not for a drink or for coffee somewhere, but tea. The only time in his life Mark had been invited to tea. A man of forty-five inviting him to tea! It had made him wonder what had gone through the mails about him between L.A. and here. Funny old faggots . . .

The elevator stopped and the inner door glided open. James pushed the outer door and held it while Mark went by. Another corridor, this one not so long as the one on the ground floor, and not so bare: placed at intervals along each side were low wooden chests, richly carved, and the floor, though still of tile, was partly covered by worn old rugs. As below, several doors gave off the corridor; James led Mark to one on the right-hand side, which had a knocker of brass in the shape of a lion's head mounted on it.

"Come in. These are my rooms. Tremper's been here," he said.

Mark looked around. The room they were presently standing in was not a particularly large one by Italian standards, perhaps twenty feet by thirty. There were two windows on the outer wall, one on each side of a pair of doors that stood open onto a balcony. The furnishings were sparse, almost ascetic—a few chairs and small tables, mostly in the same style as the dark carved wooden chests in the corridor. No rugs. In the center of the room was a large table supported on bulbous legs, which was piled up with books. The plastered walls had some faded ornament painted directly on them, and in addition, two full-length mirrors in heavy gilded frames were hung by stout cords from the picture molding, one on either side of the door to the outside hall. Another door, at the end of the room, led to another room, into which James disappeared to prepare the tea.

He reappeared carrying a tray. "We'll take it out on the terrace," he said. "I've been working all day inside, and the air would be nice." The terrace had its own low white metal table and some canvas chairs. "Pull up so you can reach things. How is Tremper?"

"He was fine when I left him," Mark said.

"I suppose he writes you." Mark shook his head. "Oh no?" James stared at Mark a moment, as if he didn't believe him. "Sugar? Lemon? I'm afraid I can't offer you milk. It's strictly light housekeeping here. I've no real kitchen, you see, only a hotplate in my bedroom for boiling water, and no refrigerator—though I can get ice downstairs if I want it. Where're you staying?" When Mark said he was at a youth hostel not far from the railroad station, James gave a little nod, as if the arrangement precluded any comment.

Suddenly he began to fire questions, speaking abruptly, almost rudely. "You said this morning that you'd just come up from Rome. How long were you there?"

"Two weeks."

"What did you see?"

"Just about everything."

"Impossible."

"Enough, anyway. And lots of places more than once."

"Such as?"

"Oh . . . the Sistine Chapel."

"That doesn't tell me much about you. It's hardly plumbing a depth, to see that place twice. What else?"

Mark chose something less obvious. "San Luigi dei Francesi."

"Hmm. How did you happen to go back there?"

"Reasons."

James smiled. "Not a bad choice. Did you see the Caravaggios at Santa Maria del Popolo?"

"Certainly."

"St. Paul's horse is interesting, isn't it? Everybody else always has the beast fleeing or rearing—at the vision. But Caravaggio shows us how Paul's conversion was a personal thing between him and God. Brute horse and brutish groom had no share in it. What did you see today in Florence?"

"Not much. I didn't do any sightseeing. I felt like a change. I went down the river to that big park. Ran awhile. Went to the public swimming pool—they told me about it at the hostel. Had a swim and some sun. Got some lunch. Then, as I was walking back along the embankment, I found this old guy who had a boat. He wasn't using it for fishing, and I got him to rent it to me. I rowed up and down for about an hour, between the spillways. And then I walked for miles back up behind the city. Ended at the big piazza where they've got the oversize copy of the David. Fooled around up there, looking through telescopes and eating ice cream, until it was time to come here."

James, thinking he couldn't have joined in any of it, that Mark's vitality was quite excluding, said quietly, "All in one day."

"I thought it wasn't enough. I should at least have gone in a church or two."

"Donatello will always be here," said James. "Though you, of course, will not. How long *are* you staying? More tea? Just put your cup on the table and I'll pour into it. Hot water? That all right? Sorry there are only these dry biscuits to eat, but I haven't been out today, really not at all, so I had no opportunity to get us anything. There. One day off, to recover from Rome, I'll grant you, but tomorrow, of course, you must go to work. Looking, I mean. You'll see we're quite different."

"Oh, I already have," Mark said. "Have seen that."

"Seen *I'm* different, you mean?" James said, amused. He sipped in silence. "So is my balcony. You can't have had one like it in Rome."

"No, I didn't." Mark looked around. "It's terrific."

"Terrific? A 'terrific' balcony? Yet it's only on the fourth floor, by European count. Surely below the minimum for 'terrific.' Go over to the railing, if you like, and take a look. If you aim to the right, the view is toward Careggi—miles across the Arno. The Medici had a villa there. You didn't say how long you were staying in Florence."

"I don't know. At least a week," Mark said.

"I'm terribly busy just now," James said, "but perhaps, even so—"

He didn't finish his sentence, nor did Mark ask to be taken around—why invite the bite Tremper had mentioned? "Thanks for taking time out to see me," he said. "And as you are so busy—well, you'll have to tell me when I should leave, Mr. Molyneux. I really don't have any idea how long you stay when you're invited to tea."

"Until you've had enough."

"Enough tea?"

"No. Enough of my balcony." James smiled. "I meant it. Go look at Careggi."

While Mark did so, James sized him up. The predictable clothes—polo shirt, wash trousers. No coat, of course—James hadn't expected that. The running shoes—they'd become almost a uniform for the young. Like many people with some pronounced physical disability, James was almost morbidly sensitive to the physical presence of other people. He found Mark's overwhelming. His vitality radiated out at one, diminishing one's own flawed corpus still further. And there were the imperfect good looks, the heavy jaw and slightly lopsided mouth. So much more interesting than mere regularity.

Mark turned around. "Well—there. I've looked in every direction. Is that enough?"

James wasn't ready to let him leave, for he didn't yet know about the all-important intellect, or if Mark would be worth more time.

"What did you do for Tremper?" James asked.

"Mostly I worked in a back room."

"Did you ever meet Ixion?" The bookshop was called Tremper & Ixion.

"Never. I don't think there is such a person."

"Nor do I. Curious name to have picked for an imaginary partner, to make your firm sound more tony. Ixion was a murderer, you know. The Greek Cain, first to do a job on somebody, I forget just who. Tremper & Ixion—it does have a nice sound to it. If pretentious. But then, pretense is at the center of what motivates most collectors of everything, including books. If they didn't find it where they shopped, they'd not come back."

Mark neither agreed nor disagreed.

"Is the business going well, d'you think?" James asked.

"Seems to be. But I honestly couldn't say. So much happens where you don't see it."

"Mmm. They're all so secretive, those dealers," said James. "I do buy old books for Tremper, and other dealers too, but I don't consider myself one of them. I'm an amateur. Don't have a dealer's manner—or methods, either." He watched to see how Mark would take the next remark. "They always seem to me, oh, maybe not Tremper so much, but most of the others, always seem faintly corrupt. Sufficiently tempted, they'd do things one would oneself prefer not to do. Do you know what I mean?"

"Sell the family Bible, you mean, if the price was right."

James put his teacup back on the table and ran his fingers back and forth over his knees, a sign that he was pleased. "Precisely. I'm glad some people I know aren't here to hear you say it, but precisely. Sell it whether they need the money, really, or not—need excuses things greed doesn't, you know. Even Tremper would, wouldn't he? It's from that sort of thing one has hoped to keep oneself, by remaining merely an amateur. And staying—alas!—so very poor."

A surprising turn in the conversation. Mark began to like James better. He'd probably offered tea because it was cheap.

"Tell me, Mark, what did you do in the back room at Tremper & Ixion?"

"Mended things. I'd worked in the shop of the library where I went to college. First aid to books."

"Ever work on old books?"

"Some. They had a good man who fixed them, and he taught me. That's what I did for Peter. Repairs—if they weren't too serious."

"Very useful around a place like Tremper & Ixion, I'm sure. And Peter wrote me you did cartwheels down Rodeo Drive." Mark slowly shook his head. "But you could have?"

Mark leaned back against the railing of the balcony, seized it with his hands, locked his elbows, and slowly, slowly, taking his time, lifted his feet off the ground. He then leaned backwards until it seemed he must lose his balance and go over the railing on his head.

James had to close his eyes. "What are you about to do?" he whispered.

Mark lowered himself. "I've put my feet back on the floor again." He'd noticed James's eyes. "Are you afraid of heights, Mr. Molyneux?"

"I'm afraid of everything," James said. "Heights and depths. It can be humiliating, sometimes, though not just now, for surely what you did really *was* dangerous."

"Only if the railing had given way, and I knew it wouldn't. I'd tested it when I was looking at Careggi."

"I see." James got up and shook the railing himself. "Sound enough, I agree." Meanwhile, he'd come to a decision. "And now I want to show you something," he said. "Come along to my sitting room."

They went back inside, James talking as they did so. "Just as you arrived, I'd come upon a little problem, and perhaps you can help me with it. I've been making a descriptive list of all these books that you see; they're from a family in the north of Italy. Anyway, one of them has something . . . I suppose one could say something 'wrong" with it. Let me show it to you. Perhaps you'd have an idea what to do."

James went to the table. "Here it is." He righted the large folio volume, bound in vellum the color of yellowed ivory, intending to open it at once.

Before he could do so, Mark's interest was, unfortunately, caught by the binding. Mark reached out a hand to run his fingers over it. "Isn't that . . . 'terrific'!" he said, grinning a little. "Like satin. And the decorations, too."

"Yes, it is an interesting binding," James said. "The tooled arabesques are pretty and, for the period, very rare. The coat of arms is, of course, standard. Banal. One of the things one has to put up with, if one plays with old books of European source."

But Mark wasn't to be put off so easily. "A shield. And that crisscross thing. And three lizards. Curlicues. And that looks like a hat above it all."

"Which is to say a portcullis, three salamanders, mantlings, and, to be sure, a hat. The family that once owned this is extinct, so the arms aren't current, one might say." James did open the book. He turned to the title page. "The subject's as boring as the coat of arms. *De Interveniendo Dei in Rebus Humanis*— 'On God's Intervention in the Affairs of Men,' is how I read it. By one Gregory of Rimini. I haven't had a chance to look it up—or him, either—but I expect it's considerably older than the book. I mean, the book must be a printed version of something written some time before." He paused, while Mark looked at the title page. "One wonders where even Tremper would sell this one. Obscure treatises on theology can't be fast-moving items, I'd think. Well, that'll be his problem. Here's mine." James opened the book further. "It's near the back." He came to the stuck pages. "There. You see? Isn't that curious? What do you make of it?"

Mark sat down. He looked at the paper and ran the tips of his fingers over it, as he had over the binding, like an insect with sensitive feelers. Sensually—that struck James. Mark asked for more light, and James moved his large brass lamp nearer and turned it on. Mark then asked for a magnifying glass, and James brought it. Mark, too, tried to insert his fingers in gaps in the paste.

"There's something between the pages," he said.

"I'm quite aware of that," James said.

Under Mark's careful prying, part of the bottoms of the pages, where there was much less adhesive than on the tops and sides, gave way, and he could insert some fingers. "Huh," he said. "Whatever it is that's in there has been glued to the second page. I think deliberately, the way they used to tip in illustrations when they were printed separately from the book." Mark felt some more. "And what I suspect happened is that the page the insert is mounted on and the page in front of it got stuck together because whoever did it was too liberal with the paste. It squeezed out from behind the inserts, got onto the backing page, and of course, when the book was closed, that page then stuck to the one before."

"Quite plausible. You know, I like the way you handle the book, and I like the way your mind works, Mark," James said, as quick to give credit as he was to criticize. "You've learned some things from your work with Tremper—never mind whether or not you go on with it. Will you, do you think?"

"After what you said about book dealers?"

"You could become the first entirely honorable one."

Mark shrugged. He went over the book again. This time he widened the opening between the pages at the bottom and looked in. "Can't see far enough up there to be useful. But here, where I got the pages apart, you can see some of the adhesive. Dry and old—it might come apart just by some careful work with a razor blade or a scalpel, though I wouldn't want to try it."

"What's to be done, then?" James said.

"Steam."

"Just . . . steam?"

"Best thing there is, if it's regular flour paste. If it's something special—well, I wouldn't know. But it looks to me like paste. And if it is, it'll let go if it's moistened."

"But what about the inserted material? If there's ink on that, handwriting or whatever, would it run?"

"Not if you're careful enough. You could slip some blank paper in wherever it'll go, to protect the insert. And not moisten the page a lot, just enough to get at the paste. That'll happen pretty quickly, I'd think, given how old it probably is." Mark hefted the volume. "Big guy. Hard for one person to handle, but we might do it together. You had boiling water for the tea, so you must have a teakettle. Want to give it a try?"

James just hesitated. "Why not?" he said, with a certain reck-lessness.

It took them an hour. James was given the task of holding the book while Mark manipulated the stuck pages over the spout of the teakettle. First he'd apply steam to them, then test the firmness of the adhesive. More steam. Another testing. Then he'd try to loosen the outer borders. More steam. The pages rippled, of course, but Mark said they'd smooth out once they'd been let dry; they could even be flattened with a coolish iron, if necessary. More steam. Another testing. Bit by bit, Mark got them to open. As each little section gave way, he put wadding inside to hold the freshly separated areas apart, so they wouldn't stick themselves back together again. It took patience, but he seemed to have that—more of it, surprisingly, than James did, who got frustrated and nervous, though of course it was fun, too—for both of them. A mystery, unraveling before their eyes.

At exactly seven o'clock—the bells in the little church of San Doroteo outside were just chiming—the thing was done. James carried the volume back to the table and laid it flat, open to the two once-stuck-together pages. The insert, now fully visible though still attached to its backing pages, was indeed made of sheets of paper, slightly smaller than those of the book, that were carefully hinged together by narrow strips of another paper run-ning along their boundaries. Moreover, it appeared that they had on their inner surfaces some kind of drawing; ink from the other side had come through here and there.

"Let's have a look," James said.

He unfolded the sheets with due respect and delicacy and laid them out flat. There were four of them altogether, hence they made a rectangle nearly four times the size of the book, one single large sheet, because of their hinges, on which was a single contin-uous drawing.

Mark said, "I was right about its being attached like an illustra-tion. A folded-up illustration. I wonder who put it in there. And I wonder what the subject is. Must have something to do with— what did you say the title was?"

"'On Divine Intervention in Human Affairs,'" said James. "We may well never know the answers to your questions, I suppose. Exasperating, given the magnitude of our discovery." The choice of words was quite unfortunate. "By that I mean simply its size."

James had realized at once that he had made a mistake in letting Mark work on the book, had gone too far, too fast. His hands were now trembling just a little—something to be concealed. Every instinct, all the years he'd spent looking at fine things and judging them, told him that what he and Mark had before them was magnificent, of such potential importance that Mark's mere knowledge of its existence was very possibly a major indiscretion. He folded the drawing back, though Mark was still examining it, and put the book to one side. "So much for that," he said. And, too abruptly, "Thanks, of course, for your help. I'd never have known how to do it otherwise."

James asked for the telephone number of Mark's hostel, as good a signal as any that it was time for Mark to leave. As he was writing it down, Mark picked up another of Ricky's books and turned it over. "That's interesting," he said. "This coat of arms is like the one on the book we were steaming, except this one has fish standing on their tails, and no hat."

James looked. On either side of the shield that bore the portcullis and the salamanders was a supporting dolphin rampant; one of them held a spear in its flipper, the other a banner with a cross on it. He said, "Venetian families sometimes have marine motifs on their arms," and took Mark to the elevator.

It was already rising, and stopped at their floor. A very large man got out, who sported muttonchop whiskers and flowing hair, and was carrying two fat briefcases.

"Hello, John," James said. "Just back from the German Library?"

"Yes, yes. Another profitable day. The edifice of my pages grows ever loftier."

James introduced Mark. "This is Professor John Battle Davenport," he said. "Professor Davenport is writing . . . the book to end all books, aren't you, John?"

Davenport harrumphed. "No book will end all books on Raphael," he said, "but if it were possible, I suppose mine might do it. It will, after all, sum up the wisdom of a lifetime."

"Back to the library tomorrow, John?" James turned to Mark. "Professor Davenport spends his days at our splendid German Art Historical Institute—one of the best libraries in the world. So— you will be there tomorrow, won't you, John?"

"Not likely," Davenport said, in no way surprised that anyone would be so interested in where he'd pass his day. "Hate to waste even an hour, but Pauline wants to do something. We'll be back for dinner, of course."

"Of course," James said, as the elevator doors were closing. "And that," he said, in the privacy of the descending car, "is the most perfect example of its species that exists in all the world. The Academic Humbug—which is by no means endangered." He put Mark out on the piazza. "I'll write Tremper about you," he said, "and perhaps we can see each other again, though I don't promise it."

James's excitement, which lasted the night and hardly let him sleep, only grew greater after he'd spent some time at the German Library himself the next day. His questioning of Professor Davenport had been purposeful; James didn't want him around while he was doing his research, for Davenport was notorious for being jealous of other people's work. As James had no photographs of his drawing yet, he had to depend on simple memory while he hunted and compared; even so, his investigation suggested something quite extraordinary and more than vindicated his first instincts.

He returned to Villa Arberoni, determined to try to free the drawing from the page to which it was still attached. He needed help, but of course it would never do to call in Mark again, and so, in the end, he cut the page with a razor blade; then, steaming the drawing loose was no problem at all. He replaced the page in the book but made no attempt to reattach it to its own stub, merely left it loose-leaf.

If what James now suspected was true, his drawing was an almost unimaginable find, so important that it was—given Italian law—dangerous, so valuable it might change his whole life, not to mention Ricky's. The only people who knew of its existence, perhaps the only people who'd known since the early sixteenth century, were himself and Mark Stapleton. Fortunately, Mark didn't know what he'd seen, and he wouldn't get a second look, not at the drawing, probably not at James. He'd simply have to be kept at a distance. He might tell Tremper about the steaming, but it would end there, for James wouldn't send the book to Tremper, and of course he wouldn't sell the drawing through Tremper. Mark, the product of the here-today culture of California, wasn't likely to say anything to Tremper anyway, was he? With luck, what had happened would go out of his head. With luck—but James, as he worried about it, wasn't so sure. He remembered how careful Mark was, and his quickness to catch the discrepancy between the two variant coats of arms. Still, the secret was presumably safe enough, so long as Mark went away without learning anything more. That meant he mustn't be given a chance to ask questions. James wouldn't telephone him. Definitely not. He'd send him a note in a day or two, saying he'd been busy and that now he was going to leave town. Something of that sort.

Which was a pity, because James had, in fact, liked Mark, and it seemed unfair to punish him for being so helpful. He recalled Mark's intent expression as he'd shaded his eyes to look toward Careggi, and his fine concentration as he'd worked those pages loose. Yes, it was a pity all this had come up to cause Mark's banishment. Otherwise, one might have done something with him, started his mind and spirit in finer directions. Otherwise, he might have become something of an ornament to one's life.

Such being James Molyneux's plan—to see no more of Mark—he was fairly nonplussed the following evening when he walked into dinner and found Mark there, as Signora Benassi's guest. And that was only the beginning.

PART

three

This time the porter, Antonio, was on duty, wearing a striped jacket and dark trousers. With a bow and a murmured *"Buona sera,"* he let Mark into Villa Arberoni and rang upstairs on the house telephone to announce him. Then, using gestures to reinforce his quick Italian, he gave Mark his choice of the stairs or the elevator to the next floor above. Mark chose the former, to see what they were like: wide and dim, three flights, electric lights on each landing at this hour, and a stool for the weary.

The upstairs vestibule seemed to him much like the parts of the building he'd already seen—except there were travertine floors and the ceiling was higher—until the maid who was waiting admitted him into the first of the state rooms.

What a difference! It was spacious and splendidly decorated; the lofty, coved ceiling was frescoed with tropical landscapes that were inhabited by exotic birds and animals: parrots and toucans, alligators and jaguars. The doorjambs were made of marble, and the floors were parqueted. Tall bronze reflecting lamps stood in the corners, turned on now to illuminate the ceiling, and Savonarola chairs, their hard wooden seats softened by velvet cushions, lined the walls.

And what a maid! She was skinny and ancient, severe in manner and dress: black, head-to-toe black—shoes, stockings, dress almost to the ankles—with, however, white cuffs and a beautiful white collar that fell from a tightly buttoned band at her throat well down onto her bosom, shoulders, and back, like an ecclesiastical vestment. She also wore, perched atop her knotted iron-gray hair, a little white cap, formed and starched into a miniature bundt cake. She held herself stiffly erect and walked rapidly as she took him down a hallway as formal and elaborate as the great foyer, past several pairs of closed doors. Then came a pair that was partly opened.

When she noticed, she stopped and waited in order to cross behind Mark to close them. Curious, he tried to get a quick look. She allowed him to go into the room for a moment.

It was easily large enough to serve as a ballroom, surely the grandest room on this floor, yet it was disused. The furniture, in-

cluding a piano, was covered with sheets. There were no rugs on
the floors, which needed waxing and polishing. Though there
were heavy gilded valances above the great windows along the
outside wall, there were no draperies. In the center of this wall, a
pair of glass-paneled doors gave onto a terrace that overlooked the
gardens and formed an extension of the same dimensions as the
great room. Mark could see flimsy outdoor chairs sitting on it,
turned on their ends to keep their seats and backs clean, as well as
marble benches, marble urns planted with flowers, and a marble
balustrade broken by the beginnings of a stairway that would go
down to ground level. But none of this was what he'd been
brought to see.

The maid was signaling for his attention. When she got it, she
pointed to the wall directly opposite the doors to the terrace—the
place of honor—where a large painting hung on silken cords that
came from the molding below the coving of the ceiling. It showed
a magnificent woman, standing, so it appeared, in this very place.
Her abundant black hair was caught up by a circlet of rubies; she
also wore a necklace of several strands of pearls, as well as gold
bracelets and sparkling gemstone rings. In her right hand she held
an egret-feather fan, while her left hand rested at the corner of an
ornate table on which was placed a spiraled seashell in a very
elaborate mounting, and a many-branched candelabra, whence
came light that touched her face and her fine bare arms and shoulders, and glittered on the sumptuous fabrics of her dress and on
her jewels.

Mark stared. He couldn't imagine anyone's having such a painting in a house, yet he'd been invited to what Signora Benassi,
making fun of his origins, had called her "rancho."

The maid waited—she, too, looking at the painting, as if in a
wonder of her own. Then she lifted the dustcover from the table
that was placed below the portrait. It was the same as the painted
table—and in its way as amazing as the portrait itself, its carcass
inlaid with rare woods about which sprouted and twined leaves
and tendrils of gilt-bronze, bearing flowers of lapis and enameling.
She replaced the table's cover and stood back for a last look. "*La
contessa*," she breathed reverently. She led Mark back to the hall
and closed the doors to the great room behind them.

• • •

Mark waited to spring his surprise until he and the signora were seated in her small drawing room, quite different in scale from the great room, and more pleasant; there were photographs on the tables, and the furniture was comfortable. She offered him a drink. He took Scotch, as did she, brought to them by the maid.

"I have to tell you something that'll amaze you, Signora Benassi. I've already been to Villa Arberoni."

"No!" she said. "It's not possible. I can't be that forgetful."

Mark explained about his visit to James Molyneux. "Your calling card has no address on it, you know. I never guessed I was at your place—and for some reason James didn't say anything."

"One doesn't reveal one's life all at once, Mr. Stapleton," Signora Benassi said. "But—what a coincidence!" she then said delightedly. "I adore coincidences. They remind us how little control we really have over our lives. And weren't you clever to wait till now to tell me about it and not waste it on the telephone. It's so important to know the right moment to spring a secret."

She'd been working, when Mark arrived, with a pencil and some sheets of paper, which she'd put down on a low table in front of the upholstered couch on which they were both sitting. When the ancient maid came in with some little crackers, Signora Benassi told her to put the papers away. "We're planning a party, Mr. Stapleton, Costanza and I are. It's almost two months away, but it will be a big party, and that takes time. We've been estimating what needs to be done to ready the rooms the party will be in; above all, we've been inventorying possessions—silver and china and the like—to see how many people I can invite." Signora Benassi made a little face. "As well as inventorying people to see how many are left to be guests. Now tell me about yourself and Florence."

Mark began by describing the hostel where he was staying.

"It sounds simply awful. Surely you don't like it?"

"I liked the place in Rome, but this—" He shook his head. "Full of kids that need baths. Noisy. Not too clean. I'm too old for it."

"No doubt," the signora said, "you find my villa, with which you are so unexpectedly familiar, more agreeable. Would you like living here better?"

The point of her teasing was unclear, and Mark made no reply.

"I have room for you. Move in."

He didn't know what to say; the invitation, if it was meant seriously, was too unexpected. And he couldn't help but wonder what strings might be attached.

Signora Benassi said, rather grandly, "Mr. Stapleton, a young man ought never to be tongue-tied. In your situation, you should say yes even though you have your doubts. That would be instinctive with any well-brought-up Italian your age."

"Like Tiberio?"

"Precisely. To Tiberio, the truth would be less important than my feelings. I daresay James Molyneux will be teaching you things about the city, but if you do move in here, you'll have some things to learn from me, as well."

Mark thought of Laurie—did he want to give up his independence? No, definitely not. "It would be for such a short time," he said, stalling.

"A rude excuse. And don't be so sure your stay will be short, once we got you settled in here." The signora began to play with her many finger rings; Mark hadn't noticed any the day they'd met, but then, he remembered, she'd had on gloves. "However, I must let you in on the whole thing, before you decide. For all its grandeur, if you will, Villa Arberoni is, at bottom—we only whisper this, mind you, never say it aloud—is at bottom"—and she did whisper—"a *pensione*."

"I don't believe it."

"Demi. Oh, very demi, but yes, a *pensione*. You see, I have much too much room. The obvious thing is to rent it as apartments, but if you do, in Italy, you can't ever raise rents and you can never get people out. And when they die, their heirs stuff them and sit them in chairs in a window for an hour every afternoon, and in the meantime move in and live there themselves, paying the same old rent. Even if you can prove that their relative is stuffed, to get them out takes years and costs a lot of money for lawyers and bribes. It's the most terrible nuisance. So I rent rooms by the week and the month, and only to foreigners who will, I am reasonably sure, move on eventually, and if they don't, have no rights anyway. I'm quite arbitrary about who I let stay here—and they come only at my invitation and with dependable connections—if there is such a thing. No small children. No salesmen. No sociologists. No bores"—she paused—"except when it's unavoidable. You'll be quite free to come and go, by the way, if that should be worrying you—as it might at your age. You can have guests to your rooms, as you were the guest of James. We're quite grown up," she said, mocking his unspoken reservations, to his embarrassment.

"Laughter and the clinking of glasses till the small hours of the night—they don't bother us. Nobody can hear. Nobody will know. And we serve some meals. That's where the demi comes in. Dinner on Tuesday and Saturday—it's often quite an event. You can have guests then, too. There'll be half a dozen tonight, invited by one of my regulars who's a professor and who really rather overdoes it sometimes. And there's lunch if you want it, but a buffet kind of thing, Tuesday through Saturday. Sunday and Monday we fend for ourselves. I usually dine with my *pensionnaires*, though I don't usually have lunch with them. I'm old, you see, and I like variety and company, and this is how I get it. As I can hardly be expected either to want or to be able to keep this absurd building filled with guests who don't pay, I keep it filled with ones that do. Well?" She waited a moment. "How does that sound to you—clinking of glasses and all?"

"It sounds wonderful, Signora Benassi. But I'm on a very strict budget."

"Oh, don't worry about that. I don't run Villa Arberoni for profit, exactly, though I try not to run it at a loss. The question is, where will we put you? It so happens that several apartments are vacant, but I think the one that would suit you best is on the ground floor. At this end, but farther along toward the corner. The garden side. The windows are high—they'll start at your shoulders—but it's quite light. Not always sunny, but light enough. You'll have a bedroom, a sitting room, and a bath. Would you like that?"

"It sounds very nice." Mark waited for her to say something more specific about money.

The signora played with her rings while she did some figuring. "To be precise . . ." She named a sum that was absurdly small for the circumstances, but—Mark, too, quickly did some figuring—was probably more than he'd pay for the same number of meals and his room if he stayed at the hostel. "It's a bargain rate, and you mustn't tell the others," she said. "Though they have views. And then, Mr. Stapleton"—here, Signora Benassi put a hand on his—"I haven't forgotten your kindness." She withdrew it and said briskly, "The sum I suggested covers your rooms and breakfast and the meals I mentioned. Guests are extra, wine is included. Other details you'll learn as you go along, and your bill will be given to you every Monday morning by Costanza, and you'll pay her. Speaking of her, tips are extra—Costanza, Velia and Anna, the other maids, and Gina the cook, and Antonio. So add about twenty percent to the figure I gave you. There's no telephone down where you'll be, but Antonio will take messages for you, and you can call out from his phone in the porter's room."

She let Mark refigure, to include the tips. "Is that too much?"

He shook his head. "Even if it were, how could I pass up the chance to have dinner with you twice a week?"

"Nicely put. Graceful words—but will you be left with a little extra money for graceful acts?"

Mark was puzzled. "Like what?"

"Oh . . . like bringing me flowers the next time I invite you in here." She was teasing him again. "Even though you pay for your dinner."

"I didn't think."

"It's no good if you have to think," she said.

There was a knock on a door somewhere nearby. "That'll be Ricky. The Marchese dei Guidoni—Tiberio is his great-nephew. Remember." Signora Benassi held a forefinger to her lips. "Nothing about my dizzy spell at the cemetery." The silent Costanza glided through the room into the next one and opened the door. "It will be nice for Tiberio to have someone his own age to talk to when he comes here," the signora added. "And he needs to practice his English. That mother he lives with has terrible English, and anyway, even in Italian she never says anything but 'I' and 'no.'"

84

On their way up to dinner, Signora Benassi, Mark, and Ricky passed through the great room Mark had already seen, which the signora called the *salone*, and the other rooms beyond it. They included a very large dining room—it, too, almost never used anymore—which had its long table and two massive sideboards now loaded with the china and glasses and flat silver she and Costanza had been looking over. She gestured at the bunches of knives and forks and spoons of different patterns, tied into bundles in most cases, in others just put in piles. "So much of it," she said ruefully. "The eighteenth-century silver is in my own little dining room. This is what my mother had for her receptions. Nothing very valuable, though it's perfectly good sterling. My mother loved parties, Mr. Stapleton, and in her day one gave huge ones all the time. You can imagine how many teaspoons got used when the Prince of Wales was here."

They went on into an antechamber behind which was the pantry where, the signora explained, the servants received the food from the dumbwaiter that lifted it up from the old kitchen in the basement. "That was the way it used to be done—the kitchen at a vast and inconvenient distance from the dining room. Of course, now we've got a kitchen upstairs where we're going, small but ever so efficient, and another one next to my own little private dining room back near where we were sitting just now." She looked at her watch. "Oh dear. Onward."

It was then that Mark observed something quite curious. The pretty little anteroom they were leaving had mirrors on the inner sides of its doors, and there was a mirror set into each panel of the walls, surrounded by more of the fantastic tropical landscapes Mark had already seen in the foyer and on the ceiling of the *salone*—painted for her mother eighty years ago, the signora said, by a young Brazilian artist whose first name was Joel but whose last name had got misplaced. As the signora left, the old marchese stayed behind, and Mark's eye was caught by a double reflection of his shock of white hair. Mark watched him, always in the mirrors, as he let the signora go ahead. He saw Ricky back quickly into the state dining room, go to one of the sideboards, pick up a handful of spoons and put them in his pocket, then turn and rejoin Mark and Signora Benassi. It had all happened so quickly she hadn't noticed his absence, absorbed as she was now with descriptions of her mother's famous desserts. A moment later, all three of them were in the foyer.

"We'll use the elevator," Signora Benassi said. When they got to the next floor, they went to a good-sized room, where things to drink were set up on a table. To the right was the dining room, its doors still closed. To the left, the drawing room, which was full of chairs and lamps and tables and had paintings three deep on its walls, a room as overfurnished as most of the rest of the villa was bare. Some ten people were already waiting, drinks in their hands; Mark recognized James Molyneux, of course, and also Professor John Battle Davenport. Signora Benassi announced, as she came in, in the voice of someone who knew quite well how to dominate such a miscellaneous gathering, "Good evening, good evening. This is a young American friend of mine, Mark Stapleton. He's coming to stay here with us. James, as you already know him, suppose you take him around and introduce him. Professor Davenport, the Marchese dei Guidoni and I are, as always, eager to meet your guests."

On Sunday morning, James Molyneux went to the studio in the garden of Villa Arberoni, to which he had the key, given him by his cousin Hilda before her departure for America. He found her Polaroid camera and a pack of film and took them, as well as a large piece of board, part of her art supplies, back to his own rooms. He carefully clipped the newly discovered drawing to the board, then took several photographs of it in its entirety, by the light from his balcony, and used the rest of the film to take some of the more interesting details.

He lined the snapshots up on his table. They weren't very good, but they'd have to do for the time being. He couldn't risk taking the drawing to a professional photographer; you never knew who'd mention what to whom in a city as small as Florence. And the Polaroid snapshots had one advantage: they'd go in a pocket without being conspicuous.

He then took the drawing to his table, turned on his big lamp and a table lamp, and spent an hour going over it with a magnifying glass, inch by inch, until he knew every smudge and blot, every pose and gesture of the main groups in the composition: the horsemen entering from the left, and the opposing groups to the right, standing on the ground and on the steps of a large building.

It was, quite simply, first-rate. One of the best sixteenth-century drawings he'd ever seen—good in detail, good in the overall. The general date? Though he was no expert, it seemed to James, on the basis of style, to be about that of the book, a hypothesis that was confirmed by the watermark of the paper: a horse's head surmounted by three stars. He'd looked that up on Saturday at the German Library, and it was the mark of a papermaker active in Rome before the Sack, but not after. That didn't mean the paper couldn't have been used later than it had been made, but it nevertheless suggested a *terminus ante quem* of 1527. If he could now find other drawings, agreed to be of the same date he had in mind for his own drawing, that were on the same paper—well, that would be choice substantiation of his dating, and might support an attribution to a specific artist, since the artist who'd used the paper for one drawing would have used it for others.

Many questions remained, which James would have to address, one by one. Who was the drawing by? He already had his ideas about that, daring, exciting, but they'd have to be confirmed. Why had it been done? If it was a model for a project to be carried out in fresco, as it appeared to be from the shape—a horizontal lower border, but a rounded upper one, such as is found in countless architectural paintings in Italy, wherever the ceiling of a room is vaulted—had it ever been executed? What was the subject? And, of course, how did it happen to be in Ricky's book? He'd start going into all that in the German Library on Monday; meanwhile, he wanted to have another look at that book.

He put it on his table and went through it page by page, paying particular attention, of course, to the pages close to the ones that had been inadvertently pasted together. The book yielded no further clue, except that his re-perusal of it led James to think harder about one thing: Why mount such a large drawing, surely considered of value by whoever had put it in the book or had had it put there, in this particular dull treatise by Gregory of Rimini—so dull nobody had opened it in four hundred fifty years? It couldn't have been merely a method of storage, and it wasn't accidental. It surely had to do with the book's subject, "On God's Intervention in the Affairs of Men," and that might be the key to the subject of the drawing. Perhaps, though it would be a chore, he should read some of the text.

His Latin was sketchy, but with the help of his dictionary he had, by midafternoon, an idea of Gregory's argument, which was a theory about the nature of miracles, in particular in those instances in which God had intervened dramatically and miraculously in an event of human history. The purpose of such miracles, so went the line of reasoning, was not to reveal the power and majesty of God, for to argue that would be to impute to Him the possibility of pride, but was rather to reinforce human determination through the recognition and rewarding of special virtue. Dull stuff—for who cared? Much of the text was made up of endless examples drawn from Holy Writ, patristic writings, and historical tradition, such as the tales of early medieval popes contained in the *Liber Pontificalis*. It was to the cases cited by Gregory that James paid particular attention; you can't illustrate an abstract argument, but you can a story. None in the text just before the page on which the drawing had been pasted seemed to fit it. It surely didn't represent Daniel delivered from the lions, Jonah delivered from the whale, or Saint Sebastian delivered from death by arrows.

Then, on the verso of that page, now of course cut loose from the book, James came on a reference to Saint Peter's miraculous liberation from prison by an angel, as recounted in Acts 12. And that sent him to his Italian Touring Club Guide to Rome.

He turned to the entry on the Vatican and to the description of Raphael's Stanza of Heliodorus, with its four great history frescoes, those monuments of Western sensibility. There, of course, was *The Freeing of Peter*, the most famous representation of the subject in all of Christian art—and a subject not so common. James couldn't think of another example. When he read about the other subjects in the room—*The Expulsion of Heliodorus*, *The Mass at Bolsena*, *The Repulse of Attila* by Pope Leo the Great—he came on a generalization about this stanza in his guidebook that made him say "Golly!" out loud. Done between 1512 and 1514, so the book said, the subjects had probably all been suggested by Pope Julius II, and all *"rappresentanti miracolosi interventi di Dio a protezione della Chiesa."* All "represented miraculous interventions by God in protection of the Church."

There it was. A small possible first clue. Miraculous interventions. Gregory of Rimini's subject, and the subject of the Stanza of Heliodorus. Added to the paper the drawing was on, it suggested a trail that led to Rome. Even to the Vatican. Even to . . . Raphael! John Battle Davenport's Raphael. Second greatest painter of the High Renaissance after Titian, and considered by many connoisseurs of various times and places its greatest artist. The connection was, certainly, tenuous, but to James it was most definitely there, for he already had a hunch, on the basis of stylistic comparisons, that his drawing belonged in the circle of Raphael. Not necessarily by the hand of the master, but of his time and from his workshop, at the very least.

James looked at his snapshots again—he'd put the drawing away—thinking of them in terms of the Stanza of Heliodorus. One of the horsemen to the left was obviously a high Church dignitary; the people to the right had some of the qualities of those frescoes, as James remembered them, their powerful groupings and sense of thrust and counterthrust. The background, a city, was less heavily penned in than the figures—not entirely legible. One could make out some buildings that seemed to have features—square towers and crenellations, like those on Palazzo Vecchio—typical of late medieval Italian civic architecture. It had no counterpart in the frescoes, as far as James could remember; but on the other hand, one didn't usually look at backgrounds all that carefully. Perhaps, on Monday, he'd find that it did. What could the drawing be about? Was it, like *The Repulse of Attila,* a subject from Church history? The presence of the dignitary, who might be a pope, suggested that. But why had it been made, if it was in some way connected with the Stanza, since it obviously hadn't been put to use? That was the touchy question. For the moment James could go no further, but he had a line of investigation to pursue on Monday.

Next, James completed his handwritten catalog of Ricky's books and typed it up with several carbons, to be sent to Peter Tremper. Then he began his letter to Tremper. He told Tremper of the "Guidoni consignment," as he called it, and explained the desires of Ricky for anonymity. There should be no problems about the books from this end, he wrote. The Italian authorities weren't too much interested in old books and wouldn't care even if they knew the books were leaving the country; still, it was probably simpler to send them out without a declaration. They could be got up to a dealer in Lugano that James knew of, who would then re-export them to the United States for a small fee. That way there couldn't possibly be any trouble. He praised several of them, and in particular mentioned the bindings and the general condition of the books. At this point he digressed to another subject:

By the way, your former employee Mark Stapleton called me, and I asked him to my place for tea. An interesting young man, and very agreeable. Something of an original, in his way. Lots of people have found Florence a museum, but he's the first person I've met who's discovered it's really an athletic facility. He spent the day jogging, swimming, and rowing—as an alternative to the Uffizi. He struck me as a youth with some potential. Terribly *new*, of course, with little as yet written on the blank pages of his *animus*, but what matters in the young is the capacity to receive a text, not the absence of one, which is only natural, and it seemed to me he might have that capacity, perhaps to a nearly distinguished degree. It turned out that he'd met Signora Benassi in Rome—you remember she's the owner of the villa where I live. After I'd had him around for tea, she had him around to dinner, just yesterday. She's asked him to stay here with us, so I'll be seeing more of him.

That ought to soften Peter up. James returned to Ricky's books:

Old Marchese Guidoni is terribly broke, incidentally. I told him I'd approach you with the idea that even though the books are coming to you on consignment, you might be willing to advance him some money. Think it over and see what you can do. It would be a kindness to him, and of course it might make him more willing to part with more treasures in the future.

While he tried to go to sleep, James worried about several things. Should he now tell Ricky about the drawing? Better not, he decided. Better he should know nothing until James himself knew more. Possibly it would be best to wait until the drawing was safely out of Italy before saying a word about it to anybody. One didn't want those in the Ministry of Fine Arts whose job was to enforce the national patrimony laws getting on its scent. For, if it was as important a work as James suspected, they'd care a lot about *it*.

And what of Mark? He did know about the drawing, and now he was going to be nearby. He might talk to Davenport. Or to Ricky. Or, worse yet, to the signora, who'd be quick to guess. It was no longer possible to hold Mark at a distance, as had been the first plan. How, then, to silence him? One would have to befriend him, get him under one's influence—wasn't that the only way? James had sat at the other end of the table from Mark at dinner last night, and could only hope he hadn't already been indiscreet. His mouth had to be sealed, that was certain, and there was no time to lose. Mark was a flaw in an otherwise neatly controllable situation. A damned nuisance.

James spent much of the next day at the German Library. It was maddening that snoopy, suspicious old John Battle Davenport had so many of the books on Raphael on his desk, where, for reasons of discretion, they were off limits. Until, that is, Davenport went out to lunch with Dottoressa Andromeda Paonese of the local Soprintendenza di Belle Arti. Then James was able to go hurriedly through some of those books; he stayed at it too long and almost got caught when Davenport returned. After Davenport left for the day, James went back to his desk, though he had only half an hour before the library closed. The next morning he went to the library early so he could work before Davenport got there. This time, however, James did get caught—he had a habit of concentrating too much on what he was doing, and he forgot to keep an eye on the door.

"Ho there." Davenport suddenly loomed at his side, like a reproachful gorilla. "Ho there, James. What's up?"

James said, "John. Good morning. Up? Oh, nothing much. I was looking for a copy of Vasari—I wanted to read his life of Leonardo—and I thought you'd have a copy here so I wouldn't have to go searching in the stacks."

"Well, I don't," Davenport said, "only a xerox of the life of Raphael." He tugged at one of his muttonchop whiskers. "Why do you want to read about Leonardo? Got something by him you're flogging? That's rather a big bite for you, isn't it?"

James shook his head. "Curiosity, that's all."

"Afraid you'll have to go to someone else's desk to satisfy it," Davenport said unpleasantly.

James drifted away. He did go then to Vasari and read the biography of Raphael. It was, of course, the most basic source of all, written in the middle of the sixteenth century by the father of art history, but it contained nothing of any particular relevance to his particular interest. When Davenport went back to the villa for lunch—it was Tuesday; the buffet would be set—James forwent both the meal and the chance to talk to Mark for the first time since Saturday night, and instead gave himself two full hours with Davenport's Raphael bibliography. At about the time Davenport would be returning to the library, James returned to the villa, stopping on his way upstairs to leave a note on Mark's door inviting him for a glass of wine before dinner.

James seemed to have gone as far as he could with his research. The drawing looked to him to be a Raphael. The style seemed to check—individual figures could be closely paralleled in Windsor, and so on. The paper was okay. It was undoubtedly the most important Raphael drawing in existence, if it was a Raphael, probably the most important drawing to have survived from all the Renaissance. Worth millions. But just because of its importance, it was certain to stir up controversy when it became known. This expert would accept it, that one wouldn't. To get the highest possible price, James needed some surer fact, an archival reference or the like, to prove the attribution to Raphael. He didn't know where to find it, but he would persevere. Sooner or later, something would come along to solve his problem. It only needed him to be ready to use it.

As Davenport was leaving the library that afternoon to return to Villa Arberoni, he was joined by Ettore Biscotti, a scholar of international renown, who knew as much about Leon-Battista Alberti as Battsie knew about Raphael, which was an awful lot. They went downstairs in unison, said good evening to the porter with one voice, and walked out onto Via Giuseppe Giusti together and headed toward Via Cavour, where Ettore would turn right, Battsie left. The small, elderly, nimble, and malicious Italian was, as always, amusing, talking about Dottoressa Paonese, in this case about how she had sown terror throughout the Soprintendenza by her high principles and intransigent morality.

"Which can be awkward," he said.

"Oh, very. But one needs such a person, now and then," said Battsie.

"In Florence? I'm not so sure. You had lunch with her yesterday."

"How did you know?"

"I see everything. What did she have to say?"

"That Italy must be grateful to me for all I've done for Italian art."

"Not lunch but a banquet, my dear fellow. By the way, what was it Molyneux wanted at your desk?"

"He was looking for a copy of Vasari, so he could read the life of Leonardo. But—how did you know I caught him there?"

"I told you I see everything."

They were at Via Cavour, and Davenport was eager to get home, but some nuance in Ettore's voice made him stop. "And what else have you seen?" he asked, bending over Biscotti as a Newfoundland might bend over a cairn terrier.

"I have seen that for two days Molyneux has been treading on your territory. First by going through all the books on Raphael that you don't have on your desk. Secondly, by going through those that are on your desk every time you're out."

"No! What do you think his reason is?"

"He's a dealer. There's only one reason I can think of. The question is, what's he got for sale?"

"The *Floriano Madonna?*"

"I'd have heard of that."

"There's the terrible portrait belonging to Principe Barletta, but who'd want it?"

"The Getty, perhaps. With so much money to spend, I suppose they have to take what they can."

"*I'd* have heard, in that case. They wouldn't dare consider it without asking me. What else?"

"There's the Nelli *Saint Sebastian.* I heard old Nelli just sold his badly mildewed Veronese to a manufacturer in Hong Kong."

"I don't think James would touch that picture. Half of it's repaint, and the other half's nonexistent."

Biscotti shrugged. "A Raphael drawing, perhaps?"

"Perhaps. But whose? From some collection around here, do you think?"

"Who can say? If so, your friend and admirer Dottoressa Paonese and the Internal Security Police would be interested, surely. Should we . . .?"

Battsie laughed uneasily. "We can hardly go to Andromeda Paonese to report that a certain insignificant dealer in anything he can scratch up to sell has been looking at my books on Raphael."

"Should we turn detective?"

Battsie reared back, as if the cairn terrier had snapped. "How?"

"You must begin to remember exactly the way in which you leave your books, where the notes are in them, and so on, and see if he tampers with them. I'll keep an eye on him when you aren't there. And we can both watch and see what he looks at in the stacks."

Battsie chuckled. "Why not?" he said. "Pauline simply detests him, you know. She'd be delighted if we caught him out at something." He looked at his watch. "And now . . ."

"So long," said Biscotti, thinking perhaps he'd have a *gelato* on his way home.

"Toodle-oo," said John Battle Davenport. And he bumbled off toward the Duomo, holding his two overstuffed briefcases like outriggers. He wondered if they'd have a good dinner at Villa Arberoni that night. A full day's thinking always left him hungry.

Ricoverino dei Guidoni had put off going to Fratelli Sulmona all day Monday. From time to time, when he thought of the little clutch of silver spoons that now lay nested among his handkerchiefs, he could hardly believe he'd done such a thing. At the same time, he was exasperated with himself for being so ashamed. He had to have them. The alternative, which was quite inadmissible, was to borrow money from Madeleine for her own gift. She wouldn't ever miss the spoons. Silver, possessions like that, unless there was a particular sentimental attachment to them, or unless they were very fine, didn't much interest her. And he'd only taken enough spoons to make the necklace. It wasn't as if he'd stolen for profit. But all the same—his feelings swung wildly, a state of mind to which he was entirely unaccustomed—what he'd done was scarcely honorable. It was ironic, yet true: stealing from the poor was one thing, and everybody did it all the time; from the rich, another. In the end he decided that if he had such doubts and regrets, he'd better put the spoons back where he'd found them, else he'd never be serene in his mind again. And so he carried them in his pocket when he went to see Madeleine on Monday.

Unfortunately, Costanza had already put the silver away and locked the sideboards, and he could think of no pretext to get her to unlock them. Nothing was said about any spoons being missing. No doubt they hadn't been counted again—if they'd been all that closely counted in the first place. In fact, that silver might not get counted again for years. If ever, it would be after the birthday party. Some unidentified guest would then be blamed, were the theft noticed, or one of the special servants brought in for the occasion. There was no longer judicial torture. A false confession couldn't be wrested out of anybody. There'd be no harm done.

It was a sign. Ricky had intended to return the damned spoons, but now he couldn't. And so, after finding reasons to delay all day Tuesday, too, he set off for the little shop near Palazzo Strozzi in the late afternoon.

* * *

Giacobbe Sulmona was most welcoming, yet there was in his manner a stiffness that indicated to Ricky he intended to stand fast on the matter of payment. Yes, he'd made a sketch, following the marchese's suggestions. He showed it and explained its details: the little creatures themselves would be made of Rio Aguaro ribbon jasper—the source was new, just discovered a year ago—chosen to suggest the striations of their shells; their bodies, as they protruded above a silver rim set into their shells, would be of Egyptian jasper the color of butterscotch. Sulmona had some pieces of it in his desk drawer, which he showed Ricky. The strands of water plants in which the nautilus would be entangled would have leaves of red and blue-green Kashmiri jasper, with here and there a touch of Malagasy agate. All held by a network of silver strands, with a heavier silver back to the necklace, to give the front part stability. The earrings would be quotations from the necklace. Everything would come in a box lined with double-thick, tarnish-proof cloth, and a sack of the same cloth in which to keep the box during periods when the necklace wouldn't be worn regularly. Sulmona asked Ricky what he thought of a detail here and there, but that was really only a formality. He was, when his interest was engaged, a fine designer.

After Ricky had approved and complimented the jeweler, he said, "I have come to tell you to go ahead." He got out a little parcel, and from it took the silver spoons. "They're family stuff, but not of any great importance. A branch of my mother's family—she was the daughter of a Count Rainaldi—hence the R on the handles. Late nineteenth-century, and perfectly expendable, as I say. As for the rest of the cost—well, I'm arranging for that, and you'll get your money. But now, so you can begin, I'd like you to melt these spoons down and use their silver."

Sulmona stood. He backed away, speechless.

Ricky, too, stood. Grandly. Quite prepared to become furious. "They have no value to me, whereas the necklace is of the utmost importance. I insist, Signor Sulmona, that this time you do as I ask."

Sulmona looked as if he might weep.

"I'll hear no excuses. It is absurd for you to sentimentalize my family silver if I do not. You will do as I wish."

Sulmona neither nodded nor shook his head. He cast his eyes to the floor. "If you say so," he mumbled.

"Then you will proceed?"

"We will proceed, Marchese."

Ricky left the shop, satisfied.

Poor Giacobbe Sulmona was anything but. He hadn't been balking at the idea of melting down the spoons, as he had the cigarette case. They were of indifferent workmanship and late date. He had balked because only that morning Signora Benassi's porter had come in with a dozen knives whose blades had, with time and lack of use, come loose in their handles, and the pitch stuffing needed replacing. Sulmona was asked to repair them, and was told they were to be ready no later than mid-July. Before, if possible. They were of precisely the same pattern as the spoons the marchese had just brought in, and also had the monogram *R* and a coronet on them—of course Sulmona knew, as anyone his age would, that Signora Benassi's mother had been the Contessa Rinuccini. And yes, it was only nineteenth-century flatware, but it wasn't all that common. It was unlikely there'd be two separate sets surviving in Florence, impossible that they'd both have the same monogram.

He and his brother owed everything to Signora Benassi, but that didn't help him to know what to do about her spoons in this case. She and Marchese dei Guidoni were a connection of such long standing, it was a situation where angels might fear to tread. Moreover, there was the matter of the necklace. How could he now not go on with it? Yet how could he, if it required melting down stolen spoons—for what else could they be? He wished that he and his brother had closed their shop a year before, as they'd talked of doing, or that he knew a lawyer he could trust.

It was Tuesday evening. Ricky had, as usual, come to Signora Benassi before the general dinner at Villa Arberoni.

"Ricky," she said, "we have to talk about something serious.

Important. You're going to find it very unpleasant, and I'm sorry, but we must."

She'd found out. Ricky's guilt seized him like a deadly enemy, by the throat. He couldn't breathe. He turned pale.

Signora Benassi glanced at the clock over on the table next to the elegant bronze and glass case that contained her Cellini piece, but both were now hidden by a great bowl of lilies. She had to put on her reading glasses, which hung by a little chain around her neck, to look at her wristwatch. "It's seven-thirty. That's good. One shouldn't have too much time, when the subject's important. We'll have to talk about it more than once, but we may as well get it started this evening. And see the nice flowers Mark Stapleton sent me, along with a charming note. I think he may work out."

"Yes, my dear," Ricky said at last, in a strangled voice.

"Are you all right?"

"A catch in my throat. I need a drink."

"Get it. And get me some gin," Signora Benassi said.

Another alarming sign—for Ricky. Madeleine only drank gin when she was quite nervous herself, and it would not be unlike her to begin a conversation that might end everything between them in this strangely offhand way. But what could she mean, that they'd have to talk about it more than once? How could they do so, when he'd be dead of shame?

"I'll begin by telling you something I'd planned to keep from you." She recounted the incident in the Protestant Cemetery. "Mark was my savior—surely you must have suspected I had more reason to invite him to live here than a mere chance conversation beside a grave. Now, it wasn't all that serious, what I had, but—it was a warning. I saw Dr. Greghi yesterday, and he confirmed that that was just what it was, as he'd told me over the telephone. On the basis of that first warning, I did certain things while in Rome. I saw my lawyer and the notary and my man of business—why do you look so cheerful all of a sudden, Ricky? What *is* going on? I tell you, what I'm talking about is very serious."

"I'm cheerful because I'm so glad your seizure wasn't worse," Ricky said. "But I am also reproachful; you should have told me before, Madeleine."

"Well, I didn't." She noticed his hand was shaking. "I think you'd better put down your glass until you hear the next thing." She waited, then went on. "Lawyers and notaries and brokers, they all said the same word, over and over: '*Matrimonio. Matrimonio. Matrimonio.*'"

"What? What are you talking about?"

"About taxes, actually. You know as well as I do that it is the practice in this country to levy relatively small taxes on the inheritances of one's blood relations or spouse, and to collect the sky otherwise. I do not intend to have all my money go to those thieves in the government. I wish to leave some of it to you in trust, and that money will stay in the United States, which is no problem—apart from American inheritance taxes, which have greatly diminished. But I want to leave some to you outright, to go to Tiberio. And that would be most horribly taxed. Therefore, I think that you and I had better get married."

Ricky sucked in his breath, let it out, sucked it in again, like someone beginning to have a nightmare. This was so vast in its implications it almost made his earlier fears of discovery fade into insignificance.

"Say something, Ricky, for heaven's sake. You're acting like a village maiden who's just had her first proposal."

"But—" he gasped at last, "there will be a scandal."

Signora Benassi laughed. "Dear Ricky," she said, "no wonder I can't resist you. If we have lived as we have lived for twenty-five years without causing a scandal, I can't see why there should be one if we get married."

"I'd have to . . . to confess."

"We'll have a civil ceremony."

He made an impatient gesture. "The Guidoni do not marry in civil ceremonies."

"Then confess to the Archbishop. I'll soften him up with a contribution—why not toward cleaning those dirty stained-glass windows at the Duomo?" Madeleine smiled. "Certainly he can't make any trouble over the religious education of our offspring."

"No, no, Madeleine." Ricky shook his head. "It's far too late."

"Yes, yes, Ricky." She nodded. "It's not too late. But it soon might be. I've had my warning. I'm not immortal."

"But"—he held his hands out pitifully—"how would we live?"

"Much as we do now. Except that you would move here, obviously, which would bring our arrangements more into accord with good sense anyway. I'll make you an apartment of your own above me; there's already the small corner stairs, and I'll put in another elevator for you. Costanza needs it anyway. You'd be as free to come and go as my *pensionnaires*—as James, for instance. In some ways you'd be more independent than you are now, if you want to know what I think. Give your apartment in Palazzo Guidoni to Tiberio. He should have a place here in the city. He's far too much alone for a young man, off there in that flyspecked villa with only his unquenchable mother and his gramophone and those peasant girls he's always getting involved with, *faute de mieux*. Which reminds me . . ."

Signora Benassi reached for a pad of paper and a pencil. "I want to get him the new Xavier Galloel recording of the Beethoven piano sonatas—it got a fine review somewhere. Where was I? Oh yes, I had Tiberio in Florence. He can meet people here, including, one day, his wife, and he could see more of us at the same time. But also, if we are married, I can put money immediately into more land for the boy, and give him something he can really work with. When I die, he'll keep the property without the state getting its hand into it. Now, you know that would be nice and that he'd like it."

"The point, however, Madeleine, is not Tiberio. It's you and me."

"Of course. But Tiberio can't be dismissed. All this will be enormously to his advantage. Anyway, they're drawing up a new will, which I'll sign as soon as you agree to sign a marriage settlement. I've already explained how I intend to provide for you in my will, and there'll be money for you sooner, too. I hope I don't need to tell you I'll be generous."

Ricky gestured—gratitude? resignation? disagreement?—it was hard to say what his gesture meant, which was, of course, intentional.

Signora Benassi frowned. "What to do with the villa here—that's really knotty, but we're working on it. The bureaucrats are likely to declare it some kind of monument and include it in the historic zone. I've fended that off, but there's a quite intransigent creature in the regional Fine Arts office, a dragon of a woman named—I think it's Clytemnestra—Clytemnestra Paonese, with whom it's increasingly hard to come to any understanding. I've heard she's a relative of the Minister in Rome, too, which gives her real power. Anyway, if we don't dodge them, they'll declare that the villa can't be modified in any way, which will mean nobody will want to buy it and it'll be nothing but a drain on my estate and fall to pieces and then they'll condemn it, lift its classification, and buy it for themselves and make millions. You know how those things go. No, a way must be found to evade them—but that's not your problem. Or even mine."

"Madeleine," Ricky said, "I can't consent to this. It's not only too sudden, but also it's the very nature of it. I do not obey commands in things of this kind. Not even from . . . your Roman lawyer and businessman."

She reached out toward him and said gently, "I'm not commanding you to do anything. I come as a beggar."

"That's unfair. And untrue."

"As a beggar—with twenty-five years' worth of vested interests," she said cheerfully. "I warn you, I do indeed intend to have my way about this, if it's humanly possible. And why not? Why should we not marry? Give me a sensible reason—now that we've disposed of your religious scruples."

"Very well. I'll be blunt, since you insist. Because everyone will say I'm marrying you for your money."

"Why do you think Benassi married me?"

"He adored you."

"That's true, but he certainly loved buying old editions of Petrarch, too. And don't you adore me? Of course you do. We'll tell everyone that you're marrying me as my seventy-fifth birthday present."

"It comes to the same thing," Ricky said, not without a pang as he thought of the present he was indeed giving her. "They'll say I'm marrying you because you're getting . . . old. That I've lived off you for decades and that now that it might be coming to an end, I've decided to make a sure thing of it. And they'll say you're a fool, that I've kept you at a distance for a quarter of a century, and now, when you're about to drop off the tree, I'm moving in. Oh, I can imagine the things they'll say. They'll say you've been trying all along to . . . to get a title. They'll say terrible things, Madeleine."

"Who cares? It's not true. I've no more wanted to marry you than you have to marry me. But now I've had my warning. I care now for more regularity in my life. Ricky, I want you nearer me. And—taxes are taxes. You know, I do have distant relatives in America who'll have a far better chance of breaking a will if I leave money to a stranger. Imagine calling you that! But it's the word my lawyer used."

"They'll laugh," Ricky said gloomily.

"Let them laugh, old man."

"I don't care if they laugh at me. I will not have them laughing at you. Anyway, they won't laugh at me. They'll sneer. They'll laugh at you and sneer at me. Maybe the Americans won't, though I doubt it, but I know the Italians."

Signora Benassi was silent for a long time. It was difficult. Ricky was a complicated man, in his simple way. Apart from his worries about the figure they'd cut in the eyes of the world, he surely felt obliged, because he was a man, to object to her proposal because she was a woman. There was, however, no way around that.

Finally she said, "You're very hard on Tiberio."

"Oh, to the devil with Tiberio."

"Sometimes, when I look at Tiberio, I think he may *be* the devil," she said. "But then he smiles, and I know he's an angel. If you really don't, in the end, agree to what I want, we're going to have to arrange a marriage for him with some scrawny old hen who owns half of Lombardy, for he can't go on as he is. His beauty will, at least, make an interested marriage easier to achieve. Well, I said we'd have to talk about this more than once, and so we will. I won't give up. Truly, Ricky, in this matter I do intend to have my way if it's humanly possible. You see, there's another reason, too."

"And what is that?" Ricky asked wearily.

"To confirm the love we've felt for one another, as our lives wind down."

He got up, took her hand, and kissed it. "I can't dispute the love, only the inference you draw from it."

"Mmm. And now," she said, "let's talk about my party."

As they went to dinner upstairs, the signora stopped to give an order to Costanza, another to Velia, with an additional several to carry to Anna and Gina, and, as she walked into the dining room, three or four of them to Antonio, who was helping to serve at table that evening. And then she interfered, as dinner was beginning, and told people where to sit, taking care to place Mark next to Iris Siswick. That was the trouble—and that was the thing Ricky could never tell Madeleine. She was too accustomed to running things. Now, with his apartment, however shabby, at Palazzo Guidoni, he could go home, get away from all this organization, all these quick do-this's and do-that's. But once he'd moved in here, he'd have lost his independence, no matter what Madeleine said. He'd be so under her surveillance he'd lack even the precarious freedom bestowed by a cup on the street—speaking of beggars. If only he had some money, he could marry her in relative peace, for then he really could go his own way—take trips and so on—but he didn't. If they married, he'd have everything he wanted—new shirts, suits, comforts of every kind—but at the price of his remaining liberty. He'd be only a pampered client. And to that there was no possible accommodation.

✺

On Saturdays, Pauline Davenport wore a long dress to dinner. On Tuesdays she didn't. If there'd been no other way of knowing what day of the week it was, that test would have been enough. Tonight, partly as a result of her simple dress, she was ready before her husband and out in their sitting room to await whatever happened next.

Iris Siswick, who lived downstairs, tapped—why wouldn't the girl use the knocker? Pauline, when she opened the door, said just that. "Why won't you use the knocker? That's what it's for."

"I didn't want to disturb James Molyneux," Iris whispered as soon as the door had closed behind her.

"As if I care if *he's* disturbed."

Iris said, "The new person was just going into his rooms as I

103

came to yours, and your knocker echoes so in the hall."

"Mark Stapleton, you mean?" Pauline wondered at Iris's shyness, which prevented her from calling Mark by his name. "They *had* already met, hadn't they? Pauline gave a meaningful lift of her eyebrows. "And Mark *is* a good-looking young man. What'll you have to drink?"

"Wine. Yes, I suppose he is. Though not like—like Tiberio dei Guidoni."

"Tiberio's too thin, if you ask me. Not that I should talk." Pauline had thickish legs and a thickish torso. Lots of freckles and all her teeth—and plenty of character to go with them.

"Less this year than last," said Iris, who rather kept track of Tiberio. It was her second stay at Villa Arberoni. She'd come for the summer last year, and for the spring term and summer this year, following her piano instructor, Hamilin Rees, who had a little house off in the direction of Impruneta. The Davenports came every year from January through August, now that John was semi-retired. "Thank you." Iris took the glass of wine and composed herself on a stool—fine, soft brown hair braided up around her head, enormous eyes, a long neck, and serious arms.

Pauline thought how graceful she was, yet how lost and unhappy she looked, and wished there were something she could do about it. But it was difficult. On Tuesdays, Pauline usually invited Iris for a drink before dinner. On Saturdays she didn't. Not as dependable an indication of the day as the long dress, but almost. The Davenports invited outside guests most Saturdays, and it was simply too difficult to work Iris in. She knew nothing but music, and would sit, lovely in her way, to be sure, but silent, silent, silent, listening while John and the outsiders talked. Eventually it made people uneasy. Eventually it made Pauline herself uneasy, for if someone was silent long enough around John Battle Davenport, she began to suspect—even in the case of Iris—that person was finding him a bore.

Battsie himself came in from his bath, wearing a terrycloth robe. "Here already, Iris? 'Scuse my informality." He put ice and whisky in a glass—no water. "Be back out *all'istante.*"

Pauline, seeing his bouncy retreat through Iris's eyes, wondered what happened when one's husband's legs got too thin to support the expanding bulk above. She said, "I wish Signora Benassi would fill the big apartment downstairs, and the smaller ones, as well. We have too few people here at the villa right now. When she and Ricky don't come to a meal and there aren't any guests, just us and James, it's below the critical mass. Of course, Hilda Guest—or Molyneux—she never did call herself Hilda Guest, you know—Hilda'll be back soon. For whatever that's worth—at dinner." Pauline liked Hilda little more than she liked her cousin James. "That poor Harry Guest. He didn't really want the divorce, only wanted her to be reasonable. And she'll be sorry, mark my words. They should have stayed married."

Iris wasn't very liberated, but she was of her generation. "If they no longer loved each other . . ."

"Who says they didn't? Anyway, that means nothing. *Nothing*, I say." Pauline gave a toss of her head. "There comes a time in every marriage when the point is to stick together, no matter what."

Both women were obliged by her sudden vehemence to wonder when that point had arrived in the Davenport union.

Battsie came back in, barefooted still, but with his pants on and buttoning his shirt. "Well, now," he said, "What're we talking about?" He left before he could be answered.

"About Hilda Molyneux and her divorce," Pauline called.

"Divorced, is she?" The professor appeared in the doorway, tying his tie. "Single mankind had better watch out. Glad I have you to protect me. But maybe I'm too old for her."

"I would have thought," Pauline said dryly. "Particularly as, judging from Harry Guest, she liked men who look like boys." More to the point, was Hilda, in fact, too young for Battsie? Or might he try to pluck her? He had so the habit of mesmerizing the front row at Sillitson Hall, back at Vassar. As Pauline had once sat in it herself, had, in fact, been plucked out of it in her day, she knew all about it.

"And what did you do today?" he asked Iris, a shoe in each hand.

"Practiced, Professor Davenport. And had a lesson."

"Funny bird, that man you study with." Iris had had Hamilin Rees to dinner a previous Saturday night. "Never have guessed the piano was his instrument. Hard to imagine he's got only one composer up his sleeve."

"He has more than one, Professor Davenport," Iris said. "He won't let his pupils have more than one." Rees's theory of pianistic education was that a pupil should study the work of a single master at a time, and Iris had been on the piano sonatas of Haydn for over a year, forbidden, on her honor, to play any other composer even when she was by herself.

"Haven't you about gone through whatever it is you've been studying?"

Iris shook her head. "There are over fifty Haydn sonatas, and I've only learned thirty-three," she said.

Pauline changed the subject; it was one thing Iris would talk about, always drearily. "What did *you* do today, Battsie dear?"

He was putting on his light tweed jacket. "I nailed down the *Madonna of Foligno*," he said. "And you?"

"I read," said Pauline.

"You hear that, Iris?" John Battle Davenport cried jovially. "It must be wonderful to be able to read books instead of eternally writing them." And then he sat and told the two women just how the nails had gone into the *Madonna of Foligno*, until it was time for dinner. It slipped his mind to tell Pauline about James Molyneux's mysterious interest in Raphael until later, though, as Iris always walked the stairs, being somewhat claustrophobic, he could have whispered it in the elevator.

Late Tuesday afternoon, before he returned to Villa Arberoni to put on his blazer—the only coat he had—and go to James Molyneux's rooms before dinner, Mark stopped by the Hotel Granduca, which was on the river a little below the center of town. He asked for Laurie Walker.

The concierge, a man of unsurpassable snobbery, who had his own desk and assistant, looked at his list. No. Nobody with that name was staying with them. Mark asked if she had a reservation for tomorrow, or later in the week. No. They had no reservation in her name. What about a Miss Emilene Ladore? Mark asked.

The concierge grew more distant, but Mark couldn't tell

whether it was because he was being asked to do too much without any chance of a tip, or because he was being discreet. Nothing under that name, either. If true, it surely meant that all the reservations were in the name of Laurie's uncle—which Mark didn't know. There was nothing to do but come back and ask again.

He then went to a florist's shop he'd seen in Via dei Calzaiuoli. He bought two large bouquets, one of white lilies, the other of lemon-yellow ones, and had the shopkeeper mix them together. He took the bouquet back with him to the villa, where he wrote a note:

Dear Signora Benassi,
    I thought it might be nice to give you flowers when you *hadn't* invited me, to show you I think of you at other times, too.
                                                              Mark Stapleton

After he'd changed, he stopped on the signora's floor, left the note and the bouquet with Costanza, and went on upstairs.

They sat out on the terrace. James pulled the cork from a bottle of red wine and poured two glasses. "Here you are," he said to Mark. He swirled his glass a bit, then sniffed and tasted. "Pretty good. From up north—the Valtellina. My cousin gave it to me when she left for America a couple of months ago. I wish I could carry what we don't drink down and have it with dinner, but Signora Benassi would be very offended. She's unyielding about the house wine, which is made by Ricky dei Guidoni's great-nephew."

"Tiberio?"

"Yes. How'd you know?"

"People seem to mention his name a lot."

"Poor kid. Burdened with worthless land, an impossible mother, and a heritage of claptrap ideology. He deserves great credit for having decided that he could go to the state wine school to study oenology and still remain a gentleman. And what've you been up to, Mark?"

"Seeing things." Mark ticked off a fair list.

"And do you like us or Rome better?"

"Rome is certainly bigger."

"True. We're small and limited up here." James then risked, "And there are so many places you should go. I'll make a list for you. Bologna, for starters." He swirled and sniffed again. "If I were you, I just might head for Bologna tomorrow. I mean it. Wonderful city. Don't waste too much time on us."

Mark said, as his answer, "And just how long is it you've lived in Florence?"

"Too long, I sometimes think." James dropped that tack. "Doing any more athleticizing?"

"I run every day. It has its dangers from the traffic along the Arno, but I've gotten pretty good at outmaneuvering it, and it's okay once you're in that park."

"Let's get back to what you've seen." James fired one of his shotgun questions. "What's most interested you so far?"

What flashed into Mark's mind was the incident of Ricky and the silver spoons. Not a story for James; the nice point was whether—or when—to tell the signora. Mark turned James's question. "You don't want to hear about my sightseeing, but I really would like to know more about the Marchese dei Guidoni."

"Why?"

"He's the first titled nobleman I've ever met; we don't have them in San Diego. Are he and Signora Benassi very old friends?"

"Oh, very. And very good ones."

"Is he . . . eccentric?"

"An eccentric titled nobleman?" James stared at Mark over his wineglass. "Eccentric? Ricky, eccentric? Is it, I wonder, eccentric to be old-fashioned?" James waited a moment. "To cling to customs most people have never practiced and which those that did have given up?" He waited again, always watching Mark. "To take forever to get ready to go out in the morning? To believe it is your duty to set a good example to your inferiors by observing the forms of religion, though you're a complete sceptic?" James smiled. "To doubt the durability of any literature after Goldoni and of any art after Guardi? And to be very nice? You'll have to decide the answers to those questions for yourself, Mark."

Mark persisted. "Has he any peculiarities? I mean, if he's like all that, he must have some other quirks. Like . . . setting fires?"

Mark tried to imitate James's swirl, but all his wine did was rock back and forth. "Or kleptomania?" he added, in as offhand a way as he could.

"Whatever in the world gives you that idea?"

"Well . . . if he's eccentric."

"But I tried to say he really wasn't," James said shortly. "Not to respond to irony is a brute trait, Mark." He softened that by pouring more wine. "There's no use not telling you what everybody else knows: Ricky and Signora Benassi are lovers. It started even before old Benassi was dead, I understand, though he was as good as dead. He and Ricky were close friends until Benassi's stroke; Ricky, for someone of his class, is something of an intellectual, and Benassi was a world-renowned Petrarch scholar. Anyway, they've been lovers for at least a quarter of a century."

Mark tried to imagine the unimaginable. "And they still are?"

"Definitely, as far as spending time together and so on are concerned. As for their intimate life—I couldn't really say."

"But they still love each other? I mean a lot?"

"Again, I say watch them and decide for yourself." James fell into the mode of instruction. "You're in a new place. Cultivate the habit of observation. Perhaps one day after you've been at Villa Arberoni awhile—if you stay—we'll talk about the people you meet here. Not mere gossip, you understand, but gossip elevated into art. Now I do want to hear more about your sightseeing."

Later, after James had cross-examined Mark about San Marco and the Medici tombs and the Uffizi, he let the conversation lag, then said, "By the way—that drawing you helped me free the other night—you remember? A great disappointment. It turns out to be more or less modern."

"Modern! But the paper it was on wasn't modern."

"Nineteenth-century," James said dismissively. "Modern in comparison with the book."

"The paper wasn't nineteenth-century either," Mark said stubbornly. "I'd bet on that just by how it felt in my hands."

James said, "Someone used old paper to draw on. It happens with forgeries quite a lot—one of the most frequently used tricks. Not that this drawing was a forgery. Just a copy after a fresco I ran down in Cadore, where Titian came from. Artists used to copy things all the time that way when they visited Italy before there were photographs to carry home."

Mark was persistent. "What about the paste? It seemed pretty old to me."

James had to bully. "That, my friend, *was* nineteenth-century. Early." He got to his feet and took the bottle and his glass. "Unfortunately, it leaves the drawing of little interest. I've tucked it away in a portfolio somewhere. Too bad."

"Then you took it out of the book?"

James was leading the way to his sitting room. He hesitated, as if it were the step down. "Well . . . yes, I did."

"You mean you held that book all by yourself and steamed it free? I can't believe it."

"You mean you can't believe I'm sufficiently . . . strong?"

"*I* wouldn't be. Not strong enough to risk that."

Caught, James admitted, "I cut out the page it was pasted to first."

There was a silence. Anyone who'd worked with old books knew that was vandalism. "I see," Mark said finally.

"It was a blank page," James said.

"No it wasn't."

"Almost. It can easily be bound back in. Give me your glass and I'll put them both in by the sink." James went off to his bathroom. When he returned, he said, "Will you be going back to work for Tremper?"

Mark shook his head. "No. He doesn't know it yet, so I'd rather you didn't tell him."

"Wouldn't dream of it. What'll you do?"

"Not sure. Something with a future, I suppose—I'm twenty-four. Time I got started. I'd like to live somewhere outside California for a while."

"Don't convert to Italy. I did, and I've scarcely left this really rather boring little city in almost twenty years." James stopped in front of one of the full-length mirrors and looked at himself in it—the evening's penance. "Thanks for coming up," he said.

"Thanks for having me." Mark added, unexpectedly, "I learned some things."

"Did you! What?"

110

"About brute traits."

"Forgive me." James looked around at him. "I mean it. What else?"

"I now know what isn't eccentric, and what isn't old."

"So," James said. He opened the door slowly and let them out. "By the way, we don't talk at the table downstairs about . . . oh, selling that book and the like. Being in trade's not considered good form. We're all for the arts or scholarship or being gentlefolk with large private incomes, downstairs." He rested a hand on Mark's shoulder, lightly. "Or lucky young Americans on the Grand Tour," he said.

"Is that a hint or an order?"

"A request, Mark. It might embarrass me."

It didn't matter to Mark. Why should he talk about the book? What did matter, a definite seasoning to his life, was that now he had two secrets, one involving silver spoons, the other a drawing said not to be old that so obviously was. And he had his anticipation of Laurie. In Rome he'd had nothing of the kind, just Brother Ninian and the monuments.

"We're going to talk about my birthday party this evening," the signora said from the head of the table, where, as always, she sat in a certain majesty in her massive, tapestried armchair, two bells at hand, a thin tinkling one and a deeper brass one, which she used indiscriminately. "Gina's tried a new recipe for us tonight—gnocchi made with asparagus tips. We'll see," she said, as Velia carried them around. "My party will be on the twenty-second of July. A Friday. The feast day of Mary Magdalene, for whom I'm named. Put it down in your calendars—you're all invited, of course. In fact, I've got duties for each of you."

She waited until everyone had bread and wine. "James, I want you to be responsible for the gardens. Whatever you think'll be nice. Japanese lanterns strung over the fountain. A dragon in it. Anything. Tiberio will help you; when he used to stay here as a boy, he'd go through the ilex trees like a monkey. Mrs. Davenport, I hope you'll help me with inside details. Professor Davenport, I'll expect you to be jolly and welcoming to the learned guests, and Ricky'll be the same to the worldly ones. Mr. Stapleton, I'm thinking about you—and don't dampen things by saying you won't still be here. Maybe I'll put you in a feathered helmet and make you my guard of honor. Miss Siswick, I'm hoping you'll play. I'm having the big piano down in the *salone* gone over, and I'll have little chairs set up. People will be told they must come on time and can't talk."

"I'd love to," Iris said, flushing with pleasure.

"It will be the keystone to the whole affair," the signora said. "More important than dancing or drinking or supper. Only—my dear, it can't be Haydn."

"Oh."

"Now don't sound that way. I want Chopin—and it's my party. I'll talk to your teacher myself. If he won't let you play Chopin, he can't come, and all Florence will be there." The signora looked at Ricky. "As well as old friends from Rome and so on. One isn't seventy-five every day. I'll never have another birthday party, but this one is going to be very gala."

When the signora let the conversation break into smaller groups, Mark asked Iris what Signora Benassi had meant about Haydn. Iris explained her piano instructor's odd method.

"Are there a lot of Haydn sonatas?" Mark asked.

"Sometimes they seem endless."

"And do you like the method?"

Iris had never said it to anyone before. "It's spoiled Haydn for me forever."

"Why don't you go to someone else?"

"Mr. Rees has a great reputation."

"Is that a reason to stay with him if you don't like him?"

"I've thought it was, but maybe it isn't."

"What're you going to do with it—I mean your piano playing?" Mark asked.

"I wanted to be a concert artist, but now I'm not so sure."

"Why?"

Iris was flustered. Something else she'd never said to anyone was that she'd come to realize she didn't have the talent.

When she didn't reply, Mark guessed it for himself. "That's too

112

bad," he said softly. And smiled at her. "It really is. Why does Rees keep you on?"

"Money, I think," she said.

As they were getting up to go into the drawing room for after-dinner coffee, Mark said, "I'd like to hear some Haydn sometime, even though Signora Benassi doesn't want it at her birthday party."

Signora Benassi overheard. "Why not now? Would you?" she asked Iris, aware that the girl never looked more attractive than when she was playing. "While we have our coffee." She gestured toward the smaller of her two pianos, which was kept in the drawing room on this floor so Iris could practice on it when they weren't eating nearby. "Sit down and Mr. Stapleton will bring you your cup."

Iris went to the piano to wait until everyone had been served. "It's not that I don't like Haydn, you know," the signora said, as she was pouring. "Only, for a birthday party, one wants more sentiment, I think. But sometimes Haydn's just right." She dropped a cube of sugar in Ricky's cup with an emphatic plop. "There are almost no differences of opinion in his music," she said, looking at him, "and when one does arise, it's quickly and cheerfully resolved. There's much to be said for that." She composed herself to listen.

Iris, taking her cue from the signora's remark, played the pretty early Sonata No. 21 in C Major, and played it very well. When it was over, the little group applauded. As Iris bowed without rising from the piano bench, the only eyes she sought with her own were Mark's, and his, the only approval she looked for.

James had grown more and more uneasy throughout dinner. He'd made a fool of himself, up in his rooms, trying to feed Mark ideas about leaving Florence as soon as possible, when his own life was so obviously their clear denial. Far worse was to have told such crude lies about the drawing. He'd underestimated Mark. It was clear from his last remarks that he'd been put on guard—just what James hadn't wanted—and had made it known to James with a manly honesty. As people were leaving the drawing room,

James went to Mark and held him there for a few moments, making a further point about the Medici tombs, then asked if he'd like to take a turn in the garden.

Downstairs, in the court that had the lemon trees in it, he showed Mark the electric switches, which turned on lights here there along the paths and among the trees. He opened the grilled doorway and, his cane hooked over his right arm, walked slowly down the path that ran parallel to the wall that divided the grounds of Villa Arberoni from Piazza San Doroteo. When they came to a crossing, he turned to the right. At the end of the new vista was a small building. He took his cane and pointed.

"That's the studio, where Hilda, my cousin, stays. But you'll probably miss her—unless you really do hang around for the birthday party."

They walked on in this new direction. "Do you think you might?"

"Dunno," Mark said. "Tell me about the villa. And why is it San Doroteo outside? St. Dorothy ought to be feminine."

James lapsed happily into his instructional mode. "You'd be quite right; if it were Saint Dorothy, it would, of course, be Santa Dorotea, but it isn't. I must now be as ponderous as Davenport for a moment. It's Saint Dorotheus. Quite different from Dorothy. Dorothy, poor thing, got it under Diocletian—died a virgin and martyr, but not before she had an angel take a basket of apples and roses, a substantiating miracle because they don't come in season at the same time—to a nonbeliever. Such was the power of her gift that he was led to the Faith, although he was a lawyer and should have known better. He, too, was martyred."

They'd come to the open circle at the point where their path intersected the main wide alley that led from the steps coming down from the terrace of the villa. Here there were more plants in great pots and tubs: oleander and camellias, as well as a circle of tree roses. Also a small fountain: a nude female figure, each of whose hands pressed a breast, whence issued two jets that plashed into a wide basin containing goldfish. Mark asked about her, and James said, "By Tribolo. Copies the Venus de'Medici you saw in the Uffizi, except the hands are differently placed. Typical Mannerist conceit, the breast-jet business." He sat on one of the marble benches and, with a gesture, invited Mark to sit at his side.

"Saint Dorotheus was later, though still early Christian," he went on. "Sixth-century Palestinian. He wrote a treatise on the ascetic life and ran a monastery. Had some influence on the Trappists, one is told. Relics were brought back here by the Crusaders, and a little oratory was founded outside the then city walls. Eventually, as the city grew, it got contained within the walls, and an Augustinian monastery was established. But it was dissolved and the grounds sold in the nineteenth century, and the villa as we're looking at it now was put together. It's the only really decent garden inside the old walls, except for the Boboli, of course. Wonderful that Signora Benassi's mother bought it and preserved it when she decided to move to Florence. Now one wonders what will become of it when the signora dies."

"So the villa's not old?"

"Oh yes. In part it is. Where you live's fourteenth-century, actually." James discussed the fabric of the building, elucidating its history, until it was time to go back inside. Then he said, "Would you like to have a look with me at a bit of Florence?"

"I certainly would. Peter Tremper said that was the best thing that could happen to me."

"Did he? That was nice of him. Let's say Thursday morning at ten o'clock. In front of Santo Spirito, not here, in case you want to do something else first. We'll introduce you to Brunelleschi. Nothing more beautiful in all the world."

Twilight had fallen as they'd been talking. One of the garden lamps was hung in a nearby tree to cast its gentle glow over the fountain near which they sat. Eyes found them out . . .

Professor Davenport looked forth from a window. "There's James Molyneux and the new fellow," he said.

Pauline came to have a look herself. "Mark Stapleton's his name, Battsie. You'd better learn it." She sniffed in disapproval. "I didn't have the impression Mark was one of the boys, but James would know that better than I would," she said.

"I can't ever tell anymore. I liked it better when people who

115

were queer were transvestites and vice-versa. But—times have changed, and we must change with them," Battsie said. "By the way, there was something I meant to tell you." He recounted what Ettore Biscotti had seen. "Probably nothing at all," he said. "But one will, all the same, keep an eye on the situation."

"Do," said Pauline. "How I'd love it if you tripped James so he fell really hard."

"That's what I said to Biscotti—that you really hated Molyneux. I don't. I almost never think about him. Well, I must to bed." Battsie disappeared into the bedroom. "I begin to wrap up the *Sistine Madonna* tomorrow," he called. "Fascinating problems. Fascinating."

"I don't hate James, I despise him," Pauline called back defensively, still at the window.

But that wasn't quite true. She did very nearly hate James—as well as despise him. It wasn't because he condescended to her. As a faculty wife, she was used to that. What she couldn't forgive was that James couldn't always conceal that he disdained Battsie, what he said, what he was. If James disdained what Battsie was, why shouldn't she despise what James was? That was justice—in the academic world and no doubt in most others.

When Iris Siswick was sure Velia would have the coffee cleared away, she returned to the drawing room. The walls of the villa were thick, her own quarters right above it. If the windows were tightly shut, she could practice at night and bother nobody. When she went to check the sashes, she saw James and Mark sitting out in the garden.

Tears came into her eyes. It was getting harder to hold back her despair, which had been growing for months. The worst of it was, she couldn't see any way out, none that she could manage for herself. She was too timid for strong action on her own, and the humiliation would be too great—to admit defeat, go home to Albany, face—what life then? She needed to be rescued, and she knew it. She needed someone she could hold on to. She had nobody here, and that hadn't bothered her until music itself began to fail her.

116

What if she were there, beside Mark? He'd been so nice, with his questions at dinner—though the questions had been painful. Could he save her? Would he ever want to? If he'd really been interested in her, *really* interested, were questions about Haydn the ones he'd have been asking? She was doubtful.

She thought about it as she returned to sit on the piano bench, then about Signora Benassi's birthday party. She began a Chopin étude from memory, but her conscience got the better of her and, with a sigh, she opened up the Haydn that awaited her on the music rack like a sentence to hard labor in perpetuity.

Ricky left right after dinner, too upset by the conversation that had preceded it to stay on. Signora Benassi and Costanza were alone in the signora's bedroom, getting her ready for bed, where she might read for hours. Costanza went to pull the draperies, but paused when she saw Mark and James.

At her signal, Signora Benassi came to have a look. "I like that young man," she said. "And it's nice to have a new face at table. I'm tired of everybody else. I do wish he'd get interested in Miss Siswick. He'd be so good for her. One of the things that's wrong with her music is that she needs some life as well as all those finger exercises. And they could so conveniently carry on an affair here. She'd never need to interrupt her practicing schedule, and he wouldn't have dreary walks home late at night."

Costanza agreed, then added, "Has the signora thought who he looks like?" The signora had not. "Like the husband of Mr. Molyneux's cousin. He looks very like Mr. Guest."

"She's returning soon. Divorced."

"If Mr. Stapleton is still here, it will be interesting to see what happens."

The signora laughed. "What a wicked imagination you have, Costanza."

"The contessa, your mother, always said people love according to patterns."

Signora Benassi thought about Benassi and Ricky. They were quite different—except for their Latin. "That was just a notion of hers."

117

Costanza shrugged. "It is, in any case, a situation that would have amused the contessa," she said, as she pulled the drapery cord.

"Certainly," the signora said. "Such things were, after all, her life."

PART

four

PART

four

Wesley Knuckles, Laurie Walker, and Miss Emilene Ladore left Rome on Saturday. They spent the first night in Orvieto, after a tour of its cathedral, during which Miss Emilene took a fierce dislike to the Signorelli frescoes of the last days of the world and what follows, said they so embarrassed her she couldn't bear to look at them—by which she meant all the mens' codpieces. On Sunday they went on to Assisi to spend the second night, after visiting the Basilica of San Francesco, where she complained about the damp in the Lower Church. She awakened on Monday morning with a slight funny feeling, but didn't say anything. They spent Monday night in Perugia; by the time they got to their hotel, she had a tickle in her throat and, without giving any reason, refused to go out and walk around the city. On Tuesday morning the tickle was a scratch, and she had other funny feelings, too. Still, she didn't say anything.

From Perugia they went to Siena, where, in the great pseudo-medieval Hotel del Palio, named for the famous race run each summer through the Piazza del Campo, Miss Emilene and Laurie shared adjoining rooms, which had a connecting door between them that could or could not be left open. Each had her own bathroom. After Laurie had laundered the seat in Miss Emilene's, she did some unpacking for the old woman, although, as their stay would be short, it wasn't necessary to get into all of her variously shaped pieces of luggage. She then went to her own room to put her own things in order, but she only got as far as opening her big suitcase and getting its contents strewn over her bed before Miss Emilene interrupted her.

Left to herself, Miss Emilene had sterilized her thermometer in her little traveling bottle of rubbing alcohol, and had then taken her temperature; by this time her throat was raw and nasty, and her whole body ached. It was when she saw the results, plain to read on the glass tube, that she knocked on Laurie's door.

When Laurie opened up, Miss Emilene said, "Laurie, you'd probably better call your uncle and tell him I'm sick and can't go outside. I've got a fever. A hundred degrees. I'm really sick." Laurie asked her other symptoms. "I ache like a roping steer, and my throat feels like a dirt road in Taylor County at the end of August."

Wesley came at once, but at first Miss Emilene wouldn't let him in her bedroom. He had to stand in Laurie's room and talk to her through the connecting door, which Laurie, as guardian, held slightly ajar—while at the same time he looked at the things Laurie had unpacked and put on her bed, with particular interest in the underwear.

"How long has this been going on?" he asked.

"Ever since we left Rome," Miss Emilene admitted.

"Ever since we left Rome," Laurie repeated when Wesley indicated he hadn't understood; thereafter Laurie repeated all of Miss Emilene's replies.

"Rome! Why haven't you told us before?"

"Because I didn't want to get stuck in either of those ungodly places we stayed in."

"Assisi? Ungodly?" Wesley said.

"Infested with monks," Miss Emilene said. "And that other place"—Laurie provided her the name of Perugia—"it was too high up. In Texas we don't build cities on precipices."

"Please, Miss Emilene. Let me in so I can see how you look," Wesley begged.

"Oh, all right." She'd gone to bed, so she pulled the sheet up to her neck after she'd clapped her red wig back on over her thin strands of white hair. "Come on in if you have to."

When Wesley saw her, he said, "Oh dear!" then, "May I?" He put a hand on her forehead. Hot. He took her pulse. Beating rather fast, it seemed to him, though he didn't really have any idea what would be normal for her. He picked up the thermometer.

"An even hundred, twenty minutes ago," said Miss Emilene, "and it hasn't changed, so put that thing down."

"I'll get a doctor right away."

"No." She hunched farther into her bed. "It's just a cold. I can tell. When I get colds, this is what they're like."

"But Miss Emilene, be reasonable," said Wesley. The learned world would accuse him of negligence if she died on his hands without founding anything, and hadn't even seen a doctor. "I think a professional opinion would be prudent."

"I don't want a doctor. My daddy hated doctors, 'specially at the end. He said if they knew as much as they pretend to, they'd all live forever, and then where would we be? Now let me alone."

Miss Emilene got worse. Her color faded, except for her nose, which turned orange. She sniffled and glugged. She wouldn't eat. She lost part of her voice. She crawled out of bed to go to the bathroom, but that was all she did do. By the time Wesley returned around noon the next day, from his official visit to the Chigi-Saracini Foundation up the hill from the main piazza, it was obvious something had to be done, and he did it. On his own authority he told the hotel to get a doctor, told Miss Emilene about it, and got her to agree to let the doctor talk to her through the door, as Wesley had had to do at first, but no more.

That done, he then telephoned John Battle Davenport over in Florence, with whom he had a tentative appointment the following afternoon, based on his previous plan to take his party over to Florence in the morning. Davenport himself wasn't yet back for lunch, but Pauline took the message, and she and Wesley arranged that the professor should wait at home after he'd eaten, not go right back to the German Library, and Wesley would call him again when he had some idea from the doctor how long they were likely to be held up.

At three o'clock Dr. Squarcione arrived, a muscular man whose face was all lines and furrows. Naturally he was outraged by the terms of his visit; it would certainly not be considered admissible at the medical school of the University of Padua to diagnose a patient you weren't permitted to see. On the other hand, he'd been told by the hotel's manager that Miss Ladore was from Texas, which everyone knew to be a land of gold, and that her group had arrived in a Mercedes limousine with a driver who had stories of his own to tell about the way his clients lived; Dr. Squarcione agreed, therefore, to go ahead with his consultation and make up for its irregularity by charging twice as much for a visit during which he didn't see his patient as he would have for one during which he did. Once again, Laurie stood in the door. Behind her stood the manager of the hotel, to translate, and beside him was Dr. Squarcione. Wesley was in the room with Miss Ladore, standing beside her bed.

The doctor asked for her pulse. Wesley took it. Was it strong or weak? Wesley couldn't say, only that he could feel it. What about her temperature? It was still one hundred. Would Wesley depress her tongue with this?—a wooden tab was handed through—and look into her throat for signs of white patches?

When the answer came back that the patient wouldn't allow it, Dr. Squarcione made a gesture of frustration and muttered some phrases in Italian that caused the manager to hold up a cautionary finger. Any heart palpitations? the doctor asked. That wouldn't be anything new, Miss Ladore said. Any chest pains? No, but this whole thing was giving her a pain somewhere else, she said, and it was time to send the doctor away. He persevered for a few more questions, then offered his diagnosis: given the difficult and improper circumstances, which made it quite impossible for him to say with certainty anything whatsoever regarding the condition of the patient, as far as he could tell she might, subject of course to every imaginable qualification, have the cold that was making the rounds of all of Italy, including Rome, Orvieto, Assisi, and Perugia—Dr. Squarcione had ascertained just where the travelers had been. If her condition remained stable, and her throat improved, there was hope that she would recover in a couple of days. If she got worse, they should call him again. But—he would not consent to a second visit on the same terms as this one.

Miss Emilene refused to take any of the medicine the doctor prescribed. Unconvinced that pills in Europe were manufactured with the same precautions as they were in Texas, she made do with her brought-from-home cough drops and aspirin.

Laurie and her uncle had dinner alone together in the hotel dining room that night. Wesley was nervous and irritable. He complained about the temperature of his pasta and the toughness of his broiled liver, and he sent back the wine because, he claimed, it was cloudy, though both the headwaiter and Laurie said it wasn't—which only infuriated him the more.

"You should have backed me up," he said to her. He waited while the waiter uncorked and poured the new wine. "Unfavorable omens," he said, glowering because the waiter, exasperated himself, had spilled on the tablecloth.

"What are?"

"Getting a bad bottle of wine on top of Miss Emilene's getting sick. I've worried from the beginning that all this might not come to anything, Laurie. Middle-of-the-night worries—you know the kind. Too much depends on one eccentric old woman. I know how to handle boards and corporate donors and your typical millionaire, but *her*—she's unpredictable—like all crazy people." Wesley had had quite a lot of whisky in his room, and it had loosened both his tongue and his imagination. "I'm full of dread," he said darkly. "Before, it was dread for fear she'd go home. And now—if she should die before she did anything firm with her money, after all the work I've done preparing things, well, it would be just too bad."

"For her too," Laurie said quietly.

Wesley looked dubiously at her. "True, but it's not the point I'm trying to make. Look, you're alone with her a lot. Does she talk to you? I mean, about our project? Or about me?" Laurie shook her head, and it was true; Miss Emilene never did discuss Wesley's projects with his niece. "Why don't you draw her out, for Christ's sake?" he said. "Find out what's really going through her head, if you can. This would be a good time to do it—while she's shut in and all. Her defenses will be down."

"I was hired as a companion, not as an informer."

"I like that. *I like that*," Wesley said furiously. "An *informer*. What a word to use, when all I asked you to do is help me a little. Well, how does it feel to be a traitor?"

Laurie said, "I think you're drunk, Uncle Wesley. I'm no more a traitor than I am an informer."

"All right, all right. Of course you aren't. But—" He tried again. "I told you once before, I think she likes you. Maybe she hasn't talked to you because she thinks you aren't interested. Show her you are and see what happens. See what she says. Do what you can for us. Don't be so cold all the time, Laurie. A girl who looks like you shouldn't be so goddamned cold."

The turn in the conversation surprised him, and he quickly turned it back. "And talk me up to her."

"I wouldn't know how to begin," Laurie said, her dark eyes snapping.

Wesley sat back and put down his knife and fork and stared at her. She'd never looked more desirable. Those wonderful lips— like Marilyn Monroe's. Which of the articles he'd seen strewn over her bed did she have on? he wondered. "You're angry now, aren't you?" he said. "Well, try to look at it from my point of view. I so much want this thing to go through. I'm . . . overwrought. So much depends on the next few days. We've got to get her to Florence. I count on John Battle Davenport to be the catalyst that'll make everything fall into place; he's the dean of Renaissance studies, and if he can't do it, nobody can. We've got to get her that far."

Laurie said, "Why does all this make so much difference to you, Uncle Wesley? You've already been head of so many things."

"Why? Because this is something new." He poured himself some more wine. "Running a college is like running someone else's hand laundry—when it isn't like running a lunatic asylum. You receive the product wrinkled and dirty, process it, and send it out clean and smooth, year after year, and your help does nothing but complain about the heat and try to do less work for more money. Add doctors and lawyers and Ph.D.'s to that, and you've got a university. Meaning you've added dry cleaning to your laundry operation. Running a foundation is strictly defensive. The only thing you worry about is giving your money away to the wrong people, you don't worry if you're giving it to the right ones. I've done it all, and done it well, but now I want something different. This thing I'm on to—do you know how I feel about it? I feel that maybe it'll be really distinguished. Really distinguished, Laurie. My monument. The climax of my career—and mine from beginning to end. Not something I'm taking over from other people. Is it so bad to have an ambition like that?"

Laurie no longer cared enough about her uncle to be moved in the slightest by his speech. "Maybe if it meant less to you, you'd get further with Miss Ladore," she said.

"I don't know what you mean by that. Probably not too much. Anyway, I'm asking for your help," Wesley said, "not begging, but asking. *Please* work on her, if you can. I remind you that you have an obligation to me."

"Yes, I know," Laurie said. "I spend quite a lot of time thinking just how big it is."

A remark that brought such a lewd thought into her uncle's mind that he had to have the rest of the wine to wash it clean away.

The next afternoon, after a long siesta, Miss Emilene felt better. Her head wasn't as tight. Things were breaking up a little. She was well enough to be bored, and asked Laurie to read to her.

Possibly there was a bookstore in Siena that sold books in English, but Laurie didn't know where it was. However, she had noticed a shelf of books, things left behind by other guests, in the hotel's writing room, where there were three desks that had quantities of the hotel's stationery in their drawers, but no chairs sitting in front of them. Laurie went there to look for something Miss Emilene might like, but the selection was terrible: out-of-date travel books with names like *My Tuscany* and *Mornings-After in Florence*, and romantic novels about the Plantagenets and Stuarts, left behind by the Siena-loving British, just the sort of thing you'd expect people wouldn't bother to carry back to Liverpool or Wolverhampton. She came on only one exception, a book that might do, though it might not. She took it upstairs, sat down beside Miss Ladore's bed, and began to read without telling her what she'd be hearing.

"'You don't know about me without you have read a book by the name of *The Adventures of Tom Sawyer*; but that ain't no matter. That book was made by Mr. Mark Twain, and he told the truth, mainly. There was things which he stretched, but mainly he told the truth. That is nothing. I never seen anybody but lied one time or another, without it was Aunt Polly, or the widow, or—'"

"Stop!" whispered Miss Emilene. "Oh, stop. Just for a moment, not for good. Child, where'd you find that?" Laurie told her. "How did you ever guess? *Huckleberry Finn* was my daddy's favorite book, and it's mine too. It was almost the only thing I ever saw him read that wasn't a newspaper or something to do with cows and natural gas. The only thing he and I agreed about entirely. Oh my. Now this is going to be a treat."

Laurie read on. And on and on. Miss Ladore couldn't seem to get enough, not in two hours, though she'd been sleeping nearly all the time up till then. Once when Laurie got tired and stopped to rest, and glanced over at her, she saw that Miss Ladore was crying. Her ugly old face was screwed into a gargoyle. She let out a sob.

Alarmed, Laurie stood up. "Is something the matter?"

"Of course there is. I'm homesick. Do you think I want to be here? I don't. I want to be at my ranch."

Laurie said sadly, "If I had a ranch, maybe I'd want to be there, too."

"You would. Oh, you would. I wonder what time it is." Laurie told her nearly five o'clock. "No, no. I meant back in Texas. I'm so addled, what with being so far away and feeling like this, that I can't even remember what the time difference would be. But it must be in the morning there. I wonder if I'd be able to reach Hap Macro."

"Reach him where? Who's Hap Macro?"

"He's my manager, on the big ranch. He grew up on it—his daddy worked there. He's someone I really trust. Even in Texas there aren't too many like that."

"I'll see what I can do if you want me to. What's the number?" Laurie reached for the telephone.

A couple of minutes later, Hap Macro was on the line. Miss Emilene didn't try to keep the mouthpiece at a distance; her voice was too shreddy for that. She risked infection and put her face right into it.

"Hap? It's me, Miss Emilene. How're things?" They spoke for ten minutes about the weather in west-central Texas, and the cattle market, and some repainting that was going on in the ranch house. Then: "Me? I'm going from one city in Italy to the next, like I was selling brushes. I'll say it isn't any pleasure. It's all about establishing a place where people can study what went on in the fourteenth and fifteenth and sixteenth centuries, which it seems were full of activity. What? No. Entirely here in Europe, Hap—I don't reckon much went on in Texas before 1492, for heaven's sake. It'll take a lot of Daddy's money. Maybe some of mine, too. What do you think?" She listened a little. "He told me to spend it this way. I mean, not exactly this way, but generally." Another silence while she listened. "That's not true. It wasn't till later that he lost touch. I don't know. I just don't know. I'm in way over my head. I tell you what, Hap. I wish I was home. I'd just like to smell Texas for five seconds—I'd give a million to anyone who could bring me a paper bag full of that air, I declare I would."

They talked a little more about the ranch, and then, when she'd hung up, Miss Ladore said, "Don't you have someone you'd like to call, Laurie, now that we know how to do it?"

"Not really."

"No boyfriend?" Laurie shook her head. "Well, now, that's too bad. And you so pretty, too. Boys must flock around you like ants around sugar."

Laurie said, "That's the trouble."

"That's what trouble?" Miss Emilene asked.

"Being pretty brings such obvious boys around—all the ones who think they'll make out all right with a pretty girl. The egotists. You know what they want, you know what they'll say. You even know what their ambitions in life are going to be. You know everything about them in advance. It's so boring."

Miss Ladore thought that over and didn't like it. "My daddy used to say, 'Emilene, just remember something. Plain as you are, the boys who come after you will really be after your money.' I believed him, Laurie, with the result that I didn't remark in time the one who wasn't. Now read some more of *Huck Finn*."

Later, during another break, Miss Ladore lay in bed, quietly. She wasn't so sure anymore that Laurie was really Wesley's spy. She glanced at her. "I shouldn't have called Hap in front of you, or said those things, I suppose, about being in over my head and all. I suppose you'll report it to your uncle. But I don't really care. He's worn me down. My daddy taught me lots of things, good and bad, but he never taught me how to get along in this world after he left me alone in it. Not really. Maybe he hoped I couldn't. Anyway, sometimes I've thought, during the last couple of days, that I was ready to give in and sign a blank check."

Laurie got up and began to walk around the room. "I am *not* going to tell my uncle what you said. I don't tell him *anything*. I haven't ever told him anything."

"Can I believe you?"

"Yes, you can. He'd like me to, but I won't. Do you want to know why? I don't trust him any more than you do. Don't you dare sign a blank check."

"Why are you traveling with us?"

"He thought you'd need someone, and he thought I'd be a help. Loyal. And I'd never been to Europe and thought it would be a good way to get here. I wish I weren't, I can tell you that."

"Let's both of us go home." Miss Emilene swung one leg out from under the covers and put it on the floor, as if, cold or no cold, she was ready to pack on the spot.

Laurie made a hopeless gesture. "I can't just leave. Neither can you."

Miss Emilene pulled the leg back under the covers. "I suppose not. But I'm getting close to it, I can tell you. I don't know how much longer I can hold out. What do you think of this Renaissance business? Do you think it's a fraud? Do you think your Uncle Wesley is a crook?"

"I don't know what he is. And I don't know what I think about the Renaissance Center, or whatever it'll be called. I don't see anything wrong with it. What I don't like is how everybody's always trying to get money out of you."

"Child, if nobody got money out of people like me, there wouldn't be anywhere for people to go on weekends. No concerts. No museums. No ballet. No theaters. I don't mind that. I'm used to it. What I don't want is to waste my money on an institution that's got no reason to exist except for your uncle's vanity."

Laurie said—the ultimate betrayal!—"Why don't you spend the money for some kind of scientific purpose?"

"'Cause of my daddy. He said not to. He said, 'Emilene, steer clear of them test-tube jockeys. If you've got the brains to,' he said, 'try and see that the name of Ladore gets added to Getty and Kimball and all the other culture people.' What you want at the end ought to have special weight, it seems to me, even though it's different from what you've thought all along. A person who's dying is likely to be more serious. Anyway, that's why I got all tangled up with your uncle. I was told that if anybody was on top of culture, he was."

Miss Emilene stopped, cleared her throat, and drank some water. "That was too long a speech for someone with my condition," she said. "Give me a cough drop."

Laurie did so, then said, "He may be on top of culture, but that doesn't mean you ought to give him a blank check. Don't let him get on top of you."

Miss Ladore sucked. "I'm not likely to. Don't you let him, either. I've seen how he looks at you."

"Good God!" Laurie said—for Miss Ladore had made sense of Wesley's odd remark about her coldness.

Miss Emilene slept awhile then, and afterwards Laurie read her more of *Huckleberry Finn*, all the way to "'. . . and so there ain't nothing more to write about, and I am rotten glad of it, because if I'd 'a' knowed what a trouble it was to make a book I wouldn't 'a' tackled it, and ain't a-going to no more. But I reckon I got to light out for the territory ahead of the rest, because Aunt Sally she's going to adopt me and sivilize me, and I can't stand it. I been there before.'"

Miss Emilene cried again. When she'd composed herself, she said, "You know, Laurie, when I'd come to that place in the book, and there I was at the big ranch, with my daddy on one of his rampages, I'd think, maybe that was what I ought to do. Light out for the territory. But where do you go, when the territory's where you're already at?"

On Friday, Miss Emilene was better. On Saturday her temperature had returned to normal, though she had some cough left, and felt a little weak. By Sunday they'd been through *Huckleberry Finn* a second time, and she felt well enough to travel. They drove over to Florence in the late afternoon.

Before they left their rooms at the Hotel del Palio, she said to Laurie, "I want to tell you something. I'm feeling just a whole lot better about things. I'm going to be a match for your uncle; he'd better watch out. While he thinks he's getting what he wants out of me, I'll get what I want out of him. And I want to tell you this, too, Laurie. I'm glad I got sick here, for two reasons. One is *Huck Finn*. That really restored me. The other is that now I've got a friend. A few days of bed rest did me some good, but a friend's what I needed a lot more than rest. Don't you let me down."

John Battle Davenport happened to mention to Iris Siswick at the villa's buffet lunch on Wednesday that he wouldn't be returning to the German Library as soon as he'd like; he had to wait for a long-distance call that took precedence, said he, over the call of

Raphael. James Molyneux overheard. Knowing that Battsie's Raphael books would be free, he took the opportunity to go himself.

He'd been thinking and thinking of his great drawing. If it was a Raphael project, as he believed it to be, it was a remarkably complete one. He'd found, in his quick go-through of the oeuvre, nothing of the kind. That was, no doubt, because any presentation drawing as complete as what he had would have been used up, thumbed and folded and so on, in the process of painting the fresco for which it was the design. It therefore seemed likely that the project his drawing had been done for had remained unexecuted. But mightn't there have been other drawings connected with this one, perhaps preliminary to it, or, more likely, ancillary to it—studies for individual figures, or even details, a head, a foot—that had then been worked into the big, finished drawing? Such had always been Raphael's practice, for he worked carefully and by steps toward the final formulation of his ideas. If James could find any such partial drawings, and they were accepted as being by Raphael, the probability of his completed drawing's attribution would rise dramatically, and with it the price. James got out his Polaroid snapshots and began a search.

The catalog of the Raphael drawings in the British Museum yielded nothing. The Cabinet des Dessins at the Louvre: nothing. Battsie himself had written on the Raphael drawings in the Metropolitan Museum, and naturally had a copy of that on his desk. Nothing at the Met. The catalog of the Uffizi drawings yielded no more. A little discouraged, James sat back. Meanwhile, another visitor to the library had crossed behind him several times throughout all this searching, but James, concentrating, hadn't really noticed, nor did he really notice when it happened now, or notice that the man paused before he continued toward the racks that contained current issues of periodicals.

It was getting on toward four-thirty. If Battsie was going to come here at all this afternoon, he'd come soon, because during his grumbling to Iris he'd said he wouldn't wait for his telephone call past four o'clock. Still disappointed, though he'd known it wouldn't be easy, James went on. He picked up a book on the drawings in the Boymans Museum in Rotterdam—a famous collection. It had a marker in it near the entry on a study for the head of Saint Sixtus in the *Sistine Madonna* in Dresden—Battsie's current victim. He looked at the reproductions of the other Raphaels in the Boymans.

There it was! What he'd been hoping for. A drawing of the shoulder, arm, and hand of a man, so close to one of the figures in James's drawing that they had to be connected. Moreover, the Boymans drawing told him something else, for one detail in it was clearer than the comparable passage in his own drawing, where there was a smudge. The hand held aloft keys. Keys! Naturally the Boymans catalog identified their drawing as a study for Saint Peter. James was therefore able to say that in his drawing the related figure was Saint Peter. Saint Peter mounted on horseback, who rode forward brandishing his chief attribute like a weapon. And that meant that the man who accompanied Saint Peter in James's drawing and held a sword would, of course, have to be Saint Paul. They were always shown that way, Peter with keys, Paul with a sword.

James, really excited now, read on. The Boymans drawing, at the time the catalog was written, hadn't been associated with a known work of Raphael, but the attribution was unquestioned by any scholar. The entry then mentioned paper and dimensions. James converted the centimeters to inches; they corresponded to each of the four single sheets of which his drawing was composed, and the paper at the Boymans bore the watermark of a horse's head and three stars. Other drawings by Raphael, in the Albertina in Vienna, in Bayonne, etc., were done on the same paper, so said the catalog—and said that as the Albertina drawing was a study of the head of the angel in *The Freeing of Peter*, dated 1514, during the second year of the pontificate of Leo X, presumably Raphael was using paper from this producer during the early years of Leo's reign. From this, and on stylistic evidence, the Boymans catalog concluded that the date of their drawing must be about 1513 or 1514.

There it was! Major evidence. James transcribed the catalog entry—unmindful of the other scholar who passed yet again behind him, slowed once more, and went on.

As James was leaving the library, he met John Davenport coming up the stairs. They nodded.

"Get your phone call?" James asked pleasantly.

"Yes, yes," Davenport said, giving him a slightly suspicious look. "An engagement I had was postponed until the weekend or early next week. All the more time for my work here."

"My congratulations, then," said James. "To Raphael, I mean."

James Molyneux was something of a solitary, not really because he was all that misanthropic—the word Ricky would put to it—or because he was poor company and people avoided him, but because few seemed to him worth the kind of intense investment he made in a friend. He was, however, always on the lookout for recruits to his small circle of the acceptable. When anyone joined it, James was fiercely loyal, even possessive. Though he had few friends, nobody could have cared more than he for the ones he did have.

Would Mark do, he wondered, as he was walking toward Santo Spirito—in what he realized was something of a reversal; a few days ago he'd planned to keep Mark at a distance, now he was wondering how close to bring him in. But if he was going to bring him in at all, how close then became a proper question. His relationship with Mark had been so muddied—by Tremper, by the drawing—that James just wasn't sure. It would require some testing, and today would be a start.

James was early, because he wanted a few minutes alone inside the church to review old impressions and perhaps receive a few new ones before Mark arrived. He hesitated in front of the building, his cane at a forty-five-degree angle from the pavement, not to admire the façade, because there isn't any, but to choose which of the two lateral doors he'd enter by. It was so obvious to use the left one, circumambulate the aisles and transepts and choir in the clockwise sense, that he wondered if he'd ever done anything else. The mere question was enough; he entered by the right door. As a result, he literally bumped into Mark, who was just leaving by it, having entered earlier by the left.

"You're very early," James said.

"Aren't you?" Mark asked.

He'd had time, had made time, to return to the villa and clean up after his morning jog and was back in his sightseeing uniform:

blue polo shirt and khaki trousers and a different pair of running shoes. James wore a suit.

"Am I? Yes, I suppose I am. I thought that as I was, I'd have a look in to pass the time."

"Well, so did I."

James smiled. "I came early deliberately."

"I did too."

"And just why did you?"

"So I'd know what we were going to look at and could sound more intelligent."

"I suppose I came early for the same reason," said James. "One does like to make as good a show as possible when one's offered to be a cicerone."

"You didn't need to bother. I'm bound to be impressed."

"You think so, do you? Take nothing for granted," James said rhetorically, leading the way back into the interior, "including the relative height of Santo Spirito's nave arcade to that of its clerestory. One knows, quite simply knows, though there's naturally no documentation for it—how could there be?—that Brunelleschi put all his heart and mind, neither less than the second finest in the fifteenth century, into the problem. And came up with a solution so simple as to be truly dangerous—as is so often the case when heart and mind are fully and harmoniously united."

Exactly the kind of talk Mark had hoped for. He passed through the columns of the arcade into the open vessel of the nave and stared at the elements James had mentioned, paced up and down, turned round and round for a full five minutes, before he dared to draw his conclusions.

"I see," he said, returning to James's side.

"If that is true, if you truly see, our architect could ask for nothing better. Its awesome originality will become clear to you when you go to see San Lorenzo—the other Brunelleschi church—if you've not yet been there. Go back if you have and remark the difference between treating the arcade as a pedestal and treating it as a partner. Now let me lead you to your own explanations of how everything works in here."

For forty-five minutes, sometimes pointing with his cane, sometimes leaning on it, James took Mark up and down the length and breadth of the church, now making an observation of his own, but more often asking a question. He brought Mark to see how every shape in the arcade was echoed in the borders of the chapels of the outer walls. That was fairly easy. Thereafter he had him pace off, measure with both eye and foot, certain intervals, and then—not without some prodding and a disdainful sniff or two—got him to perceive how the floor plan had been laid out on a module determined by the dimensions of the crossing under the dome, and how these horizontal dimensions worked in conjunction with the vertical ones, and how the bays of the nave were linked to the bays of the aisles, and how, pulling transepts and choir into the scheme, it all knit together, finally, into a splendor.

Mark, at the end, was grinning with sheer delight. "I'll be damned," he said.

"Sum it up. Find a phrase to sum it up," James urged.

"It's . . . architecture without accidents," said Mark.

"Not bad. Not a bad phrase at all." James's quick initial smile gave way to an expression more serious, yet hardly severe. "But not quite true—if by it you mean the church lacks feeling," he said. He was singularly pleased. Mark hadn't had—that had become clear—the slightest notion in advance what to look for, despite his preview, but when he was edged onto course, he'd soon found his way. He was receptive. And willing. Possibly perceptive—or of that bent. Certainly he was attentive. James had never butted anybody up against Brunelleschi so remorselessly for so long a time, yet Mark's attention had never strayed. He'd listened, looked, walked, listened, queried, thought, queried, looked, thought, walked, and listened until James, not he, was too tired to continue. And, James surmised, he was doing it not only for his own interest but also to please his mentor.

"That's enough," James said. He held forth his cane as a reminder, thus insisting on a reference to his disfigurement—as he was likely to do when he felt himself too set up by something he'd accomplished. "I get tired faster than those whose bilateral symmetry is more perfect."

He walked, limping more now, toward the west entrances. "How long had you been here? Before I arrived?"

"Almost half an hour. Without seeing anything," Mark acknowledged.

136

"And did our tour live up to what Tremper led you to expect?"

"I've never spent a more interesting hour in my life."

"What else did he say about me?"

"That you were prickly."

"Not quite true. Discriminating to a fault, perhaps. How well do you know Tremper?"

Mark hesitated, then said, "I've never been to his house."

"I have," James said, wondering just how much Mark's statement was meant to tell him. "There are no books in it."

"So he's told me."

"If I could afford it, I'd never sell any of the books that come through my hands; I hope I don't have to tell you that it almost killed me to cut that page, but I saw no other choice if I wasn't to damage the drawing. No, if I could have my way, my rooms would look like a bookstore that never has a customer. I'd keep them all for myself. That's the difference between Tremper and me."

"I've noticed others."

James glanced sideways at Mark, put just a little on edge by his last statement. "Do you now suppose you know quite a lot about Santo Spirito?"

Mark knew James well enough already to be guarded. "I think I know more than I did."

"We would disagree," James said. "For I hope you realize that unless you can forget all the business of harmonies, consonance, and proportions, of *pietra serena*, the Brunelleschian order, stilt blocks and modules, and go into the church next time with your former innocence of mind and eye artfully reconstituted, and truly see it as it is, our morning here will have been wasted."

"I don't know if I can."

"You must."

"But . . . how can I? You've educated me."

James turned on him, an unexpectedly passionate expression on his thin dark face. *"Don't use that word.* You must realize that the proper replacement for a lack of knowledge is a finer innocence, not an educated ignorance. Else you'll be no better than those so very educated scholars who steep perpetually in the tepid pot of the German Library and think that when they've talked to each other about treatises on perspective and neo-Platonism, they've said something worth hearing anywhere else."

Mark looked curiously at James. "Please tell me what this is all about," he said.

"Certainly. Glad to. Learning, as they have it, is a pox that spots and spoils the pure love that is the only foundation for a true knowledge of what our eyes see."

Naturally, Mark made no comment.

"And of course, if we ever get to people, as I suggested we might, you and I—that will make Santo Spirito seem like simple addition. We'd need a year to get started on people. It's a pity we don't have it. But you'll have returned to that back room at Tremper & Ixion long since, I suppose."

"I told you I didn't intend to return there," Mark said.

"You'll change your mind."

"I don't see why you say that."

"Tremper'll beg you back, and so you'll go."

"Don't spoil the morning," Mark said quietly.

A moment of silence followed. Then James, suddenly cheerful, said, "How like me to try. Let's go have a coffee. You know what? I'll pay."

The next day, at a leisurely hour, James went back to try his luck again at the German Library. Davenport had gone there bright and early. Twelve or fifteen books were open in front of him. A pad of legal-length lined paper and half a dozen freshly sharpened pencils were beside his right hand. A mountain of the same paper, already written upon, lay in a disorderly pile in front of him. James, who was anything but professionally trained, for once envied Battsie his robot methodology. He considered the possibility of asking his guidance, in a guarded way—If you had such and such a problem, how would you proceed?—but decided that, given how suspicious Battsie was of other scholars, it would be too dangerous. With him, there would be no safe questions. And so James went to the place where the catalogs of museum collections were kept, more specifically to the shelf devoted to collections of drawings. He looked up the Albertina drawing, and the one in Bayonne. Both seemed to him stylistically to resemble his own, though neither was of a detail he could find on his Polaroid snapshots. He tried to think where there might be other groups of important Raphaels. Berlin? He looked. Nothing of any interest. Stockholm? Nothing. He went through perhaps ten catalogs, with no results. Then, in the collections at Hannover, he came upon another drawing that he felt almost certainly was connected with his: a study for the head and, separate from it, one for the body (the latter drawn nude, as was often the practice of Raphael) of the young man of about twenty who accompanied, seemingly as an attendant, the figure dressed in ecclesiastical garments in James's drawing. James carried the volume out to the reading room and took down the information in the notes on the plates. Such was his concentration, in his efforts to make sure he had the German right, that he didn't notice another reader who glided quietly behind him, paused to look over his shoulder, then went on, and who, a short while later, when James, fired with enthusiasm, returned to the drawings catalogs to look further, found a book in a facing aisle to be interested in, and from there watched James closely.

Battsie had lunch at a nearby trattoria on Via della Colonna, in order not to waste time, then returned to his desk, where he made good progress with the *Sistine Madonna*, settling at least part of one of the puzzles connected with it once and for all, as he saw it. When he was leaving for the day, Ettore Biscotti joined up with him. Once more they walked together toward Via Cavour.

"Day before yesterday, while you were gone, our friend"—Ettore looked comically behind them, as if afraid they were being followed—"spent hours with your books—which, moreover, he was very careful to replace exactly as you'd left them."

"So? Which ones? What did he want with them?"

"Books on drawings—you have out a lot of them. The Uffizi, the Louvre, and so on. He compared their illustrations to some little snapshots that he took in and out of his pocket for that purpose. There seemed to be no end to his curiosity."

"There's no end to mine, I can tell you. Looking at those catalogs behind my back? Outrageous!"

"They are, from one point of view, general property, I suppose," Ettore said.

"Nonsense. Raphael's in my pocket for the time being. I'm going to have to speak to that . . . amateur."

"Hear me through." Biscotti clasped his hands behind his back and walked a little more briskly; he and his wife were going away for a long weekend, and he was late. "He found a drawing in one of the books that interested him sufficiently to copy down the entry. It's in the Boymans. I checked it later. Studies of a man's shoulder and arm and hand. Keys. Saint Peter."

"That one, eh?" Battsie slowed to a stop so quickly that Biscotti was carried by his momentum several feet ahead of him and had to come back. "Curious. I've written it up, you know. An article in the *Zeitschrift für Kunstgeschichte*. It's one of a group on identical paper, wrongly interpreted by Daphne Nickerson, in my opinion. She associates them largely with rejected ideas for the tapestry cartoons; she'd have been better off if she'd stuck with crewelwork herself, instead of warping and woofing her way into art history. I sometimes think it's a pity there's no other *grande dame* of Raphael studies to unseat; it's just too easy to topple Daphne. Built like a pear, anyway."

"A group, you say? One of a group of drawings? And is there another of that group in Hannover?"

"Yes. How'd you know?"

"Today Molyneux was also very interested in a drawing in Hannover. It shows the figure of a nude youth on horseback, turning to the right and gesticulating, and also has the head and eyes of a youth—quite portraitlike—as a marginal note."

"Nobody's ever figured out who it's of, unfortunately. How fascinating! What a detective you'd make, Ettore. What do you suppose he can have got hold of? Maybe I should ask him. Say I've been told he's been using my books every time I go off somewhere, and what's he up to?"

"And give our game away?" Biscotti was shocked. "Certainly not. He'd run for cover instantly. I have a much better idea. I assume you still dine together at Villa Arberoni; I recall with pleasure the last time my wife and I were there. Now why don't you introduce the subject of Raphael at your dinner table?"

Battsie laughed. "I daresay some might opine that I do it too much already."

"But make this different. Lead him into a—how do you say it?—into *un agguato.*"

"I see what you mean—what a devil you are!" Battsie cried, so enthusiastically that people looked. "Good idea. I'll camouflage the ambush with a little erudition, perhaps. Something I've been working on. Then, at the end, I'll slip over toward these drawings we've been talking about, bait the ambush with them, and steer him in a certain direction and we'll see if he takes it. If he does, we'll know more about what he may have in his hands."

Mark was invited for drinks again on Saturday evening by Signora Benassi. They first talked about the dress she'd wear to her birthday party; she'd had a phone call from her dressmaker, and would have to go to Rome, just for the day, on Monday, for a first fitting. Then she asked him how he'd been spending his time, and he told her of his visit to Santo Spirito with James Molyneux.

"An interesting experience for you, I'm sure, Mr. Stapleton. But don't let James take you too far. He sometimes grows into an overly impassioned guide." She paused, her little nose pointed at Mark quizzically, to let the remark sink in. "I wonder where Ricky is." The Marchese dei Guidoni was expected, but was late. "We'll have to go up to dinner without him, I'm afraid."

When they reached the elevator, there was Ricky, just come up. He apologized. "I couldn't help it. Sorry, Madeleine. Sorry, Mr. Stapleton. My great-nephew came to see me and only just left."

"Tiberio was in town? But why didn't you bring him to dinner?" she said. "I've been wanting Mr. Stapleton to meet him."

"I suggested it, but he couldn't stay. He had to get back to his vines."

"And why did he come over?" she asked sharply.

"Nothing important," Ricky said, preferring not to talk about it in front of Mark.

Signora Benassi wouldn't wait. "I'm going to whisper to Ricky for a moment," she said to Mark, who immediately stepped ahead of them when the elevator arrived. "Now tell me what it's all about," she said to Ricky, "so I can think about it during dinner.

There'll be nobody here but the regulars."

"Some property has come up for sale, at a distance from the villa, but not too far for him to manage. A parcel—forty-three hectares of good vineyards in the Colli Aretini—that has the classification of Chianti. Not Chianti Classico, to be sure, but a very respectable property all the same. Two peasant houses, and a nice owner's house, too—modern, the latter is."

"And Tiberio wants to buy the property?"

"He'd like to. But of course it's quite impossible—though it's rather cheap for what it is. I had to say I couldn't help him."

"Not couldn't," Signora Benassi said. "Wouldn't."

"It comes to the same thing," Ricky said.

"Not at all. The early Christians were forbidden to seek martyrdom, but they were allowed to accept it joyfully if it was forced on them."

"Where did you ever learn that?" Ricky asked.

"Probably from Mama." Signora Benassi caught up with Mark. "May I take your arm, Mr. Stapleton?"

As there were no outside guests that night to enrich the mixture of company, Professor Davenport talked almost uninterruptedly. Nobody else could say anything. Or perhaps nobody wanted to. The signora was in a mood. Ricky, too, was depressed and silent. James had just heard from his cousin Hilda; she was returning to Florence sooner than expected, and he was preoccupied thinking about her—her advents were reason for a certain amount of apprehension. Iris was silent, as usual, and because Mark would have had to talk across the professor in order to reach anybody else, he couldn't say much, either. The subject of Davenport's disquisition was, of course, Raphael—his ins and outs, his ups and downs. In particular, the captive little group heard the recitation of Battsie's entire chapter as written thus far on the *Sistine Madonna*. By the end of dessert, when even the faithful Pauline was ready to rise up against him, he was ready to spring his trap on James.

"Of course, one of the worst mistakes Daphne Nickerson made in her monograph was to dispute my claim that two drawings, one in Helsinki, the other in Budapest, should be dated at roughly the same time as the *Sistine Madonna*, and grouped with a number of other drawings—in Hannover." Battsie waited. "In the Boymans." He waited again. "All of them stylistic sisters, and some of them obviously connected with Raphael's fresco projects that were going on at the same time as he was painting the *Sistine Madonna*. Daphne asserted—"

James had opened his eyes. "What was that again? What you've been saying is extraordinarily interesting. Please elucidate."

Pauline looked angrily at him. "Why don't you listen in the first place?" she said, driven almost mad by the possibility that Battsie might begin *da capo*.

But he didn't. "There're a group of drawings I wrote up once upon a time. All on identical paper. Some can be associated with known paintings, most can't. That's all I was saying. Daphne thinks they're later by as much as two years than the Stanza of Heliodorus. I don't agree. She thinks they may have connections with the tapestries, and even goes so ridiculously far as to suggest one of them may be connected with a project for the Loggia. The *Loggia!* Isn't it ludicrous?"

"Budapest and Helsinki, you said?"

"Mmm. I think another of them, in Leiden, is possibly to be connected with a fresco Raphael is said to have had in mind right after the election of Leo X, an incident in the life of one of the early popes—*The Return of Leo the Great to Rome*. Same pope as appears in *The Repulse of Attila*. Daphne Nickerson denies there ever was such a project, if you can believe it, yet it's mentioned in Vasari."

Mark raised his hand a little, like a timid freshman, and asked who that was.

Battsie said, "Giorgio Vasari. A painter and an architect—he designed the Uffizi. And he wrote a *Lives of the Most Excellent Architects, Painters, and Sculptors*. It's where one begins, even now. First brought out in 1550, and a second edition in 1568, much expanded. That's where Daphne Nickerson fell flat on her face— which is only a manner of speaking, because a spheroid body can't fall flat on anything." Battsie chortled. "The second edition's not only expanded, it's also sometimes contracted. I mean, Vasari cut things out. Daphne argues that whenever he cut something it was because he'd discovered that his original information was erroneous. Fine. So he happens to cut out the reference to the Leo-back-to-Rome picture, and therefore, argues Daphne, he's come to realize the project never existed. Sometimes, you know, reason alone won't take care of one's colleagues' mistakes; it wants ridicule. In my review of her book in *The Burlington Magazine*, I said I supposed that if a printer had inadvertently dropped old Vasari's discussion of the church of St. Peter's, Professor Nickerson would claim it didn't exist either—and walk through it with her eyes closed to prove her point to herself." Battsie shook his head over the folly of his adversary.

James had opened his eyes wide. "Two editions, you say?"

"Mmm. Of course, I can't explain why Vasari makes some of the changes he does; oddly enough, there're a surprising lot of them in the life of Raphael. But Daphne Nickerson is certainly guilty of gross misjudgment. That's what comes of never leaving Bryn Mawr."

The signora had had enough. "We will have coffee now," she said, rising, and when they were in the next room, she took hold of things.

She had Ricky sit by Pauline Davenport. She herself talked to James. She arranged for Iris to sit on a couch between Mark and Ricky, and she put Battsie all by himself. But the evening was by then ruined. Conversation just wouldn't go. Mark tried with Iris, but she was hopelessly unresponsive. Bored, Ricky decided to smoke. He took out his case and offered a cigarette to Iris and one to Mark, who both refused. He sighed, and lighted one for himself. As always, he put his case down on the table in front of them, to allow for a change of mind.

At once Mark leaned forward and looked closely at it. "That's interesting," he said. He touched the embossed decoration on it with his forefinger.

"My family coat of arms."

"Are you Venetians?"

"Good heavens, no. We're Italians. Why do you ask? Oh, I see. You mean the dolphins. Curious, aren't they? That's a rather late addition to the arms, actually. As you probably know, a great many states were represented in the Christian fleet at the Battle of Lepanto, including Florence, which sent a small contingent of gal-

144

leys under the command of Admiral Tullio dei Guidoni, my ancestor. In recognition of the victory, Grand Duke Cosimo, who was of course reigning in 1571, granted Tullio the right to dolphins rampant, to flank the shield and all the rest that we'd had since the time of Countess Mathilda."

Mark picked up the cigarette case. "Do different families ever have identical arms?" he asked. "I mean, could these arms belong to a family elsewhere in Italy?"

"Heavens, no. There'd have been a war over it."

Mark looked at the case a moment longer, then put it down again. "I learn something new every day," he said—and quite pointedly did not look at James Molyneux.

James, horrified by the turn of events, which caught him out in his lie about the arms on the books Mark had seen, had stopped talking to Signora Benassi in order to listen. Thank God, Mark didn't give anything away, not right then. But what about later? Somehow James would have to explain. He asked Mark to go into the garden with him again, just for a short walk.

They were earlier tonight than they had been the other time, and the day was a few minutes longer, too. James turned on no lights; nevertheless, they were observed from the villa.

Pauline said, "There they go again. I've never seen James Molyneux be so obvious."

Battsie was reading some notes. "Eh? Oh, you caught on, too."

"I'm talking about the play he's making for Mark Stapleton—and which is being welcomed, I'm sorry to say. It's like a courtship dance, whose consummation's foregone. I just wonder whether it'll take place on our floor or down in the basement. Caught on to *what?*"

"Caught on to the way he jumped at the bait in my trap. All that stuff about the *Sistine Madonna* was a smokescreen. It was the drawings at the end that mattered. Biscotti and I want to see if he'll go looking for the ones I mentioned. If he does, it may mean he's got one of the group to sell, and we can figure out which. Or maybe he's identified another."

"Maybe you can get him deported," Pauline said.

"Maybe," Professor Davenport said, "though all I really want is to scare him into leaving my stuff alone—and perhaps find out if he's onto something I ought to know about. It'll be my last book, and I don't want any oversights in it for Daphne to cackle at. You'd think he'd tell me as a duty, wouldn't you? But dealers—they own no duty to any higher aspiration, only to gain."

Ricky and the signora stood at the window and spoke of Tiberio.

"How much is the land?"

Ricky mentioned the price. "I told him that I had no money at all, and no real way to raise any. He wondered if it was possible to mortgage the palazzo, since it'll come to him. I told him it was already so mortgaged he'd be lucky to get the key to the lavatory when I died."

"I could easily let him have the money. But I won't, unless . . ."

"Please, Madeleine. I feel sad enough."

She was neither very sympathetic nor at all discouraged. "Not quite," she said. "Not quite sad—or bad enough. Not yet. Look! There's James and Mark again. James has taken him in hand. I warned Mark about it. James can be so overwhelming. And then he gets those fierce attachments. I doubt if Mark took my meaning, though. Well, you can tell people only so much. There are certain things one must learn for oneself."

Iris Siswick, when she returned to the drawing room to practice, leaned pensively against the window for a moment. She remembered how Mark had tried to talk to her after dinner, and how mute she'd been, partly because Ricky was on her other side. Couldn't think of replies to Mark's sallies. Had only blushed when he said how he admired her, because she had something she cared as much about as she cared for music. How could she let him know how ready she was to try something besides another Haydn sonata? There he was, walking again with James Molyneux. James was always so clever, when he wanted to be. Nice to her—he'd talk and talk and not expect her to answer. Never at a loss for

146

words. She envied him—in some ways. Were it she who was walking with Mark down there, what would she find to say to interest him? Probably nothing.

"You had a drink again with the signora tonight," James began. "That's twice you've been in her apartment. Often enough for you to have noticed things. What have you seen there that's choice?"

"There's a big picture of her mother. Costanza showed it to me the first night."

"Big, indeed! It's a John Singer Sargent portrait. Probably one of the four or five best he ever painted. It's even said he may have had a walk-out with Contessa Rinuccini—as who did not?"

"Really? You mean she—"

"Oh yes, indeed. Famous for it. If you could be rich and married and have every social connection and still be a courtesan, that would be her proper classification. A long string of liaisons, many of which lasted only a few weeks. They used to call this place 'Villa Aphrodite' because of her scandalous life; Florence was much stuffier in her day than it is now, but from what I've heard, she'd have shocked Paris itself. Then, later in her life, at about the turn of the century, when a Belgian prince, first cousin to the King of the Belgians and like him fearfully rich on loot from the Congo, took her over, she had to reform—it was thereafter, by the way, that Signora Benassi was born, though she never had his name, of course. He wouldn't put up with any nonsense, and Contessa Rinuccini ended rather a proper lady, they say. I never knew her, I'm sorry to say. Dead for a generation at least. What else did you notice at the signora's?"

Mark admitted he hadn't noticed anything else in particular.

"I'm disappointed in you," James said. "You didn't see the nautilus cup? It's right there in a case on one of the tables in her little sitting room, where one has cocktails. A shell, mounted in enamel and gold and baroque pearls. It is, along with the saltcellar in Vienna, the most famous piece of sumptuary art to have survived from the sixteenth century. Attributed to Benvenuto Cellini—he did the *Perseus* that's in the loggia on the Piazza della Signoria."

147

"I know that," Mark said.

"*Do* you? And then there's the art nouveau furniture. Made by a famous Belgian cabinetmaker, Geerhardt DeBoeck, on commission by the Prince, for the Countess. Last of its kind—art nouveau was already on the way out, but princes hear of such declensions later than other people. Or don't care as much, being in the same situation themselves. Matching cabinets in the room where you had cocktails. Other stuff too—like the big table that's under the Sargent. Worth a fortune these days."

"I didn't notice it. I'm not sure I'd have known what I was seeing, anyway."

"Pity," James murmured. He walked on silently. When they'd completed their turn of the garden and were back in the vestibule, where they'd separate, he paused at the elevator door, holding it ajar.

"About the coat of arms—" he began, not sure, even at that late moment, what he'd say.

Mark said lightly, "What coat of arms? Good night," and turned and walked down the long dim corridor toward his door.

While James worried and surmised, Mark tried to read, but he was restless. At about eleven o'clock, he went into Piazza San Doroteo. It was Saturday night. People were coming and going, even way out here, far from the center of town. He strolled slowly to Piazza della Signoria and stood quite close, in fact, to the statue of Perseus to which James had alluded. The crowds in the city were increasing daily. Students were beginning to come now from northern Europe and the United States, and tourists were pouring in in ever greater numbers, too. Miscellaneous floaters were gathering for the summer—one of the sights on the piazza that night was a flame-swallower, of undetermined fatherland, who danced half naked in the midst of a circle of spectators to the accompaniment of some little gourd-shaped drums, thumped by a partner. After he'd swallowed some flames, he'd skip around with a plate and beg money—this, in the very place where, five centuries before, they'd burned Savonarola for preaching too effectively against vanities.

Mark went to one of the cafés, ordered a beer, drank it slowly, then left and began to walk again.

Halfway down Via dei Calzaiuoli he encountered a very pretty girl. She had long blond hair, and was wearing a man's shirt much too big for her, and faded pants rolled up to the knees. She was barefoot, but she was carrying shoes. She hadn't anything on under the shirt, which was partly unbuttoned. Mark had a look and decided he was interested. He said hello, she said hello back. She put on her shoes, they walked a little, had coffee, and he asked her to come home with him. She was German, from Düsseldorf—her name was Ortrud—but she spoke some English.

She was wide-eyed when she saw Villa Arberoni. She was also high on something; her mind slipped in and out of focus and she spent time in Mark's bathroom, pretending to admire the monograms on the towels while she looked in the cabinets for interesting pills, and was cross when all she found were vitamins. But then her mood changed, and she came back and sat on the bed. She kicked off her shoes, and swung her bare feet, whose bottoms were dirty. If they got on the sheets, it would be something Mark would have to explain to Velia.

They began to make love.

When they were naked and had got to the point that he was eager to enter her, however, she pushed him away. *"Muss' es wie Schwestern machen,"* she said slurrily several times, by which, it turned out, she meant sixty-nine. Mark didn't like the method. When she insisted and it was obvious things weren't going to work out, he got her up and dressed and got dressed himself and walked her back into town. She said she was hungry and wanted a sandwich. He bought her one and left her with it. He didn't want to watch her eat.

He awakened the next morning, bored with life. He was wasting time. He had only so much money, and a lot of things to see in Europe. He'd been trying each day to reach Laurie Walker at the Granduca; it had now got to the point that the operator was insolent to him. He didn't know whether Laurie's plans had changed and she hadn't come, or whether she was already at the hotel and they wouldn't tell him, perhaps because of orders from her uncle—or something having to do with Miss Ladore and security. He'd try one last thing. He'd write a note. Perhaps they'd give Laurie mail, even if they wouldn't put through a phone call.

Dear Laurie,

I've been trying to get in touch with you by telephone, but haven't had any luck. I want very much to see you. I've stayed in Florence just on the chance. Maybe you're not here, but maybe you are, and they won't let me through to you.

If you are, how can we arrange it? Here's my idea. For the next couple of days I'll go each noon and wait near the statue of Perseus by Cellini in the Piazza della Signoria. I'll stay for fifteen minutes. Try to come and meet me.

I've got a terrific place to live in, a big villa at the edge of town near Porta Romana, owned by this amazing American lady. Lots of privacy. I'd really like to show it to you. It might change both our lives.

Love,
Tiberio

The next day Mark took it to the Granduca, handed it to the man on duty, and hurried off before he could be told there was no Laurie Walker staying at the hotel.

When Wesley Knuckles, Laurie, and Miss Ladore arrived, they left their passports, as one must, at the desk and went upstairs, Miss Ladore to rest, Laurie to soap Miss Ladore's toilet seat, then help her unpack. Wesley immediately called John Battle Davenport to tell him they were in town.

"I'm very eager to have you meet Miss Ladore," he said. "Frankly, she's getting . . . restive. I want to have a good talk with you first, then I want us all to talk together. Perhaps over dinner."

"How about Sabatini, on Via de' Panzani?"

"The obvious place, of course. Yet—well, I hesitate to say this, but she's ever so tired of restaurants. If it were in some way possible for you and Mrs. Davenport—"

150

Battsie took the hint. "Delighted," he said. "Tuesday night. And you and I can talk tomorrow."

When Wesley went downstairs to get himself a drink in the bar, the man at the desk handed back the three passports. When he'd been entering the names on the forms required by the police, he'd noticed that of Laurie Walker, and connected it with the note that had been left that morning, which had been put to one side, since nobody knew what to do with it. The reservations were indeed all in the name of Wesley Knuckles; they hadn't been lying to Mark. The clerk gave the note, too, to Wesley, who opened it, over a martini.

He was furious. So Laurie *was* carrying on behind his back. He thrust it in his pocket and, naturally, didn't say anything to her, but he instructed the clerk at the desk that no calls were to go to either Miss Ladore or Miss Walker. Any calls for either of them were to go first through him. The security police, he said, would explain the reasons for this if they wished to check with them. He mentioned the name of the officer he'd talked to in Rome, and gave his number.

The next day, at noon, he took up a position in the Piazza della Signoria, half hidden behind the Ammanati fountain, from which, with his binoculars, he could get a clear view of the base of the Cellini *Perseus*. People came and went, lots of tourists, lots of Italians. He didn't quite know what he was looking for—doubtless a handsome youth, but that wasn't much to go on. There are always a lot of them around any public square in Italy. None who fitted that description, however, came and waited at the proper place for the time span the letter had indicated. Only a feeble old man with a spotted dog on a lead, and an American boy in a blue polo shirt and khaki trousers, did just what the letter said. The old man was surely not Laurie's lover, and as for the American youth—his name might be Jimmy or Johnny, but it certainly wasn't Tiberio.

It was a waste of time—and humiliating, too. Wesley did not go back, and therefore missed Mark on Tuesday.

When Laurie Walker didn't show up that day either, Mark determined to leave Florence on Thursday, since he'd got a note from James Molyneux asking him to visit more Brunelleschi churches with him on Wednesday. They'd do San Lorenzo and the Pazzi Chapel. Mark didn't want to miss that; however, it would be his last act of tourism in this city.

But naturally, when Laurie came to dinner at Villa Arberoni on Tuesday night, he changed his mind.

PART

five

On Monday morning, James Molyneux returned yet again to the German Library. He checked on the Helsinki, Budapest, and Leiden drawings that Battsie had mentioned on Saturday night. The first two bore no relationship to his drawing. The Leiden piece, however, was another matter. It was of the torso of a woman, lightly sketched, then corrected and drawn in more firmly—indubitably the same woman who, in James's drawing, was standing to the far right, turned halfway around to reach out toward a group of other women who were on the steps of the building behind her, one of them lifting a child so it could see the central action. There was no doubt about it. The drawing in Leiden was a study for his own, and James took down information on it.

Another voussoir in his arch. Next he had Vasari to work on.

The library, thorough as always, had both the 1550 and 1568 editions in many examples. James got one of each date and took them to a table where he could compare their biographies of Raphael, sentence by sentence, paragraph by paragraph, page by page. He noted plenty of inconsistencies, mostly very minor, and none that seemed to lead him anywhere until, in the midst of Vasari's description of Raphael's work for the papal apartments at the Vatican, he came upon the discrepancy that Battsie had spoken of. The later edition passed from one painting in the Stanza of Heliodorus to the other as they presently exist, but in the earlier edition of 1550 that was not the case. Quite to the contrary. In it, Vasari recounted at some length an incident all mention of which was deleted from the later edition:

Fortune deprived Julius II of his life, removing that patron of talent and admirer of every good thing. On Leo X succeeding he wished the work on the chamber to continue. It had been planned while Pope Julius was still alive that one wall would be covered with a scene showing the sainted Pope Leo the Great meeting with Attila upon his coming toward Rome and driving him away with a simple benediction, with the aid of Saint Peter and Saint Paul, who with drawn swords were coming to defend the Church. But the Bishop of Arezzo suggested that the subject be changed, although Raphael had already begun it, and that instead another story from the life of Leo the Great should be used, that is, how it is recounted in the *Liber Pontificalis* that after the sack of Rome by Genseric, King of the Vandals, the people of Rome, though their lives had been spared through the pope's intervention, were nevertheless reduced to the utmost misery and held him responsible for what had happened. Being incited by certain evil men they drove him from the city, which he had to leave in the night like a common criminal, with only a few attendants. But as he passed through the countryside not far from the place where Saint Peter encountered Our Lord and asked Him whither He went, the fleeing pope was met by Saint Peter and Saint Paul, who told him to go back, that God would protect him, for he was His vicar on Earth and a virtuous man who had been unjustly driven out. He therefore returned to the city at dawn, accompanied by the two saints, who rode with him just as if they were soldiers, the former holding aloft his keys, the latter his sword, a sight most magnificent to see. And the people were terrified at this sign of divine grace and fell down and begged for forgiveness, which the pope granted. This change of subjects was suggested to please Pope Leo, because of the way in which his older brother Piero de'Medici and the rest of his family had been unjustly driven out by the Florentines in the days of the Friar of San Marco and were soon to return in triumph. The pope commanded Raphael to make a drawing that would show how he would paint that story, if he were to put it on the wall in place of *The Repulse of Attila*. Raphael, to whom any beautiful thing came easily, did it in the surprising length of only five days, very large and fine, on several sheets joined together, with many of the details worked out as the figures would look, and using the likeness of Pope Leo as the earlier pope of the same name, in pontificals, accompanied by the Cardinal de' Medici, and by their nephew Lorenzo, and by Giuliano, the brother of the Pope, and in it Raphael showed Rome with the buildings of the great square as they are in Florence, as had been done earlier by Domenico Ghirlandajo in the chapel for Francesco Sassetti in S. Trínita, as I have already recounted. When Pope Leo saw it, he laughed and said it was very fine, but he thought it was better to remember that Florence was not Rome and that he did not reign in the former city as he did in the latter one, the Medici being only its first citizens. The pope said he thought that it was better not to change what the old pope had wished, and he ordered Raphael to complete the other fresco. It is said that Raphael gave his model for the new fresco to his friend Orazio Sinicropi, a man of great learning and love of the arts, who had in his charge the papal library, but that after Raphael died the Bishop of Arezzo, who had been made the Cardinal of Santo Stefano and was always with the pope, with many threats and unpleasant remarks, forced Sinicropi to give him the drawing, saying it had been his idea and that the drawing should be his. Although I have seen many of the beautiful things that belonged to the cardinal, some of which are still in the palace of his family in Florence, I have never seen this famous work of Raphael, which, it is said, disappeared many years ago. And some say it is one of the things that were taken away by Fra Pietro da Cracovia, a learned monk who lived in the household of the Cardinal of Santo Stefano, when he returned home after the death of the cardinal not long after the election of Pope Paul.

Once again, James took his Polaroid prints out of his pocket. There could be no doubt about it. The drawing that had been in Ricky's book was the drawing Vasari had written about. Beautifully documented. Moreover, John Battle Davenport was already committed to its having once existed and would take up the cudgel to defend its authenticity.

James was now so excited it was hard for him to get back to work. He arose and walked around a little, overwhelmed by his incredible good luck. He pulled the Polaroid snapshots out of his pocket again and looked closely at the face of the figure in pontificals. Yes, it could be Pope Leo X, though it hadn't at once occurred to him—but then Leo was younger here than he was in the portrait in the Uffizi collection, and of course the drawing, done quickly, was not so precise.

When he'd calmed down, James returned to his desk to transcribe the 1550 passage. So hunched was he over his books and his paper that he didn't notice when spry, sly Ettore Biscotti tiptoed up behind him and remained there for several minutes, reading over his shoulder, before he moved stealthily away.

There remained, of course, the problem of how the drawing got into the hands of the Guidoni, but James had a hunch that would be solved when he knew who the Bishop of Arezzo, later Cardinal of Santo Stefano, was. His transcription of Vasari completed, he left the German Library and went to the National Library over on the Arno near Santa Croce and worked there for an hour. He was able to find listings of those who had held important ecclesiastical positions in Tuscany in the sixteenth century, including the man who was Bishop of Arezzo in 1513 and, from 1517 to 1534, Cardinal of Santo Stefano.

Anselmo dei Guidoni.

He would have been the first of the Guidoni cardinals Ricky had mentioned. But he'd also mentioned another, given the hat through the influence of Cosimo I, which would mean he was a prelate at just about the time Vasari was bringing out his second edition. No doubt a man of power and influence at the court in Florence as well as in Rome. The Admiral dei Guidoni, probably the cardinal's brother, would have had power, too. There was every reason that Vasari, who so depended on Medici commissions, would have cut out the story, which did not show the earlier Guidoni in a very flattering light. Vasari had, in other words, cut it out for political reasons, not because he'd discovered that the information on which his earlier account had been based was untrue.

Chalk up another plus for Battsie. He'd have some real fun with Daphne Nickerson when this drawing became known. The learned fur would fly.

In the meantime, back at the German Library, Ettore and Battsie had gone to hold a council of war in the little room, sealed off and separately ventilated, open to those who must smoke cigarettes.

Ettore told Battsie about James's investigations of the Raphael drawings in Helsinki, Budapest, and Leiden, and that he'd copied the entry on Leiden out of the catalog.

"The very drawings I mentioned on Saturday—following your genial suggestion, Ettore." Battsie tugged on his muttonchop whiskers with both hands, as if they could be raised and lowered. "So he's onto one of that group, is he? Very curious. You know, I've thought about it, and there isn't a single one of them left in private hands. So he must be onto an unknown one—as we always held to be a possibility."

"He also transcribed an entire passage from Vasari about one of the frescoes in the Stanze, in the early edition, not in the later one." Biscotti waited a moment, so Battsie's mouth would have time to fall ajar. *"The Return of Pope Leo to Rome,"* he then said, with due solemnity.

Battsie gasped. "I put him onto that, too. You don't suppose, do you, that— Are you aware of what Vasari says?"

"I am now. I read the passage. A full-scale *modello*. Is it possible?" Biscotti seized one of Battsie's arms.

"Of course it's possible. I've argued myself, not necessarily for its survival, but for its original existence. Only someone like Daphne Nickerson could doubt all that. What a tumble she'll take, if that drawing should surface. Even though you're only an architectural historian, I'm sure you understand, Ettore, how major a work of art it would be. It would be the greatest find of our century."

Biscotti drew back into himself, offended by Battsie's chance slur on his specialty. His normal expression of amused malice was replaced by a nobler one. "It must not leave Italy," he said.

"If it's here."

"Molyneux is here. Where else would it be?"

"I'm sure he has connections in lots of places."

"But why, if it's somewhere else and belongs to someone else, would Molyneux be looking it up here in this library? Surely if a dealer or some other owner, who was beyond the reach of our national patrimony laws—in Germany or Switzerland, for instance—wanted such a drawing documented, he would apply"—Ettore made a too elegant and deferential gesture—"to Professor Davenport."

"True."

"I think it's evidence enough. One can waste too much time worrying about innocence if there's a reasonable suspicion of guilt. I think we should inform Dottoressa Paonese. Or rather, you should. It would be better if it came from you; she might think I was settling a grudge. Let's at least get her pecking at James Molyneux. No. More than that." Biscotti's eyes became sardonic slits. "Let her flog the truth out of him with the whip of her principles, and rub his wounds with the salt of her morality." They laughed together at the image. Ettore added, "You know, there might be a decoration for you in all this. I wouldn't be surprised. La Paonese has relatives in the highest circles. Speak to her, John."

"Oh, very well. If you insist," Battsie said. "I suppose it can't do any harm. If the drawing is out of the country, James is in the clear. If it isn't, it really should stay, I suppose. Is Andromeda here today?" He went to the door and looked out into the reading room.

She wasn't. He telephoned her office. Unfortunately she was on a trip to Rome, Naples, and Brindisi, and wouldn't be back until the following week.

Wesley Knuckles sent Laurie and Miss Emilene off to lunch by themselves on Monday, while he took Professor Davenport to Sabatini. They talked generalities during the meal; afterwards, when he brought the professor back to his rather magnificent hotel room, their discussion turned more serious.

He uncorked a bottle of cognac, and they settled into facing armchairs, Davenport with a pad of paper and a pencil in his hands. "Now then," Wesley said, "let's get down to brass tacks. Here's what I have in mind." For half an hour he outlined his final thoughts about his institute, stopping only when Battsie asked a question.

"How does that sound to you, John?"

Davenport took a little time before he replied. He reviewed his notes, and in fact used them when he did speak. "Research library. Visiting professors. Senior and junior fellows. Concerts of period music, using old instruments—delightful idea! I could hear them squeak and scrape as you were speaking, Wesley. Madrigals too, of course. Lectures. Seminars. Symposia and colloquia. Auditoria."

"Ium, in that case, I'd think."

"Very well, but—refectory and cloister. Gardens. Residential mansions and apartments. The occasional acquisition of the rare

160

and choice work of art or artifact, to contribute to the atmosphere of the place—good idea to have one room like the Gallery at the Huntington or the Music Room at Dumbarton Oaks, to give people a feeling of what it's all about. And for receptions. Oh, I quite agree with that. Let's see . . ." Battsie went back to his notes. "A scholarly quarterly and a full program of occasional papers and monographs. I can't think of anything you've left out. And, as a ringing justification, a call for interdisciplinarianism. As you put it, 'Not only more scholarship and better scholarship, but perhaps even different scholarship.' Sound. Both sound and stirring, Wesley."

"Do you think it will work?"

"Quite a different question." Davenport thought about it. "I suppose it comes down to staffing. How, if you manage to get funding for all this, will you go about staffing the professional side of it? I mean, your basic appointment. Your scholarly chief. For on that rock will you build your church of learning, Wesley. Make no mistake about it."

"By *how* will we staff, I assume you mean *who?*"

"One way of approaching it, certainly."

"Any suggestions?"

"I can think of lots of people who'd be qualified for your visiting appointments. But the permanent scholarly chief will be a more ticklish matter." Davenport held out his glass, and Wesley poured an encouraging dollop of brandy in it. "Take Daphne Nickerson, for instance. At Bryn Mawr. She'd qualify as a visiting scholar, but you'd no more want her for your permanent chief than you would an ostrich. You need someone with the authority of years. Who has both learning and wisdom. An idea of how the world works, as well as the stature needed to rise above it. Someone like yourself—except that it's not quite your field, is it?"

Wesley added to his own brandy. "No. And"—he swallowed, then had to clear his throat; he had a little tickle—"well, I have other hopes for myself. There'll have to be a general director to coordinate all this."

"Quite." Professor Davenport eyed his glass. "But as for your scholarly chief—Who? Who? Who?" he said.

Wesley sipped and again gave a little cough. "Am I not right now looking at the very wise old owl I need?"

Battsie raised his eyebrows, and touched his chest with the fingers of his free hand in surprise.

"We'd work well together, John, would we not? It would crown your long and distinguished career."

"I've so looked forward to the serenities of retirement."

"Yes, of course you have, and quite right, but think of Cincinnatus. Isn't it your duty to do this?" Wesley leaned forward, speaking intently. "There'll be impressive fringe benefits, of course. You can't imagine how much money these people have. We'll make the National Gallery look like the county poor farm. Moreover, though it's not the main point, patronage is always fun, too. Reward old friends and make new ones. Cast enemies into outer darkness—all in a good cause."

"And for you?" said Battsie.

"Oh, I'm just one of those guys who like to set clocks to ticking," Wesley said.

"And I'd be seeing that it kept good time," Battsie said. "It *is* rather a duty; you're quite right."

The mutual-assistance pact being more or less signed, they had a little more brandy and sat for a moment. Wesley was thinking that Battsie, with all his pedant's vanity, would be easy enough to manipulate, and would give great legitimacy to the institute. Battsie, whose stock-in-trade was images, was envisaging two fine houses, facing each other across a formal garden, in design a bit like Villa Rotunda, all Palladian rhetoric and swagger: one temple portico where he and Pauline would stand upon occasion to receive the respectful salutations of visiting scholars, the other where Wesley Knuckles would receive Ministers of Culture and Heads of State.

"I'd have to consult my wife, of course," he said.

"I've never had the pleasure, only spoken to her on the telephone, but I can't imagine any wife not wanting to join her husband in an adventure like this."

"Mmm. Pauline'll sign up, or my initials aren't J.B.D. Where do you expect to locate, by the way? Cambridge? Princeton? You might have trouble finding land there. Washington? I hate the thought of the climate. Of course, there's California. Didn't used to be, but there is now."

Wesley had to clear his throat. "And Texas," he said.

"*Texas!* That throws a different light on things," Battsie said, frowning. "I'm not so sure I'd be interested, not if it were to be in Texas."

Wesley's answer to that was to return to inducements. "Naturally, nothing's been figured out about salaries, but I should think that the top salary in the academic end of things would be about eighty thousand. Plus expense account. Free house and so on. And I shouldn't be surprised but that we might take an apartment in New York for the occasional use of our staff. All that . . . plus eighty or ninety thousand."

Battsie stared, startled by the figure. "It can't be said you're not slathering the butter on the bread," he said.

"Thickly, I'd think."

"Still—*Texas?*"

"There's nothing firm in all this," Wesley said, to bring the professor back to a recognition of who was deciding what. "I haven't absolutely made up my mind about any of it, and Miss Ladore hasn't committed herself. I'd planned, you know, to take her all over Europe to visit scholarly institutes and so on, but I think she's going to balk. I'll be lucky if I get her as far as Venice and the Cini Foundation—which'll be so useful to nudge her in the right direction, as far as architecture is concerned. So things have got to go a little faster than I planned. I want you to help me. I take it I can, in general—I mean Texas aside—count on your support? You concur with the scheme I've outlined to you, do you not?"

Davenport nodded, not so vigorously as to seem greedy, but not so weakly as to seem uninterested. "Absolutely," he said.

"Good," said Wesley. "Then let's sit down with paper and pencil—and the rest of this bottle of brandy, not bad, is it?—and spell out a plan in detail. A proposal, something we can show not only to her, as soon as possible, but also to the rest of the trustees of the Billy Abilene Ladore Foundation—although basically they'll do what she says. She's got a lot of power under the will, and so much money of her own I'm told she weighs it. How does that sound?"

Battsie reached in his inside coat pocket. "Here. I just happen to have a fistful more of sharp pencils I meant to leave at the

163

German Library this morning. My contribution to the cause."

Wesley took one of them and with it wrote at the top of a sheet of paper, in block letters, THE LADORE CENTER FOR RENAISSANCE STUDIES.

"Let's go," he said.

Mere hours later Battsie was in a dark suit, pocket handkerchief distinguishedly aflop, muttonchop whiskers fluffed, and his best glasses on. Pauline was in a long dress, though it was only Tuesday. Iris had long since been disinvited for cocktails. Antonio rang from downstairs. The guests had arrived. John went down to bring them up himself in the elevator, which would just accommodate four people. Pauline stood in the open doorway to await them, not yet quite sure how to act. In her long career as Mrs. John Battle Davenport, she'd bumped up against many different kinds of people, but Miss Emilene was the first billionaire—as Pauline somewhat hyperbolically thought of her. It would be a comfort to have Signora Benassi's help at dinner.

Signora Benassi, after exchanging one sentence with Miss Emilene, had gone against custom and placed her, not Wesley, on her own right, and they'd talked together through the meal. She was too good to waste, Signora Benassi knew it instantly. One didn't meet her like every day—or any day, necessarily. James Molyneux, who was on Miss Ladore's other side, only occasionally got a chance to speak to her, but the signora noticed that he seemed to feel the same way. In short, Miss Emilene was something of a success, perhaps because she was so enjoying herself, eating a home-cooked meal at last, even if it wasn't exactly a Texas menu. After dinner, Signora Benassi proposed a tour of Villa Arberoni.

They began with the great frescoed foyer, then moved on to the state rooms along the front of the building; Miss Emilene and the signora, continuing the chumminess begun at the table, formed one group, more or less accompanied by Laurie and Ricky, Wesley and the Davenports another. When they reached the great dining room, Miss Emilene said, "My daddy, Billy Abilene Ladore, always used to say that if there's something you want to know, the best thing is to ask about it." She waited while Costanza turned on lights and, as she passed them, checked the doors of the two huge sideboards in which the silver was locked up. "You've got this great big place with all these big rooms in it, painted up and so forth. You're my age, so you have to worry about what will happen to it. Do you have any children?"

"I had one son, who died long ago," replied Signora Benassi. "A daredevil, I suppose you'd say. He was killed climbing in the Dolomites when he was only fourteen." They moved into the *salone* and stopped to look for a moment out of the window. "I've lived here all my life, both as a girl and after I was married. It didn't seem right to leave it, even during the Second World War. My mother went home—she wasn't in good health—but I stayed on, with my husband, of course, though I'm an American citizen."

Miss Emilene thought about that. "I guess I wouldn't leave the big ranch, either. I mean if the Mexicans moved in on us or something like that. I've missed the bluebonnets by coming to Europe, and now I'm missing my roses." She leaned on the handle of the window as if she were, in her imagination, about to open another door at another place. "It's not easy to grow roses where I live, but I do it. They're famous for miles around. Once when I'd put a bowl jammed full of them in the living room, too many, really, my daddy said I made the place look like a funeral parlor, and he said, 'Well, here's the corpse,' and he reached up with the long-handled poker and knocked the head of a pronghorn antelope off the wall so it fell in the bowl and broke it." She looked at Signora Benassi as if she'd just surprised herself by a thought. "He had a mean streak," she said. "What was the war like for you?"

"When I think about it now, I think of such odd details. Of how we buried all the silver down at the bottom of the garden, under the dog kennels, for instance. I had three whippets then, and only Costanza here, and we left their droppings on the ground. By policy, I mean. The German officers billeted upstairs didn't go near, as a result. They couldn't imagine anybody not cleaning up over the place where they'd buried table silver—such an unsanitary idea! For a while, at the end, we were able to conceal two men in those kennels, whose father was a jeweler and did a lot of work for my mother. Two brothers, who are jewelers themselves now. The Nazis were after them, and we saved them from deportation."

She then took Miss Ladore to the portrait of Contessa Rinuccini, which Costanza had just lighted. "This is my mother."

Miss Emilene looked at the painting, then at Signora Benassi. "I suppose it flatters her."

"Not all that much. Mama was a perfect subject."

"You still have those rubies and pearls?"

Signora Benassi nodded. "They spent the war in the bank. Odd, but the Germans didn't systematically rob our bank vaults, only, casually, people's houses. I don't wear them often. One doesn't often get dressed up enough. And then, there're so many of them—for me."

"My daddy said the jewelry a woman wore told you all about her, and it usually wasn't what she wanted you to know."

"Sometime I'll tell you more about Mama, and you can see if you think it's true of her."

Miss Emilene said, "I'm getting tired. I've been sick, you know. I'm going to have to go back to the hotel. But first tell me why you have all these people living and eating here."

Signora Benassi explained her arrangements. "It's convenient to have the money," she said, "but the real reason is to keep myself amused. You have no idea how boring it is to be seventy-five in Florence."

"Try Abilene, Texas," said Miss Ladore. "That's why I live mostly at the big ranch." Wesley and the Davenports came to admire the portrait, then went to the windows to look out at the terrace and the gardens, but Miss Emilene lingered for a moment. "Tell me one last thing. If I should want to talk to you on the telephone, when's a good time to get you?"

"Nine in the morning, when I'm having breakfast. I always talk on the telephone when I'm having breakfast," said Signora Benassi. "May I look forward to your call?"

They, too, moved to a window, where they were joined by John Battle Davenport.

Miss Emilene said, as she looked out, "There's that young

man—Mark was his name, wasn't it?—and that other man who stays here, whose mamma came from Tulsa. Sitting on a bench by your fountain. I wonder what they're talking about."

Signora Benassi said, "Why, about us, I should think."

Wesley Knuckles and Pauline Davenport stood at another window. "Where do you live when you're in the States?" he asked.

"We still keep a house in Poughkeepsie."

"And aren't you tired of Poughkeepsie, after all these years?"

"I was tired of it by the time I was a sophomore at Vassar."

"What would you think of a move?" Wesley said.

Pauline, who'd of course been told all about the Renaissance project, turned improbably innocent eyes to him. "Move to where?"

Wesley's smile welcomed her into the conspiracy. He then changed the subject. "Who is that young fellow who's talking to James Molyneux out there by the fountain?"

"Mark Stapleton's his name. Signora Benassi found him in the Protestant Cemetery in Rome."

"I think I saw him yesterday, hanging around in the square, there by the loggia and Palazzo Vecchio."

Pauline looked disapproving. "I shouldn't say it, but—"

"Go ahead," said Wesley. "I file all indiscretions in the wastebasket."

"He may have been hoping to be picked up by someone—except that he seems to be developing such a strong connection right here."

Wesley took that in. "You mean . . . ?"

"Look at them," Pauline said. "You can't miss what I mean."

Wesley cleared his throat; the damn tickle wouldn't go away. "So Molyneux's gay."

"As big a pansy as any you'll find in the W. Attlee Burpee seed catalog, Dr. Knuckles."

That was interesting, in view of the fact that Wesley was likely to do business with James. Had an appointment with him, in fact. And of course, it also put Wesley's mind at rest. Mark and Laurie had talked together after dinner for a bit, rather intensely it had seemed, until Wesley had broken it up. But if Mark was Molyneux's boyfriend, he was one young man Wesley didn't need to worry about.

Ricky and Laurie looked out at the terrace. "Have you enjoyed your travels?" Ricky asked. Laurie nodded. "And do you like Italians?"

"I don't really know any. Except, now, you."

"I have a nephew—a great-nephew, actually. A delightful boy—I think of him as a boy, though he's very much a man. Your age, I should think. Twenty-four. Perhaps you'll meet him, if you stay long in Florence. I think you'd find him charming, and I know he'd find you delightful."

"I'd like to meet him," Laurie said politely, her mind on whether—or how—she was going to arrange things later that evening.

"I'll try to fix it up. A pity he hasn't a sister for Mr. Stapleton. Maybe Miss Siswick will do, however. Perhaps next Saturday? If you're free. You can all come back here again. We could set up a table apart from us old people for the four of you at dinner."

Laurie looked amused, in a cool way.

"I'll have Signora Benassi speak to Dr. Knuckles and your aunt."

Laurie corrected him. "I'm not related to Miss Ladore. I'm Dr. Knuckles's niece."

"Knuckles's niece?" Ricky tried to keep the disappointment out of his voice. "Oh. I got it confused. Stupid of me."

"I've been brought along as Miss Ladore's companion."

"I see. I have to say my nephew's so busy tending his vineyards that it's very hard to get him away. I will try, though." But of course, Ricky didn't. If Laurie had to travel as someone's companion, she wasn't going to be able to bring that parcel of fine land to Tiberio as a dowry, and Ricky was back where he'd started.

Wesley, just before they left the *salone*, beckoned John Davenport over to the window where he now stood alone. He pulled some papers out of his pocket. "Here," he said. "Check these over; it's what we agreed on, with a couple of little changes. If you could type them up with some carbons, it would be a big help. I don't expect there'd be a typing service here that could handle English."

"Pauline'll do it. Does all my typing. I trust that'd be all right."

"For her to know about it? Oh, quite. I think she's just what we'd need as the wife of our scholarly director, by the way. Handsome dress, eh? She seems none too attached to Poughkeepsie. Quite willing to move, I'd say. By the way, she tells me Molyneux's gay."

"I suppose so," Battsie said, "though he's never made a pass at me."

"That'll be awe," Wesley said. "I'm glad to know about it. It gives you a certain edge over a man if you know more about him than he knows about you. I've set up an interview with him for tomorrow." Wesley had to stop again to clear his throat. "He was recommended as just the person to act as our agent in building the new library—if Miss Ladore approves our proposal. I'm rather thinking we ought to make him one of our team. What would you think of that?"

Davenport said, "Well, he's very intelligent, of course. Knows languages marvelously well. Good memory for books. But I wouldn't move too fast on it."

Wesley reminded Battsie of the facts of life. "Miss Ladore seemed to like Molyneux—his mother was from Oklahoma, I heard him tell her. That's all she needed."

Battsie said, "So—it might come to pass that James and I would be colleagues?"

"He'd be yards underneath you on the table of organization."

"That changes things a bit."

"Changes what?"

"Nothing important, just a little something that's come up at the German Library," said Battsie.

Iris Siswick came back into the drawing room, sat down at the piano, and ran through a few finger exercises. Then she tried the fine Sonata No. 50 in C Major—Hamilin Rees, no doctrinaire, was letting her learn the sonatas out of order—but when she reached the rondo, she stopped. Her heart just wasn't in Haydn. She got up and went to the window. There, as before, down near the fountain on a bench, sat James Molyneux and Mark.

Iris thought of dinner. Mark had sat next to her. The pretty girl the Davenports had invited had sat opposite them, but Mark had paid almost no attention to her. He'd talked to Iris almost all the time, only just once in a while looking at the other girl and saying something to her, so she'd sat alone and quiet and listening while Mark told Iris all about his visit to a church with James Molyneux, and about the University of Arizona, and about what it was like to do gymnastics, and also about growing up in San Diego, and what it was like in Los Angeles, where he'd worked for some friend of James's, and then how he'd inherited a little money from his mother's elderly aunt and was using it for this trip. He'd wanted to talk about himself—that's what it came down to—and Iris was a good audience. But wasn't it more than that? It was as if he'd been offering her his credentials.

And yet . . . there'd been that one time, after dinner, when he and Laurie had gone to a corner of the room together almost as if they were keeping an appointment long postponed. They'd talked as if it didn't matter in the slightest what anybody else was doing. Not for long, though, because her uncle had gone and interrupted them. A funny name, Knuckles. If he'd been a concert pianist, he'd have had to change it.

"Quite the gala occasion, wasn't it, Mark?" James said. When they'd broken up after dinner, the Davenports and their guests going off for the obligatory tour, he'd first taken Mark to Hilda's studio, where Mark had looked at her drawings and many sculptural projects (no comment had been made on the fact they were so largely male nudes) while James searched out her good camera and a roll of black and white film. Now he and Mark were walking toward the circle and the fountain and the same old bench. "Pauline Davenport in her ankle-length peach-fuzz skirt, and it's only Tuesday. Imagine wearing something that color when you have Pauline's hair. It's simply stupefying—the poor thing." They took their place, looking up toward the villa. "I wonder what that spectral Texas woman is making of our signora's state rooms. She's a wonder, in her way, is Miss Emilene Ladore. It must be so easy, I would think, for someone as rich as she and with such an odd

170

background—if you can believe the stories—to be stupid and unpleasant. Data is so screened before it reaches them—like laboratory animals deprived of a full range of sights, sounds, and smells. But she isn't stupid. Only simple. And nice, actually." Mark wasn't very talkative. "You seem preoccupied," James observed. It was beginning to matter a great deal to James that he shouldn't bore Mark. He tried something new.

"I think we might have a lesson on people," he said. "Good time, when there've been strangers to dinner. Are you willing?"

Mark nodded. That was all.

"Well, we'll start with Dr. Wesley Knuckles. Did you notice anything unusual about him? I mean about his manner?"

"I couldn't really see him from where I was sitting."

"You didn't need to see him more than once to know that he is vain of his face and ashamed of his hands. Didn't you see how he curled his fingers inward?" Mark hadn't. "Mark, you don't use your eyes. Damn it, that's what they're for, man," James said, but not nearly so harshly as he'd have said it a week earlier. "Notice things." Troubled by Mark's continuing indifference, James risked a lot. "Have you not noticed how I work at concealing my . . . awkward leg?"

Mark, jerked to full attention, said, "Yes. I saw that the first day."

"What a relief!" James said, in only partial irony. "Without that, I'd have almost given you up—not for the sympathy part, I hope you understand, but for the rest. But back to Knuckles. He sat across from that mirror that's in the heavy frame, and if he looked at himself once, he looked at himself a dozen times, and each time he did, he turned a profile. He was liking what he was seeing. But if he had his hands on the table and, as you spoke to him, you looked at them, he'd curl his fingers into his palms and in a few seconds he'd hide them in his lap. Even stop eating in order to hide them."

"Why did he do that?" Mark asked, becoming interested in this part of the conversation, too.

"Because they're the hands of a lout. His head is, in its way, rather patrician. Self-indulgent, perhaps, the face, and indulged, but still fairly handsome. Hair too carefully arranged, but rather attractive. Skin tone good, etcetera. But the hands don't go with the rest of it. He thinks they give him away. By which I mean he's got some kind of secret. Possibly he's ashamed of himself, of aspects of himself, and thinks they're all described in those hands for anyone to see."

Mark was even more interested. After all, Wesley was Laurie's difficult uncle. He asked, "If you found out what he was ashamed of, could you make Knuckles jump, do you think?"

"Not quite that—he'll have ways of striking back. All the same, knowing he's on a double level of some kind—it gives one a certain superiority. One knows more than he does; even though he's got all the power, one has one's advantage, too. He asked me to come and see him tomorrow morning, by the way, on the recommendation of Peter Tremper. I put him off till afternoon, because of our Brunelleschi tour. One doesn't too obviously jump oneself when the Wesley Knuckles of this world snap their fingers," James said. "Now tell me what you thought of the girl."

"What'd you think of her?"

"That's she's unhappy. Not the way Iris Siswick is unhappy— not, that is, profoundly—but all the same, she should be careful; her kind of unhappiness is habit-forming, like all luxuries. And she has a secret, too."

"How do you know that? What kind of secret?"

"I know it from the way she looks away when you engage her eyes too directly. As she's obviously not merely shy, and certainly has no reason to be diffident, given that she's such a great beauty—and isn't she that?—she's got something she'd prefer you not get at. Maybe it embarrasses her to be the old woman's companion. But I think it more likely she's embarrassed by her uncle. Perhaps she's ashamed of him. Not so much of what he says— that's perfectly plausible if somewhat jejune, he's a type, after all—but ashamed of his essence. It'd be something soft and rotten, yet corrosive."

Mark was very, very interested now. "How do you know all that, James? Excuse me. Mr. Molyneux."

"Do James me if you'd like to; I'd like you to. I know it from how she looks at him when he's trying to be charming. When he was trying to charm Signora Benassi—he didn't succeed, by the way. Anyway, when he was really putting on the flattery, telling her how magnificent her villa was, and how she must be one of the most fortunate of all women, the girl was watching him. Just . . . watching him. And there was a look on her face that told one she has long since passed her final judgment on him: guilty!"

"Do you think she'd turn against him?"

"At least that," said James. "Did she hint at such a thing? For that'd be fun to know, too, given how close she's bound to be to Miss Ladore." Mark shook his head. "Look. They're all standing in the windows of the *salone* now. And there's Iris, too, on the floor above, where she practices. All looking out and talking."

"I wonder what they're talking about," Mark said.

"Why, about us, I rather think," said James.

At eleven-thirty, Mark went to the Piazza della Signoria to wait yet again, seated beside the base of the Cellini *Perseus*. At about a quarter of twelve, in accordance with the arrangement they'd hurriedly made after dinner, Laurie arrived, out of breath, her face flushed.

She looked wonderful, but Mark didn't tell her so. "Nice going," he said calmly, as if he'd never had a doubt. He waited a moment before he stood up—not what she'd be expecting. "Nice going for the second time. Did you have any trouble getting away? It's really weird you have to worry—you'd think this was Arabia. Anybody suspect anything?"

Laurie shook her head. "Uncle Wesley went right to his own room, complaining about his throat, and I know Miss Ladore was asleep when I left, because I could hear her snoring. I just hope she doesn't wake up and want me. She doesn't like hotels, so she doesn't sleep well."

"Let's walk around the piazza." Mark took Laurie's hand, and they drifted to the left, past the rest of the sculpture that stands under the Loggia dei Lanzi, to the entrance to the Palazzo Vecchio, which loomed high and severe in the dark. "There's not much going on—Tuesday night. You ought to see this place on Saturday, though. It's like Fort Lauderdale, only without sand. When did you get to Florence?"

"Sunday afternoon. We were held up because Miss Ladore got a cold in Siena; she spent yesterday in bed here, too. Uncle Wesley's got it now."

"That means he'll be out of the way and we can see a lot of each other."

"No it doesn't," Laurie said. "It'll make Miss Ladore entirely my responsibility."

Mark let that pass. They stopped to look at the replica of the *David* that stands on the platform in front of Palazzo Vecchio. "Overrated and underhung," he commented. "I couldn't believe it when you walked in the room tonight. I'd given you up. I was going to leave Florence day after tomorrow. Didn't you get my note?" When Laurie said she hadn't, he explained about it to her.

"That means Uncle Wesley must have got it. The bastard. Think what he'd have said when he heard your name at dinner tonight if you hadn't used 'Tiberio.'"

They smiled over the way they'd made a fool of Wesley. Mark said, "Did you think when you were traveling about how you might see me here in Florence?" Laurie nodded. "Like—how much?"

"I didn't have anyone else to think about."

"That's why I've thought about you, when I did," he said. "Last resort."

They both smiled again, pleased to be finding a way to get along. He put an arm over her shoulder.

"Do you want to come back to my place at the villa?" he asked. "It's down, kind of in the basement. Very private. We could . . . talk."

Laurie shook her head.

"That figures." They walked in step, off to the left again, to look at Ammanati's flabby Neptune who, pigeon-splashed, rode his crazy chariot above a basin of littered water—the very fountain behind which Wesley had hidden himself. "Overrated and underhung," Mark said again.

"Where'd you get the name Tiberio?"

"It's real. He's a relative of the old guy you met at dinner tonight, the Marchese dei Guidoni, who's the lover of Signora Benassi—what do you think of that? James—James Molyneux, the dark guy with the limp—told me they've been lovers since before we were born. The marchese has this great-nephew named Tiberio people are always mentioning."

"He's the one his uncle was telling me about after dinner, I guess. I think he wanted to set us up. He lost interest, though, when I told him I was a working girl."

They wandered over to look at the equestrian statue by Giambologna of Grand Duke Cosimo. "Overhung and underrated," Mark said. "I mean the horse. Why does your uncle curl his fingers up and hide his hands? Is there something he's ashamed of? Did he strangle his wife or something?"

Laurie got loose and turned to stare at Mark. "She left him before he got around to it. So you noticed about the hands." Laurie was impressed; it wasn't the kind of observation the boys who bored her were likely to make. "Mom—she's only his half-sister, by the way—says he got in the habit when he was little and used to bite his fingernails, and then he began to do it every time he'd done something he shouldn't have, she says. I imagine that was pretty often, and still is, though Mom doesn't say that. She's impressed by him. I've noticed he does it more whenever he's unsure of himself. Like right now he's very nervous about Miss Ladore. He should be." Laurie had no loyalty left to Wesley, and didn't in the least mind being indiscreet. "He's trying to get a lot of money out of her, but she's very likely to turn on him. If she does, I'll be right at her side." Laurie looked at her watch. "I can't be gone long."

"I liked her," Mark said. "She's simple, but not stupid—and she's nice." He put the arm over Laurie's shoulders again. "About tomorrow—when and where can we meet?"

"Maybe we can't. I'll have to see."

Mark didn't force it. He found a piece of paper in his billfold and wrote a telephone number on it. "I'll be out from nine to noon, but I'll stay in my room from then till one o'clock, and wait for you to call. Do you run?"

"Some. At home."

"Maybe you could get away by saying you were going jogging. There's a good place down the river from the Granduca where I could meet you. There's this old guy who'll rent his boat, too. I'll take you rowing."

Laurie liked the idea of the boat. "I can try, though Uncle

Wesley's got this idea he owns me."

"He doesn't," Mark said. "I've got a receipt for a down payment—my entrance fee to the Vatican Museums."

"He acts like someone who's jealous." Laurie told Mark all of it. "You won't believe this, but Miss Ladore thinks he has something on his mind."

Mark was shocked. "You've got to be kidding. Your own uncle?"

"Half-uncle. That's what she says."

"No wonder you look at him as if you've passed a kind of final judgment on him: guilty!" Mark said, surprising Laurie again. "Let me know if he ever makes a move on you. I'll flatten him, and then we can tour Europe together. That's what my plan is, for you and me to travel together."

Laurie said, "Even if I were free, what makes you think I'd want to travel with you?"

"I take it for granted. When you call tomorrow, you'll get the porter, Antonio. Just say to him, 'Signor Marco, per favore,' and he'll come and get me, or his wife will, or one of their kids—I don't have my own phone. You will call, won't you?"

"I'll try," Laurie said.

Mark walked her down the Arno to within a hundred feet of her hotel lobby, where they kissed. Pretty good!—she was more in it than he'd expected. After a bit, he drew his face a little back and, looking at her, his voice hungry, said, "Saturday night I was feeling really—you know—too long by myself, and all because you hadn't come to Florence, because I'll tell you the truth, I've thought about you a lot and it wasn't a last resort, either. More like first choice. So anyway, I went out and found this German girl and took her back to the villa. Guess what? Nothing happened. She was a little kinky, but that wasn't the real reason I couldn't carry through. She just wasn't what I wanted most."

Telling the story was dangerous, and Mark knew it. Laurie might have swung either way. But it was all right. She shrugged as if to say "So what?" but she didn't stop the kissing, mixed with a little whispering, not right then. When she did, it was to say that the night porter at the hotel was watching them from the door and enjoying it too much, and she'd better go inside.

176

Mark and James finished the second round of Brunelleschi the next morning in just enough time to get Mark back to the villa by noon. Almost. Unfortunately, James wanted to stop in the Cathedral on the way home and show him some things about the great Brunelleschi dome. Mark tried to put it off until another day, but couldn't; once James was in pedagogical mode, he was hard to deflect. As a result, they were late. After they'd left the Cathedral, Mark walked faster than he should have with James, who had trouble keeping up, but of course wouldn't admit it. When they came to the Arno, the traffic was solid in front of them at Ponte Vecchio, the light against them. Mark turned an abrupt right, never stopping. They could cross at Ponte Santa Trínita. It was faster anyway—you weren't held up by all the tourists buying coffee spoons, as you were on Ponte Vecchio.

They went downriver on the built-up side of Lungarno Acciaioli, at something close to a trot. Suddenly there was a break in the traffic, which otherwise surged up the river as fast as the drivers could push their cars between lights. Mark, accustomed by his running to quick maneuvers in the Florentine traffic, said, "Let's cross to the river side right now." He started to do so at high speed. James attempted to keep up, and almost made it across, but a little short of the curb he stumbled, lost his cane, and fell hard. He sat up, half stunned, and turned his head to look at the traffic that was thundering toward him only yards away, brakes screeching. He put his hands over his eyes. Mark sensed that James was no longer at his side, and turned back. Realizing it would take too long to get him to his feet, he scooped James up in his arms. He leapt to the sidewalk. Horns honked. Curses were howled. But they were safe.

He put James down. "I'm so sorry," he said. "I'm *so sorry.*" Another brief break in the traffic allowed him to retrieve James's cane. "I'm *really* sorry," he said, as he handed it back. He tried to brush dust from James's coat, but stopped when James recoiled from his hand.

James leaned against the wall of the embankment. "Sorry for saving my life?" he said at last.

"Of course not. Sorry I was rushing us so."

"You were doing that, all right. Now, please, let's just be quiet a minute or two." James remained where he was for that long, then turned toward Mark, who, awkward and contrite, stood at his side awaiting the inevitable sharp reproaches. "It was so quick, what you did," James said, his voice tender. "You didn't even have to think about it. You knew what had happened and what to do and you saved me. It was really . . . rather splendid, Mark. All those gymnastics paid off for me today. Bought me my life, I'd say. I'll never forget it. I mean either the grace or the speed. Or the debt, either."

"Please, Mr. Molyneux—"

James smacked his cane against the embankment wall. "For Christ's sake, call me James," he said. "I thought we'd established *that*, at least."

James was badly shaken up and had to go slowly; he had a sore knee, too, where he'd fallen—on the short leg. It was twelve-thirty when they got back to the villa. James went upstairs immediately; Mark knocked on the door of Antonio.

He made a sign toward the telephone and toward himself. *"Telefono per me?"* he asked.

"Sì, sì, Signor Marco," Antonio said. He was usually very correct, being a former peasant and a family man, but he did smile just a little knowingly when he said, *"La signorina Americana ha telefonato. Signorina Laura."*

"Shit!" Mark said. "Goddamn it." He'd missed her. He looked in his pocket dictionary for "message." *"Messaggio per me?"* he asked.

Antonio shook his head, but then gestured furiously. *"Qui!"* He jabbed the forefingers of both hands toward the floor. *"Qui. Qui."* Then he flung his arms wide. *"La villa."* He pointed to the clock. *"Adesso!"* he cried, just as the bell rang. *"Ecco."* He beckoned Mark to come with him. When he opened the door, a uniformed driver was standing outside, and behind him was the big Mercedes, with Laurie and Miss Emilene and all their luggage in it.

James didn't go to lunch that day. He was too unnerved by his fall and in some curious way too exhilarated by it to want anything to eat. Instead he rested until midafternoon, then got up and got out his drawing.

Each fresh exposure reaffirmed that it was superb. The pope on his mule, his retinue, all coming in from the left, the magnificent figures of the two saints on horseback ahead of them, that of Peter one of Raphael's noblest inventions, then the foremost figures of the Roman multitude, some with spears and axes, rushing forward from the right, yet drawing back as they realized the awesome presence of the saints, the women on the steps behind them—all so marvelously orchestrated in choruses and counterpoint, like a great Handelian finale. That same solemnity and energy. Raphael the decorator, at his best. What a fresco it would have made! A far better one, James thought, than *The Repulse of Attila*.

Once again he clipped his drawing to Hilda's piece of board, loaded her 35-millimeter camera, and took a whole role of pictures of the drawing. He'd settled on black and white film, both because it was more accurate and because there was nothing much to be gained at this point by color, and getting the latter developed and printed took more time. When he was ready to go to the Granduca for his talk with Wesley Knuckles at five, he was able to leave the roll at a shop where they could have it ready for him in about an hour. He didn't ask for prints. That was still too dangerous. But no shop technician was going to bother to scrutinize the frames of one more roll of 35-millimeter film.

"I've got a perfectly horrible cold," Wesley said weakly over the house telephone; James was calling up from the lobby of the Granduca. "But would you mind coming to my suite anyway?" He sneezed four times. "It's nearly as big as the lobby, so you can keep a healthy distance from me."

The suite was new. After Miss Emilene and Laurie had left, Wesley had had himself moved into it. He'd had no wish to take his cold to that villa, even if Signora Benassi had had room for

179

him; if he was going to ail, he'd ail in style. Handkerchief in hand, and smelling of nosedrops, he opened the door to James, brought him in, gave him a moment to be impressed by the view of the square in front of the hotel and on up the river toward Ponte Vecchio, then sat him in a chair. Wesley himself went to lie on a couch, his glass of brandy by his side. "Best thing there is for a cold," he said. He indicated the bottle and another glass. "Have some yourself, if you want it. Good prophylaxis, too. Sorry to see you when I'm in such bad shape, but as I have only very limited time in Florence, I thought I'd better keep our appointment—as best I could." He sipped, coughed a little, sniffled, and lay back, his eyes closed.

He then described something of the projected Center. That done, he said, "The point of my telling you about all this is that we're going to have to create a library almost overnight. We'll want to have the best library in the world on Renaissance things, if that's possible, and we *will* have it, if money can buy it. Old books and new ones. Books in all languages. It will be a tremendous task to assemble it so quickly. Tremper—he's going to act as one of our stateside agents, I hope; we'll have others, naturally—tells me you know a lot about the book market over here, and that you might be able to help us."

"I'd certainly be glad to try," James said.

"Frankly, I've already checked your credentials. Alfred Mitchel at the New York Public Library and Lee Bush down at the Library of Congress have assured me you're legit and very able. You'd have to come back to the States from time to time to consult with our librarian, but otherwise we'd want you here in Europe. You could purchase for us almost as you saw fit, certainly at first. I'd hope you'd get us private libraries before they were put onto the open market and dispersed. I'm told that's very efficient—buy the whole thing, keep what's wanted, and sell the duplicates. I think, by the way, that we'd rather have you on a salary and an expense account than have you work on commission." Wesley was too weak to be entirely tactful. "Cheaper for us and less of a temptation for you," he concluded.

"What kind of a salary did you have in mind?" James said, aware that he was in no position to take offense.

Wesley named a figure that would keep James handsomely in Florence, in fact would enable him to repay Signora Benassi out of his first check, if he didn't go deeper into debt to her in the meantime.

"I think that generous," James said. "And I'd like doing it, too. One has grown weary of so much day-to-day."

"Of course, it all depends on Miss Ladore; I must emphasize that. I'm proceeding as if she were in accord, because I want, when I present her with my full program, to have it worked out as closely as I can, right down to details of staffing, where that's possible. For people like her, it's better not to be too general—not the way their minds work, y'know. But—*but*—she hasn't yet said yes to any of it. However, I'm full of hope." Wesley swallowed, making a face as he did so. "Worse and worse," he said. James said how too bad it was, to get sick when he had only a few days in Florence. "You're right. It *is* bad luck." Wesley closed his eyes again and leaned back, ready to end the conversation. "And now—well, frankly, the longer you stay here the more likely it is you'll catch it."

But James had something more to say—and to do. Nothing less than to initiate a campaign. "I bring something up precisely because you *won't* be long in Florence, Dr. Knuckles, and because there's a kind of urgency about it. I mean, it's something I wouldn't want you to miss out on, just because you might be unavailable at some crucial moment."

"What's that? Eh?" Wesley said, sitting up.

"You mentioned, when describing your new Center, having at least one 'period room'—wasn't that how you put it?"

"Yes. That's one idea. Dignified. Properly furnished. Not institutional. You know—something like the East and West Rooms at the Morgan Library, or the Music Room at Dumbarton Oaks. For receptions. Perhaps small meetings."

"And you mentioned getting things to go in it. Would you be acquiring *really* important works of art?"

"Mr. Molyneux, if this goes through, whatever we do'll be done lavishly. We won't be buying works of art in the quantities the Getty's doing, but they'll be the same, quality-wise, and we'll pay top prices."

"I may know of something for you. The most important work of Renaissance art to have come on the market in decades."

Wesley, in order to pull himself together for subtle negotiations, poured himself more brandy. "May I ask you what it is?"

"A drawing."

Wesley frowned. "Only a drawing?"

"Dr. Knuckles, you will simply have to believe me when I tell you it's a drawing such as nobody has dreamed of."

"That's not much to go on. Have you got photographs of it?"

"No, but I will soon."

"Why is it you're telling me this now? You're not asking me to commit myself, I take it."

"No. I bring it up so I can inform the agent of the owners you'd like the right of first refusal—providing they do, in fact, decide to sell, to you or anyone else. I can't commit them, as far as that goes, or even tell you who they are, because I don't know. I know only that they, and the drawing, are, shall we say, transalpine."

"I understand." Wesley looked a little suspicious. "Nobody told me you were a dealer on *this* scale."

"A happy stroke of fortune brought the drawing to to my attention," James said gratefully.

"Have you any idea what the price might be?"

"For a work of this magnitude, one expects to pay, nowadays, millions, Dr. Knuckles."

"*That* important!" Wesley was impressed, and rather pleased. "The only kinds of things that make any sense to the Miss Ladores of this world are the things that cost millions—and they may be right. Your happy stroke of fortune may work for both of us.

"Whereas," Wesley added, thinking of his cold—and, as ever, apprehensive of Miss Ladore—"fortune can so easily bring us down like—like a stray dog on a superhighway."

James flinched as if Wesley had struck him. How could the man have hit on that metaphor? It brought back to his mind his near accident with all the force of rushing water, and pushed out the present. He lost interest in where he was and who he was talking to and relived the morning, strong as a hallucination. Felt the sudden startling pain as he fell. Saw the oncoming juggernaut of traffic. Knew again the shame of putting his hands before his face, the way he'd done when, as a boy, he'd fallen while at play and tried to hide his tears. And then, like a change from minor to major key, felt again the sudden lift of his salvation.

"Mr. Molyneux?" Wesley said crossly. "Are you listening to me?"

"What? Oh, you'll have to excuse me. I—" James, to explain his apparent rudeness—and at the same time to boast of Mark's rescue of him—told Wesley of the incident. "It's come back to me, the way things will, over and over—I'll have it most of the night, I already know that. It was brought back by your remark about a dog caught on a highway. That's just what I was today. That overpowered. That helpless. I don't believe in miracles, but I understand now why people do. When Mark picked me up, it was quite as if a messenger of God had snatched me from the jaws of death; I wish I could think of a less pretentious way of saying it that would still convey my feelings, but I can't. His strength and his swiftness, Dr. Knuckles . . . It's quite simply one of the most vivid—and moving—things that have ever happened to me. I'll remember it to the last day of my life."

"Obviously he's a *very* good friend," Wesley said, his effort to sound both knowing and pleasantly urbane somewhat spoiled because he had immediately thereafter to sniffle again.

It went clean over James's head. "More a savior," he said. "And he didn't have to think. People like me—we have to figure out whether something is possible and all that, and by the time we make up our minds, the chance has passed. The bewildered beast lies bloodied on the asphalt. To act so well, so instinctively—it's a remarkable gift."

Wesley was bored. This was all too analytical. It was, he supposed, lover talk, basically, and therefore better said by James to Mark in bed than spread all over the place. He got back to the point. "I was telling you that one of the major figures in my plans is John Battle Davenport. I assume he'd accept this work of art you speak of."

"I'm sure of that, yes," James paused, faced now with the need for secrecy until he had his drawing safely out of Italy. "But I think it would be best not to mention it to him as yet. Scholars' gossip. And if news of this gets out prematurely, it may never come on the market at all. The owners are concerned about their price and about inflation. They're in no hurry, so I'm told. They need to be carefully brought along, d'you see? So it should be a secret between us. When I have photographs and full documentation to show you, and their final decision, and perhaps a price, you then may, if you wish, consult Professor Davenport. I can almost guarantee his enthusiastic endorsement."

"I'm dying of curiosity," said Wesley.

"If you're dying of anything, I'd say it was your cold." James got up.

"It is miserable." Wesley let the corners of his shapely mouth turn down. "No. Keep away. We won't shake hands. But there's one other thing," he said. "You probably know already that Miss Ladore and my niece have moved to Villa Arberoni."

"No! They have? When?"

"This noon. You didn't encounter them at lunch? I understand they had it there."

"I didn't eat. Too upset because of my near accident."

"Well, they have. I'll stay here, but they'll be your villa-mates for the next several days, until we move on. I called Professor Davenport and asked him if he could do a little sightseeing with them during the next days; I'm going to have to stay pretty close to this room. He suggested that you might take them instead, so he can work on his book. He said you were the best possible guide to Florence. Said you'd done it for—well, for pay. Would you mind? We could recompense your help rather generously. Two hundred dollars a day, and you need only take them out for a few hours each morning."

"There's a legal problem," James said. "Guiding is a closed shop here, pretty much restricted to Italian citizens. I got into trouble; that's why I quit doing it."

"But now that they're staying at the villa? It can appear that you're merely being neighborly."

"Would it be all right if young Mark Stapleton joined up with us?" James asked.

"Of course. Of course—if it would be an inducement. You plan it. Out of town, too. You can have the car, for I certainly won't be needing it. I've canceled everything for the moment, even

Villa I Tatti. Take them to Pisa. Miss Emilene might like the Leaning Tower." Wesley sniffed vindictively. "She's rather one herself."

And so, except for Friday, when James was out of town, he spent part of the next days with Miss Emilene, Laurie, and Mark, lecturing them impartially, but interested only in Mark's responses. So circumspect were Mark and Laurie that even the sharp-eyed James never guessed how well they were coming to know each other outside the fine bright world of the Florentine achievement, which James built for them from their encounters with paint and marble and bronze. Because his terrace faced the other way, he never knew, for instance, that they spent part of each afternoon together in the gardens of Villa Arberoni, while the benign Miss Emilene, who did have windows on the garden, and used them, took improbably long siestas.

James picked up his film, carried it outside, and looked at it as he stood on the sidewalk. The negatives seemed adequate. He was fairly confident they'd make decent enlargements, especially some of the details.

Now that he had a possible buyer, it was time to decide about the mechanics of marketing the drawing, including how best to cover its trail. James had thought of all that, naturally, and had come up with the procedure he believed would work the best, as well as be the safest. It involved his going to Munich for a day, and the sooner the better—tomorrow, in fact. He could take Miss Ladore and the others sightseeing in the morning, tie up a few loose ends in the afternoon, and take the night train over the Brenner; flying was expensive and, out of Florence, not all that convenient.

He'd need a reservation, which meant he'd have to go to the station—yet another expedition, and he was stiff and tired from the day's events already. He was in luck, however; the line at the reservations window wasn't long, and there was a seat for him, too. When he returned to the villa, he went out into the garden to rest and think for a moment. Late afternoon and early evening were his favorite times there. Signora Benassi was on the terrace in front of the *salone*, seated not far from the top of the stairs, a stroke of blue-green silk against the pale, lichen-marked stone. She saw him and beckoned with a wave of her arm.

She noticed he was limping more than usual when he climbed toward her. As she never knew how, tactfully, to express concern over his deformity, she said, "You're looking tired around the eyes this evening, James, and they're usually so bright and penetrating. You've been overdoing."

He told her about his narrow escape that noon. "Mark picked me up out of danger like an angel of the Lord," he concluded, in a variation of what he'd said to Wesley. "He really did. An angel of the Lord."

"Come sit down," Signora Benassi said, directing James to a nearby garden chair. "We'll watch the sun cross behind my sun-dial cypresses and talk about coincidences. You are the second inhabitant of Villa Arberoni whom Mark has rescued." She spoke lightly of her experience in the Protestant Cemetery. "What a strange thing—that he's salvaged both of us. I wonder what it means."

"Nothing at all to him," James said.

"That's not fair. He's hardly what I'd call mindless, James."

"I meant it admiringly, Signora Benassi. That's the wonderful thing about what he did—at least for me. It was as instinctive as for a good soldier to be brave. As natural and beautiful as a horse taking a jump. To Mark it was simply . . . what one does. But to me—it will always mean an enormous lot to me."

"I don't wonder," she said, "that you've grown fond of him."

James gave thought to the word he'd use. "Devoted."

So that was settled. She didn't need to be told more, James didn't need to tell it. But Signora Benassi would now have to worry about James. She'd seen him infatuated before, and knew how he could suffer. "He'll be moving on, of course. He must, after all. It's his first trip to Europe. He can't just get stalled with us here in Florence forever. He will leave."

"I'm afraid so," James said numbly, already unable to imagine it.

"As I like him too, our problem is to see that he stays with us here as much as he reasonably can, given his circumstances, isn't it? I've already suggested to him that he should keep his rooms, the way Hilda has kept the studio. Leave his things in them indefinitely, until he finally returns to America, and go on short trips elsewhere in Italy—or outside, as far as that goes. Take a few things, travel lightly, and make this his headquarters. He's more or less agreed—though he seems in no hurry to leave Florence right now. I know he'll come back toward the latter part of June for the first run of the Palio, because I promised to have Tiberio get him a ticket right on the square. And he'll come for my birthday party. He's now promised that."

"Better to have him come and go than to leave forever," James said.

"I'm afraid it's the only way we'll have him at all—coming and going is. We must both work on it, then," Signora Benassi said. "I count on your help."

James said, so openly that Signora Benassi grew even more worried, "As you well know, you'll have it to the limit."

Late the next morning, after visiting the Carmine and Santa Maria Novella (excluding the Spanish Chapel) with his three pupils, James went for the last time to the German Library, to see if he could learn anything about other Raphael projects that had never been completed. He did: a most pertinent bit of bibliography which, for once, Battsie didn't have out, a long article by a scholar named John Shearman in a book put together in celebration of the ninetieth birthday of Walter Friedlaender. The article was called "Raphael's Unexecuted Projects for the Stanze," and had been written in 1965. It contained nothing unexpected related to James's own drawing, but its opening sentence, which James copied down, would make a splendid quotation for the documentation that would have to be presented to any potential buyer: it stated that most of the Stanze frescoes had preliminary projects that varied from the completed ones, sometimes even in subject matter. Shearman, too, would not be hostile to the existence of James's piece.

That was as far as he needed to take things. He went home to marshal his information and to pack for the night train to Bavaria. It was his intention to carry the drawing with him.

•   •   •

Ettore Biscotti found John Davenport, got him to one side, and reported on the article James had gone through.

"We have him," he concluded triumphantly.

Battsie wasn't as eager as he ought to have been. "It might be. I've had second thoughts, however. So improbable, you know. I think, Ettore, that you led me into acting far too precipitously when I telephoned Andromeda Paonese; thank heavens she was out of town. I'm not at all sure we know enough to justify dropping even the merest hint to anyone, much less to that high-principled woman, whose unbridled morality might easily lead her to accuse someone unjustly, you know it well. In fact, I'm inclined to forget the whole business."

"I don't agree," Biscotti said shortly.

Battsie shrugged. "Your privilege, of course. However . . ." He did have a means of calling Biscotti off, though it necessitated being a little bit premature in discussing the new Renaissance Center. Battsie told about it—for the first of many, many times, no doubt. "There'll be visiting scholars from over here, of course, Ettore," he concluded. "Full-year appointments, very possibly renewable. The stipends will be, to put it modestly, extravagant. If it goes through, naturally you'd be one of the first to be invited. Molyneux, by the way, will probably act as the European agent for the library, buying used books and the like. We shall be quite dependent on him—a good thing, I believe. He's an honest man, at bottom."

Biscotti made a counteroffer. "I'd be delighted to be a part of your institute, naturally. Publications, you say? A good place to put my book in English translation when I've finished it. You on Raphael and I on Alberti would make a nice beginning of all that, would we not?"

It wasn't a bad bargain. The Renaissance Center would probably want to publish Biscotti's book anyway. "Agreed," Battsie said. "We can honor one another."

"Perhaps you're right—about the Raphael thing," Ettore thereupon conceded. "Perhaps we *had* better forget about it."

That was how it was left. But both men had *arrières-pensées*. Biscotti, as he returned to his own desk, was wondering how it might be possible to drop a hint himself to Dottoressa Paonese, without having Davenport know about it, thus keeping the chance for an appointment to Davenport's new Center abroad, and at the same time having a grateful government here at home. One never knew when one might need a local favor, too. As for John Battle Davenport, he knew Ettore too well to think he'd sealed his lips for sure. That wasn't all he knew, either. When he'd spoken to Wesley that morning, Wesley, from his sickbed, had told him about the drawing in strictest confidence, including its being from a transalpine source. Maybe it was, but Davenport had heard that story once too often; one remembered the scandal over the Metropolitan Museum's Greek vase, for instance, which the Italians claimed had come illegally from an Etruscan necropolis. James Molyneux might be in some danger.

When he got back to the villa about seven o'clock, he knocked on James's door. James, who was just packing, was quite surprised. Davenport had never come near his rooms before, except through express invitation, though over the years they'd lived across the hall from each other for months at a time.

"Knuckles tells me you may be going to work for his new Center for Renaissance Studies, James. It seems very likely I'll be there too," Battsie said. "Congratulations. I know our library will be the better for you."

"Why, thank you, John."

There was an important silence. "People tell me you've been showing quite a bit of interest in Raphael recently," Battsie said finally. "I mean . . . it's been noticed."

"Has it?"

"Mmm. I've no objection, you understand. Such a great master—there's room for more than one of us, eh?" Battsie hung on to James's half-closed door, as if ready to leave. "Still . . . do watch your step, James. Italy is an odd country. One never knows where they'll pounce, and one never knows why or when, or what it'll be over. The best policy is never to be pounceable, that's what I always say." Battsie opened the door wide again, as if he'd just had a thought. "You've been interested in discrepancies between the two editions of Vasari, it's reported. Amazing, isn't it, that business about the project for *The Return of Leo the Great to Rome?* Wouldn't it be something if *that* turned up after all these years? A discovery to arouse even the most torpid bureaucrat to excited action. Do take care, James."

James was in a turmoil. It was almost certain that when Wesley had talked to Davenport about James's appointment to the staff of the Institute, he'd told him about the drawing. But who could have discovered the investigations James had been doing? James had to go lie down on his bed, he was so plain frightened, and try to think. He had some dim sense that as he was working at the German Library, a quiet—and now, it seemed, sinister—figure had gone back and forth behind him. Sometimes paused, as if looking at something else. And hadn't someone been across the shelves from him from time to time as he was searching? It was all very ill defined, but—yes! Someone had made it a point to spy on him. Who?

Bisotti!

Who else? Nobody more likely. What bad luck, to have been watched by that most delightfully malicious of men. Would he be up to making trouble? Most certainly, if it could be done in safety.

James almost went over to the Davenports' apartment, to talk some more to John Battle and find out what it was he really knew, so James would have a better idea from which direction an attack might come, but he decided against it. Better not to give himself away too much.

Davenport's warning had been clear enough, in any case. The next question was what to do about it. Should James cancel his trip? He didn't think so. It was urgent, now, to substantiate a foreign source for the drawing as quickly as possible. But—quite another matter—should James take the drawing with him? Absolutely not. He didn't want to be pounced on at the Italian side of the border, or somewhere between here and there, and have his drawing confiscated by the police. No, the drawing would have to be got to Germany in a different way. For the time being, it would have to stay in Florence.

It seemed best to leave it somewhere outside of his own apartment, so when he returned Hilda's camera half an hour later, just before he left for the train station, he took the drawing with him and put it, folded, in the drop-front bin where she kept her paper.

190

It fit easily, was smaller than some of her own uncut sheets, and wouldn't ever be noticed. Even if the police should search his rooms, as seemed unlikely—after all, they didn't have much to go on—they almost certainly wouldn't come to the studio or search anywhere else in the villa. Signora Benassi had too much influence for them to treat her house as if it were a nest of thieves.

PART

six

James arrived in Munich very early and somewhat frazzled; he'd not come by sleeping car. He went to the day hotel in the station and hired a room, where he shaved and took a shower, then rested awhile. At nine o'clock he went to see his friend Hans Lochner, with whom he'd done business many times, and who owned perhaps the best of the newer art galleries in Munich. The Lochner Gallery wouldn't open to the public until eleven, but James had telephoned from Florence for an early appointment. He rang the doorbell to the showrooms just off Maximilianstrasse, and in a moment Lochner, a brawny, curly-haired man in his early thirties, still tan from late skiing in the Alps, came to the door.

He cried, "Jimmy! How wonderful!" and they hugged each other. Then he led James through the showrooms, where a late-season exhibition of anguished German Expressionist paintings hung, to his office in back, which was furnished in quite unanguished chrome and black leather and cool enameled metal. Spotted green-and-brown lady-slipper orchids, which Lochner, the son of a famous botanist, hybridized as a hobby in a greenhouse on the roof of his gallery building, were grouped on his desk and on a row of low filing cabinets.

James looked at their name tags and admired them while Lochner started the coffee machine going in a little closet adjoining the bathroom. As the coffee was brewing, James described his drawing, using the Polaroid snapshots as illustrations, and summarized his discoveries at the German Library.

When he was finished, Lochner said, "Where is it?"

"In my hands, Hans."

"And whose is it?"

James told him. "That's what makes it tricky."

"The national patrimony laws, you mean?"

"Yes. Because of the way they restrict any Italian who'll have to keep and resell the thing in Italy, no legal buyer could pay more than a fraction of what the drawing's worth on the international market. In fact, if the drawing were to be made known, the government would probably force sale to somewhere like the Uffizi, at a confiscatory price. Therefore, it must be exported and sold outside the country—illegally! And one must be sure the thing can't be traced to Ricky, no matter where it's sold."

James got the roll of film out of his briefcase and Lochner looked at it through a magnifying glass. He whistled. "You've got something, Jimmy," he said. "You really do." He made a note of the six or eight frames he thought would enlarge the best. "But why have you come to me?"

"I want you to sell it."

"Wouldn't you be better off using one of the big houses that specialize in old masters?"

"You mean like Colnaghi or Agnew? They might not want to touch it, given the circumstances. Also, I can trust you absolutely."

Lochner grinned. "Are you so sure? Merely because we were once lovers for three years—"

"Three and a half. Yes, I'm so sure. And you do deal occasionally with old masters. The big houses are apt to be ponderous, too—you agree?—whereas you're inventive and intelligent. Why wouldn't you be? I taught you a lot of what you know."

"All of it, Jimmy. All that's best." Lochner thought for a moment. "The public question will, of course, be that of provenance: Where does it come from? I could refuse to discuss it. There's nothing in the laws of this country that can oblige me to disclose anything."

"Remember that last sentence in Vasari, Hans? About the learned monk Peter of Cracovia—which is, of course, Cracow. By the way, I wouldn't be surprised but that it was he who pasted the drawing in the cardinal's book—a clumsy act, and more expressive of a pedant's values than those of a collector, certainly. Anyway, Vasari as much as says he stole it and carried it to Poland."

"Quite right. I could start rumors that the drawing came from behind the Iron Curtain. Poland. Czechoslovakia, as far as that goes. Even Hungary. Allude to the thieving monk—maybe we can find out what happened to him when he got back up here. Fill that part of the thing out a little—I'll put a graduate student from the university on it. The beastly bureaucrats over on the other side are so suspicious and malign, they'll snap and snarl at one another. Maybe we'll have a few trials. And such a story can't damage anyone who's vulnerable. No poor little librarian *did* steal it, after all, and the aristocrats who might have had it in their libraries or collections are all in exile or prison, or are dead. Let them cry murder, from the other side. Nobody listens to them, not even in their own countries, and they'll never be able to put a case together, because they won't have one. Yes. A mysterious source from the Soviet Zone. But only implied. I'd need whisper to no more than two colleagues over a coffee one morning, and the thing'd be spread from here to Tokyo within hours, fully ornamented and magnified. And speaking of coffee . . ."

He went to the machine, where the coffee was long since ready, and brought them cups. James, meanwhile, reached forward and turned the orchids on the desk to different angles and admired them—a welcome change of thought, but not a long-lasting one.

James said, "As for the other obvious question—to whom should we sell it?—I've got an idea for that." He told Lochner a little about Wesley and Miss Ladore. "So if she comes through with funding for the Center, they'll have the money and the need. What do you think the drawing would be worth, Hans?"

"Hard to say. Nothing like it has come on the market, not ever, I suppose. But if all the appropriate scholars back it . . ."

"I can guarantee John Battle Davenport. I think Shearman will have no a priori objection. Daphne Nickerson, at Bryn Mawr, will. In the end, its value will depend on judgments of its artistic quality, so Pope-Hennessy's opinion will count enormously. Knuckles and his board will certainly consult him, as well as the others, before they buy."

"Indeed. So, then, assuming all that's favorable—what will it bring?" Hans scratched his curly brown hair. "If nothing goes wrong, we're talking about millions of dollars, I should think."

"Three? Four? Five?"

"Or six." Hans thought about that, too. "It would depend on how rapid and private a sale one wanted to make. I mean, if quickness were desirable, one might ask five."

"And speed *is* fairly important."

"One can always raise the price if a first buyer proves reluctant, too, Jimmy. Next, how will you get it into my hands?"

"I won't carry it up. Too risky." James told Hans about John

Davenport's warning, which disturbed the dealer as much as it had James.

"I don't like the sound of that, Jimmy. Once it's up here, why don't you get out of Italy for a while? Come and stay with us for as long as you want—months, a year—here in town or at the mountain place. Ulrich would like that as much as I would. We don't see enough of you." Ulrich was Lochner's friend.

"There are things to keep me in Florence for the moment, though I'll remember your offer. As for moving the drawing—I'll send someone to you with it."

"What a responsibility!"

"But how else to do it? You can't come down for it, any more than I can bring it up. The question is, who to use? There's my cousin Hilda. She's coming back, maybe next week or the week after, and she's not too badly cast as a lady Goldfinger. She could carry it mixed in with some of her own stuff, in a portfolio, as she's an artist. It'd look perfectly natural. But she's perhaps too close to me. Also, I don't like to wait on her convenience, and I'd have to. I do know of a young man—"

"Bruno? I wouldn't think that Bruno—"

"Lord, no. Never Bruno."

"So Bruno's out of favor."

"He's gotten to be a little much. I mean, when you've just fucked with someone and you're feeling rather good about it, and that someone starts to talk about emigrating, it is something of a discouragement. But there's a young man staying at Villa Arberoni right now who'd do as a messenger, I think."

Hans smiled and tilted back in his chair. "Tell me more."

"Signora Benassi is letting him use Villa Arberoni as his headquarters while he takes trips, comes and goes; you see, we don't want him getting bored with us," James said, going on longer than he needed to. "Why not have him come to Munich? He won't need to know what he's carrying, but he's very honest. I trust him almost as much as I do you."

"Why?" Hans asked. "Better tell me why, Jimmy."

"He saved my life." James described the incident on the Lungarno Acciaioli. "It was like finding oneself in a baroque painting, Hans. I was about to be martyred, and suddenly strong arms carried me out of danger. I can still feel it. You can't know what it means to someone like me, with my limp and my cane and my inability to do anything physical quickly, much less well, to be borne to safety by . . . unflawed creation."

"And is he handsome?"

James thought for a moment. "Very pleasing. Strong—maybe even more than you, Hans. Splendid. But not handsome like—oh, like Tiberio dei Guidoni—you met him at dinner last time you were in Florence, and remember him, I'm sure. Mark is handsome enough, but he's no Tiberio. In any case, he's . . ." James gestured, at a loss for words.

Hans was looking less amused now. "Jimmy," he said, "you're in love."

"Terribly," James admitted, deliberately choosing the word he'd made fun of Mark for using. But then he dropped the quotation marks from his voice. *"Terribly.* And it's happened almost just like that." He snapped his fingers. "I don't look forward, I don't look back. It's happened, that's all. Can you believe it?"

"Of course. As happened thirteen years ago—do I have the count close enough to suit you this time?—in San Miniato at eleven-thirty in the morning. A Wednesday. I never looked back, either. And what about him? Is he . . . ?"

"Not a bit. He's . . . straight as the dive of a falcon, Hans. I don't even care. All I care about for the moment, all I can think about, is having him near me. Or the promise of it. Just how much I'm in love came to me last night on the train, when I couldn't sleep, and realized that whenever I wasn't positively trying to think of something else, I thought of Mark. Felt him save me. Saw his chagrin that he'd got me into it. Saw his face when he'd figured out how Santo Spirito works; I put him through that just the way I once did you. When I realized he occupied all my head except just what's in front, I realized that it's true. I'm *terribly* in love. He saved my life, and as for me, I'd die now to save his. I mean it."

Concerned and, it seemed, a little sad, Hans said, "A man who'll never care for you? An American at that, with the thoughtless way they have? What have you set yourself up for this time, Jimmy?"

"I don't know. I don't care. But of course I shall continue to keep it from him. As long as he thinks I merely—merely like him, like to teach him things, it will be all right."

"As long as that's true, perhaps. And would you put him in such danger—to carry your drawing out of Italy?"

"There's no danger, if the police aren't forewarned. I came through last night, and the only people we saw were the ones who stamp passports. No customs at all, anywhere. The magic of the Common Market. He'd be just one more of the millions of young tourists who cross back and forth with their rucksacks and parcels."

"But if something should go wrong?"

"Why, I'd come forward and say it was my doing. If I'd die for him, surely I'd go to prison for him."

"You sound almost . . . eager for that, Jimmy."

"It would be a proof, wouldn't it?" James turned aside. "And if he can carry me to safety, surely he can carry my drawing."

Hans shook his head slowly. "I don't like it. Let me see if I can't think of a better way."

James shrugged. "So long as you realize how much I trust him."

"Oh, I do. But something else might be neater—though I hope you'll send him to see me in any case." Hans changed the subject to one less troubling. "Fascinating as your love life is, Jimmy, we must get enlargements made."

James said, "And they must have 'Munich' stamped all over their backs. I'll want to carry a set of them to Florence with me, in your official gallery envelope. Nothing must suggest an Italian origin."

Hans rumpled James's hair. "Wily old Jimmy," he said, but as he was then standing above and behind James, so James couldn't see him, he shook his head again. James was his oldest friend and, after Ulrich, his closest one, and he was worried for the future.

The prints were ordered at a shop not far away—Hans took the roll there while James napped in his chair. When he returned, he and James worked the rest of the morning on the documentation. First James wrote it in English, then Hans rendered it into German. Both versions would accompany the photographs, the German coming as the pretended original, along with a letter in both languages from Hans to James, containing a tentative offering of the drawing, which would leave the price fuzzy—to test the ground. The prints wouldn't be ready until late afternoon, so, after leaving the dossier to be typed by a secretary, they went off for lunch down at Kloster Andechs—bread and cheese and some of the wonderful beer—and talked for hours, before returning to Munich in time to get the enlargements.

Considering the circumstances under which James had taken the pictures, they were very good. The quality of the drawing sang through them.

As he was putting everything in a folder, which would then go in a very official-looking envelope, Hans said, "Jimmy, you've got something this time that makes the Sustermans I sold for Guidoni look like a penny postcard. Shouldn't we have come kind of agreement?"

"I wanted you to have the full feeling of the situation before we came to this, Hans, that's why I've not brought it up before. What would be an appropriate amount for you and for me?"

"Will my commission come out of yours, or from the owner?" James said it would come from Ricky. "Then I think I should get five percent, and you fifteen, in this case. You've done quite a lot more than merely mail a package, after all. And as for me—I wouldn't be at all surprised if there were many difficult moments ahead. Think of Davenport's warning. I may have to do a lot of negotiating—and bluffing. And of course safeguard the drawing. I think I'll earn five percent. And by the way, costs such as a frame—I'll try to find an old one—insurance, and space in a bank vault, and perhaps even a printed offering to replace the stuff we've just done, if that Center doesn't buy, should come from the owner. He should count on netting about three-quarters of the price, when all the bills are in."

James agreed. He assured Lochner that Ricky would agree, too. He'd not have much choice.

James did take a sleeping car for his return trip; Hans insisted and paid the extra fare on the early night train. As a result, James got plenty of sleep and arrived in Florence in time to spend the morning with Mark and the others, sightseeing as usual. Afterwards, when he was removing his drawing from Hilda's bin of paper, he got an idea.

She was a good draftsman, loved to draw almost as much as she loved to model in clay, and her studio was full of drawings of every size—in pen and ink, pencil, charcoal, crayon, pinned to the walls, framed and hanging, sitting in piles on top of tables and her bookshelves. James folded his own drawing, then looked for one of Hilda's that was just a little bigger. He soon found it—an amusing one at that, and already matted. Hilda had had a phase—she was always going through phases with her art—when she'd visited the museums and churches of Florence to make what she called "re-thinkings" of famous paintings, sometimes of a detail, sometimes of the whole work. By a "rethinking" she meant that she extracted from the painting and put into a drawing the volumes and relationships of its figure composition; as a sculptor, that was what particularly interested her. It was one of these "rethinkings" that James had come upon, a study after the *Madonna della Sedia*, in the Pitti, that most popular and seemingly sentimental of all of Raphael's depictions of the Virgin Mary with the Christ Child. Hilda's rethinking of it went, in fact, right to the point of the powerful interlocking spheres of its design. She'd exaggerated so subtly—made the great chubby legs of the Child almost but not quite monstrous, for instance—that her drawing was like a distorted precis of the original, perfectly recognizable for what it was, though reduced to pen and ink instead of colors, yet seen in a funhouse mirror. Indeed, it struck James, when he found it, what fun it was, in that the sentimentality came through, in Hilda's version, as irony. It was perfect for James's purpose, and was, moreover, boldy signed and dated at the lower left, the signature illegible, but the date—from last November—clear. No customs official, or anyone else, could claim it was old, certainly.

Hilda used a standard-size mat and had frames to fit, so James was able, temporarily, to put his Raphael between Hilda's drawing and the backing of the frame, close it, and hang it on her studio wall.

He then telephoned Wesley Knuckles to tell him he had more

material on the drawing. Wesley was too sick to see him, but said he'd let him know when he was better. Frustrating—James was eager now to move the sale along.

James took his group to Pisa the next day, Sunday, and on Monday to Arezzo for the frescoes by Piero della Francesca; they tried on that excursion to stop and see Tiberio dei Guidoni, but he was off on some errand, and they missed him. On Tuesday they stayed home and went to the Uffizi Gallery, where James showed them the paintings in reverse chronological order—beginning with Titian and ending with Cimabue—to cut the fetters of evolutionary development with which scholars shackle art, said he. After lunch that day, John Davenport took him aside.

"Wesley Knuckles called just now. I'm seeing him this afternoon," Davenport said, his tone of voice definitely conspiratorial. "He wants you to come to his hotel at the same time. He's sending the car for us at three-thirty. I gather you have something of *the utmost importance* to show him."

James nodded. "The phrase, John, is, in this case, surely inadequate."

$$\approx$$

One after another, James tossed his eight-by-ten photographs of the great Raphael drawing on the writing table in Wesley's suite. "There it is," he said, affecting a certain disdain. He pulled out the documentation. "And here's its pedigree."

Wesley and Professor Davenport looked long and carefully at the photographs, particularly Davenport. Then, always without comment, he read the dossier, both in its English and its German versions. Then, once again, he returned to the photographs. He picked up the one of the entire work and carried it to a chair.

"Have you seen it?" he asked James.

James was leaning against the window, pretending to admire the view. He didn't turn around. "Yes. On Friday. I went up to Munich Thursday night, saw the drawing and got this stuff—one couldn't entrust it to the mails—and came back Friday night. It's superb."

"Went up on Friday, did you?" Davenport muttered. "That was quick. A word to the wise, eh?"

Wesley was waiting to see what Battsie would say, but Battsie held back; one didn't, in such a situation, blurt, after all. He reread the dossier in both languages. "The German's so much more convincing than the English translation," he observed. "This kind of information just seems to go better in German, doesn't it?" Then he got up and looked at the rest of the photographs again.

"I'd have to see it, of course, before I make my final judgment," he said, "but going on what I've got here in front of me . . ." He stopped to look some more.

"Yes? Yes?" Wesley prompted him. "Can't you yet come to the point?"

Battsie straightened up, stood like a reviewing colonel, and in a commanding voice said, "It is unequaled in importance in the preserved oeuvre of Raphael—I mean the drawings, of course. A magnificent discovery. What more can I say?"

"I just wanted you to say it in the first place," said Wesley.

Davenport, who wanted James's connection with the drawing clarified, in case of any trouble, said to James, "Just for the record, would you mind telling us how you came to be involved with the drawing? Are you acting as the dealer's agent?"

"I've known Hans Lochner for years and years. He sent me snapshots of it originally—it hadn't yet been properly photographed—so I could look into it at the German Library here. He's primarily a dealer in nineteenth- and twentieth-century art, not old masters, and he wanted my advice about selling it in America. As for the research I did—well, John, it was your chance remarks about the discrepancies between the two editions of Vasari and about the group of drawings on similar paper that turned the trick. Without knowing it, *you* wrote the most essential part of the documentation on the drawing."

"That sometimes happens," Davenport said.

"If all goes well—and the owners still, even at this late hour, seem to have some doubts—" James put in, to explain why the drawing couldn't be seen in Munich immediately—"but if they do decide to go ahead and sell it, you'll be able to see it at the Lochner Gallery in perhaps ten days. I mentioned you and your Renaissance Center to Hans, Dr. Knuckles, and I think you will have first choice."

"And just who *are* the owners?" Battsie asked.

"I don't know. Hans wouldn't say. But when I asked him if it could have come somehow from behind the Iron Curtain, he didn't flatly deny it."

"Perfect," Battsie said, smiling.

"Don't forget Peter of Cracow," said James.

"Don't worry, I won't. Before I'm through, his name will be a household word."

"It's really important, John?" said Wesley. Davenport nodded. "And it will make for a wide coverage in the press? All that sort of thing?" Davenport nodded even more emphatically. "Would it call for a special publication—one that might initiate our series?" Davenport nodded until it seemed he'd never stop. "Well, then—how much is it?" Wesley asked.

"You'll have to talk to Hans about that," James replied, "but I think between five and six million."

Battsie whistled. "A bargain, too."

"Marks?" Wesley asked.

"No, dollars," said James.

"A real bargain," said Battsie. "For some reason, I assumed you meant pounds."

Wesley said, purring now, "It all depends on Miss Ladore—but how can she resist? Which reminds me, what kind of a mood does she seem to be in, gentlemen? You see her every day."

James said, "I think she'd probably agree to anything to get out of having to follow me around any longer."

"I got that reaction from her, too, when I had your job in Rome," Wesley said. "She actually told me to stop reading from"—he remembered just in time that the author of his Roman guidebook was present—"from Fodor one morning. Well, I'm feeling almost myself. John, I think it's time you and I presented her with our formal proposition for the Center for Renaissance Studies. Have you got the typed version with you?"

Davenport did, of course; to show it to Wesley was the main reason he'd come to the Granduca. "Let me have it," Wesley said. "Here, Mr. Molyneux. As you're to be on the team, why don't you read one of the carbons?"

An hour later, after some changes had been made in all copies, Wesley went to the telephone and called Miss Ladore. The three men then drove to Villa Arberoni together, where James went on up to his own rooms, after dropping Wesley and Davenport off on Miss Emilene's floor.

They spent an hour with her, talking and explaining—even, now and then, listening—until she said she couldn't take anything more in, and they should give her the papers and let her read them by herself, and should go away.

Battsie went down to the courtyard with Wesley, to be sure nobody overheard them, before they compared notes. Wesley said, "So far, so good—wasn't that your impression?"

"If I may use a vulgar expression, I'd say it's in the bag, Wesley. What a coup! One feels like doing a hornpipe right out there in Piazza San Doroteo."

"I agree. And you're reconciled, I take it, to the where of the thing. That's *really* settled. We no longer have to decide between Princeton, Cambridge, or Washington. It's between Amarillo, San Antonio, or Abilene." Wesley, gleeful, clapped Davenport on the back. "Though I still think she might consider Dallas. Don't despair."

"One does reach the point," said Battsie, "where one is grateful for small favors."

Wesley had inquired after Laurie, whom he hadn't seen since he'd got sick. Miss Emilene was flustered into telling the truth, because she couldn't think of a lie fast enough: Laurie frequently went to read in the villa garden in the afternoons. Wesley said good-bye to Davenport and went to look for her.

He saw her from a distance, half hidden behind oleanders, and realized she wasn't alone. There was a man with her. Filled with suspicions, Wesley sneaked toward them.

It turned out to be Mark Stapleton. Merely Mark Stapleton. Both the young people stood up, as Wesley approached after a warning cough. Mark was smiling, Laurie's face so expressionless Wesley decided to be abrupt with her.

"Well!" he said, the single syllable a reproachful disquisition on her sins and errors.

The temptation to elaborate was too strong. "Not a word out of you for days—I could have died, for all you cared. I hope you've been having a good time."

206

"I have, thanks," she said. No apologies. No contrition.

Wesley was really going to have to do something about her, but this wasn't the place. Wait till he got her in Venice, where there was no alternative but water. He said, "I've just been with Miss Ladore. My health is more or less normal, thank you, and our business in Florence will soon be finished; I'm taking her to I Tatti tomorrow for tea, after a visit to Villa la Pietra. Nothing to hold us here, so we'll be leaving for Milan on Friday." As he turned and walked stiffly away, she stuck her tongue out at his back, while Mark bent over and kissed her ear.

Wesley would have been a little worried at finding Laurie alone in the garden with that young man, given all the talk one heard about bisexuality, except that Pauline had assured him Mark was James Molyneux's active boyfriend—hadn't she?—and it didn't seem possible he could be deceiving James right under his nose. If there was an attraction between Laurie and Mark, it would be the pull of youth, not of sex. Or could Pauline be wrong? No. It was the kind of detail the Paulines of this world always got right; that was what made them so useful. Wesley rather fancied that he and Pauline Davenport would in time become quite chummy. Thereby he'd learn of things that went on at his Center that her learned husband would know nothing about.

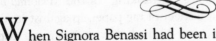

When Signora Benassi had been informed that Miss Ladore and Miss Walker would be leaving on Friday, she invited Miss Ladore alone for dinner in her own small dining room on Thursday evening, without Laurie or Dr. Knuckles. Miss Ladore wanted to take things easy that day, so James took Laurie and Mark off alone to Pistoia for sightseeing and lunch. After they returned to the villa about four o'clock, James got onto something that had to be done before the formidable Hilda returned, which would be any day now—she'd written the signora to have her place put in order and her bed made. While Mark and Laurie went off somewhere, he went to the studio in the gardens, got Hilda's tape measure, and took very exact measurements of the matted drawing behind which he'd concealed his Raphael. He went with them to the little shop near Santa Croce where Bruno worked and got him to knock together a simple frame out of precut moldings, one that would fit the drawing but was a little deeper than the ones Hilda kept on hand; several layers of board backing would be needed to hold the mat of her drawing tight against the glass.

Bruno, it turned out, had been trying all day to reach James by telephone. He'd got notification from the Canadian Embassy in Rome that his application for immigration papers was now on line, and that he would probably receive his visa in about four to six months; they gave that much notice so a person could get his affairs in order. When the frame was finished, James, in lieu of paying cash for it, said that though he was short now, he'd have the money for the passage for Bruno, his wife, and his two children when the time came. And some more, to help him get started—though Bruno's brother Sandro had already got the promise of a job with a picture-framing company in Victoria.

The grateful Bruno suggested in a low voice, so that Tino, the gilder who was nearby, couldn't hear, that he and James might get together that night. James, who'd been thinking as he watched Bruno work, that Luca della Robbia's choirboys didn't age all that well, said he was busy—and then, because he'd hurt Bruno's feelings, had to talk to him out in the street about his plans for a full ten minutes before he took the frame to a shop nearby and had glass cut for it. When he got it back to the villa, he went once more to the studio, put Hilda's "rethinking" of the *Madonna della Sedia* in the new frame, put a sheet of rag paper up against it, then put his folded drawing in, and backed it with more rag paper. Then he filled the remaining space with ordinary cardboard, to make a snug fit. He took the picture to his own rooms and hung it on his sitting room wall, right by the bedroom door. All it needed was to have tape crisscrossed over the glass and be wrapped in brown paper, and it would be ready to travel.

He had nobody to have dinner with, and went looking for Mark, but Mark was out. James then had second thoughts about Bruno, but by the time he telephoned the shop, Bruno had already left.

Mark and Laurie had never been out in the city alone together. They walked down past Santa Maria del Carmine, went inside for another look at the Masaccio frescoes, then went past Santo Spirito to the Arno. They turned left, crossed the river, and eventually found themselves on the embankment near the public gardens and the racecourse. Mark hired the boat he'd been using from the old man who owned it and rowed Laurie down to the lowest spillway and back.

It was a perfect day. A cool dry wind had driven off the pollution; the sky was almost clear and, as the sun lowered, began to take on a little of the luminous green for which Florence was once famous. They beached the boat and, hand in hand, not talking much, slowly walked toward town. When they passed a place where three men were fishing from the bank, seated at intervals of fifty feet, they stopped to watch, and Mark put his right arm loosely around Laurie's shoulders. One of the men caught a little fish, and there were cries of encouragement and envy from his two companions. Mark and Laurie smiled at each other. A little later the men put away their fishing equipment, and each dumped whatever bait he had left onto the grass. They went together to a single car, got in, and drove off to the ramp that led up to the street.

Mark and Laurie lingered on, while the late rush-hour traffic grew heavier behind them. Mark saw something down on the bank: a rat—he pointed it out to Laurie—which had come out from underneath the embankment wall. It hopped through the tussocks of coarse grass and weeds to the leftover bait. Then came another. When a third one slithered forth, Laurie shuddered. Mark pulled her closer to him. Gradually he lowered his hand.

Pauline Davenport, who was driving up the Arno after an afternoon spent taking care of one of Battsie's students, who was living with her husband and a new baby in the direction of Prato—all three had the cold that was going around—got stopped by a light near Mark and Laurie. She watched them. She saw him drop his hand to Laurie's waist—and a little farther. And then her light changed, and she had to charge ahead.

"He was pawing her ass," she said to herself. "Why—they must be screwing." She thought some more about it, and began to smile. Wasn't that a good joke on James Molyneux!

When Wesley and the Davenports had a farewell dinner together that evening, Wesley spoke of the problem of traveling with Miss Ladore, now that she was so restless. Then he got on the subject of Laurie, and of how unfriendly she'd become, which complicated his problem. His voice had a sound to it that alerted Pauline; as a faculty wife of thirty years, she'd heard of everything. She kept quiet about what she'd seen on the Lungarno. Given Wesley's dirty-old-man tone of voice, he might interfere. Spoil the joke on James. Her loyalty to him as her husband's new ally didn't go that far.

✂

Signora Benassi was in her sitting room, reading a book that had been sent to her by friends in the United States. She put it down when Ricky arrived. "You deliver me from a bad novel by being early," she said. "Thoughtful as always."

"Yes, yes," he said. The nautilus cup gleamed in its case on the table beside the clock. Ricky made a point of going to look at it, though he'd seen it more times than he could count.

Really a little overdone. Typical of that bragging blackguard Cellini. The necklace would have more real elegance, more real style; Ricky had just been to see how it was coming, and Giacobbe Sulmona had showed him the first shells, carved from the ribbon jasper. Lovely. And once they were strung to their fellows and put in their setting of water plants, the effect would be ravishing. But Madeleine was talking to him. Ricky turned around.

"I'm glad to be able to tell you something before Miss Ladore arrives. Do you know who came here to see me this morning? Tiberio. He was dreadfully embarrassed—poor angel."

"Embarrassed about what?" Ricky said, arming himself.

"Embarrassed to be asking to borrow money from me for that land he wants so much to buy."

"How dare he do that!" Ricky drew himself up. His shock of white hair bristled.

"He has nobody else to go to," Signora Benassi said.

"Did you . . . lend it to him?"

"No. I said there were problems."

"Did you tell him what they were?"

"I did."

"You discussed our private affairs with him?"

210

"Oh, don't look so fierce. I had good reasons to do so. I was sure it had occurred to him that it would be easier to have you speak to me for him, given your special position, but he felt it was more manly to speak for himself. I wanted him to know that he was right—that he'd done the right thing, done it in the right way. That you weren't a better avenue at all. Just for his own peace of mind."

It was a somewhat subtle point. Ricky spent a few moments over it, then said, "But now he'll think I don't care sufficiently for his welfare. He'll blame me."

"Why shouldn't he? But don't worry. Before he's self-interested, he's a Guidoni. He'll think that whatever you do, according to your sense of honor, is the right thing, even though he suffers for it."

Ricky sat down. He sighed.

"I quite agree," said Signora Benassi. "And it's all your fault."

Costanza appeared to announce Miss Ladore, who came in, walking unsteadily, as she'd been doing from time to time ever since she'd had her cold; something was still wrong with her inner ears. She wore a long woolen skirt, electric blue flecked with black, and a cloak that matched—just the thing for a windy late winter day in Texas, but odd for Florence toward the end of May, and a contrast to the signora's paisley print suit.

"No, thanks. I've had too good a lesson in my life where it can take you," she said, when she'd been offered a drink. "Though my daddy sometimes said that the only thing worse than having him drunk was having him stop. Now I want both of you to have a look at this." She waved Wesley's proposal, which she was carrying, and explained what it was.

She thrust it in Signora Benassi's hand, sat down, and accepted some fruit juice from Costanza. Signora Benassi read the proposal slowly, page by page, and as she finished, handed the pages to Ricky.

"Will you do it?"

"I don't know," Miss Ladore said. "That's why I brought it here—to see what you'd think about it. I know we only just met, but that's the way I am, when I like people. I trust them. Being careful may save you some mistakes, but it costs you other things.

I hope you don't mind. I mean, it's your world, this thing he's proposing. Like your villa. It's got nothing to do with the big ranch or me. So . . ."

Signora Benassi asked, "Must you do it right away? Why not let it go for a year or two? Sometimes that gives a perspective."

"We have to spend part of my daddy's trust each year; that's the way the tax laws are written. So we have to get going."

"Sensible people don't argue with a reason like that," said Signora Benassi, with a glance at Ricky.

"And I'm never going to know much more than I do right now, no matter how long I wait. I'm satisfied Wesley is what everybody says he is, though I don't trust him as far as I could throw a yearling heifer. And Professor Davenport, who's in on all this in a big way, is certainly on the level."

"Very, I should think," Ricky put in. "Though, for poor Raphael's sake, one might prefer he were on an inclined plane."

"They write of residences and dining rooms and lecture halls and an auditorium for concerts. And a major library. That will be very costly," the signora said.

"Art, too." Miss Ladore told them about a Raphael drawing that had been mentioned during her interview with Wesley and John Davenport.

"And is there enough money?" the signora asked.

"I've got all the money in the world," Miss Ladore said. "A lot more of that than I do sense."

"What do you think, Ricky?"

"As a friend? I don't know. As an Italian—I can't help but think the Renaissance is worthy of every attention."

"It won't be just Italian," Miss Emilene said. "There's that phrase in there. 'The Renaissance, from Poland to Portugal.'"

"One of a number of phrases in there one might want to modify. Your report, Miss Ladore, is scarcely marked by its stylistic elegance."

Signora Benassi's next question was more practical. "Who'll run it?"

"Wesley intends to, I suppose. Professor Davenport'll be in charge of that part. Your James Molyneux will have a job with us, too, buying books."

"Now that's interesting," Ricky said.

"*Good!*" Signora Benassi cried. "'My' James needs a job—as I well know. And he'll be very useful to you. Two thoughts occur to me. One of them is this: since we agree that Dr. Knuckles is a little slippery, why don't you get all the work you need out of him, but keep him dangling?"

"How do I do that?" Miss Emilene asked.

"Make him director—what is that Italian phrase that means 'for the time being,' Ricky?"

"*Pro tempore,* and it's Latin, my dear."

"Do that. 'Wesley Knuckles, Director Pro Tem.'" The old women laughed merrily, joined by Ricky, as they thought of how that would sit in Wesley's ear. "My other idea is quite different," Signora Benassi went on. "With this involvement in the Renaissance, don't you want some kind of place in Europe, where it all got started? A place where your scholars could spend time close to archives, and so on? In Florence, for instance. Yes, definitely, it seems to me that what your Center will want eventually is a presence in Florence. In a nice place. A place from which to fly its colors. Make itself known, alongside I Tatti and the Acton Villa and the German Library and so on."

"I suppose that's a good idea," Miss Ladore said. "You wouldn't happen to know of the right piece of real estate, would you?"

"I might," said Signora Benassi.

Laurie and Mark had gone back to the villa, so Laurie could help Miss Ladore get ready for dinner. Laurie changed into her best dress and came downstairs as soon as Miss Ladore had left to go to Signora Benassi. Mark was waiting in the outer courtyard, in his blazer and a necktie. It was, after all, an occasion. He took both of her hands.

"Ready?" He put a lot of meaning in the single word.

She nodded. "I had a message from Uncle Wesley to come and have dinner with him and the Davenports, but I called and said I wouldn't do it. I said I'd brought a pizza home and was going to eat it cold while I packed. They're going somewhere expensive over on the other bank."

"Then we'll eat on this one," Mark said. "And it'll be as expensive as I can afford."

"Don't be silly. We'll split the bill."

"Not tonight," he said.

They found a trattoria where they could sit outside. Mark was subdued, though he did everything he could to be nice. Laurie was quiet too. Both felt the effect of its being their last night together in Florence, and maybe for a long time thereafter—and it wasn't just Mark who wondered what would happen before they separated. After dinner they walked through the city, looking at the Cathedral, at the various shop windows, at other churches, at the sculpture and fountains, all the things they'd been seeing every day together. Walked and walked, and talked about everything but tomorrow.

Until, that is, it was almost eleven o'clock, and they were in the square in front of the Foundlings Hospital. Mark said, "When'll I hear from you?"

"I'll write from Milan or Venice, where we go next."

"When will I see you?"

"When I don't have Miss Ladore on my hands."

"That could be a long time." Mark started them moving back toward the center of the city. "I hate to see you go."

"I know," Laurie said.

"What does that mean?"

"It means I'm sorry to be going."

"Then why can't you say it?"

"I just did."

There was a little impatience in his voice when he said, "You realize we've been walking all over this city tonight, holding hands and feeling heartbeats and going in for a lot of silent communication, just as if we were lovers. But we aren't lovers."

"Yes, I know that, too."

"Why aren't we lovers?"

"How am I supposed to answer that?"

"Being with you sometimes, Laurie, is like being with a girl I've just had a fight with, who's freezing me out. Only we don't ever argue about anything. Maybe we'd do better if we did—but not tonight."

"No," she said quietly. "Not tonight."

Mark frowned, and suddenly sped them up. "We're going back to the villa now. We'll go to my rooms. And we're going to talk about us. I've got wine—there'll be the tinkle of glasses into the small hours—which was what Signora Benassi promised me, or I wouldn't have moved in."

Laurie said, "All right. But it gives me funny feelings. I mean, Miss Ladore and all the others right upstairs."

"Signora Benassi also promised me nobody can hear," Mark said.

When they got to Villa Arberoni, the door beyond the elevator, which led into the corridor, was closed. Unusual. Mark's key would unlock it, but it required a lot of fiddling, and the noise might, even at this hour, bring Antonio out. Instead they walked to the front of the building, crossed the gardens at the foot of the terrace stairs, and went into Mark's rooms by way of the far outside door.

He turned on a lamp while he poured two glasses of wine, then turned it off again. The only light came from the moon. Laurie sat in the comfortable chair, Mark on the floor beside her. He leaned his head against her left thigh and closed a hand around her left ankle. He looked straight ahead.

"I have to tell you," he said slowly, "it's never happened to me before, to like a girl as much as I like you and not have her like me as much back." He rotated the hand.

"Does it bother you a lot?"

He ran his finger up over her calf, but that was all. "I suppose it depends on how it turns out."

"How do you know whether you *do* like me more than I do you unless we know for sure how much you do *like* me?" she said dreamily. "Good wine."

"From the Valtellina," he said. "Up north. It's better than the wine we have at meals here, I think—which Tiberio makes. I like you lots." He waited for a possible reciprocation; then, when none was forthcoming, he asked, "Have you ever been in love?" He could feel Laurie's head move, through her leg, but couldn't see. "Was that a nod?" Another movement, which he guessed at. "What was he like?"

"You really want me to tell you?"

"If it's over."

"It is. He was crazy. He'd been through everything—all the drugs. He ended up getting a job with a man who raises goats and sells the milk to people like my father, who's a health-food nut. His name was Lewis. Lewis the milkman—only he was nineteen at the time. Strange. Couldn't stand still or sit still."

"How about lie still?"

"He wasn't good at that, either. Actually, he was even restless when he was asleep. Twitched a lot—like a sleeping dog. Ground his teeth. Probably he'd blown part of his central nervous system—I never knew. But he was different from the other boys I'd known. They were more like you."

Mark's hand, which had continued active on her ankle, stopped. "I can't help it if you know nice guys."

"Lewis wasn't nice. But something about him got to me."

"How'd you do it? I mean, where do you go to make love with a goat-milk delivery boy? Not in the truck, I guess."

"I saw him sometimes at night, at his room at the dairy, and also he planned stopovers at the house when I'd be the only one home—both my mother and father work, and I was in my last year at Gaucher and didn't want to live in a dormitory, so I was living at the house. My mother found out about it one day when she came home sick. She had a fit. She's very conventional. So conventional she's boring—I told you she approves of Uncle Wesley. My father is unconventional, but he's boring too. It's hard to choose between them."

"I wish we'd talked about this before. Why didn't we?"

"Why waste the gardens outside on talk like this?"

"It's no waste," Mark said sharply. Then he asked, "What happened to Lewis?"

"He got fired."

"I mean, what happened between you and him?"

"It stopped being satisfactory."

"Any others?"

"One or two. Not like him, though. He made me hurt for him. He was really screwed up."

"I'm not," Mark said. "I'm really not."

"I know."

"Do you hold it against me?"

"I don't know. I could."

"Do you want to hear about the girls I've been in love with?"

"I don't think so. No, I don't."

"Good. I'm tired of talking." Mark turned his head sideways. He pressed his lips against Laurie's knee, right where her skirt ended, then, with his free hand, pushed the skirt up a little and followed its hem with his mouth. "I could so easily fall in love with you," he said. "I mean, almost as crazy in love as that other guy. Please. Let's. Now. See how it goes. It might make a difference."

He rose to his knees, put his head in Laurie's lap for a moment and inhaled the smell of her, then got to his feet and drew her to hers and took her in his arms. He wanted to be sure he knew what was happening, to her, to him, to them, before he stopped all thinking, but he couldn't figure out exactly what was. Laurie still seemed undecided. Willing, yet undecided—he sensed that. He moved his hands behind her and drew her forward, and she began to relax. He could feel it. It was going to be all right, after all. They'd make love, and make peace with each other, and plan things.

"I'm going to get you happy if I can," he said. "That's all I want to do."

"Shhh," she said.

Some kind of commotion started up outside. Voices. Then all the lights in the garden came on.

"My God! What's that?" Laurie said, pulling back.

"Who cares? Come on." He tugged on her hand. "Let's go to the bedroom."

"But listen, Mark. Something's gone wrong. It could have to do with Miss Ladore—she hasn't gotten over her cold. Go look out of the window and see what's happening."

"When'll you stop worrying about her?" Mark said angrily.

"Go see, Mark. Please. What if someone starts knocking on doors, looking for me?"

"Jee-sus!" Mark went to the window of the sitting room, but he couldn't see much because of the shrubbery. "Come on to the bedroom window. I'll hold you up so you can see too." He went next door. "I hear a woman's voice. Someone I don't know. And I hear Antonio, I think. Yeah. There he is, coming down from the parking lot on the path on this side. And there's someone crossing down by the fountain. A woman. You know what? I think it must be James Molyneux's cousin, just arriving. That's who it is. Antonio closed the door up near his end of the corridor so that when she arrived I wouldn't be bothered by the noise, but she's managing to make it sound like the President of Italy is arriving. Probably has lots of luggage—there goes Antonio's oldest son, carrying some more of it."

Mark became aware not only that Laurie hadn't come to join him, but that she wasn't saying anything. "Laurie? *Laurie?*" Silence. "Oh *no!*" He ran to the sitting room.

Empty. The door was open. So was the nearby door from the corridor into the garden. He ran outside, but she'd disappeared. Where? He ran a short distance down into the garden, but if she'd gone that way, he'd have seen her from the window. He turned around, and of course the other gate, that led from the parking area on James side of the villa, was open so Antonio could carry luggage through it. Laurie must have gone through the back lot around to the main vestibule. Mark followed her, sprinting as fast as he ever had in his life.

Iris Siswick had had dinner with Hamilin Rees, her piano instructor, at his house near Impruneta. He'd had his other pupils, too—he had four scattered around the area that spring. He gave them tuna fish and shells, and not much else except a monologue, quite up to the standards of John Battle Davenport, on his experience as an accompanist for several operatic stars when he was younger, and how it had turned him against all sloppy musical method and led him to devise the clean, spare pedagogy he now espoused so unyeildingly. Iris waited until she was the last to go, then told him about Signora Benassi's birthday party, and that she was going to play Chopin.

"No," he said. "Absolutely not."

"But, Mr. Rees, please make an exception. I'll need your coaching."

He went around, pouring whatever was left in the different wine glasses into his own. He drank.

"Think of what we've been doing together as if it were a psychoanalysis, Iris. You're the patient, I'm the doctor. We made a pact: you'd follow my method and obey the rules I set up. Suppose you had some unfortunate disorder—nymphomania or whatever—and asked for one night's exception to its proscription. I'd say no. One fall from chastity, I'd say, will ruin months or years of work; that's how psychoanalysis achieves its results. Flexible where flexibility is indicated, rigid where the situation calls for rigidity. I will not give you permission to play at this ridiculous party if your landlady won't have Haydn."

"That's too bad," Iris said. "I'm going to play for Signora Benassi, whether you agree to it or not."

Rees coiled like a small, dangerous snake. "If you do, then your therapy is at an end."

Iris had enough courage to point out, "I believe I said so first."

"You're fully aware of what you're doing? You know I don't relent. I don't forgive."

"I'll not want it—your forgiveness," she said.

Scornfully he motioned her toward the door. "Thank God you've done it. I've rarely had a pupil less talented in searching out the profounder meanings of things. You can run a scale, all right, but nobody ever said that was music. My advice to you is to sell hats. And don't think you'll get away without paying my last bill."

Iris burst into tears and ran for her car.

She kept herself more or less under control on the drive home, but her life looked fairly grim to her. She'd got out of one thing, but had no other to take its place. She couldn't go home—she really had no home to go to, since her father had remarried. She was close to despair when she parked behind the villa—surprising how all the lights were on back there!—and went to the entrance. She stopped to look at herself in the mirror before the climb to her floor.

Mark came in. When she saw him, her shyness left her for once, and she ran to him and put her arms around him, and he quickly put his around her. Crying again, she told him what had happened.

"That's too bad, Iris," he said gently.

"At least it's over now and I know where I stand."

"And that's good." He moved his hands over her back, comforting her. Then, very carefully, he pushed her away. He didn't want any misunderstanding that might lead her into further hurts. "Iris, did you see Laurie?"

"Where would I have seen Laurie?"

"Maybe when you came in. I guess she'd already gone up in the elevator. Shit!" He turned to the wall and slammed a hand against it. "*Shit!*"

Iris, perplexed, said, "What's the matter?"

"The matter? I'll tell you what the matter is. You've had a fight with your piano teacher and lost him. I just *didn't* have a fight with my girl, but I've lost her anyway. I've had enough for one night, Iris. We'll talk some more tomorrow."

He walked back out of the villa to his own room, using the front way, just as Antonio was coming in from the studio. They wished each other good night.

Iris, all tears now, over yet another defeat, went upstairs to her music cabinet, took the sonatas of Haydn, and threw them into the bottom of her closet. Then she unwrapped the copy of the nocturnes of Chopin she'd bought only that day. It was late, but she didn't care. She carried the music down to the drawing room and opened it to the Nocturne in B from Opus 62. She began to play. After a while, all thoughts of Hamilin Rees and of Mark, and indeed of everything but the magical line of ornament being traced by her right hand, were driven from her mind. Music hadn't failed her after all, only Hamilin Rees and Haydn.

As Costanza was preparing Signora Benassi's bedroom, she saw Mark and Laurie cross in front of the villa. When, after a while, there was a great racket downstairs and out in the gardens, she looked out again and saw the arrival of Hilda Molyneux, which Signora Benassi had been warned of only at nine o'clock that night, by telephone. A moment later, Laurie darted into the gardens far over to the right, then turned and ran in the other direction. After a bit, Mark did the same thing. Some minutes later, Mark crossed in front of the villa alone, despondently kicking gravel off the path. When the signora came into her bedroom, Costanza told her all that she'd seen, and said it was too bad.

"But," she said, "I'm sure Mr. Stapleton will try again."

"Miss Walker leaves tomorrow, Costanza."

"Villa Arberoni has worked its magic on them, as the contessa always put it. He'll try again somewhere else."

"What a romantic person you are. Magic, indeed!" said Signora Benassi, then asked a question she'd never cared to ask Costanza before. "Did my mother ever refer to this place as Villa Aphrodite?"

Costanza continued to look out of the window as, one by one, the lights went off, except for those in the studio. "Only once, when the furniture was delivered, on the first anniversary of her connection with the Belgian prince. It was moved in, you know, while she was away. She returned, and there it was. He wasn't in Florence, either; it was a gift given from a distance. That night, when she lay down for the first time on the bed that was later stolen by the Germans for that fat general—"

"Goering. They told me I was 'lending' it to him."

"Yes. She lay on it in her negligee and said to me, 'In this bed, you know, I do feel like the goddess of love, being wafted across the seas to that island she landed on.' You remember the bed had all those snail shells and flowers, Signora Benassi. 'It would serve them right, the gossips who call it so, if I renamed this house Villa Aphrodite.' That was the only time she ever said it—at least to me. What a loss it was, that beautiful bed."

"It'll turn up one day, though you and I may not know about it."

"There. Mr. Stapleton has come out of his rooms again. He's walking up and down—a young man in the throes of lovesickness. But—the game is over for tonight, I think." Costanza drew the draperies.

The next morning, Miss Ladore and Laurie left the villa at nine o'clock; they and Wesley would stop off in Bologna for a little sightseeing and for lunch, then continue on north. Mark didn't appear to say good-bye. When she realized he wasn't going to, Laurie wrote him a note.

Dear Mark,

I know I played a really mean trick on you last night, and I'm sorry about it. I would have come back downstairs after I had a chance to think it over, but unfortunately Miss Ladore was still up and wanted to tell me about her evening, and I couldn't leave. Forgive me for it. I'm not usually like that. I may have my problems, but being a tease isn't one of them, usually. I'll write you and I hope you'll answer.

How to sign it? She decided on her name only. She couldn't just say 'yours,' because she liked Mark too much. But 'love' might be more than she wanted to say. As the car went along the *autostrada* toward Bologna, Laurie felt discontented and dissatisfied, with herself and the world, and was very short with her uncle, and wasn't all that nice to Miss Ladore. Miss Ladore noticed and worried and wondered what had gone wrong, after all she herself had done to make it go right.

PART

seven

PART

SEVEN

Mark lost interest in Florence overnight. On Friday, when he went into the city after Laurie had left, he compared it unfavorably, with respect to air pollution and congestion, to San Diego. The Duomo was a barn, the Ghiberti doors to the baptistry fussy and hard to see. If the Campanile, made of pink and white and green frosting, were built in Forest Lawn Cemetery in Los Angeles, snobbish people would make fun of it. Even Santo Spirito, when, despondent, he revisited it to try to recapture some of his earlier excitement, seemed to him a monotonous boneyard of skinny gray columns.

He gave it up and went swimming. He avoided an invitation to join James Molyneux on a trip to Fiesole that afternoon, and that night went off alone to the same trattoria where he'd had dinner with Laurie, and he spent Saturday alone, too. He almost cut Saturday-night dinner, bored by the thought of James and his endless analyses of things and people, bored by Signora Benassi's talk about her birthday party, bored by the urbane and ironic Ricky, so predictable—except for the theft of the silver. He had no interest left in Iris—a loser, just like him—or in the Davenports, who turned meals at the villa into a curriculum. Even the idea of meeting someone new—Hilda Molyneux—bored him. She could only be more of the same, someone else who lived a life that was off on the edge of the real world, where people spent their time worrying about perfection in small things because they hadn't any big things to worry them. Precious, all of them, and all of it bored him.

Yet he had to stay for a few days. Laurie had promised to write as soon as she got to Milan. She deserved a kick in the ass; still, he was curious to know what she'd say.

He kept thinking of one sentence from her note: "I have my problems, but being a tease isn't one of them." The hell it wasn't! And somebody ought to tell her so.

He did go to the regular Saturday-night dinner at the villa—he was paying for it anyway—and he did meet Hilda Molyneux. And she was, it turned out, different. Her body was big and voluptuous and required a lot of space around it; she elbowed even John Battle Davenport into less than his share of the table. She singled Mark out to talk to, and over coffee she asked him to pose for her—only portraits, she said—until she found a permanent model. She'd pay for it—a good wage, it seemed to him, for doing nothing.

James, whom Mark had scarcely spoken to, interrupted. "Is it, I wonder, the best way to spend the time you have left with us, Mark? And do you really think you'll relish it?" he asked.

"How do I know?"

Hilda said, "Of course he will. It's fun for most people to be drawn, Cousin James, though you so dislike it. It's the highest form of attention there is, and attention has endless appeal, as you know perfectly well."

James looked long and hard at her, until she tilted back her head and laughed, more loudly than Mark had heard anyone laugh in these rooms before; Pauline Davenport looked grimly at her, while Signora Benassi, who was talking to a guest of the Davenports, paused in mid-sentence until the sound died down.

When Mark got to the studio the next morning at ten o'clock, he found it considerably changed from the day he'd gone in with James to get Hilda's camera. At that time her drawings had been neatly stacked in piles, or filed away in one of her large bins, or in portfolios, and her sculptural projects had all been put back against the wall and covered with old sheets. The pillows had been neatly lined up on the daybed against the wall, and the chairs placed in careful arrangement around the coffee table in front of it. No clothes had been in evidence, and the curtains were drawn. All that had been turned into disorder in only thirty-six hours, as Hilda righted for habitation the order she'd created before she left for America some months before. The chairs were pushed into new places; one of them faced a wall so it couldn't be used at all. The tables were covered with dirty ashtrays and a couple of coffee cups and boxes of pastels and charcoal, as well as loose crayons and pens and pencils. She'd moved forward two pedestals that had half-finished clay figures on them, vaguely visible through their swaddlings of plastic wrap, put on to conserve their moisture. And she'd unhooked the front curtains and taken them off their rods. Privacy was no problem: she had one screen she could pull to block the windows, and another to close off the alcove where her bed was placed, in the rear anyway. The studio had been transformed into a place where someone worked.

She was very businesslike. "Oh, hello, Mark. That's for you to sit on." She pointed to a solitary, straight-backed wooden chair.

He watched her get out paper and thumbtack it onto a board. Then she came over to him and moved his head so he was looking partly into the room but could also see a little of the gardens, down the crosswalk toward the fountain; the window began almost at the floor and ran eight feet up the side of the building.

She didn't talk much, once she got started, just looked and drew, looked and drew, occasionally rubbed something out, and drew some more. Mark could have been a pile of apples or a pitcher of sunflowers. It was a strange feeling, not exactly pleasant; certainly it didn't feel like the highest form of attention. After a while she got up and moved around. She didn't look at Mark, but he could follow her most of the time with his eyes, without changing the position of his head, which she'd warned him not to do.

She resembled James more this morning than she had the night before, when she'd had on makeup. She had his dark coloring and dark eyes; the skin under her arms, when she pushed up the loose sleeves of her smock, was smoky. But Hilda was full of a physical force very different from James's nervous energy. When she was ready to do a new drawing, she said gruffly, "Get up," then lifted the chair with one hand and tossed it along the floor to another place about six feet away. When she got coffee for herself, she banged the pot on her little electric burner, and clattered the cup and saucer as if she'd like to break them. Altogether, and in this utterly unlike James, she seemed to have little respect for things.

She crumpled up and threw away the first drawing without showing it to Mark. When she'd finished the second, she brought it over. "Not very good, is it?" she said. "I'm out of practice. We'll change your pose again and do another, then I'll let you rest."

This went on all morning. Mark got bored with posing, too, but it did turn out to have one great interest—Hilda was right; he got to see himself after each essay. She did seven, all told, and two of them weren't bad, she thought. She didn't ask him to come back in the afternoon, but did tell him to come on Monday morning, same time, and he agreed to do so.

She paid him cash on the spot. "Am I worth it?" he asked, as he shoved the lire notes in his billfold.

Hilda wore her dark, luxurious hair pulled up over her head when she worked—last night it had hung down her back, drawn through an ivory ring—and when Mark had arrived at the studio, it had been wrapped in a bright blue kerchief. But she'd long since pulled the kerchief off, and strands had tended to straggle as she was moving around so energetically. She pushed them out of the way and smiled at his question. "That remains to be seen," she said. "All models aren't."

James Molyneux, on Friday morning, had made a point of going down to the vestibule of the villa to see Laurie Walker and Miss Ladore off, and was surprised when Mark didn't show up too. But perhaps, having said good-bye to them already, he'd gone on one of his early-morning athletic jaunts. James put a note of his own beside the one Laurie had left for Mark, suggesting they might go to Fiesole that afternoon, if it turned out to be convenient, and that Mark should get in touch with him if he was interested. When, by four o'clock, he hadn't heard anything, James went downstairs to see if Mark had ever got the note.

Yes. It was missing from the table. James asked Antonio if he happened to know when Signor Marco had come in, and whether he'd gone out again. Antonio said he'd come back once to get his swimming suit late that morning, then had come in after lunch, and he'd gone out again just a little while ago.

Wasn't that a bit strange, considering that they'd become daily companions? Strange that Mark, if he didn't want to climb to James's floor, hadn't even telephoned up on Antonio's line to say he couldn't make Fiesole? Of course, James had said, "if you're interested"—a mistake. Mark might have thought the invitation lower-key than it was intended to be. Still, it seemed distant. Inconsiderate. Indifferent. James began to worry, not much, but enough. And, almost in spite of himself, and certainly knowing better than to let it begin, he started to keep track.

He and Hilda had an early dinner nearby on Friday evening; she was still worn out from her plane and automobile trip. After they'd separated, she to go to the studio, James asked Antonio again about Mark. He'd gone off to dinner. By himself? Yes. James thanked Antonio—he couldn't keep asking questions of him so directly, but for today it had probably been all right. That night James was awake, his mind in a state of threatening clarity, until almost three o'clock, then, on Saturday morning, he couldn't sleep. He awakened at six-thirty, restless, feeling almost ill, and apprehensive; if one day of Mark's absence could do this, he was really in for it. He read for a while in bed. Couldn't concentrate. Got some tea. Left it to get cold in its mug. Tried to resist temptation. Eventually he couldn't. He went downstairs, where he found Antonio in the courtyard, watering the lemon trees. James reminded him of the time they'd got some kind of scale, just at this season, too. Antonio put down the hose, and he and James looked the trees over, carefully—Antonio, a countryman, didn't have too much use for Signora Benassi's city gardener. Only after they'd concluded there was nothing wrong with the trees this year did James quite casually say how lonely it seemed at the villa without the two American ladies. Had Signor Marco found something to do to keep him busy today?

Antonio glanced at him, a little surprised—it wasn't a question he'd usually have been asked. Signor Marco had gone away just a little while ago, he said, carrying his swimming suit again.

James nodded and sauntered out into the gardens. He thought of going to the public pool down on the Arno, just to see Mark and reaffirm that he existed, but what would he say to explain why he was there, if Mark saw him?—he who never put on a swimming suit except when there was nobody else around, when he was alone on a beach at dawn or had Hans's cold mountain pool all to himself.

Velia's last act, on Saturday afternoon, before she left for her two days off, was to bring fresh towels around. When she came to

James's rooms, about four o'clock, he talked a little to her: Where would she be going tomorrow? Church. Which parish did she belong to? She mentioned one in the suburbs which James had never heard of. James then said, casually, that he planned to go up to Fiesole in the morning; it would be a nice day for an excursion, he thought. He'd asked Signor Marco to go on Friday, but he couldn't—maybe tomorrow would be better for him. He hadn't seen Signor Marco in a couple of days and wondered what he might be up to. Velia, who, after years of trying, still had trouble understanding James's very good Italian, was the last person in the world who was likely to know where Mark might have gone. She had no curiosity about people; also, she was so simple she rarely remembered anything for more than ten minutes. To have dropped the question to her was itself an embarrassment. But, for a wonder, she happened to know the answer. Signor Marco had been going out when she took him his towels, she said, repeating herself several times so James would understand. He'd said something about—she searched her memory—Piazzale Michelangelo.

Where he'd gone his first afternoon, before he'd come to have tea with James. Mark was revisiting things, then—which would be a preparation for his leaving. The thought of that made James feel bleak and left out. He simply couldn't, not now, stay in his rooms.

He caught a bus that took him, with a change, up to the hill above the city, but he didn't go into the piazzale, whose monstrous oversize reproduction of the Michelangelo *David* and general vulgarity and crowds were an offense, and where Mark would be as surprised by an encounter, almost, as he would have been yesterday at the public swimming pool. Instead, James climbed the road that led toward the church of San Miniato. He would wait there, on one of the benches, and read the newspaper he'd brought with him. Surely, if anything he'd been teaching Mark had taken, he would all reverently visit San Miniato. It would be a test.

Half an hour later James saw him, coming toward the church by a different route, by the stairs. Mark was eating an ice cream cone, which struck James as an act of unbridled innocence. To approach San Miniato with a cone in your hand—that was truly pre-Fall. After Mark went inside, James sat a few minutes longer, imagining the familiar interior, took Mark to the chapel of the Cardinal of Portugal and gazed with him at the Antonio Rossellino tomb, marveling at its serenity. Then, quieted if not content, he folded his newspaper and returned to the villa.

He wasn't too troubled by the way Hilda overwhelmed Mark on Saturday night—not even, really, by her invitation to Mark to model for her—he was rather glad she had a target other than himself until she'd calmed down a little from her post-travel excitement, when she was always at her worst. And on Sunday morning, James didn't have to wonder. He knew precisely where Mark was—at the studio—though when he was on his way in from the central post office, where he'd gone to make his long-distance call to Hans, James did go into the gardens and look down the long cross-alley to make sure. Yes, Mark was there. James could see him, sitting by the window; it was so like Hilda to let the whole world know what went on. James then pushed a message under Mark's door, asking him for supper.

He'd gone to the post office to call Hans, just in case the Italian authorities might be tapping his own telephone line—improbable as it was, it would be the easiest thing for them to do if their curiosity was really aroused, as Battsie had hinted it might be. He'd got Hans at his place outside Griesen, not far from the Zugspitze, and after James had told him the latest developments with the Center for Renaissance Studies, they'd talked about how to get the drawing into Germany. Hans had a new plan. He would drive to Milan and stay at the Hotel Il Moro. James should come up secretly by train—perhaps take a local to Prato, then change to an express, to avoid being followed. Bring the drawing with him and put it in a locker at the train station in Milan, then come by the hotel and give Hans the key. Hans would go and collect it in a taxi and take it back to Munich. Hans had a busy schedule for the coming week, so they agreed to execute his plan a week from Tuesday. Relieved that James had raised no objections, though it meant he had to go back and forth to Milan, Hans remarked that he was happier to be doing it this way. It was better, he said, than to entrust the drawing to someone who didn't know what he was carrying.

"And speaking of that, how are things going with your new friend, Jimmy?"

"I don't know. I haven't seen him, at least not to talk to, in several days."

"Not to talk to?"

"I followed him this afternoon to San Miniato. He didn't know."

"That's a bad sign, Jimmy. Well, you have my hope—and love. And remember, we want you to come and stay with us."

"I think I may need both your hope and your love, and perhaps also your invitation," James said.

Something was wrong. Primed as he was, James knew it within seconds of the time Mark got to his rooms. Mark didn't look at him in the old way. Bewildered, panicky, James was too grateful for the bottle of wine Mark had brought with him. Then, "Supper's bread and a cold Italian omelette and squid salad and cheese and fruit," James said. "Will that be enough?" Mark nodded. Didn't even flinch at the squid. Lest there be silences, James was driven as they ate to give a really quite brilliant summary of all they'd seen together, a monologue about everything in Florence from Giotto to Leonardo and beyond, though he knew perfectly well he ought to have shut up, that another silence is sometimes the first's worst enemy. It was a disaster. Mark hardly bothered to pretend to be listening, and actually refused to answer one or two direct questions when James asked them. Nothing like it had happened in all the days they'd gone places together. Nothing quite like it had happened to James in years.

"I thought . . . thought you'd come further since Santo Spirito than it seems you have," James said, sick at heart. Desperate, he changed the subject. "How'd your modeling go?"

"All you have to do is sit there."

"As, apparently, here." James's smile was thin. "Sometimes, perhaps, a little more," he suggested. "There, I mean. Cousin Hilda's really quite good. I shouldn't wonder but that she'll give you a drawing of yourself before you leave—she usually does. Have you any idea when that'll be?"

"Sometime later in the week."

"And then come back for the Palio and again for the birthday party?" Mark nodded indifferently. James couldn't stop himself from trying: "I should like to go to the Palio with you—I've had it on my mind. That's why I didn't propose we go to Siena with Miss Ladore. We'll do Siena together, as we've done Florence. It's narrower—and for that reason has both its special refinements and unexpected reaches."

Mark nodded again—non-committal. James could stand it no longer. "Whatever in the world's the matter with you?" he said. "Don't you want to see Siena with me?" Mark looked unhappy—which didn't answer James's question one way or another. "I have to say I feel insulted."

Mark said, "You shouldn't. It's not Siena, James, it's . . ." he began, but broke off, gave it up, and that made things worse. He needed to talk to someone about Laurie; she was a subject he and James shared that he could have shown an interest in this evening, but, though he might have told James about a lot of things, Laurie didn't seem to be one of them. There'd be no reason to expect much sympathy, or any good advice, not because James was gay, but because Mark's problem with Laurie was too simple and straightforward for James's methods. To try to make James feel better, Mark used the worst of excuses. "Maybe I'm catching the cold Dr. Knuckles had. I feel a little under the weather."

James said, "You don't look it, and if you are, you shouldn't go swimming so often."

"How did you know?"

"How? Oh—Antonio mentioned it," James said evasively. "Speaking of going places, I was rather wondering if we shouldn't try Fiesole."

"I never did answer your note, did I? I was in a hurry, I guess."

"But—tomorrow?"

"I'll be modeling for Hilda again."

"You should, you know, give priority to completing your Florentine experience."

"I've already promised her."

James slowly put down his napkin and fork. "Which amounts, I suppose, to assigning another priority."

When Mark got up to help carry dishes to the bathroom sink, he noticed Hilda's drawing on the wall. "That wasn't here before," he said.

"It's one of Hilda's. You'll recognize it—I hope—as a parody of the *Madonna della Sedia*. I'm taking it to Milan in about a week—meeting a friend there from Munich, who's a dealer. Only about ten years older than you, but he's made a great success of his gallery."

"You mean you're going all that way, just to take him this one drawing?"

"Well, yes, more or less. I'm hoping he'll have an exhibition of her work. We're splitting the travel."

"Why don't I take it to Milan for you? Or to Munich, as far as that goes, if your friend is coming down just for it? I'm planning to see Munich."

"No, no," James said. "You'll have enough to carry."

"But I don't. Almost everything's in a backpack, so my arms are free."

"Your arms? Yes, of course. Well, but my friend's got it all arranged."

"Think it over," Mark insisted. "Seriously, I'd really like to do it."

James gave way a little; the offer of this small favor was at least better than Mark's former indifference. "It would only make sense if you went directly there. I mean, right through."

"That's what I plan to do."

"If you perhaps feel you owe me some slight debt, in return for . . . Brunelleschi, it would save me an unpleasant trip."

Mark lifted the drawing off the wall. Not too heavy, though it did have glass on it. "Easy," he said.

"You'd like my friend Hans," James said. "He's an athlete, like you. Still wins amateur skiing competitions. I met him here in Florence, quite by chance. We were both at San Miniato—something you should see, Mark, if you haven't. Have you?"

"I was up there this afternoon—for the first time."

"Were you? And what did you think of the chapel?"

"The chapel? I didn't see any chapel. I didn't have a guidebook with me, so I didn't know what to look for. All that marble inlay up in front is nice, though you can't help but think how much work it must have been for somebody."

"Better to think how beautiful it is. So—you walked right by the chapel and didn't notice it. That rather defies credibility. Hans was looking at the chapel; it has one of the finest of all fifteenth-century wall tombs in it—of a young cardinal whose countenance is so pure it purifies even the pomp of his robes— among other things. But—never mind." James, to show his disappointment, took away the chance of Mark's errand. "I doubt that it will work out, about the drawing. I'm sure, now that I think of it, that Hans has many reasons to come to Milan, and for me it's always a treat to see him, even if it takes a train ride."

Mark said, "Well, the offer stands." He put the picture back on the wall, and started to continue onward with the dishes, but he saw something else he hadn't seen before, in the corner, on a stout triangular table: a bronze statuette, the nude torso of a young male, about a foot tall.

James said, "Also by Hilda. I was wondering if you'd notice it. Of her former husband. I don't terribly like it, as a matter of fact—it's really too literal; her work's improved quite a lot since she did it—and usually put it away when she's out of town. She did it for me—which was too bad, since I had to take it whether I liked it or not." He added after a pause, unnecessarily, for Mark had surely guessed about all that already, "The male nude is one of her specialties."

"Times have changed, haven't they?" Mark said.

James came to the studio the next day while Mark was posing for another series of portraits. He watched for a few minutes, then asked Hilda if she didn't have something he could use to carry a framed drawing; he was arranging to get the one he'd just asked her to give him up to Munich. She interrupted herself to dig down into a big chest, in which she found a canvas satchel, shaped like a huge envelope, with a flap that came over the top and tied on the other side. "Perfect," James said. "Just what may be wanted."

He hesitated at the door, said, "I'll have to make sure the drawing will fit, of course," and left suddenly.

When he was safely out of earshot, Hilda remarked, "Checking up."

"On what?"

She said, "What do you think?" She smiled and answered her own question. "On how my work is going."

There was no letter from Laurie that day. But then it was Monday, and she'd only left on Friday. And no telephone call—not that Mark expected one, for she hadn't suggested it. He stayed on another day, most of which he spent posing; Hilda now had a dozen fair portraits of him, and the fun was going out of that, too. No letter that day, either.

On Wednesday he got up early and went running. When he came back, he went into the garden to the circle by the fountain, where there were some areas of grass kept green by watering. He did some exercises and, just for fun, some tumbling—leaps and somersaults and handstands. Hilda saw him at it and came out of her studio, dressed in a bright yellow and black striped robe that eddied around her legs and sandaled feet. Something he'd never seen her in—usually she wore cotton knickers and her cotton smock that came down to above her knees. Her dark hair was unrestrained, and fell all around her shoulders.

"I'm impressed by what you can do. You've a beautiful body, Mark. Don't change for our morning session. Come as you are. I'll do figure studies of you."

Mark, who was sitting on the grass, looked up at her, panting. "I'm pretty sweaty," he said.

She shrugged. "If you're too modest . . ." She turned—he blinked when the robe brushed against his face—and strode back into the studio, the stripes billowing out behind her as if she were walking into a wind machine.

Mark did shower. Then he put on his other pair of shorts, which were clean, and went to her that way. She had him pose both seated and—this turned out to be lots harder work—standing. Standing still and not moving, for half an hour at a time. He commented on the small bronze of her husband he'd seen in

James's room. After that, she made an occasional remark about Harry Guest and her divorce, all the while doing a series of pen-and-ink drawings of the whole Mark.

"Watch your head, Mark. You lowered the tilt of your chin—by quite a lot. Modeling, you know, takes a certain kind of negative concentration."

"I don't think it's possible not to move," Mark said. "A person's body changes, just with the passage of small amounts of time. Watch someone who's taken a position on the—"

"Of course, of course. It's a question of tolerable limits." Hilda worked on. "People change more than their poses, you know. I just loved my husband Harry in the morning. He was so innocent-looking when he woke up, you wanted to take a towel and wipe the dew off his face."

"How about later in the day?"

"You looked at that towel and wondered."

She hummed to herself a little—probably a song with some personal meaning. Then: "Another thing that went wrong—he found me too bohemian."

"What does that mean?" Mark asked.

"That I wasn't altogether faithful."

Mark laughed at the "altogether," and tried to see what kind of expression she had on her face.

"Don't roll your eyes to look at me—you'll almost inevitably change your angle when you do. Being faithful is a really tricky business, I mean particularly since Harry worked in Milan and I lived down here—except on weekends."

"I guess you're either faithful or you're not," Mark said.

"Of course, neither was he—altogether. In more ways than one."

And later she said, "I'm missing Harry too much. I may have made a mistake."

When they took a break—she was now giving Mark coffee whenever he wanted it, a favor she'd not shown him when he was only posing for his portrait—he sat on a stool, and she came over and stretched out on the daybed close to him, her head against the pillows, her feet thrust out on the floor; Hilda was tall. She gave him her cup to put on a table, then clasped her hands behind her head.

"One important difference: I wasn't jealous of Harry," she said. She lay there, relaxed and thoughtful. "Funny, because I was older than he was—he was only twenty-five when we were married, and I was thirty-five—and that usually is supposed to mean lots of jealousy, for the woman. It didn't work that way—but then I never had any real doubts about him. I knew he'd come back, and he always did. So did I, but he had doubts. Not that we really fought, except over the studio here. He couldn't stand the mess and insisted, when he came for weekends, on staying at the villa, or in a hotel if Signora Benassi didn't have any room. I thought it probably confused the servants—except for Costanza, who's seen everything at least once before. Now we'll go back to work, and you can tell me about yourself. It won't bother me, your talking, as long as you don't take deep breaths or begin to paw the ground."

Mark started in on California, but she stopped him. "Tell me the important things," she said. "For instance, do you like boys or girls? I don't even know that about you."

Mark didn't think it an amusing question. "Girls," he said shortly.

Hilda laughed at his tone of voice. "Exclusively?" she asked.

"Yes."

"Not even an occasional venture around the block? No ducks, geese, or chickens?"

He shook his head.

"Better to answer with words. Tell me about your love life, then. Do you have anybody now?" He forgot and nodded. "Stop that!" she said. "Where is she?"

Out it came, all about him and Laurie, a little modified, for reasons of pride. At the end he said, "She was in my rooms with me Thursday night when you arrived and made so much noise. She was sure something had gone wrong with Miss Ladore, so she wouldn't sleep over. Ran upstairs. I don't know when we'll see each other again." He hesitated. "It's not going just right."

"Sorry about that," Hilda said. "Does Cousin James know any of this?"

"I've never told him. I don't think he noticed anything when he was taking us sightseeing. We were pretty careful—made a good game of it—not because of him."

"Will you tell him?"

"Why should I?"

Hilda took her time answering. "Well, he'd be interested," she said. She had to brush away strands of hair from her face, and got some ink on her cheek. "And rather put out, I think. He prides himself on noticing things—if he *didn't* notice, that is. We haven't talked about you, he and I, so I don't know. I guess the moral is the more we care, the less we see—*if* he didn't."

"I'd say the opposite. When he's trying to get people to look at a building or a statue or a picture, he's absolutely wrapped up in it. I don't think he knows who he's talking to, half the time."

Hilda said, "But there is the other half."

She worked quietly for a while, then stopped and went to an album and got some snapshots from it. "Don't move. Here." She came and stood in front of Mark and showed him the pictures—of a young man, most often with her, sometimes alone, sometimes with her and James. Smiling and youthful and healthy. "Harry," she said. "Does he remind you of anybody you know?" Mark said he didn't. "How about these?" She showed him a couple more, of Harry posing in this very room, once in the nude.

"Only of that small sculpture in James's sitting room."

She laughed. "You fraud," she said. "If James hadn't told you that, you'd never have guessed. The bronze doesn't have a face or moles. You wouldn't know Harry's mole-count anyway—never having gone around the block."

When the modeling session was finished, Mark went to the vestibule to look for mail. No letter from Laurie, and it was Wednesday, which meant that she probably hadn't written him over the weekend. She knew he was leaving soon, too. He decided to give her one more day, then leave Florence, having made an arrangement with Costanza about forwarding a letter to wherever he went next. A Friday departure. He told Hilda, who asked him for dinner that night in her studio, and James, who was also going to be

239

at dinner, and of course the signora, who invited him to dinner in her private apartment on Thursday night.

James was tense, and hardly ate at all. Hilda was noisy and in a party mood, laughed a lot and drank a lot of wine. She'd put on lime-green pants that were too tight, and a blouse whose wandering magenta patterns did unusual things to her coloring—and were in deliberate defiance of good taste. When, after they'd had coffee, she knocked a glass of red wine over on the floor and simply left it there, James excused himself, and Mark, against Hilda's wishes, left with him. He didn't want to get stuck with Hilda, who was in a smoking, drinking, and talking-late mood. Before he and James parted in the vestibule, he repeated his offer to take the drawing to Munich.

James, preoccupied, said, "Oh, well, but you know, it's my idea. I shouldn't avoid the trip."

"Can't you understand that I'd like to save you the trouble of it?"

James looked sadly at him. "Yes, I understand that. And," he added, "I think I understand why."

Mark, tired of reproaches, didn't ask James what he meant.

James lay on his bed and stared at the ceiling and tried to analyze what was happening. Mark's offer about the drawing was easy: one does small, impersonal favors for those from whom one withholds greater ones—and comes to believe they are equal. James also reviewed every word of conversation he'd had with Mark during the last week, pondered all the nuances, weighed the tones and inflections. What had gone wrong? Was it Hilda? It didn't seem possible; it had started before Mark even met her. Had James said something? Nothing he could discover. A change of mood? It was far more serious than the shifts of mood that take place in old and young alike when they're about to travel. To James it was a sea-change. One day he'd had a friend, the next he'd lost him. For there was no doubt about it: the old intimacy, based on things seen and talked about, on Mark's admiration, nothing less than that, and on James's gratitude for his life and for Mark's efforts to learn—and on fondness—it was gone. Missing from Mark, on his side, and as a result, disappearing on James's side, and something far less pleasant taking its place. Preoccupation. Obsession. James simply couldn't think of anything else.

At length he got up—he'd never taken off his clothes—and went downstairs and out into the dark garden. He was without his cane; nevertheless he walked all the paths, over and over, thinking. He saw the Davenports' lights go out. He saw the signora's lights go out. He saw the lights go out in the guests' drawing room; Iris would be finished at the piano for the night. Finally—and when this happened he was standing and staring at Mark's windows, had been for five minutes—he saw Mark's lights go out. Only Hilda's remained on, in the studio.

James knocked on her door.

She'd put the leftover food in her refrigerator—she had a small one of her own out here—and she'd wiped up the wine. She'd changed into her yellow and black robe. She was looking over some of her old drawings. When James came in, she tossed them to one side, and they talked.

Eventually he had the courage to say, "Now that you know Mark Stapleton, what kind of a reading do you get of him?"

She shrugged. "Lots of animal magnetism."

"Yes, but otherwise?"

"What's 'otherwise'?" She laughed. "Whatever word you might find to put to it, Cousin James, there just isn't any 'otherwise,' when you're dealing with someone like him."

James said, "Oh, come on. Don't pretend to a grossness you don't have. I feel a change in Mark—that's why I asked you what you thought of him. An indifference. A coldness, not of my making. I'm suspended somewhere, without clues as to what's happened. I thought you might have one."

Hilda was thoughtful. "Do you blame me for it?"

"If I did, I wouldn't be here."

She knew that for many people bad news and the person who brings it are indistinguishable; better not to tell James about Mark and Laurie. Instead she said, "James, are you in love with the kid?" James nodded. "Oh God!" she said. She stamped out one cigarette and lighted another. "Really in love?" He nodded again. "Now that's a catastrophe. He isn't for you, James. Less, even,

241

you should know yourself, than Harry was. What a waste of your talent for passion. I mean it."

James described how his life had been saved. "Now do you understand that I can't help myself?"

Hilda, who, like Mark, had physical vigor, wasn't all that impressed by the feat. "Oh pooh," she said. "That's only an excuse you're making for having got yourself into something stupid. If not unseemly."

"What I feel, unseemly?" James said, in disbelief. After a moment he said, "Talking to you is never uneventful, Cousin Hilda. I suppose that's why I continue to do it, no matter what happens."

"And always will," she said. "And always will. It's your fate. Mine too."

When Mark arrived for his last session in Hilda's studio, the next morning, she surprised him by saying, "No more nonsense about those running shorts, my friend. We're going to start something serious today. I'm going to do a torso of you like the one you saw of Harry, and it'll be in the nude or not at all. So get ready."

"But I'm leaving," Mark said.

"And'll be back. I'll work on it each time you come and go. Take off your things and stand right there." She pointed to a spot fully lighted from the garden window and went to an armature to which she'd already attached lumps of clay.

Mark didn't like the idea. Shyness apart—and he felt some of that—he didn't like simply to become an inert exhibition, a man without secrets and also without will. Moreover, Hilda's bluff professional manner didn't quite convince him. She seemed to be making a greater point when she lay on her couch and pulled her arms back so her smock was pulled tight and her big breasts shoved up in the air, and when she let her legs, in those knickers that she never buttoned properly, lie open. But in the end he did what she asked. It would have made him look like a fool to refuse.

She worked long and hard, and the pose she'd put him in—his right leg forward, left one back, his weight falling on the right foot, his torso turned to one side, his right arm raised—was a difficult one to hold. Hilda knew it, and was easy on him. Repeat-

242

edly she tossed him one of her smocks and told him to stretch and move around, while she smoked or drank coffee. She also let him take his pick of the portrait drawings she'd done of him, and put it in a mat for him, so he could pin it to the wall of his sitting room, leave it there while he traveled back and forth, and if he still liked it when he was ready to go back to America, keep it—or make an exchange.

At almost one o'clock she had him strike his pose for the last time that morning; they'd be going to the buffet over in the villa at one-thirty. Hilda found fault with him. She came and lifted his left foot and moved it an inch or two backwards. And she said there'd been more tension in his waist before and manipulated his shoulders to recapture it. Then she pulled on his left arm, and turned the hand more outward. When she was finished, she ran her hand over his shoulders, like a connoisseur of horseflesh. "You have wonderful skin—it's a pity one can't capture that in clay. But I hope I can get the elasticity of it as it rides over the muscles." She touched him once more, and this time let her hand rest on his scapulars.

And then, of course, he knew where it would lead, if he kept on posing for her. His body made his knowledge known, and Hilda must have read of it, but she made no comment, and it went away.

~❧~

Shortly after James had gone into the garden, driven to make another visit to Hilda's studio, but had turned back when he looked through her window and saw Mark posed like a nude ephebe by Lysippos, he received a telephone call from Dottoressa Paonese. She was back in Florence and asked him to call on her at her office at three o'clock that afternoon. James would have been quite uneasy under any circumstances, but she'd caught him at a really bad time, when he hadn't any resilience, no reserves of courage. Unlike what was happening in Hilda's studio, this didn't have to be suffered in silence. James went to see John Davenport, but he was at the German Library. He would, however, be back for lunch.

James bided his time till lunch was almost over. Iris and Pauline had left the table. Hilda and Mark had never come, and James had imagined them, all the while Pauline was talking to Iris about their dresses for the signora's party, down in the studio, another wine glass kicked over on the floor beside the daybed, last night's cheese uncovered and hardening on a plate next to last night's anchovies, and the two of them coupling on Hilda's spread-open smock, those absurd knickers she wore pulled down around one ankle. Once he and Battsie were alone, however, James put that scene out of his mind and told about Dottoressa Paonese's call.

Battsie said, "So she's after you, is she? I was afraid of that. Someone, never mind who, has probably been feeding her tidbits of half-cracked innuendo. Hmm. So what do we do? I talked to Knuckles last night—they're on their way to Venice today, as a matter of fact. He said Miss Ladore is ready. Someone's holding something up in Texas, but she'll have final word tonight or tomorrow. It's almost certainly going to be favorable, she's more or less promised him that. Which means it would probably be all right if I ran a little interference for you, James. I'll go see Andromeda myself, after you do."

"I'm scared, John. If she decided to make me a scapegoat—and you know how such things are done in Italy out of political expedience, particularly when the government's as tottery as this one is—she wouldn't need evidence that I'd done something wrong. She could hound me out of the country merely because she wanted to—and that might be the least of it."

"Even La Paonese is human," Battsie said comfortingly. "And whoever is human has a place where, if you put your finger just right"—he poked the air to show what he meant—"you'll find a tickle spot." He had a second thought. "Except maybe Daphne Nickerson. God forbid the try, in her case; I for one wouldn't know whether to hope for failure or success. Anyway, be careful when you talk to the fair Andromeda. Admit nothing, agree with everything. And I remind you of the case of that idiot Aston-Brown, who kept phoning everyone under the sun when he had the Zannoni Titian for sale, and they'd put a tap on his telephone. Don't use yours for anything but complaints."

"Thanks for the warning, John. As a matter of fact, I'm already being careful with the phone."

"Of course, it's not as if your Raphael drawing was in this country. If *that* happened to be the case—*well!* But of course it's not—you were, after all, in Munich just last week and saw it there, eh? And of course, it *did* come from a source up north."

"Quite," James said.

"Except," said Battsie, "that source remains anonymous. Legendary, so to speak. It's not as if you belonged to Banker X or Y in Brussels or Basel. Not quite. So they can believe what they want to, and act on what they believe. Be very careful—but don't worry overly. We'll take care of you now."

James, grateful, wondered how he could ever so have undervalued Battsie.

He went to the headquarters of the Fine Arts Superintendency at the appointed hour—and how appropriate it was that it should be located on Via del Carcere, the Street of the Prison, where once, under the half-mad Alessandro, first of the Medici grand dukes, had been located the infamous building in which so many of his enemies suffered and died. James, feeling like a victim of that prince, was told to wait in an office decorated with posters of Italian monuments—the same posters one saw in trains, and at least as faded. Then he was summoned.

Dottoressa Paonese was very mild in appearance, and very plain—which made her the more formidable. She was dressed in unbecoming spring-weight knitwear and sensible shoes; indeed, one would have taken her for a bureaucrat from one of the People's Republics rather than for an Italian; she was dumpy and dowdy, like that. Her office, where she worked every afternoon—her mornings were spent at the German Library—was drab, too, not even any posters. She looked over some papers on her desk while James stood waiting. She marked them in their margins with a ballpoint pen. Then she sent him to a chair and began.

"I have asked you to come here," she said, in an Italian that was bizarre in the perfection of its diction, "because of certain information that has reached me." She paused. "Information that I"—she paused again, to underline her high moral integrity—"must take with the utmost seriousness." She looked at the papers—notes on the rather elliptical conversation she'd had with

Ettore Biscotti, during which he'd talked about books but had meant, he'd allowed her to surmise, something else. "We understand that some Americans who were recently in Florence are going to establish a Center for Renaissance Studies."

James nodded, so nervous and scared he couldn't even squeak out a reply. If this was going to end in a pounce, then he would prove to be terrified-rabbit-like in his inability to run.

"And you will be acquiring things for their library?"

James nodded again.

"Books?"

"As it is for their library—yes," he managed to say.

"Other things as well?"

"Not that I know of."

"I see. Well, it is primarily because of books that you are here. Naturally, almost no printed books are unique, and where it's a question of a book that exists in several copies, at least one and preferably two of which are in Italy, we would have no objection to an additional copy leaving the country. I am speaking of old books. But if it were unique, then we would object."

"Yes, of course. Perfectly reasonable."

"We will, therefore, expect you to be scrupulous about clearing any shipments with us that are going to this Center. If you didn't, there might be embarrassments. Let me remind you of the provisions of our national patrimony laws regarding significant cultural monuments and artifacts." She did so for ten minutes without stopping, her manner in no way becoming less stern, though her breath, by the end, became a little short. "If you conform to the procedures I've just outlined, we will be glad to cooperate. I, as an Italian, cannot help but be proud that yet another tribute to my country's civilization is about to be founded, and in a place as far away as"—she checked her notes——"Ah-bee-*lay*-nay, Texas."

"Even there, they owe Italy so much," James said.

"But," she reminded him, "if this Center becomes interested in works of art—well, you know the rules now. Be prudent, Mr. Molyneux. We have many eyes and many ears."

"Thank you. I shall certainly try to be."

As James left, Battsie came in. He winked at James and said to Dottoressa Paonese, "Ho there, Andromeda. Here's James Molyneux to see you this afternoon, too, also from Villa Aberoni. Quite the reunion, eh?"

"One wonders at the coincidence," she said.

By the time Battsie had left, there was another sheet of paper on her desk, of an interest different from the others. He'd spoken of the new Center in general terms—and had answered some more questions about its library. But he'd also spoken of the inaugural ceremonies he was already beginning to plan. If all went well, she would be asked not only to attend—that was a matter of course—but also to speak, as an expert on Arnolfo da Cambio, the most graceless sculptor of the later Middle Ages in Florence, and putative architect of the old part of the Duomo. It was Davenport's idea that the first art-historical symposium should be on architecture, so people wouldn't think he was prejudiced, and in addition to her, he also had in mind Biscotti, to talk on Alberti. As the final speaker, perhaps Coffin of Princeton—one would want to have a native son—to talk about the sixteenth-century garden. "Every symposium can use some fresh air," Battsie had said jocularly, "and the subject would please Miss Ladore." A nicely rounded sort of program. All speakers' expenses paid, of course, and a serious honorarium.

Andromeda's surface manner didn't change, though her subsurface underwent an awkward modification. She didn't, under the circumstances, want to bear down with perhaps unjustifiable harshness on the Center or its agents. On the other hand, she had her relentless principles. They and a true compromise being incompatible, she temporized—but only just. She telephoned Rome and spoke briefly to her uncle at the Ministry, told him of Biscotti's hints, but rather minimized them, and suggested they were not worth calling the police in over; one would keep an eye on Molyneux, call him in now and then for a bit of intimidation, but no more. Among other things, Biscotti had been impossibly vague. Covering himself, as usual. Uncle Carlo, not for the first time, flew into a rage at the unnecessary interruption, for he was just then trying to deal with a scandal at the Ministry having to do with the procurement of the grasslike plastic used to cover buildings that might one day be restored—ten million square meters had been ordered instead of two; the manufacturer had excellent connections, even with the Communists—and now it would all somehow have to be used, to conceal the irregularity, and would turn half of Italy's antiquities green. Hastily, Andromeda hung up, her principles satisfied by the call—nor was she disturbed by Uncle Carlo's temper, for in him the family integrity had long since turned to bile.

But James didn't know of this development, so he continued to be frightened. He could well be facing a real crisis—police and all—and Battsie might not be able to fish him out. Was Hans's plan safe now? He didn't think so. He himself certainly couldn't take the drawing to Milan, nor should there be any record that Hans had recently been to Italy. The drawing must go as soon as possible, and it should go in a stranger's hands.

When he got back to the villa, James went to Mark's rooms. Thank heavens, he was in.

"Let's talk out there," James said. He tipped his head toward the balcony. "Like the first time. Wine?" He had a bottle open already.

A fine evening. It was almost seven, and Mark was expected at Signora Benassi's at seven-thirty, but because of Mark's errand to the train station, and James's thereafter to the telephone service at the central post office, they hadn't been able to get together earlier. It was quite warm, yet James shuddered as he was pouring, so much so that he had to call attention to it. "Absurd of me." He waited until the fit had passed. "You'd think I had no internal combustion going at all."

Mark was apprehensive. James had been quite strange when he'd come and said he wanted him to take Hilda's drawing after all—jumpy and distracted, several times stopping as if he'd lost his train of thought. Mark had the feeling he wasn't going to get away from Villa Arberoni without something unpleasant happening—making love with Hilda this noon wasn't it, though a return visit would be—and James's shudder suggested it might be on its way.

"The thing's all packed," James said, "and waiting. Hilda gets five hundred dollars for her drawings. Do be careful."

"I'll be careful."

"Yes, of course you will. I've seen you in action—with my own drawing. The one out of the book." James seemed to fold in on himself. "I have things to tell you, Mark. Confessions to make. I'm doing it so there'll be no barriers between us, lingering in your mind as you travel—I've wondered if questions mightn't have occurred to you. I want you to have no unspoken doubts."

Mark grew more uncomfortable. Misunderstanding, he said, "I don't want to hear any confessions on my last night."

"About the drawing you liberated?" James stared at him. "Why not? It *is* old, Mark. And very valuable."

"I guessed something like that," Mark said, relieved.

"Of course you did, led to it in part by my stupid lies. But you see, at the time I didn't realize I could entirely trust you. You hadn't yet saved my life."

Mark made an impatient gesture. "They'd have stopped in time, those cars."

"Never. Not with me as their victim," James said. "Anyway, I'm going to tell you all the things I should have admitted right off. The drawing was in a book belonging to Ricky, as you'll have guessed from the arms." Mark nodded. "It's a Raphael, and only you and I know where it came from. Only you and I. And only you and I must ever know. I'm quite at your mercy in this. One day it will be famous, much talked about—by John Davenport, for instance."

"A Raphael? No kidding? I almost said when I saw it that it was the same shape as the frescoes in the Vatican—I'd been there just the day before."

"You'd have been exactly right. It's connected with those very frescoes."

Mark observed, "If it does get talked about a lot, I might have found out about it anyway."

"Of course. And then it would be your own information to tell to whom you pleased. You've caught at once, as I expected you would, the weakness in my confession." James smiled. "I'm hoping, you see, that by having told you before you made the discovery on your own, I've bought your silence."

"It was yours anyway, James."

"I hope so. As I say, Ricky doesn't know about it, either."

James made the first step toward a kind of perdition. "Perhaps *he never will,*" he said in a strange voice. "The risks in selling such a thing are great." James explained about the national patrimony laws, and the need to sell outside Italy. "It's done all the time, but every now and then they catch someone red-handed, or choose to make a fuss over something—like the Raphael bought by Boston some years back, which they had to return with much humiliation."

"Where is the drawing now?" Mark asked.

"Already gone," said James. "Thank God. The reason I didn't tell you at once whose books I had on my table was that Signora Benassi has a fit at the idea of Ricky's selling anything old that belonged to his family, so he's doing it on the sly." James took another step. "I'll see to it that he gets the money from the drawing, but it can't be done just like that. I'm an American, and they can't do but so much to me. They could crucify Ricky. So the whole thing, from beginning to end, has to be kept a secret, even from him." James waited a moment. "You will, won't you?"

"I've already said so."

"You sound annoyed that you have to repeat yourself. But perhaps you can understand that I can't hear it too often. Well, we'll now forget about all this. More wine?"

James shuddered again, as if lifting the bottle affected him. "Isn't it ridiculous?" he said, resting it on the table. Mark took it and poured. "Thanks. Now I want to talk a little about *my* plans. I've been thinking and thinking about the future, especially yesterday and today, knowing you were leaving, knowing *you* had plans. I believe I might open a place in America. Get myself into the rare books and manuscripts business directly. Drop my connections with Tremper & Ixion and use my contacts here to set myself up in business. And on a rather grand scale. Gutenberg Bibles and all the rest. Primary documents, too—letters, journals, manuscripts, and so on."

Mark glanced back into James's sitting room, so underfurnished, so austere. "Won't that cost a lot of money?"

"I think I can raise it."

James was growing noticeably agitated. His shorter leg, crossed over his normal one, was swinging. He got to his feet and paced

his balcony, without benefit of his cane. Thu-*thump!* Thu-*thump!*
Thu-*thump!* "I'm talking about establishing a major new anti-
quarian book house, don't you see?"

"Yes, I do," Mark said quietly, listening to the sound of James's
walk.

"Even if it costs millions," James said excitedly.

Mark nodded. The unpleasantness seemed to be getting closer.

"Let's go back inside, Mark. It's too reminding of your first visit
out here—which only reminds that now you're going away."

They moved in, where James continued to walk up and down.
Suddenly he stopped in front of one of his mirrors. "Look at—"
He gestured toward his own image. "And then think of yourself.
Try to understand what a difference it's made."

"Don't say things like that."

"How could you understand—and why should you try? I promise never to say them, if . . ."

Mark saw James was watching him in the mirror. Closer and
closer, that unpleasantness.

James leaned back against his table, holding the edge with his
hands. "Do you remember how you did that acrobatic thing the
first time you were here? Using the handrail of my balcony? I've
wondered since that you guessed so quickly how to convert me—I
mean to a sense of your competence. But to get on—I'm going to
need people to work for me, people who know something about
the business and are prepared to learn more. Let's suppose that it
all happens. Would you, in that case, be interested in a job?"

"I don't know how long I'll be in Europe."

"Not for the rest of your life, certainly," James snapped. "I'm
talking about something that will go on a long time. Perhaps I
won't have a shop, actually. I'll get a barn or an apartment, or
even just an office. Work out of somewhere like that. But whatever I finally decide on, I'd very, very much like to have you come
and work for me. You'd be most useful. I'd put you in charge of
conservation."

"James, I don't know that much."

"You'd learn, man. I've seen you. I've taught you. I know you
can learn. After you finish your Grand Tour, you're going to have
to do something—get into something permanent. You said so

251

yourself. This would be permanent, Mark. It's really a considerable opportunity, what I have in mind."

"I still don't see how you can pay for it. I know what even little
things cost at Tremper & Ixion."

"I don't need you to tell me that. Look, I said I'd have the
means, and I will. I have a backer in mind. That sort of thing."

Mark changed the subject to one that might calm James down
again; he'd started to walk once more. "Where would you have
this place?"

"It wouldn't matter. How does Cambridge strike you—near my
alma mater? Or New York?"

Mark shrugged. "Never having lived in either place . . ."

"Philadelphia? Baltimore?"

"I don't think I'd want to live in Baltimore," Mark said, remembering that Laurie didn't intend to return there.

"Washington, then?"

"You're putting things backwards. You should decide where the
business will go best, and if I don't like it . . ."

James's pacing brought him directly in front of Mark. "You
don't seem to get what I'm saying. I'm offering you the chance to
choose where we'll be."

Mark didn't reply. He wouldn't meet James's eyes.

"Damn you," James said, and swung away. "Of course you know
what I'm saying. I'm saying you can have your pick of where we'd
go. Why not, as it doesn't much matter to me—so long as it's not
Detroit. I'm saying I'll give you a job and train you, and I'll move
you up. Eventually, if it all works out, there's no reason why you
shouldn't come to own part of the business."

"But maybe I'm not suited to the rare-book business. I've honestly never been able to decide whether I liked working for Peter
Tremper."

"Fuck Tremper! I'm not Tremper. You have a talent; he said so
in his letter to me about you. I know it, too. You'll be independent—free to come and go. We'll arrange for you to travel now
and then. For Christ's sake"—and here James tried to laugh—
"you can even continue with my cousin Hilda if you want to, eh? I
don't mean posing, either." He looked closely at Mark. "I thought
so. Well, I won't care about that. All I want, you understand, is

252

to have you work for me. Watch the place when I'm gone. Someone to talk to now and then. Someone I can trust. Someone, Mark, who saved my life and who I'm now trying to repay. To whom I'm offering . . . all that I can offer."

Mark was silent a long time, identifying the disagreeable thing. "Actually," he said at last, "it's a good idea. A great opportunity. I'd like it."

"Then you'll give it a try—if I can work things out?"

Mark nodded.

"Should we shake hands on it?"

"Is there any need to?"

"None, now that I have your word. You decided just like that. It's the way you do things, isn't it? Just like that."

"We'll have to talk about it some more," Mark said slowly. "When I come back for the Palio."

"Oh, we'll have lots of talking to do. I shall, I think, be happy with the arrangement," James said gently, "and I don't think you will ever have a reason to complain about me."

Before Mark left to go to Signora Benassi, they went over the details of his travel arrangements. He'd been unable to get a seat on the Brenner Express, and instead was leaving a little after eleven the next morning for Milan, where he'd change to a local train, the Alpenstock, that wound slowly up through the Tyrol to Innsbruck, where he would have to change yet again for a train to Munich that got in late on Saturday morning—a long trip, but everything was very crowded now, and he'd been lucky to get a seat on the Alpenstock at the last moment. James had called Hans Lochner. He would come into Munich to meet Mark and take the drawing. Mark could drive back with him to his place in the country for the rest of the weekend, if he wanted to. After that, Mark would do what he pleased—until the Palio.

"You'll be careful with Hilda's drawing, won't you?" James said for the last time.

"Look," Mark said distantly, "I'm dependable."

"Of course you are. Of course you are. Don't I know it? You'd snatch it from in front of an oncoming car." James smiled wanly. "Save it—like an angel of the Lord."

Mark didn't say anything. He just wanted to get out of James's rooms.

James held the satchel in his own hands until the last moment, only put it in Mark's keeping when they said good-bye at his door. And then the greater force of their parting, and the continuing alienation—he was getting all that again from Mark—drove his worries over the drawing out of his mind.

"It'll only be days, really, before you'll be back here," he said. "It will be nice to see the Palio again with someone who will so respond. Now just go off. I won't see you in the morning—don't want to. I'm not good at farewell scenes. They undo me."

James closed his door and leaned his forehead against it, full of anguish: over his loss, though it would only be until the end of June; over his love, which was scarcely much joy right now and which, he knew, would bring anything but joy in the end; over his hopeless body, which compounded it all. And over his shabby treatment of Ricky, which he couldn't help.

He made his way to his bedroom. This time he lay with his face in the pillows. Ricky was perhaps the worst of it. He thought of some of the ways he could make it up to Ricky. Buy his books one at a time, at multiples of their true value. Find some way eventually to transfer cash to him, once the business was going well. Certainly make Tiberio a major legatee in his will. All the same, it was going to come down to stealing, and James knew it. But he couldn't help it. It was the only way he'd been able to think of to keep Mark nearby. James knew he'd gone from obsession to utter folly, but he couldn't help that, either.

He groaned, a man on the rack, pulled in two directions—by honor and love. He recalled Ricky's last remark, that day in Piazzetta Guidoni: "You and I can surely trust each other," Ricky had said. But he was wrong.

After his dinner with Signora Benassi, Mark went down to his rooms. He didn't turn on any lights, except one in the bathroom, which had a ventilating fan but no window. He packed by that distant source, unwilling to light his bedroom or sitting room, lest Hilda see and come to his window or his door and want in.

No good, all that. No good, any of it. He went to bed in the dark.

The next morning he got up early and had a run; a man could think clearly when he was running. When he got back, he knew exactly what to do.

He repacked, putting everything he had with him into his back-pack and shoulder-tote this time. Then he unfastened James's parcel and added the portrait Hilda had done of him to it, and tied it all up again securely, and put it back in the canvas satchel, with a flannel shirt and some underwear packed around it to protect the glass. And then he went to the house phone and called up to Signora Benassi and asked if he could see her.

Nobody came to the door when Mark rang the bell. He rang again. And again—just as, at last, there were sounds from inside, the clicking of locks, and a voice. "Stop ringing, Mr. Stapleton, I'm doing all this as fast as I can." The door was shortly thereafter opened by Signora Benassi herself, in a very plain dress. "I'm sorry. Sorry, sorry, sorry. But things are completely upended here this morning. Costanza locks us in, I must say, as if we were a seraglio." They went to the room where Signora Benassi had first received Mark for cocktails. "Now what is it that's so important?" she asked. "I thought everything was taken care of when we said good-bye last night."

"I wanted to tell you that I've changed my mind and to thank you for everything, and to really say good-bye. I've decided to leave for good."

She sat down at her usual place at the end of the couch and began to turn her finger rings. "Once trouble starts . . ." she murmured. She didn't argue with him, but she did ask, eventually, "Why?"

He didn't try to lie; there'd have been no point, with her. "I think it's better." Her look obliged him to add, "Things have closed in a little here."

She thought that over. "Whom have you told?"

"Nobody else. I only decided while I was jogging this morning."

"Not Mr. Molyneux?"

"No." Mark turned coward—and had his first real misgivings since his morning run, when it had all seemed so simple. "Maybe . . . maybe you could tell him for me."

"Certainly not."

"Then I'll leave him a note. He said he didn't like to say good-bye to people. Said it undid him."

"He'll be very disappointed. He was looking forward to your return. Going with you to Siena and all that. Are you being fair to him?"

"As fair as I can be, I guess."

"And what about the sculpture Hilda Molyneux's doing? She spoke of it with such enthusiasm when we met this afternoon in the gardens. Said you were a—a promising subject."

"I guess it'll never get done."

"And is that fair to her?"

Mark said, with more confidence, "I think so."

"In her case you may be right, but—"

They were interrupted by sounds coming from another part of the building—from the direction of the state rooms. Loud voices, growing louder. Crying and replying.

Signora Benassi put her hands to her ears. "I can't bear it. I'm so tired of this; it's been going on since eight o'clock. It's quite impossible to think about anything else."

Costanza, not at all herself—she wore no little starched cap, and her wrinkled face was tear-streaked, her eyes wild—came hurrying in, Antonio and Velia with her. There was a scene. The three of them argued with one another and appealed their points to the signora, who tipped her head back and looked at the painting on the coving of the ceiling opposite her, and refused to say anything. Until, that is, she brought her head forward, frowned them into silence, said some quick Italian herself, and sent them from the room.

She eased farther down into the plump overstuffed cushions, draped her right arm over the arm of the couch, and fingered the tacks that held the upholstery in place. "Such a crisis!" she said wearily. Mark asked what it was about. "About nothing." She sighed. "Yet about a great deal. I sent some knives out to have their handles fixed, and they were just brought back yesterday evening by the silversmith, on his way home. I should explain to you that it was always the practice, in great houses in the old days, to count the silver when there was a change in its status—pieces taken away, as in this case, and brought back, or the household moved from under one roof to under another and the silver went along. That is Costanza's job here, was even when my mother was alive; Mama'd never have a butler and always said nobody was ever more aptly named than Costanza. And so, this morning early, she did a count of the silver. Seven teaspoons are missing."

"Seven?" Mark asked—something he hadn't known before.

"Seven. A fraction of what we have, but—they are missing. There were four dozen of them, all alike, when last counted—it happens that I helped Costanza with that particular pattern, and I know. Now there are forty-one."

More commotion. This time Costanza brought in Gina, the cook, who still carried a large ladle, which she waved in great agitation during the shouting that followed, then held before her like a mace when she stalked out of the room.

"They're coming one at a time to declare their ignorance and innocence, except Antonio, who's been here twice," the signora said. "Now what was it we were saying? Oh yes. About the really rather thoughtless way you're treating James . . ."

"I don't mean to be thoughtless—and I've certainly thought about it," Mark said defensively, and returned to the spoons. "What'll happen—about your silver?"

"That's the worst of it. I don't care about losing seven spoons, in the widest sense. But Costanza's at stake. The silver is her responsibility. If the spoons aren't found, I ought, technically, to dismiss her—and she's worked on this place for almost sixty-five years, came when she was still a young girl. I won't, of course. Couldn't. I know she didn't steal them, but then she did let it somehow happen. What I do may not be the heart of the thing, however. She may leave. She says she will, and she may even be right to. She says she'll have no authority if she stays, when everybody knows she's let seven silver spoons slip through her fingers. She says it has to be one of the other servants, and that she can't work with them, knowing that. And she's going on about how

257

she's too old. Everything you'd expect."

"But you can't let her leave," Mark said. "She's so wonderful."

"If she insists on retiring, I can't stop her. And then what? I'd fix her a place here, of course, but I won't have her spending her days sitting in a corner by the kitchen fire, being mistreated and made fun of as she fades into a senile old creature, because she's in a kind of disgrace, instead of being honored. I'll have to send her to a place for old women. It's too awful."

"But there must be another way," Mark said. "How can you even talk about letting that happen?"

Signora Benassi looked at him until he grew uncomfortable. "Are you, I wonder, a very good judge of how to treat people, Mr. Stapleton?" Mark, who'd never sat down, looked at the floor. "At bottom," she went on, "the thing isn't funny—to have silver stolen, even if you don't care about it, by someone who works for you. The principle of the thing is disturbing; there is, after all, really valuable silver here, and other things. My nautilus cup, for instance." The signora waved a hand toward it. "If I can no longer depend on Costanza to keep the silver, she can no longer hold her job as it presently is. That's the other side of it."

"What would your mother do?"

"Mama? Ha! She'd have changed costumes at least three times already this morning."

There was another commotion, and in came Costanza with Anna, who so forgot herself in the middle of her protestations that she mopped the sweat off her forehead with her dustcloth. Antonio also came back in, to provide a bass to the chorus.

Signora Benassi held up a hand. "Enough!" she said. Talking among themselves as if they'd never stop, they left.

Mark said slowly, importantly, "What if you found out none of them had done it and that it wasn't Costanza's fault, either?"

"What do you mean by that?" Signora Benassi asked. Mark didn't reply. "Don't say things you don't intend to follow up on," she said sharply.

"What if I told you I know what happened to the spoons, and they weren't stolen by anybody who works here, and it wasn't Costanza's fault?"

Signora Benassi leaned forward. "What if you said that? Why, I'd ask you to explain. You didn't take them yourself, did you?"

Mark didn't owe the situation so great a lie. "No," he replied.

"What *are* you trying to tell me?" Signora Benassi thought about it. "The silver was all out the first night you were here, but it was locked up in the dining room after we went through, and put away the next morning. How could you know anything at all about the fate of the spoons?"

"I'm not going to say anything more. But I swear to you that Costanza couldn't help what happened."

Signora Benassi began to play with her rings again, in some agitation herself now. "There was only one other person with us that evening." Mark said nothing, but he began to back toward the door. "This is *extraordinary*," she said. "You know what I'm thinking now?" Mark nodded. "Are you absolutely sure? You can't be. You're making up some kind of wild story. How. . . ?"

"The mirrors," Mark said.

"What? Oh. The antechamber." Signora Benassi slowly turned her head away from him, toward the nautilus cup on the table. "Dear God, how awful—if it's true," she said. Her sudden anger revealed that she believed it. "How dare you tell me this?"

"I didn't want to."

"Then why did you?"

"Because of Costanza."

"Costanza! Do you think she, of all people, would have wanted you to tell? What about him? Can you imagine what he must be feeling—to be driven to do such a thing? A man like that? Thank heavens I can't see how I have any responsibility for bringing him to the act." Signora Benassi eyed Mark coldly. "Your telling me is detestable."

Mark was outraged. "What about stealing and letting someone else take the blame? What do you call that?"

"Oh, what do you know about it?" The signora stood. "As you have seen, I am very busy this morning, and must send you away now. You will have managed, in leaving Villa Arberoni, to hurt one person deeply and destroy another's reputation. And neither had done you the slightest harm, or ever would have."

Mark, guilty about Ricky despite his conviction he'd been right to tell, answered only her first accusation. "James comes on too strong," he said.

"As I warned you."

"So what am I supposed to do but leave?"

"Something else. Anything else. Tiberio would have found a way to resolve things without such damage to other people. It turns out to have been bad luck that brought us together at the Protestant Cemetery, and you've learned less from your stay at Villa Arberoni than I had hoped. Good-bye, Mr. Stapleton." She held her hand out. "I must deal with the calamity you've just dropped in my lap. I do not thank you for it."

After Mark had left, crestfallen, Signora Benassi got the volume of Keat's letters that had belonged to her husband, in which she'd put the leaf Mark had picked for her at the poet's grave. She took the leaf and walked to the wastebasket with it, in the mood for a symbolic gesture. But at the last moment she changed her mind and put it back in the book. Perhaps the gesture was premature. Life at her villa had made rather excessive demands on Mark—and perhaps he'd redeem himself later, somehow. She almost called down to Antonio to intercept him as he was leaving and have him come back up for a more cordial good-bye, but she really didn't want to have to talk to Antonio at the moment. Also, she had to think.

She turned to the problem of the spoons. There was only one place in Florence to take old silver if one were to get paid anything like its value. She went to her telephone table, looked in her book under S, and dialed the number of the Fratelli Sulmona.

Her call over, she summoned Costanza and told her the whole matter of the spoons was to be forgotten for twenty-four hours. Then, when everyone had had a chance to calm down, a recount would be made in the signora's own presence and before the entire staff—she demanded, and was given, the keys to the sideboards where the silver was stored. In the meantime, Antonio was to have the car ready in an hour. Signora Benassi had errands to run, including a stop by the silver shop, so she could pay for the knives and thank Giacobbe Sulmona for having repaired them so quickly—and so well.

Mark, smarting from his dismissal, went to his rooms and wrote a brief note.

Dear James, I've changed my mind and am leaving Villa Arberoni for good, so this is to say good-bye and good luck. I'll write you a real letter later, but don't have time now. I'll keep Signora Benassi, who knows I'm going, informed about forwarding addresses, etc. Don't worry, I'll keep your secrets, and I'll get your drawing to your friend, as we agreed. Mark.

He looked at his watch. Not quite ten. He had a few minutes before he'd have to leave for the station, so he went to say good-bye, first to Iris, who was practicing—he made that very brief—then to the Davenports, though he risked running into James by going up to their floor.

The professor was already off to the library, but Pauline was in. When Mark told her he was leaving forever, she said, "What a disappointment! Practically everyone at Villa Arberoni will be heartbroken."

Mark ignored her remark. "You haven't heard anything from the Ladore party, have you?" he asked. "Laurie said she'd write me, but she hasn't."

Pauline told all. "They're in Venice now, just went over yesterday from Milan, but they won't be there long. Miss Ladore is going home—maybe as soon as tomorrow or the next day. But for the time being, they're at—" Pauline got a piece of paper and wrote on it for him.

"'Hotel Palazzo Loredan,'" he read. "'Grand Canal.'"

"It's *the* hotel. Just up from San Marco." Pauline couldn't resist asking, "What are you going to do?"

"I might try to call Laurie when I change trains in Milan," Mark replied. Though a disappointment to Pauline, it was better than nothing.

As he left Villa Arberoni with backpack, shoulder-tote, and canvas satchel, Mark put the note on the table in the vestibule, where James would find it when he came down to pick up his mail.

The train came in from Rome on time, and left Florence on time, too. But the crew went on a three-hour strike over nothing in Bologna. As a result, Mark missed his connection in Milan. By

261

that time he didn't care. He'd changed his plans yet again. He wired the gallery in Munich that he'd been held up by a strike and would bring the drawing to them on Monday.

Mark got to Venice a little after nine. He was lucky enough to find a room in a hotel not far from the railroad station, where he changed into his blazer and a tie. He got a map and instructions at the hotel desk and set out for the Hotel Loredan.

After getting lost only twice, he found the hotel; its entrance was on a narrow way that led off to the Grand Canal from the main walk up from San Marco. He was so nervous he went past the doors and on to the gondola landing, and stood there a minute, looking out at the lights of the boats that were running back and forth, and listened to the water lap against the steps and the gaily painted mooring posts. Then he turned around and went inside.

He had his story ready. "My name is Mark Stapleton, and I'm the nephew of an elderly American lady who's staying here—Miss Emilene Ladore. She was expecting me earlier, but there was a strike on my train, and I was late getting in. I don't want to wake her up if she's gone to bed, so I wonder if you could let me speak to her companion, Miss Walker."

The night concierge was convinced. He asked Mark's name again, then gave the operator instructions to call Laurie. He motioned Mark to the house telephone.

When Miss Emilene went upstairs after dessert, Wesley, in a conciliatory mood, asked Laurie to join him and celebrate the happy outcome of his efforts by taking a coffee and brandy on the square opposite the Ducal Palace, and she, because she'd never been to Venice before and might never get there again, accepted. It was chilly. The wind that always blows between the palace and the Library of St. Mark's opposite it was making the pennants on the flagpoles snap, but the scenery was worth the chill: the cusped arches of the palace, softly lighted; to its left the exotic outline of San Marco, dome upon dome; to its right the end of the Grand

Canal, then the harbor, a great field of black water that swept away to San Giorgio and the Lido.

Wesley was ebullient, boastful, self-satisfied. He crowed and preened. He couldn't stop talking about the wonderful future, now that his Center had been approved, in principle, by the trustees in Texas.

"There's only one thing that isn't going the way I'd like it to, Laurie. You and I aren't on as good terms as we were before we left America."

"I suppose not."

"Would you like to talk it through?"

"Not particularly, Uncle Wesley. I'd rather sit and look."

"I like you so much," he went on. "And now, more than ever before, I'm in a position to do something for you." Odd how words connected things in one's mind. *Position* led Wesley to the old limerick about Venice's greatest painter. *Her position to Titian suggested coition.* Wesley sniggered unaccountably; Laurie gave him a doubtful look. "I really do like you, Laurie. Always have. We should cooperate, not disagree." *So he leapt off the ladder and had her.* Wesley sniggered again. "I can make it worth your while. I've got the will, and now I'll have the way, of being a very indulgent uncle to you—if you'll cooperate." Laurie gave him another doubtful look. "I know cooperation can mean a lot of different things, but I'm not implying anything except just simple . . . well, cooperation—though I have to admit"—he lidded his eyes and smiled urbanely—"sometimes I think the Ptolemies had the right idea. You know, I'm going to be spending a lot of time out in Texas. I'd like to have a member of my family nearby. What would you think of that? I can't specify the job, but I can promise the pay would be good." He put a hand on Laurie's.

Though she stared at it, he didn't take it away. He left it, a thing coarse and suggestive. "Well?"

"I'm not interested."

"How do you know, if you don't know what the job is?"

She said, "Not interested is not interested," and removed her own hand.

Wesley got mad. "And just why aren't you interested?"

"Because I don't like you," Laurie said.

"Then maybe you'd better go back to Miss Ladore."

Laurie stood up. "I will."

Before she got away, he said, "You know what you are? A prig. A self-righteous, self-loving little prig—and don't think your looks are going to save you for very long. You get your mouth from your father, and you've seen what's happened to him."

She ran toward the upper end of the square.

Wesley finished his brandy, then had another, gradually calming down, as he thought of what a strange girl Laurie was. Taking a goat's-milk delivery man up to her bedroom at nine-fifteen in the morning to fuck with him in her own bed, smell and all. Him in and out of drug programs and the rest, too. Bad blood, coming from that crazy father, who thought food additives dissolved your skin from the inside out, and when he wasn't eating yogurt, he was rubbing himself with the oils of wild plants. Wesley didn't waste much time on regrets. He'd pay no more attention to Laurie, once he got her on the plane with Miss Emilene the day after tomorrow.

He signaled for another brandy. Laurie *had* left him with a hot spot. He wondered how you cooled that in Venice. Eventually he walked over to the edge of the water and spoke to a gondolier who was waiting there for a chance late customer.

Yes, the man knew where there was a girl. It would cost a hundred and fifty dollars, including the gondola ride, round trip. Wesley teetered in, and they sculled quite a distance, with many turns and reversals, to an old house that still had its traditional Venetian conical chimney pots, well away from the center of town, near the church of the Madonna del Orto. The gondolier knocked at the door. Wesley went in.

When they got back to the Loredan, he tipped the gondolier rather handsomely, then hurried by the night concierge, his hands in his pockets. As a result, the man didn't get a chance to tell him of the arrival of Miss Ladore's nephew.

When the telephone rang, Laurie almost didn't answer it, thinking it might be Uncle Wesley. On the other hand, he might keep trying until he awakened Miss Ladore. She took the call.

It was Mark. Laurie was so glad to hear his voice that she cried out his name. He asked if his Aunt Emilene was awake or not, and could he come up. Laurie gave him their suite number.

She was waiting in the hall when he got out of the elevator a few moments later, so she could get him through the sitting room without his having to ring the bell. She held a finger to her lips, and they tiptoed into her bedroom, where he at once took her in his arms.

When she began to ask him questions—how had he found out where she was, and so on—he said, "Don't talk. Give me a chance to do this my way."

They made love in the darkened room, the windows on the Grand Canal open so they could hear the sound of the motorboats and the calls of the gondoliers, and see the reflections of the lights from the hotel terrace below them, shining on the ceiling. Afterwards, Mark said, "Maybe that wasn't textbook wonderful, but it was better than I expected, considering how scared I was."

Then they did talk. She told him about Wesley, and cried a little when she repeated Wesley's insult to her in sending her away. Mark didn't ask, but she brought up the reason why she hadn't written him from Milan. She wasn't sure from day to day where they'd be, and she didn't want him coming up, perhaps only to find her gone.

"And you weren't absolutely sure you wanted to see me, either," he said, "and didn't trust the part of you that said yes. Being unhappy is not only a luxury, Laurie, it's also habit-forming."

It was another remark Laurie wouldn't have expected him to make. She said, "Well, maybe . . ." And then, "I wasn't sure where it would take us."

"Now you know." Mark turned to face her; they'd been lying side by side. He put his right hand on her flank. "Nice," he said. "Now tell me what it is you don't like about me."

"Less and less," Laurie said. "And it really isn't anything I don't like about you. It's just that I've always before liked boys who weren't quite so conventional."

"Who says I'm so conventional?"

"Nobody has to. It shows. Pure captain-of-the-swimming-team

type." She put her hand on his flank, so their arms crossed. "Of course, I know the team always won," she said.

Mark thought about it while he was in the bathroom. "I'm not much of a swimmer," he said when he came out, "but I'll show you what I *can* do." He did a handstand. He held it. And held it. And held it.

Laurie sat up in bed. "Get down," she said. She began to laugh. "Get down. Honestly, get down. You're making me nervous."

"I'm not ready to get down yet, and conventional people don't make other people nervous." With that, he lifted his left hand free of the floor and did something really difficult, balanced only on his right one. He used the left as a counterweight until he was absolutely secure, then slowly brought it in to his body. He took his limp penis in it, and waved it at Laurie.

"*Ciao,*" he said.

She couldn't stop laughing. "Please, get down. Please, Mark. I'm going to wake up Miss Ladore."

(Miss Emilene, though she slept heavily the first hour or two after she went to bed, like many elderly people didn't sleep so well later. She'd been awakened by what she thought was the sound of voices, not coming through the walls—which, at the Loredan, were thick as a fortress—but from the open window right by her bed; she, too, had windows on the Grand Canal. She got up and put her head out. Sure enough. She went to her door. Peeped out—the sitting room lights were still on, but it was empty. Stealthily she crept forward. Something was going on in Laurie's room. Miss Emilene would normally have been lady enough to return to her bed, but she was bothered by the fact that she'd left Laurie with that uncle of hers. If he'd somehow got the lovely Laurie to . . . It just couldn't be, but Miss Emilene had to make sure. She tiptoed forward and put her ear next to Laurie's door. Giggles. She bent over until she could see through the keyhole. See Mark Stapleton, naked as a jaybird, standing on one hand in the middle of Laurie's floor, using his left arm to balance himself until he— *Well!* And she could see Laurie, with no more clothes on than he had, sitting up in bed, laughing. Miss Emilene tiptoed back to her own room, relieved that it wasn't Wesley.)

Mark lowered himself and got back on the bed. He pulled Lau-

266

rie so she was pillowed on his chest. "Your conventional swimming-team captains don't do things like that," he said. "You know, Laurie, I'm not here because I wanted to make out—not that I didn't, but that's not why I'm here. I'm here because I'm in love with you."

"Yes," she said.

"Lie still and feel what it's like with me." He let some time pass. "Don't you see how right the vibes are? I mean for the future?"

"Well, maybe," she said.

He asked about the plans for the return to America, then said, "Don't go. Let Knuckles get Miss L. on the plane, but you stay here with me."

"I can't, Mark. I told her I wouldn't ever let her down."

"That's not letting her down. Jee-*sus*, but you're perverse. You just won't give being happy the way you know you feel right now lying here with me a chance. If you go, maybe I'll never get you back; I seem to do better with you when I've got a hand on you than when I don't. I don't trust distance, not with you. Come with me tomorrow."

Laurie didn't reply.

(Miss Emilene, meanwhile, was at the keyhole again, using her ear this time. She heard Mark's appeal—and Laurie's silence.)

Mark said, after a while, "Let's make love a second time, okay? If it was almost wonderful before, think what it's going to be like now, when I'm only about half as scared."

(A short while later, Miss Ladore withdrew to her bedroom. As she pulled up the sheets, she remarked to herself, in a whisper so it wouldn't carry around the window to the next room, "I suppose Daddy would have a fit over all this, but I think it's nice to know some young people nowadays still do it nature's way.")

When it was time to leave, and Mark had got dressed, he handed Laurie the card from his hotel. She was still lying naked on top of her bed, and he knelt at the side of it and put his face against her breast. "Come with me," he said. "If you don't, it will mean that it probably won't ever work out for us, and that will be your fault. All your fault, because I've done all I can, now. Think about it. I'll be at my hotel until ten-thirty tomorrow morning. Call me there. Then I'll leave and go to the railroad station. I'll wait there until noon. If you haven't come by noon, I'll catch the first train for Munich. And that," he said, as sternly as he could, under the circumstances, "will be that."

Laurie, surprised, said, "Why Munich?"

"I have to be there Monday morning. After that we can go wherever we please."

Mark jumped to his feet. From the door he said, "Don't forget to remember me to Aunt Emilene. Tell her how much I love you."

Miss Ladore went out by herself early the next morning. Venice was confusing, but with help from foreigners and Venetians alike, she was able to accomplish her errand, and returned with a bottle in a paper bag. The concierge would probably think it was liquor, but she didn't care. She put the bag on the coffee table and called Laurie Walker to come to the sitting room.

Laurie came out, looking sleepy and unhappy.

"I heard things going on in the middle of the night, Laurie. I got up to check on what it was."

"Oh God. How embarrassing," Laurie said. She went to the window to hide her blushes.

"Now I like a good blush—a girl like you can do just about anything she wants, providing she still remembers how to blush. He's a nice young man—I've thought so ever since Rome." Miss Ladore pretended to know less than she did. "What does he want to do about it?"

"He wants me to stay in Europe with him. Go off to Germany with him today."

"Do it. Go with him, Laurie. If you don't, you'll be sorry." Laurie made a hopeless gesture. "You've decided not to, haven't you? Don't be like that. Go off with your young man."

"But what about you?"

"Me! I'll be all right. My mind's in Texas already. It only remains for my carcass to get there."

"But what about . . . ?" Laurie glanced toward the bathroom.

"There's where I've been ingenious." Miss Emilene reached for the paper bag and took a dark bottle out of it. She waved it in the air. "My daddy always said a person shouldn't ever travel anywhere without a bottle of Lysol, and just look what I found right here in Venice. The very thing. The bottle must be fifty years old—covered with dust—but I reckon Lysol doesn't get weak with age. All I need is this and the corner of a towel, and I can take care of myself until I get back to Texas. I don't need you anymore, Laurie."

Miss Emilene was sitting on a couch. She opened her arms to Laurie and drew her down to her side. Laurie began to cry, and so did Miss Emilene, but time was running out, and she got control of herself. "I'll bet you haven't even thought about money. Well, I have. Child, if there's one thing I can provide you with as a going-away present, that's it. I've got a package of lire and two or three thousand dollars of mad money in the safe downstairs, just in case. Now that I'm leaving, I won't need it here, and once I'm home in Texas, I guess my credit's about as good as there is."

Laurie jumped up. "If I'm going, I've got to hurry, or he'll leave without me."

"Never," said Miss Emilene.

"He really will—and this time he won't come back. I'll call his hotel."

Laurie went to her bedroom door, but stopped. "Now what?" Miss Emilene said—she was reading the instructions on her bottle.

"You said something when we were in Siena about being so sure every man was after your money that you missed the one who wasn't. Did you ever almost run off with someone?"

"Never by train," said Miss Emilene.

Mark waited on the front steps of the railroad station, his backpack at his feet. His eyes were on the platforms where the water taxis discharged their passengers, or on his watch. It was close to noon, and there was a train to Austria at 12:17.

He'd never been happier in his life—provisionally; he'd be more sure of it once they were on that train. Laurie had run out on him before.

But there she was. He did a dance to catch her attention. She was too dressed up to be traveling with him, but she'd held herself to two suitcases, one big, one not so big. They hurried into the station, where they put their luggage down. Laurie stayed to watch it, while Mark got her ticket and found out if they could get reserved seats. As she hadn't a Eurail pass, she gave him some of the big wad of lire that Miss Ladore had given her "on account." He took with him only the canvas satchel, which he didn't want to let out of his hands.

It was a busy Saturday. People were crowding forward, the clerks getting irritable. There were the usual number of ambivalent travelers, who had to ask about alternatives before they bought their tickets, and of the confused, who couldn't understand what was told to them. Foreigners, lots of foreigners, who had trouble making it known what class they wanted to go, sometimes what their destination was, and couldn't get the money straight. Mark changed lines twice—always a mistake. At last it was his turn. He asked for Laurie's ticket to Munich via Trent and Innsbruck, and asked about seats—that was another window, he was told. Meanwhile, as he needed both hands to handle the payment, he put the satchel down on the floor at his feet.

One is probably safer from petty theft in Venice, as far as the natives are concerned, than in any other large city in Italy; the Venetians, considering all they've had to put up with from tourists over the centuries, are a remarkably honest folk. But that is not always true of their foreign visitors. Three of these, youths of about nineteen, had noticed how carefully Mark was holding the satchel. When he put it down, one of them tried to shove into the line a few people back from Mark. There were complaints, which he answered insolently, in broken Italian, then spoke loudly to his friend, and both of them did some pushing. There were more complaints. Voices went up, and arms were waved. While everybody's attention was taken by this performance, youth number three edged along the ticket counter until he was close enough to Mark to reach with one foot and pull the satchel toward him. He pulled it a little farther. Then a little farther. Mark, still engaged in paying, didn't notice and neither did anyone else, not even when the youth stooped, took the satchel, and backed away.

When he was in the clear, he broke into a run. He left the station, crossed the bridge to the other side of the canal, then rounded a corner and was out of sight. His friends soon joined him.

They opened the satchel and took out the parcel. After they'd torn the brown paper off, they cursed in disappointment, in whatever language it was they spoke together. A picture! Of the Madonna! And a portrait of a man, not even framed. The latter totally worthless, but they pulled the tape off the glass and tried to sell the framed drawing to passersby for a quarter of an hour. When nobody was interested, they left it leaning against the side of one of the water-bus landings and went away.

Young Arturo Bianchini, a student at the University of Padua, who'd just arrived in Venice to spend the weekend with his grandmother, noticed it and picked it up. He waved it ostentatiously in the air, so the owner could claim it. Nobody did. It was strange, because someone must have cared enough to have had it framed, yet had left it. Or—Arturo hit on an explanation, all too plausible during the rising tourist season—it had been stolen and left. However it had come to be where it was, it would make a nice present for Arturo's grandmother.

The old lady lived on the Giudecca, in an apartment she shared with another old widow, both of them very devout. Arturo explained that the drawing was after a Madonna by Raphael, which he remembered from visits to Florence. She was very pleased and took it to the tiny room in the corner of her apartment where now hung one of those all-too-blue devotional pictures of Mary that are sold in religious stores. She put it aside, and in its place hung the drawing her beloved Arturo had brought her.

That evening, and the next morning, she and her friend knelt in front of Hilda's "rethinking" and told their beads. When Father Campo came to lunch after Mass, she showed it to him. He rather disapproved of it—a little of the irony in it reached him, though he was only a simple parish priest—but he said nothing. He wouldn't have hurt her feelings for the world.

After James got the note Mark had left for him, he went to his rooms, where he remained all day without eating or speaking to anybody. His despair gradually became mixed with disbelief. Mark wouldn't really do what he'd said. He'd come back. As James imagined the ways in which the change of heart would take place, he always had Mark in quite specific places: in the office of the gallery off Maximilianstrasse; in a train compartment full of students, all bare knees and empty bottles; or in Griesen, at Hans's rustic weekend house, just coming out of that ice-cold plunge. In every case Mark would say to someone—Hans, or the secretary at the gallery, or one of the students—"You know, I think I'll go back to Florence." Just like that. James also imagined the various ways in which he'd find out—a letter, a telephone call. Most often, there'd be a knock on his door, and there Mark was, looking contrite, as he had after James's fall on the Lungarno. James imagined a dozen different variations on such a return—the apologies, the excuses, and of course the forgiving.

On Saturday, at noon, he got a call from Hans, who'd come up to Munich as planned, only to find Mark's telegram. He'd checked the story, he said, and there had been strikes on all services in and out of Milan. He'd be back in touch on Monday. The conversation had to be very guarded and oblique, with no names mentioned—and James didn't tell Hans of Mark's defection. For one thing, Hans might have reproached Mark with it, and James didn't want that.

Hilda knocked in midafternoon. James didn't go to the door. She knocked harder, until he had to answer.

"What's the matter with you?" she asked when she saw how he looked. "You didn't come to lunch. You haven't shaved. What in the world . . . ?"

It was easier just to hand her Mark's note.

"My God," she said. She sat down at the big library table. "He's run out on us."

"On . . . us. Yes," James said. "And it will probably kill me."

Hilda, as she got to her feet, pushed back the chair she was sitting in so hard it skidded an extra foot. She walked swiftly toward the balcony, swinging her arms. The doors were closed. She banged them open and went out, stayed a few seconds, then came back in. She lit a cigarette, though smoking was, in principle, banned in James's room.

"Is it my fault, do you think?" she asked.

He shook his head. "Nothing you could have done would have made any difference if I had been able to find the right things to do and say."

She hit on her own version of James's desperate optimism. "He'll come back. Be sorry and come back, just as it's planned. Back for the Palio and the birthday party—and his sculpture— after he's had a chance to think it over. As a matter of fact, this may be lucky. We're warned now. He's a bolter. We'll know better how to handle him."

"That's all I have left to hope for," James said. He looked away from her. "How was he, Hilda?"

"Sweet," she said. "A little *too*, do you know what I mean? I should have known from that."

Hilda returned to take James downstairs to dinner. He guessed at once, from the way Pauline Davenport kept looking at him when she wasn't talking to someone else, that she must know something. As they were all getting up to go to coffee, she said in a quite loud voice, "Is it all right if I tell them what you found out today, John?"

Davenport, taken by surprise, said, "What? What? Well . . . yes, I suppose so."

"Everyone will be interested, I'm sure," Pauline said. "Wesley Knuckles—you all remember him, don't you?—called John today to say good-bye. He flies with Miss Ladore to America tomorrow morning early. And, Signora Benassi, it seems that Cupid's been flying around your villa recently, firing off arrows like mad. Wesley's big news was that his niece ran off to Germany this morning with Mark Stapleton. It seems they were in love all the time—and I never guessed. I think it's very romantic."

Hilda had good control of herself. She didn't pause in stride— and she didn't look at James. Iris had no such control; she turned and left the room. Signora Benassi coughed delicately and turned to James, who'd stopped and was standing quite still. "I think I'll forgo coffee. I'm not quite myself tonight. Ricky, dear, you stay here and make sure everybody gets what they want. James, let me take your arm. Would you mind seeing me downstairs? If you want coffee you can come back, but you so often don't take it."

She steered James out of the room. When they were in the hall, she said, "I'm quite all right, but I thought you'd want to leave, and I didn't want Pauline Davenport to have the satisfaction of hearing you say so." He nodded, still speechless, and they descended to Signora Benassi's floor, where he remained in the elevator, to go back up to his. She held the door a moment. "Remember, everything has happened before, and nothing lasts forever," she said.

The next morning, after a sleepless night—during which he at last faced the truth, that Mark would never return; how could he bring Laurie back here, given all the circumstances?—James telephoned Ricky dei Guidoni and asked if he could come and see him.

Ricky answered the door in a dressing gown that might have belonged to his father. He took James to his library, where, to his surprise, James, who looked so awful, sat down without taking the slightest interest in the old books Ricky had hurriedly pulled off the shelves and put on the table.

James said, "I have something to tell you, Ricky," and forthwith gave the story of the Raphael drawing. "I've waited to tell you until it was out of the country. It's now gone to Munich, to the dealer I've chosen to handle it—a friend of mine, entirely dependable. Mark Stapleton took it with him, though he doesn't know it." And then James told Ricky about Dottoressa Paonese, and the need for secrecy.

Ricky asked few questions; he didn't know enough to ask many. Finally he came to the matter of money, and when James told him how much would be coming to him, if all went well, he said, "I'll be rich."

"By the standards of most people, if not those of Miss Ladore."

"I can live as I want. Go where I want. Do things for Tiberio. All that."

James nodded. "All that and, I should think, more."

Ricky said, "More, indeed. Oh yes, indeed more. I must make a telephone call."

He dialed a number. "Madeleine, my dear, good morning," he said. "I have a favor to ask of you. I want to come and see you this afternoon. Yes, I know we're dining together, but I want to see you beforehand. I have something important to say to you. No, I prefer not to squeeze it in over cocktails. Please, Madeleine, just for once let me be the judge of what's best. I wish to call on you at five. We will have our conversation. Then I'll leave. And I'll come back before dinner. I don't care whether it makes sense to you or not, Madeleine. In this case it is I who will decide the correct thing to do."

He put down the receiver. "One does need to be able to assert oneself, even against the wishes of the most benevolent of despots," he remarked. "And to be rich is to be free—in some respects." Then he remembered James's great sorrow. He put a hand on his shoulder. "James, I'm so sorry that a time that's brought such good news to me has brought such bad news to you. Madeleine has . . . mentioned it."

James's reply made no sense to Ricky, but then, he was too experienced in the ways of the world to expect much sense in social discourse.

"I must be grateful to him, Ricky," James said, without mentioning Mark's name. "He has given me back my honor."

PART

eight

The invitations read that the music would begin promptly at ten o'clock, and Signora Benassi, in talking about the schedule of things, had said with a firmness even her most dilatory friends dared not ignore that nobody who arrived late would be allowed in the *salone*. Guests could, of course, come in after the music was over—that was their affair—but she didn't intend to have her artist disturbed by late arrivals. Therefore, on the evening of the celebrated birthday party, people began to appear as early as nine-fifteen.

The *salone* itself was filled with little gilded chairs, set out in four blocks facing the narrow end of the room where the large piano sat, its lid up, to the left of the doorway that led toward the dining room. Between the blocks were wide aisles, one directly in line with the piano, the other on the main cross-axis of the room, running from the terrace doors to the portrait of Contessa Rinuccini. Plenty of space, almost a semicircle of it, had been left around the table under the portrait, and there were wide passageways along the walls, the back of the room, and in front of the piano. The signora received her guests, Ricky not far from her side, out on the terrace, which was decorated with terra-cotta urns filled with sprays of yellow broom that had been brought down from the Apennines where it was still in season, and lighted by standards that carried clusters of frosted-glass globes. Tables, covered with cloths and decorated with bowls of summer flowers from the villa's cutting garden, were set up at either end of the terrace, where bartenders in white jackets offered anything one wanted to drink. Though it was certainly a summer night, the heat, fortunately, was not stifling; nevertheless, by far the most popular choice, leading even champagne, was a fruit punch.

Many of those who arrived early drifted down the stairs into the garden, which James Molyneux, faithful to his promise, had prepared for the occasion—almost the only thing he had been able to get done in these last unhappy weeks. He'd had rows of torches placed down the main alley, so that as one looked from the terrace one saw a double line of them that ran straight to the fountain, which was festooned with ivy like an antique shrine, then swelled to follow the circle (where they intersected more torches set along the crosswalk) and continued, straight again, all the way to the far wall. With Bruno's and Antonio's and above all Tiberio's help, he'd also placed blue, yellow, and green electric lanterns in the trees, not according to any geometric pattern, but rather according to a principle of artful disorder, as one best puts lights on a Christmas tree. Now, in the warm Florentine night, scattered as they were amongst pine and ilex whose boughs were in constant motion because of a cooling breeze, they seemed to blink on and off like fireflies, so unpredictably that one of the guests, from Lucca, offered to bet the friends he was with, from Cortona, that Signora Benassi, a magician at everything she touched, had somehow managed to find floating lanterns, which, like kites, were moored to the trees but not fixed in place. The person who took the bet claimed, less amusingly, that they were worked by a computer that turned them off and on. As neither theory was correct, no money was gained or lost, and everybody agreed that in any case the whole villa looked just right, a little old-fashioned—imagine torches!—but such a suitable statement, in opposition to the plastic tents and balloons and Plexiglas fountains and all the other things one heard were used at outdoor parties not in Florence.

Gradually, arriving now by fours, fives, and sixes, the company gathered. The ladies, most though not all of them elderly, without exception wore long dresses of a conservative design, accompanied by such jewels as they possessed. The men were in black tie, even the youngest of them, grandchildren and great-grandchildren of the signora's friends, or friends of Tiberio, who himself hadn't arrived yet, having driven back home to change and get his mother after the morning's ceremony in Florence. Signora Benassi, in the midst of receiving, asked Ricky to go look for him, but Ricky refused. Tiberio had said he'd be back by ten o'clock, and he would be. He'd not only said so, he'd confirmed it on the telephone when he called to say his mother wouldn't come after all—that she felt too weak, meaning too envious. Signora Benassi nevertheless fussed; someone should go watch for him.

"You know, Madeleine," Ricky said, talking sideways between

his greetings to old friends from Rome, "I may need taking care of, but Tiberio does not."

"He needs it even more than you do—now," she said. "Ah, Dottoressa Paonese, how nice that you could come. And Signora Biscotti, good evening. I'm flattered you came in from your country place. Professor Biscotti, you are so welcome." Signora Benassi took Biscotti's hand in hers, but it was Dottoressa Paonese to whom she spoke. "Isn't it amusing that an old lady in faraway Texas has linked us all together? I count on your help, when the time comes to make the necessary renovations to my villa to make it useful to her foundation, to be sure they're done in the best scholarly taste. Do get yourselves something to drink, if you want it. It's almost time for the music."

At a little before ten, the signora gave a signal to Antonio. The lights on the terrace were dimmed and raised, dimmed and raised; thereafter the guests were urged, by Signora Benassi and Ricky, by Costanza and Antonio, and by several borrowed butlers and maids, to take seats in the *salone*.

"*Where* is Tiberio?" the signora asked Costanza. "Tell Velia to come running as soon as she lays eyes on him and let me know. That will be our signal to begin—I will not start without him, not even if we have to wait until midnight. Miss Siswick will fade to nothing, in that case; heaven knows she's been going in that direction."

Signora Benassi left Ricky to move the stragglers along, and went to the room just inside the *salone*, the same room from which Mark, on his first visit, had been taken in by Costanza to see the portrait of Contessa Rinuccini. There the signora received the latest arrivals, who came all in a throng, complaining of traffic and poor service at the restaurants where they'd been dining, and of the hordes of tourists who made it impossible to get anywhere on time, and of their wristwatches—always slow, never fast.

It was minutes before ten o'clock. Several hundred people were seated in the *salone*, reading their programs or talking. Iris, no doubt all atremble, awaited her call. At last Velia appeared in the far door. She had programs in her hand; she'd been assigned the task of giving them out. To get the signora's attention, she waved them, and when the signora looked in her direction, Velia, in order to signal her with all possible import that Tiberio had just arrived, made the most solemn gesture she knew: she held the programs like a holy text and made the sign of the cross. Signora Benassi broke out laughing and went into the *salone* and took her place, standing close to the portrait of her mother; for this occasion the nautilus cup had been put in the center of the table underneath the portrait, where it always used to sit, along with the pair of silver candelabras, one of which appeared in the portrait beside Contessa Rinuccini.

Conversation subsided as everyone turned, to the degree made necessary by the placement of their chairs and made possible by the condition of their arthritis—some almost one hundred eighty degreees. And wasn't it odd La Benassi had chosen to speak to them from over there to one side, not up by the piano, as one would have expected?

Then, to those who had the necessary distance vision and imagination, it all became clear. A murmur of appreciation arose and subsided. It was the gown. Signora Benassi's magnificent gown of café-au-lait satin, ornamented by a blue sash and by ruffles, cut low, but with the outer shoulders full, was clearly modeled, though it was less flamboyant, after the gown in the Sargent. The room was silent again. One ancient lady, sitting rather close to the signora, remarked to her equally ancient neighbor that it was strange Madeleine hadn't worn the pearls or the rubies or carried a fan, and did she remember how Daisy Rinuccini, on the occasion of the visit of the— People around her frowned, and her friend shushed her.

The signora welcomed her guests and thanked them for coming. She also thanked them for the presents they'd sent or brought, although they'd been told not to—the signora made a little gesture of helplessness. There were so many now on the tables in the hallways that Costanza—she looked toward her, for many of the guests had known Costanza as long as they'd known Signora Benassi—had been assigned to keep a register.

Signora Benassi went on. "I will open them in private, slowly, tomorrow, to get full enjoyment of them, and to think fondly, in each case, of the giver, and remember how we met and how long

282

we've known each other, and to take the measure of our affection. I will open them in private, that is, with one exception, which will stand for all the others." She paused. Antonio thereupon handed a package to Costanza, who approached the signora carrying it in her hands like an offering. The Signora took it, with a gracious smile.

She bent almost imperceptibly toward the elderly maid and whispered, "Velia signaled that Tiberio had arrived. Where is he?" Costanza whispered that he had indeed arrived but had gone to the back of the room. "Tell him, as soon as this is over, that he is to sit beside me," the signora said, and turned her attention back to her guests.

"That exception is this." She held the package so everybody could see it.

She removed the modishly subdued wrapping paper and handed it to Costanza, who folded it as if she intended to use it again—as she had already, for the signora had, of course, opened the gift that morning, and thereupon had decided on the present ceremony. Inside was a box, of typical Florentine make—oxblood leather with a few lines of gold tooling on it. Signora Benassi placed it on the table, then opened the lid. She hesitated a moment, to allow a certain anticipation to grow, even turned to look at her guests, as if too amazed to do or say anything; then she used both hands to lift Ricky's necklace from the interior, where a mazelike series of ridges had been built so the different parts wouldn't rub against each other and the jasper or agate or silver get scratched. She held it up so everyone could see it, whereupon Costanza came forward and fastened it around her neck, and put on the earrings, too.

Signora Benassi said nothing about who the present was from. She didn't need to, because Ricky himself came forward, quoting from the one hundred fifty-ninth of the *Canzoniere*—

> *Per divina bellezza indarno mira,*
> *chi gli occhi de costei già mai non vide,*
> *come soavemente ella gli gira . . .*

—and, for the benefit of those who couldn't follow Petrarch's Italian, then translated:

> He seeks in vain where heavenly beauty lies
> who has not seen my lady and has still
> not marked the gentle glancing of her eyes . . .

It was flattering to the signora, of course, and at the same time a delicate reference, for those who remembered, to her husband and his friend, Giulio Benassi, who had established the canonical text of this very sonnet in one of his many articles on the poet.

Ricky kissed Signora Benassi's hand, while the guests applauded, not without several of them whispering to each other that such a relationship had not been so openly recognized in the old days. Together, he and she then walked across to the center aisle and down to the front row, where three seats had been saved. Ricky took the innermost, the signora the middle one. She glanced around, looking for Tiberio, but he wasn't in sight. It was ten after ten—too cruel to Iris to have her wait any longer. Signora Benassi therefore nodded to Antonio, who disappeared into the next room and closed the door. A moment later he opened it, stood to one side, and Iris, pale, thin, and elegant in a sleeveless gown of watery green silk, came to the piano, just as a young man slipped into the seat beside the signora. She glanced at him for a moment. There was a flash of perfect white teeth in a sun-darkened face. He lifted her hand to his lips, and kept it in his hand as the music began.

Iris played Chopin, without intermissions, the program designed to last a little less than fifty minutes. She offered two of the Ballades, the First in G Minor and the Fourth in F Minor. These heroic pieces were followed by a group of the Mazurkas, to rest the ears of the assemblage and perhaps suggest the dancing that would follow, and the music concluded with a selection of the Nocturnes, ending with the Nocturne in G. Upon the hesitant trilled return of the opening melody, Signora Benassi got tears in her eyes, not about anything in particular. She turned toward Tiberio. The expression on his handsome face was quite different from any she'd ever seen there before, rapt and passionate and, to her, as poignant as the music.

It gave her an idea.

It had been planned that she would rise and present some flowers to Iris upon the completion of the encores, which were to be two Preludes, but when Antonio brought the bouquet to her, she handed it to Tiberio. He quite charmingly, as not only the signora thought, offered them to Iris, who accepted them with great style.

As the ladies and gentlemen were leaving the *salone* for the terrace and gardens, the menservants were already rearranging the chairs, to allow for dancing and to provide seats during supper; Antonio, who was directing them, broke off and approached the signora. He handed her an envelope.

She didn't recognize the handwriting, but she noticed there was no stamp. It had been hand-delivered. She asked Antonio who it was from.

"Signor Marco," he replied.

"No! Is he here?" Antonio shook his head. "But—how did you get this?"

"He brought the letters and went away early this afternoon. He asked me to give this one to you in the middle of the party, when there was a good time."

"Letters? More than one?"

"He left another for Signor Molyneux."

The signora opened the envelope.

Parma, July 22

Dear Signora Benassi,

I'm on my way to Rome—returning home tomorrow. I'll stop over for a couple of hours in Florence so I can leave this at Villa Arberoni, to be sure you'll get it at the right time.

I've thought a lot about the things you said when I left. Maybe Tiberio wouldn't have told you about the spoons, but I think he'd have stuck up for Costanza, too—or he's not the man you say he is. As for the other—maybe running wasn't entirely right, but staying would have been entirely wrong.

Whether you think so or not, I think I did learn a lot at your villa, and I certainly don't think it was bad luck that brought me there. I thank you for everything and hope our next meeting will be more friendly than the last one. Laurie Walker joins me in saying—

Happy Birthday!

Mark

Signora Benassi put the letter in a pocket that Signora Martelli, her dressmaker, had concealed among the ruffles of her skirt, found Antonio, and asked if he'd yet given the other letter to Mr. Molyneux. He had, just now.

She had things to do. First Tiberio, then gossip, then James.

It took her a little while to get to Tiberio, because she was stopped so many times by people who wanted to admire her new necklace and earrings. When she did reach him, he was talking to Ricky—a striking pair, both with the Guidoni blue eyes and regular features, but Tiberio's thick helmet of hair was black, and he was taller than his uncle. After he, too, had had a chance to admire the necklace, she said, "Would you do me a favor?"

"Tonight? Anything in the world, Aunt Madeleine."

"Take care of Iris Siswick for a while. Take her down to the garden, first of all, so she can recover from playing. Then get her some supper. She's had such an unhappy time for the last weeks, I've been worried about her." Signora Benassi explained about the quarrel with the piano instructor. "She needs people to be nice to her—and who better than you? And, more generally, what she needs is a change of scene, to get out of Florence for a while. Not necessarily be with lots of people—she's very self-sufficient, as long as she has a piano. I wish it were possible for her to go somewhere like—oh, like the house on the edge of your new vineyards, for a rest away from our heat and noise."

"*Your* new vineyards, Aunt Madeleine."

"*Your* new vineyards, and *your* new house," Signora Benassi said firmly. "One could, after all, send over the smaller piano while she was there, since she wouldn't need it here. Some such thing would do her a lot of good and be a favor to me because I so like her, but perhaps she'd be in the way. In any case, do take her to the gardens." Signora Benassi turned to other guests.

While upper-class Italians do not gesture like street boys, and

Florentines do not gesture like Neapolitans, nevertheless all Italians can use that language when they want to.

What's this all about? Tiberio signaled.

How should I know? came the return signal from Ricky.

Iris stay at the house? How could I ask her to do that?

Don't ask me. But remember, Madeleine is your aunt now. If you don't do what she suggests, you'll have to deal with the consequences.

But what if I *do* do what she suggests?

Ricky just smiled, then said aloud, "In any case, there can be no harm in the first part. Take care of Iris right now. She was very nervous about playing, and she did, to me, play exceptionally well."

"It was beautiful," Tiberio said feelingly.

He led Iris to a bench deep among the trees, where they wouldn't be disturbed by people coming to tell her how their grandparents had heard Liszt play Chopin in Palazzo Corsini in 1871, and so on.

Tiberio was self-conscious about his English. It took him several false starts before he said, "I liked the concert very much."

"Thank you."

"I liked it very, very much."

"I'm glad you did. Thank you."

"I would like to hear you play more."

"I'd like to. Thank you."

He smiled at Iris. She smiled back, then shyly looked at her flowers, which she was still carrying.

"You must be very tired."

"Well . . . yes. And excited."

"I, too, am excited. The F Minor Ballade was beautiful."

"Thank you." Iris looked up. "The lanterns are very nice," she said. "I saw you putting them in the trees."

"I am an ape, so says Aunt Madeleine."

"She says you're a monkey," Iris said, as if it made an important difference. Then, "*Aunt* Madeleine?"

"I forgot—but she'll be telling everybody by now, and it's no longer a secret. I'm glad I could tell you, Iris."

Iris got tears in her eyes.

"It makes you sad?"

"No, it makes me happy."

"I, too. I was at the wedding this morning. It was in San Doroteo, right here, not at the Annunziata or in our chapel at Santa Croce—so nobody would know. At eleven o'clock."

"I was practicing my program for the last time."

"Do you know any Schumann or Beethoven?"

"I used to. I'm going to relearn things by them now."

Signora Benassi's suggestion was beginning to seem less impossible to Tiberio.

"How long will you be in Italy?" he asked.

"I'll probably go back in September."

"And you'll spend all summer in Florence? That is too bad. Wouldn't you like to get away for a while?"

"There's the problem of a piano. I need a piano wherever I go, you see."

"But—if that could be arranged? Let me ask you something," he went on.

Ricky had followed after Signora Benassi when Tiberio went in search of Iris. "Are you serious—about the piano and all?" he asked her. "You know Tiberio has begun to spend nights at that farmhouse. If he continued to do so, they'd be there alone, for his mother won't budge—as you see."

Signora Benassi laughed. "Ricky, you've developed the most sensitive nose for propriety since Madame de Maintenon," she said. "And why not Iris rather than some local girl? You know that's going to lead to trouble eventually."

"But would it be right for her?"

"Yes. Perfect for her. He is gentle and good, not to mention dashing. Moreover, she's a sweet girl and a good musician, and I think he'd enjoy her. That's all one need worry about."

Ricky said, "I submit my resignation, then, as prude. The rest is up to Tiberio—his wishes and enterprise and, perhaps, need. Probably he'll do as you'd want. Even after twenty-five years, I marvel at the way you manage to get people to do what you want."

288

"That's because what I want them to do makes such good sense that it becomes what they want to do themselves instead of what I want them to do. Think about it, in this case. For the first few days he'll only stop by to be sure she's all right, then go home to that cavernous room where he listens to his records—with earphones, because of his mother. Then one day he'll stay longer, with many apologies lest he be interrupting. Iris will play for him. He'll listen and feel refreshed. He'll say he ought to go, but she'll play something else. He'll get the look on his face he had just now when she was playing in the *salone*, and she'll see it. And then— he will go. That time. But the next—surely not. She'll soon stop being shy around him, as his English is improving, and all the while they'll be falling in love. And so he'll begin to spend his nights there. One reason she looked so beautiful when she played—did you notice?—was because I insisted she let Costanza give her some color. Paleness is one thing, pallor another. Tiberio will put real roses in her cheeks; at least he would have in mine, at a certain time."

Ricky confessed, "Looking at it from the other point of view, I rather envy him. She has a most graceful neck. One would—"

"Tut-tut. No unfaithful thoughts tonight, Ricky. Which reminds me—we must spread the news."

"Quite right," he said. "Old love, on this occasion, takes precedence over young."

Ricky went off in one direction, to the Roman delegation, while Signora Benassi went in another.

"Wasn't Iris splendid, Mrs. Davenport?" she said. "In fact, everything is just right—and I thank you for all the help you've been. I've never given a party that's gone better—and I'm so out of practice, too. Also, I wanted to tell you that Ricky and I were married, very privately, this morning."

Pauline, resplendent in her favorite color, this gown more diaphanous than fuzzy, however, fairly inflated at the news. She wanted to know about a honeymoon.

"I rather think we'll go to Montecatini for a few days. We'll be taking a real trip at the end of the summer. I only heard yesterday—from Texas—but perhaps Professor Davenport already knew. I've been put on the board of directors of this Renaissance Center he's so interested in."

"No!" Pauline said, not entirely pleased. She didn't underestimate the signora's capacity to interfere.

"Yes. So we'll be going over often. I think it's what's called a trade-off, in return for my agreeing to make much of this villa available to them for their use in Ricky's and my lifetime, all of it later."

"That I did know about," said Pauline. "Nice that we'll always be able to stay here, now."

"Yes. Villa Arberoni preserved, and all through the enthusiastic cooperation of Dottoressa Paonese, who saw that it was a good way to protect a place that will need protection. Principles *have* their place, when one knows how to temper their application, Mrs. Davenport. I must go off and talk to other people. Do pass the word around—I mean about Ricky and me. I thought a public announcement too absurd, at our ages."

Pauline hardly needed that admonition. Within a quarter of an hour she'd told everyone she knew, and some she didn't.

The signora started the same news going in other circles—Anglican and Episcopalian, and consular—then looked around for James, to tell him personally. Apparently he'd left the party, so, not reluctant for a few minutes' intermission herself, she took the elevator to his floor.

"Here. You might as well read it for yourself, Signora Benassi," James said. "I think I couldn't summarize it for you, much less read it aloud, without . . ."

Parma, July 22

Dear James,

I'm on my way to Rome and America, and I'll drop this off on my way through, along with a birthday note for Signora Benassi. I should have written you a long time ago, as I promised to do, but I've kept putting it off, partly because I was so embarrassed about Hilda's drawing.

Hans Lochner will have told you all about what happened to it, so I don't have to repeat it. He was pretty upset, but I think he agreed I'd done all I could before I left Venice—police, newspaper notice and so on, including a reward, and information on how to get in touch with him. The police said things so much more valuable get stolen all the time that my case wasn't very important, but it's never happened to me before, and I feel like a moron. I'd like to repay you for the drawing and will do so as soon as I've earned some money in the States. As I remember, you said Hilda sells her drawings for five hundred dollars. Expect a check one of these days. But I'm not getting off the train to say that.

I wanted you to know how much it's meant to me to have spent those hours with you looking at Brunelleschi—and everything else in Florence. It's changed the whole way I see things—and some of our other conversations have changed the way I think about other kinds of things, too. I only wish we'd had more of them. I've been looking at paintings and buildings, and people, too, in a different way, a better way, because of you. I really mean it when I say that as life has calmed down and I can judge my stay in Florence with some objectivity, I think it's undoubtedly one of the most important few weeks I've ever lived through—or ever will. That's because of you. People don't change other people's lives all that often, I'd think.

Laurie Walker and I are going to Texas when we get home. I've been traveling with her, as you may have heard. Miss Ladore has offered to put us both to work—doing what, I don't know—she says not a cowboy, in my case, though I'd probably be better at that than I ever would have been as a book dealer. And Laurie and I will be together this way. Also, since you're going to be working for Miss L's foundation, it seems likely we'll be meeting from time to time. I certainly hope so, and I hope that when we do, we can take Brunelleschi up more or less where we left off. There can't be a better guide in the world to all I've still got to learn than you.

You do realize, I hope, that I was in love when I left. That should help explain why I ran off the way I did. I'm very happy about it. Laurie says hello. She wants more sightseeing, too.

Best,
Mark

P.S. Hello to Hilda. Sorry about that torso.

"What a difficult letter to write!" the signora said. "It would take a Proust to do it full justice—and then one wouldn't want to read it. He did, didn't he, go right to what's enduring."

"Brunelleschi, you mean."

She nodded. "You're probably proud of your effect on him, but I think, after reading your letter—and the note he wrote me—that it was perhaps I who had the more influence." She handed James's letter back. "It's definitely not a bad beginning," she said, and added, "I was quite right to save the leaf."

James, too preoccupied with his own thoughts to wonder what she meant, said, "I'll see him now and then, which was really all I ever could have hoped for, until one day it won't matter anymore."

"Thus we all get part of what we want—which is perhaps all that we deserve," said Signora Benassi, including herself as a matter of modesty.

"It's the stuff of comedy," James said, "but one must always remember that in comedy it's only the audience that laughs."

"You're too clever for me. Now—come back to my party, James."

"I thought I'd just stay up here, if you don't mind."

"But I do. You really must come back. You did hear Iris?"

"Extraordinary. She played quite beyond her capacities. Everyone seems to be able to turn misfortune to advantage but me."

Signora Benassa had only a limited tolerance for self-pity. As James was verging on it, she said briskly, "Well, I think I've taken care of her immediate future in a rather nice way, and I have to say that with your new job, your own future's not too bleak. So come along. You haven't yet been exposed to all the stories that Ricky and I have put in circulation."

James had put his dinner jacket over the back of a chair. He reached for it. "What stories are those?"

"We were married this morning—isn't that nice? He'll be moving to Villa Arberoni, though for the moment he's still at his palace. And Tiberio is now my great-nephew, and—alas!—his mother is now my niece. I count on him to look after Ricky and Costanza and me in our old age."

"He's a wonderful lad," James said. He took both of her hands in his. "And you, Marchesa, are a wonderful lady. I'm very glad for your news. Give me five more minutes by myself, out on my

292

terrace, looking over toward Careggi—that's not unreasonable, is it, five minutes to grieve?—and I'll be down."

When James did return to the party, the little orchestra was playing in the *salone*, waltzes and considerately slow foxtrots. Ricky, who'd been looking for him, came up and told him the news of the marriage, and James congratulated him in turn. "And where's Tiberio? I think I should congratulate him, too. He has acquired a marvelous great-aunt."

"You'll have to do that when you can. He disappeared three-quarters of an hour ago into the gardens with little Miss Siswick and hasn't been seen since."

James smiled. "Villa Aphrodite," he said.

"Precisely. It's a little much. Oh, and James—you will have guessed why I wanted to see Madeleine the very afternoon you told me about the drawing, and now, this evening, you know all the consequences of that visit. I want to say something to you, because only you will realize the irony of my new position. I want to say that I don't in the slightest regret that I am where I am now, married and all, because of—what should I call it?—a misunderstanding? All that money, you know, it was never real to me. Oh, I was angry, perhaps even felt a little—well, snared, when you first told me of the mishap, but I truly am over that. The whole story was a fairy tale, and when something in a fairy tale turns out not to be real, one isn't overwhelmed with disappointment. One has half expected it all along."

"All the same, Ricky, I can't forgive myself."

"Madeleine never guessed anything at all, you know. She thought you were so extremely agitated because of—other reasons. Needless to say, I've never said anything to her about it—the drawing, I mean—whether found or lost—or that it made a difference." Ricky smiled. "She thought, after the theft, that I was just generally tense because of the strain of our engagement. Anyway, I didn't explain any of it to her at the time, and I never will. Not now. I count on your discretion, too. As I once said, we can trust each other."

"It seems we not only can," James said, "we must."

• • •

Hunger brought Tiberio and Iris inside at last. She had the musician's post-performance appetite, and Tiberio was always hungry. James Molyneux went for some supper right behind them, and Iris told him of her plan to take a vacation—from Florence if not from the piano—at a house Signora Benassi and Tiberio owned in the hills not far from Arezzo. James said he and Hilda would come over and take them both to lunch one day.

"Speaking of Cousin Hilda—I wonder where she is."

"She and Professor Davenport were waltzing together when we came through the *salone*," Iris replied.

"I'll go watch," said James.

But the waltz was over, and he found Hilda and Battsie on the terrace, cooling off. Battsie had, as always, to make a reference.

"No further news, eh, James?"

James shook his head—he'd carried his plate, and his mouth was full of rice and wild mushrooms. When he could, he said, "I'm afraid not. Hans says the same thing every time I talk to him: the owners refuse to budge. He says it's gone back into a bank vault somewhere."

"It'll come out one day."

"I daresay it will, John."

Battsie had found consolation. "I'm having my fun with it anyway. I only today had occasion to write Daphne Nickerson, at Bryn Mawr. In connection with the new Center. I've already hinted about the drawing to her, said I'd seen photographs and so on, and I rubbed it in again. It'll drive her crazy, hanging over her head. I wouldn't be surprised but that she'll publish some sort of recantation without ever having been accused of anything; that's the kind of scholar she is. There's Pauline, been hopping around with Ettore. I expect she'd like a twirl with me next time they play Strauss, so please excuse me."

James finished his supper quickly, then he and Hilda got glasses of champagne and carried them down to the garden.

"The lighting works, you know, James," she said. "It really does."

"Largely thanks to Tiberio. I could only wave my cane, but he and Bruno did the scrambling, while Antonio hooked up the wires." They turned down one of the diagonal paths that radiated toward the bottom corners of the property, away from the fountain. "I just heard from Mark. A letter. He stopped off in Florence on his way to Rome to deliver one to me and one to Signora Benassi. Got off a train, in this season, and had to get on another. I wonder at it."

"Did he mention me?"

James gave Hilda Mark's letter to read. Everything considered, he thought she deserved the punishment.

"You have a way of keeping people your friends, once the smoke has cleared away," she said, when she was through. "It's a talent, James. I wish I had it."

"You're thinking of Harry."

"I suppose. But he's really out of my life. I'm not like you."

"Don't be so sure."

She didn't want to speculate about it. "How do you think I look, by the way?"

Hilda had her hair coiled around an enameled serpent whose golden head rested on her forehead above her eyes. Her dress, cut low to show off her breasts, was of a dazzling shade of robin's-egg blue. She wore many bracelets of gold on her right arm, along with several of ivory. She looked barbaric and splendid, and James told her so.

"Although," he said, "I think the iconography of your costume has more to do with how you wish you were than how you are."

"Thanks." Hilda took the compliment and ignored the analysis. "I rather like the effect myself. You know, I was thinking earlier of a line in that book by Walter Pater you gave me to read when I first got to Florence, do you remember? Something about how the path to success lies through a series of rebuffs."

"You don't have it quite right." James quoted: "'For the way to perfection is through a series of disgusts.'"

"Well, I was fairly close," Hilda said. "Let's both go on in search of new perfections." She put a hand through James's arm. "No matter how difficult you can sometimes be, it's nice to have you around."

"I, difficult? I?"

"Now I want some supper—and then some sleep. Bruno comes tomorrow early and again on Sunday. I've got to work fast if I'm to finish the piece before he leaves for America. But I'll take time out to get you to your train to Munich, never fear."

Many of the guests left by midnight, but many stayed on; hours are late in Florence in the summertime. At one-thirty, the music stopped. By two o'clock nobody was left but Tiberio and Ricky and Madeleine. Ricky, too, said good-bye, and Tiberio took him home to Palazzo Guidoni.

A little later, all but the very last lights were out at the villa. The torches in the garden had long since been extinguished, and the electric lanterns had been turned off. The silver had been washed and locked in the dining room, to be counted in the morning before it was put away; Costanza would be at it at dawn, apprehensive because of the way in which those spoons had disappeared mysteriously, then even more mysteriously reappeared, and she'd have to get the job done early, because the signora, feigning a deadly ennui, had forever forbidden talk about the spoons by the servants, to each other or to anybody else, on pain of instant dismissal—which included Costanza. She and Signora Benassi spoke of the events of the evening. Tiberio and Iris were mentioned.

"It would be convenient if it continued for a while," the signora said. "I don't want to have to think of too many things at once."

"It will, Marchesa," said Costanza. "The contessa always said that speed in such things, both starting and especially ending, was a matter of practice."

They walked slowly through the state rooms, both of them weary. Costanza turned on the picture light over the Sargent, which glowed like a pagan altarpiece in the dark sanctuary of the salone. "It was an evening quite worthy of her," she said.

"Why, thank you. I think it was." The signora removed her necklace.

Costanza put it in its leather box, which still sat on the table beside the nautilus cup. She turned off the light and they went toward the bedroom, where all was ready. "There's more than Tiberio and Iris." The signora told Costanza about Mark, about his note, and about how he and Laurie Walker would be returning to America together.

Costanza nodded sagely. "As I predicted. Will they marry? They seemed of that kind."

"A more interesting question: if they marry, will it last?" Signora Benassi said. "But, yes, I think they will. Will try it."

"Even that might please the contessa," said Costanza.

"Mmm." The signora began to remove her rings. "Though on that particular subject, you never knew which way Mama would jump."